DESIRES OF A PERFECT LADY

DESIRES OF A PERFECT LADY

VICTORIA ALEXANDER

THORNDIKE
CHIVERS

This Large Print edition is published by Thorndike Press, Waterville, Maine, USA and by BBC Audiobooks Ltd, Bath, England.
Thorndike Press, a part of Gale, Cengage Learning.
The text of this Large Print edition is unabridged.
Other aspects of the book may vary from the original edition.
Set in 16 pt. Plantin.

LIBRARY OF CONGRESS CATALOGING-IN-PUBLICATION DATA

Alexander, Victoria.
  Desires of a perfect lady / by Victoria Alexander. — Large print ed.
    p. cm. — (Kennebec large print superior collection)
  ISBN-13: 978-1-4104-2964-3
  ISBN-10: 1-4104-2964-4
  1. Large type books. I. Title.
PS3551.L357713D47 2010
813'.54—dc22   2010017878

BRITISH LIBRARY CATALOGUING-IN-PUBLICATION DATA AVAILABLE

Published in 2010 in the U.S. by arrangement with Avon, an imprint of HarperCollins Publishers.
Published in 2010 in the U.K. by arrangement with the author.

U.K. Hardcover: 978 1 408 49233 8 (Chivers Large Print)
U.K. Softcover: 978 1 408 49234 5 (Camden Large Print)

Printed in the United States of America
  2 3 4 5 6   15 14 13 12 11
ED012

DESIRES OF A PERFECT LADY

PROLOGUE

London, 1867

"We aren't supposed to be up here," Sterling Harrington said in his best I-will-be-the-Earl-of-Wyldewood-one-day voice. Even at age eleven he was well aware of what his future held. Not that his younger brothers paid him any heed whatsoever.

"I daresay, it won't be a problem if we don't get caught." Quinton Harrington, two years younger than Sterling, pushed past the future earl, candle in hand and ventured farther into the attic.

"It's rather too dark to see anything." Nathanial, the youngest of the three hesitated. A year younger than Quinton, Nathanial was often hard-pressed to keep up with his older brothers, especially Quinton, even if he would never admit it aloud.

In the rest of Harrington House, the sound of the rain that pounded on the roof was not unpleasant. But here in the vast at-

7

tic that seemed to stretch on into eternal shadows, if one were only eight years of age, one might feel a certain apprehension. Sterling resisted the urge to take his brother's hand but Nathanial was not fond of any reminder that he was the youngest and might still need his hand to be held. Instead, Sterling laid a comforting hand on his brother's shoulder, telling him without words that Sterling would always be there for him. It was who he was and who he was expected to be.

Miss Thompson, their governess, had always said Sterling had a fine sense of responsibility, as befitted the future Earl of Wyldewood, who would bear a great many responsibilities. Nathanial, she said, had the heart of a poet. And Quinton had the curse of an adventurous soul which, no doubt, Miss Thompson did not mean as a compliment; but Quinton nonetheless took it as such. Every now and again, Sterling would quite envy his younger brother and wonder what it would be like to have an adventurous soul rather than a fine sense of responsibility. Regardless, it was his duty in life to inherit the title and become the head of the family. Most of the time, aside from the nasty fact that his father would have to die first, Sterling was not dismayed at the prospect.

"So." Quinton held the candle high and glanced around the attic. "Where should we begin?"

"The trunks," Sterling said firmly. As they were looking for pirate clothes, this seemed the logical place to start. "There will be pirate clothes in the trunks." He started toward the far recesses of the attic, under the eaves, and its darker, deeper shadows. If truth were told, Sterling might have felt the tiniest twinge of apprehension, which he promptly ignored. The earls of Wyldewood were expected to have courage in the face of adversity, even if adversity took the form of unknown shadows in an attic on a rainy day, and one was still only a boy.

He did wish they'd get on with it, though. Every minute spent in the attic was another minute closer to discovery. To chastisement and possibly punishment. While it was usually Quinton's fertile mind that came up with whatever adventure the boys embarked upon, it was Sterling who accepted leadership of the exploit and Sterling who stepped forward and took the blame when their transgression was discovered. Be it something as enormous as evading the watchful eye of whichever governess was in residence to slip off the grounds and explore the streets of London in violation of all the rules or something as relatively insignificant as borrowing every umbrella in the house to fashion a tent.

They wouldn't be up there at all had it not been for the rain and Miss Thompson. The usually placid governess had not responded with her typical calm to finding a frog in her desk drawer. Perhaps that was attributable to three days of rain and three days of her charges being more boisterous than normal. She had sent them off to read and retired to her private sitting room, something she did on occasion. Often when it rained.

Sterling stopped before trunks that looked very much like treasure chests if one discounted the fact that their original owners might well have been maiden aunts or spinster cousins. "Which one?"

"The biggest, of course." Quinton grinned at Nathanial as if he was imparting excellent advice from an older, wiser brother to a younger. "The biggest always has the best treasure."

"Very well." Sterling resisted the urge to point out that the biggest was not always the best and lifted the lid on the largest trunk. Almost as one, the boys leaned forward to peer into the trunk.

"There's only clothes in there." Disappointment rang in Nathanial's voice. No doubt he was hoping for real treasure although surely treasure was not so easy to find.

"These aren't just clothes." Quinton handed Nathanial the candle, then reached into the trunk and pulled out a red uniform coat, exactly like those on their painted tin soldiers. "These are clothes for pirates and knights."

"And adventurers." Sterling nodded. "And explorers."

"I want to be an explorer," Nathanial said eagerly. "Or an adventurer."

Sterling spotted a book amidst the jumble of laces and old wools and pulled it out. "Look at this."

Quinton grimaced. "It's a book."

"It's a journal." Sterling moved closer to the candle and flipped through the journal. "It's Great-grandmother's."

"It's still just a book," Quinton said.

"I know." Sterling turned the pages and studied the old-fashioned, feminine hand. Here and there a word caught his attention. *Goods . . . France . . . ships.* "But it might be a good book."

Quinton scoffed. "How good can a book be?"

"You like books about pirates," Nathanial said in a helpful manner.

Sterling paged through the journal, an odd sort of excitement growing with every turn of the page. "This one is about smugglers."

Quinton brightened. "Great-grandmother knew smugglers?"

Sterling glanced from one brother to the next and adopted a serious tone as befitting his discovery. "I think Great-grandmother might have been a smuggler."

"Read it," Nathanial demanded.

"Very well." Sterling nodded, and they all settled down, cross-legged, on the floor.

Sterling took the candle from Nathanial, positioned it to cast the best light on the pages, and began to read to his brothers of the adventures of their great-grandmother, who apparently had indeed been a smuggler. And was pursued by a government agent — a previous Earl of Wyldewood he noted with pride. He read of clandestine meetings and dangerous encounters and harrowing escapes until the rain stopped. Finally, he closed the journal and considered their discovery. "I don't think we should tell Mother about this."

"Because we'd have to tell her we were in

the attic?" Nathanial asked.

"No." Quinton cast a superior look at his younger brother. "Because she might not like having a smuggler in the family."

"Oh." Nathanial thought for a moment, then his eyes widened with excitement. "Let's be smugglers instead of pirates."

"We can't today." Sterling shook his head. "Miss Thompson will be wondering what became of us. But we can come up here again and read and play smuggler perhaps."

"Can we have smuggler names as well?" Nathanial said eagerly.

Quinton laughed. "Smuggler names? What are smuggler names?"

"They're like pirate names only for smugglers," Nathanial said in a lofty manner. "And I shall be Black Jack Harrington."

Sterling and Quinton traded glances. Sterling chose his words with care. "We don't think that's quite right for you."

Nathanial frowned. "Why not?"

"Because your real name isn't Jack for one thing. We're not just playing, you know," Quinton said firmly. "It's quite a serious thing to have new names. Even smuggler names. Your smuggler name has to make sense with your real name."

"Nate," Sterling announced. "Sounds like a smuggler." He nodded at Quinton. "And you can be Quint."

"It's not very exciting," Quinton — now Quint — muttered, then brightened. "What about Peg Leg Quint or Quint the Wicked?"

"More likely Quint the Scamp." Sterling smirked.

"And who will you be?" Nathanial — now Nate — looked at his older brother. "What will your smuggler name be?"

"I shall remain Sterling," he said in a lofty manner, not that having a smuggler name wouldn't be rather enjoyable.

Quint scoffed. "Not much of a name for a smuggler."

"Oh, I shan't be a smuggler." Sterling cast them a superior smile. "I shall be the intrepid Earl of Wyldewood, agent of the crown, fearless hunter of smugglers." Just as his ancestor had been. After all, it was his heritage as well as his fate. "And I shall be the rescuer of the fair maiden, her hero."

"Girls can't play," Nate said with a shake of his head. "They're girls."

"Then I shall be Quint." Quint planted his fists on his hips and puffed out his chest. "Daring, bold King of the Smugglers."

"Who am I to be?" Nate looked from the intrepid earl to the King of the Smugglers.

"Very well." Sterling heaved a long-suffering sigh. The things one did for one's family. "I shall give up fearless. You may be the Fearless Smuggler Nate."

"I'd rather like to keep daring, but I shall give you bold." Quint grinned. "You are now the Fearless Smuggler, Nate the Bold."

Nate grinned.

"We shall have a grand time playing smuggler and smuggler hunter," Sterling said, ignoring the touch of longing that stabbed him. In this day and age, Earls of Wyldewood were more likely to study accounts than pursue smugglers. "And we shall amass great treasures and have grand adventures and rescue fair maidens."

"And wander the world and discover new places." Quint nodded.

"And . . . and . . ." Nate shrugged.

"We need a pact, I think." Sterling thought for a moment. "A smugglers' pact."

Nate's brows drew together in suspicion. "Do smugglers have pacts?"

"I don't know." Quint shrugged. "You mean like musketeers? One for all and all for one?"

"That's a motto." Sterling rolled his gaze toward the rafters. Surely even Quint realized there was a difference between a motto and a pact. "Besides, we're brothers. We'll always be one for all and all for one."

15

Nate narrowed his eyes. "Forever and ever?"

"As we ever have and ever will be," Sterling said solemnly as befitting such a pledge. Indeed, this was a promise that would last forever. "Brothers one for the other."

"One for the other," Quint agreed.

"One for the other." Nate grinned.

It was a very good pact, an excellent vow, and a promise he would keep always. Sterling knew that whatever paths his brothers might take in the future, whatever life might hold for the next Earl of Wyldewood, they would always be one for the other. He would see to it. It was, after all, his responsibility, his duty.

And he would not fail to live up to it.

ONE

There was no doubt as to the significance of his title. He wore it about him with an air of confidence known only to those born and bred to position. His appearance was at once handsome and aloof although there was no lack of warmth. And a woman knew, the first time he kissed her hand, that here was a man one could depend on. Only those especially astute would sense that in many ways his lordship was wound as taut as a tightly turned spring. And only the most daring would wonder what might happen when the spring snapped.

Reflection of an astute female upon observation of Sterling Harrington, the Earl of Wyldewood

London, 1885
"And I want you, sir" — Lord Newbury raised his cane and aimed it at Sterling Har-

rington, the Earl of Wyldewood — "to rescue my daughter."

Sterling sipped his brandy and studied the older man. He'd agreed to allow Newbury to meet with him at Harrington House, the scene of their last meeting a decade ago. That had not gone well. This looked to go no better. "I fear you have me confused with my brothers. They are the adventurous members of the family, prone to rescue and that sort of thing. I am not."

"Your brothers do not interest me."

"My brothers interest everyone." Sterling considered Newbury for a moment. "I confess, I granted you this meeting out of an absurd sense of curiosity. Now that I have heard what you have to say . . ." Sterling rose to his feet.

"Sit down, boy," the old man snapped. "You have heard nothing yet."

Sterling narrowed his eyes. "Still, my curiosity has been assuaged."

"You loved her once."

Sterling nodded. "Once."

"Then do me, do her, the courtesy of listening to the rest of it." The old man paused, then drew a deep, shuddering breath. "I beg you."

Lord Newbury was not the sort to beg. Sterling studied him coolly. It was obviously

18

difficult for him and equally obvious the man was not in good health. It would do no harm to hear what he wished to say. Sterling retook his seat. "Very well, go on."

"You are aware that Olivia's husband, Lord Rathbourne died a fortnight ago."

"I am."

"And I assume you are aware, as well, of the nature of his death."

"Nasty business," Sterling murmured.

Viscount Rathbourne had been found by Sterling's soon-to-be sister-in-law in the garden of his London home with his throat slit. Gabriella Montini was to wed Sterling's youngest brother Nathanial in a few months. Highly educated, brilliant, and lovely, Gabriella was the sister of a man who had made his living as Sterling's own brothers did. Nathanial and Quinton were — at best — archeologists. At worst — treasure hunters. Gabriella had briefly worked for Lord Rathbourne cataloguing some of his vast collection of artifacts and antiquities.

Newbury leaned forward and pinned Sterling with his beady gaze. "As you may or may not know, nothing was taken from the house. I fear whoever killed Rathbourne did not find what he was after and will return. The manner of Rathbourne's death was cold and callous. Such a fiend would not hesitate to dispatch anyone in his way. Including Rathbourne's wife."

Sterling ignored an unexpected stab of fear. Olivia was not his concern and had not been his concern for the last decade. As was her choice. "Perhaps you should take matters in hand then."

Newbury shook his head. "She would never accept anything from me. She has not spoken to me in nearly ten years." His gaze met Sterling's. "Nor, in truth, can I blame her."

"I daresay she would not welcome my interference."

"Not at first, perhaps. But her life may be at stake." The old man's eyes narrowed. "And you owe her this."

"I owe her nothing." The words were sharper than he'd intended. He drew a soothing sip of his brandy and willed himself to remain calm. "If you recall, and you should as you were the one who delivered the news to me, Olivia severed our relationship and chose to marry Rathbourne. It was her decision, not mine. I feel no obligation toward her."

"Would you feel differently . . ." Newbury paused for a long moment. ". . . if you discovered that what you thought was true was not?"

20

Sterling's heart twisted in spite of himself. "What do you mean?"

"I made her marry Rathbourne." The old man passed a weary hand over his face. "I have not lived a good life, Wyldewood. I have secrets Rathbourne threatened to reveal if I did not give him Olivia. I would have been ruined. She would have been ruined. She married him to save me, but she has never forgiven me."

Sterling's mind reeled, and at once he was swept back to the darkest days of his life.

Sterling had known Olivia in a casual manner for much of his life. Her family's country estate bordered his own. But he'd never really noticed her until she was out in society, and they met anew at a ball in London. She was bright and beautiful and clever, and he'd fallen in love with her with an intensity and a passion he'd never dreamed possible. She was a scant two years younger than he, and for a few short months, she had held his heart in her hands. And he had thought he held hers as well. They'd met frequently at public events and privately whenever possible, slipping away from a ball to share a kiss on a terrace or arranging a chance encounter during a morning ride in the park. He'd planned to marry her, and she'd agreed, but they'd yet

21

to make their intentions public even though their feelings were apparent to anyone who chanced to look.

Until one day Lord Newbury arrived to tell him she was to marry Rathbourne. Newbury said Olivia had realized Rathbourne could offer her a better future, and she would be a fool to refuse him. He said she wished never to see him again. Sterling had been stunned by the news and hurt beyond comprehension. Everything happened quickly after that. Two days later, Olivia was wed. Within a week, his father had abruptly fallen ill and wished to see his heir settled before he died. Sterling had turned to Alice, whose family had long been friends with his own and who had loved him since childhood. Dear Alice who was good and kind and far too fragile for this world. When Olivia had sent him a note the day after her father's visit and the day before her hasty marriage, he hadn't so much as opened it. What was the point? Olivia had made her decision. And weeks later, when his father was breathing his last, Olivia had sent him two more notes, and again he failed to open them. There were weightier matters on his mind, and Olivia no longer had any part in his life. She was his past and was best left in the past. His father passed on shortly thereafter, and Alice succumbed to a fever within a year and died as well.

In the decade since, Sterling had scarcely set eyes on Olivia. On rare occasions, he had seen her across a ballroom floor and had taken pains not to be within speaking distance. His mother had once said in passing that Lady Rathbourne had become quite reclusive, spending most of her days in the country. Not that he cared. He had put her out of his mind as thoroughly as if she too were dead. And if, now and again, her face would haunt his dreams, her smile linger in his soul, he ruthlessly thrust it aside. She had broken his heart, and even in his dreams, he would not permit that kind of pain again.

"You should know, she did not go into marriage willingly." Newbury studied him. "You said you would never let her go. She thought you would save her."

A heavy weight settled in the pit of Sterling's stomach.

Newbury drew a deep breath. "But I knew a man like you, a man with your kind of pride, would never pursue a woman who didn't want you."

"She could have told me." At once the memory of that long-ago note slammed into him. *She tried!*

"Rathbourne would not have allowed that." Newbury shook his head. "He insisted I keep her locked in her rooms until the wedding. I did try to renege before the marriage. I offered Rathbourne money, property, whatever he wished, but all he wanted was Olivia. He laughed at me. He said she was his now." Newbury's eyes took on a faraway quality, as if he were looking back to those days. "She and I had never been close, you know. If she had been a boy . . ." He shook his head. "Regardless, I should have done better by her. This is my last chance." He met Sterling's gaze directly. "My days are numbered. My physicians say I am not long for this world."

Sterling raised a brow. "And you hope to earn salvation now by having me help her?"

Newbury laughed, a dry, cackling sound that said far more than any words about the state of his health. "I have no illusions as to where I will spend eternity. I have made any number of mistakes in my life, Wyldewood, the most egregious in regards to my daughter. I cannot make amends for my actions. But you can atone for yours."

Sterling shook his head. "I don't think —"

The old man leaned forward. "Rathbourne tossed me a bone of sorts when he

24

married Olivia. I told him I was concerned for her welfare. Even then, there were rumors about him. He said he would keep her as safe as his other possessions. But I know he did not treat her well. Still, she is alive . . ." Newbury paused, and what might have been genuine remorse passed over his face. "Rathbourne said if he came to a violent end, I should take steps to protect her."

Sterling cast him a look of disgust. "And that was a comfort to you?"

"No," Newbury snapped. "Nor did it come as a surprise. Now, however, it seems prophetic."

"I don't know what you think I can do." Sterling shrugged. "I can't imagine she'd even be willing to see me after all this time."

"You can at least warn her. Urge her to take precautions." Newbury sighed and at once looked like the aged, dying man he apparently was. "Please, do this for her. You owe her that much."

"I don't . . ." Sterling drew a deep breath. "Perhaps I do. It seems little enough, I suppose."

"I am grateful, not that you need my gratitude. Nonetheless, you have it."

"I don't know —"

"You failed to save her once, Wyldewood,"

25

the old man said sharply, his gaze boring into Sterling's. "Do not fail her now."

Olivia Rathbourne, the newly widowed Viscountess Rathbourne, studied the two pieces of her stationery laid out before her on the desk in her husband's — no — *her* library. Her stationery was of the finest quality vellum, embossed with her name and title. But, of course, everything she wore, everything in the house or in the manor in the country, everything she now owned was of the finest quality. Her dead husband permitted nothing else.

The sheet of stationery on the left was crisp and new, the list of items that needed her immediate attention written in her precise hand. She smiled, dipped her pen in the inkwell, and crossed off *replace butler* with an unnecessary but nonetheless satisfying flourish. In the scant two weeks since her husband's death she had replaced the housekeeper, the cook, the entire upstairs staff, and now the butler. Within another week she fully intended not to have a single servant who had been part of her husband's household anywhere in sight. The butler as well as the housekeeper, cook, and other newly hired staff might not be as experienced as those they replaced, and it would

26

take them all a bit of time to become familiar with the house as well as their new employer but she scarcely cared. A certain amount of inconvenience was a small price to pay for beginning her life anew.

Her gaze shifted to the leaf of stationery on the right, soiled and worn. Folded and refolded until it barely remained in one piece, that page too hosted a list of sorts. None of the items written on it had yet been crossed off, but they would be eventually. Olivia was in no hurry. After all, this list had been compiled over nearly a decade, and she had the rest of her life to cross off the items. A life that at last was indeed hers.

There was no title to identify either list, but had there been, the one on the left would be: To Do At Once. The list on the right: To Do When He Is Dead. It wasn't a very long list, but, through the years of her marriage, she had clung to it like a drowning sailor clinging to a shattered mast. The tattered piece of stationery was the only thing in her life that was truly hers. Here were her dreams, her private desires, those silly and those profound. The practical, the possible, and some that were nothing more than fanciful notions. The list had been her secret, her salvation. If her husband had known of its existence, if he had known of the way in which it had sustained her, she had no doubt he would have punished her although it had been years since he had done so. Or he might have laughed. Which would have been worse.

She'd been at their house in the country when word had reached her of his demise. She had at once sent a quick prayer heavenward for the redemption of his soul because that was what one should do. Not because there was any possibility that his soul could be saved or that toward heaven was the appropriate direction. And she had sent a longer prayer directed at whatever saint watched over helpless women and answered their prayers. Not that she had prayed for his death. That would have been wrong in a moral sense. Besides, he was more than thirty years older than she. It was to be expected that he would precede her in death. No, she had not actively prayed for his demise. Nor, however, had she ever prayed for his continued good health.

And now she was free.

A discreet knock sounded at the door.

Freedom and privacy. A smile curved her lips. Her husband was certainly not in heaven, but she was.

"Yes?"

The door opened, and her new butler —

Giddings — stepped into the room. His references were excellent, and Olivia had no doubt that, within the week, he would have her household running smoothly. *Her household.* It had a lovely ring to it.

"There is a gentleman to see you, my lady." Giddings stepped closer bearing a silver salver, a calling card precisely centered on the gleaming surface. He held it out to her. "He says it's most important that he speak with you at once."

"Does he?" she murmured, and plucked the card from the salver.

There had been scandalously few calls of condolence since her husband's death. Not surprising really. He'd had no friends. Those who had come to express remorse and offer sympathy, however feigned, had been primarily those who'd had dealings with her husband including his solicitor — whose dismissal was toward the top of her list of items to be accomplished at once — officials from the London Antiquities Society, representatives of several museums, and a handful of private collectors. Viscount Rathbourne might have been many things, but his eye for antiquities and art had never been disputed. His collections rivaled those in any museum. They would soon follow the way of the solicitor.

She glanced at the card in her hand. The engraved name was neither expected nor a complete surprise. Indeed, his mother, his brother Nathanial, and Nathanial's fiancée had together called on her. One of the handful of calls she'd judged prompted by genuine concern for her welfare. But, of course, she no longer had any friends to speak of. While members of his family had come in person, he had seen fit merely to send a note. Formally worded and eminently proper, she had wondered, before she'd tossed it in the fireplace, if his secretary had written it and if he'd seen it at all save to sign it.

Giddings cleared his throat.

Would she see him? It struck her as odd that she could consider the question calmly, without undue emotion. But then she had exhausted her emotions in regard to him long ago. After all, it had taken some time, but hadn't she at last understood that neither he nor her father would save her? That only she could save herself? And she had. Oh certainly, she had done nothing through the years but pretend to be accepting of her fate and compile her list and survive. But her husband was dead, and she had indeed survived.

She had survived Sterling's betrayal as

well. She distinctly remembered the last time she had spoken to him. She'd been filled with joy and the promise of what the future would bring. A future she had planned to spend with Sterling, as his wife, bearing his children, growing old with her hand clasped in his. That last day they had spoken of the future and life had never seemed brighter. He was going to speak to her father, and they planned to marry at once. It was expedient to do so.

She'd said good-bye to him that day, her heart filled to overflowing. That was the very day her father had told her she had to marry Rathbourne. She'd refused at first, of course. Then her father had told her his vile secret. They would both be ruined if the truth were known. Still, she'd held out hope. Sterling loved her. He wouldn't care about such things. He had the position and the family name, the money and the power to overcome even scandal of this nature. No, he was her knight, her hero. He would most certainly save her. But he hadn't.

She'd tried to save herself. She confessed her own misdeeds to Rathbourne, confident he would not want his perfect bride to be anything less than perfect. He had not been happy, had taken his ire out on her for the first time then, but had not set her free.

31

Even in her horror and her pain she had tried to escape, but Rathbourne had threatened to destroy Sterling as well. His words had left little doubt as to exactly what he'd meant.

She'd had no choice. She would have abandoned her father to his fate, but she could never risk Sterling's life. She'd saved him, not that he would ever know. And she'd paid the price.

"My lady?"

Giddings's voice jerked her back to here and now. Why not see him? She did not intend to remain the recluse she had become during her marriage; nor did she intend to avoid Sterling or anyone else. Seeing him would be a first step.

"Show him in." She thought for a moment. She hadn't redecorated the house yet, hadn't ripped out every lingering influence of her husband's, although it was on her new list. Still, she might simply sell the blasted place and be done with it.

"Show him into the parlor." She squared her shoulders. "I shall be in momentarily."

"As you wish." The butler nodded in an efficient manner, turned, and took his leave.

The tiniest bit of apprehension fluttered in her stomach. Surely, the earl had simply realized it had not been sufficient just to

32

send a note. Perhaps his mother had encouraged him to pay a call. His appearance was nothing more than proper etiquette really. If it bore any significance at all, it was only in that this meeting would serve truly to mark the end of her old life and the start of her new one. A life she fully intended to live without regrets.

And in many ways, this meeting would serve her own purposes.

She folded the worn paper with its list of the dreams and desires that had sustained her through the years and slipped it into the desk drawer. There was no need to hide it anymore. It scarcely mattered any longer who saw it. Still, she would much prefer he didn't see it. Not today.

Today, it simply would not do for Sterling Harrington, Earl of Wyldewood, to know that his name was at the top of her list.

Two

In spite of his firm resolve, regardless of his best intentions or the fact that he thought he had hardened to her long ago, Sterling's heart twisted the moment Olivia stepped into the room.

Livy.

She nodded coolly. "Good day, my lord."

"Good day," he murmured.

Her gaze met his, and at once he was swept back to the last time he'd spoken with her, the last time he'd been so close to her. When the world had seemed a wonderful place, and he had known that the rest of his days would be spent with her by his side. She was every bit as he remembered, every bit the woman who lingered still in the unguarded recess of his dreams. He'd never seen her in black before, but the gown, almost severe in its simplicity, molded to her like the caress of a hand. She looked exactly the same. Her eyes were as green, her skin as fair. Her blond hair still rivaled that of any Renaissance angel, and her lips still begged for his kiss. She looked exactly the same, and she was entirely different.

There was an air of subtle strength about her, as if she had faced adversity and survived. She carried herself straighter, with the quiet grace of a woman who knew without doubt who she was and her place in the world. The look in her eye was cool, measured. Ten years ago, she had been a product of nature. An untouched gem. Beautiful as it came from the earth yet only a hint of what it might become. Now, she had been cut and polished and shaped. *Forged by fire.* The thought flashed through his mind, and he winced to himself.

He, along with everyone else, had heard the rumors about Rathbourne. About the kind of man he was. Yet there had never been talk about his relationship with his wife. Odd in itself, as the ongoing battles, affairs, and scandalous relations involving husbands and wives in society were the lifeblood of gossips, in spite of the queen's disapproval of such misdeeds. And in truth, did anyone ever truly know what transpired within the privacy of a marriage?

Shortly after their marriage, Olivia fairly vanished from public sight. She attended few social events, stopped calling on her friends, and, for the most part, retired to the country. Sterling had been well aware of her disappearance but had had other matters to occupy his mind. He was ashamed to admit, even to himself, that her absence from society had made his own life easier.

Looking at her, he couldn't help but wonder how much of the gossip about Rathbourne's nature was true. And what Olivia's life had been like.

"Why are you here?" she said without preamble.

"I am here . . ." He said the first thing that came into his head. ". . . to offer my condolences."

"You sent a note. It was sufficient and appreciated." Her cold glance swept over him. "If there is nothing else?"

"There is." He drew a deep breath. "Your father came to see me."

Her expression hardened so subtly he wasn't sure he had seen anything at all. "I no longer acknowledge my father's existence. If you are here at his behest, my apologies, my lord. There is nothing he has to say that I wish to hear." She smiled, nothing more than a slight, polite curve of her lips. "Now then, as I am confident you have

36

any number of other matters to attend to —"

"Livy, this is important."

Shock and anger flashed in her eyes, as if she'd been slapped. Her brow rose, but there was no softening of her expression. "I can't imagine anything my father would have to say that would be the least bit important, *Lord Wyldewood.*"

He stared for a moment, realization slamming into him like a fist to the stomach. She hated him every bit as much as she detested her father. Knowing what he now knew, he couldn't blame her. And hadn't he hated her for just as long?

A tiny voice in the back of his head whispered, "No, never." He ignored it and drew a deep breath.

"My apologies, Lady Rathbourne, for my impertinence." His tone was clipped and controlled. "For a moment I forgot myself."

"A great number of years have passed since anyone has called me that."

And I was the only one who ever did.

"Like all else in the past, it is best forgotten. Don't you agree?"

"Yes." He nodded. "However, it is because of the past, our past if you will, that your father came to me. I gave him my word that I would speak to you."

37

"Ah yes." She studied him. "And do you always keep your word?"

"Yes," he said sharply, ignoring the one time he hadn't.

"Very well then." Her expression remained unchanged. "Go on."

"I'm not sure where to begin."

"I scarcely care where you begin as long as you finish quickly."

"Yes, of course." He certainly didn't want to be there any more than she wanted him to be. Furthermore, she had no right to hate him. He didn't desert her or abandon her. His only crime was believing her father. In truth, there'd been no reason not to believe him. Certainly, he hadn't read her letters, but he'd been in too much pain himself to read the first. At the time, he'd assumed it was no more than an apology of sorts. She had at least owed him that. The others had arrived during those days when his father had been so very ill. He hadn't ignored them as much as put them aside and forgotten about them. No, she had no right to look at him the way she did. "Your father is concerned about your welfare."

"My father is concerned about my welfare? My father?" She stared for a moment then laughed, an odd, mirthless sound not at all like the laugh he remembered. The

38

laugh that had once filled his soul now tore at it. "I can scarce believe that, my lord."

"Nonetheless, he came to me because he is worried."

"Worried?" She shook her head. "It is far too late for him to be worried about my welfare or anything else regarding my life."

"He is concerned about the manner of Lord Rathbourne's death."

"Is he?" She crossed her arms over her chest. "I would imagine anyone who had ever crossed paths with my husband would be concerned only that someone had not slit his throat long ago."

He winced. "Liv — Lady Rathbourne, I scarcely think —"

"What? Has my candor upset your delicate sensibilities?"

"Not at all." He met her gaze directly. "It's the bitterness in your voice that I find distressing."

"My apologies, my lord, for distressing you. However, you are mistaken. Any bitterness I might have felt was replaced years ago by resolve. I feel no bitterness whatsoever regarding my husband or my father or anyone else."

Or me?

"I have outlived my husband, and my father no longer exists as far as I am concerned. Indeed, I feel nothing at all for either of them." She shrugged. "You are confusing a complete lack of regard for bitterness. But then you should understand that. If I recall, you were always quite good at keeping your own emotions in check."

He ignored her. He had come with one purpose, and it would be better for them both if he got on with it. "Your father fears there is more to your husband's death than might at first appear. He is further afraid you too could be in danger, that whoever killed your husband might return. I understand nothing was taken?"

"No, nothing at all. Which leads me to believe that my husband's killer was here for the express purpose of taking his life. As that is what he accomplished, I see no reason why he would return."

"Regardless, you don't know that."

"No, I don't know that, but I am fairly confident given that my husband has been dead for two weeks now and there has been nothing out of the ordinary whatsoever. And as you can see, I am perfectly all right."

"I understand the terms of his will have not yet been disclosed. Perhaps the villain is waiting for that."

"That makes no sense. It is no secret that I am his only heir." She paused for a moment. "Admittedly, a few days before his death, my husband had decided to establish a trust to found a museum to house his collections. His solicitor was in the process of arranging the necessary papers when my husband was killed. Although they had not been completed or signed, their preparation has left my husband's affairs a bit muddled, according to his solicitor. Stupid, annoying man." She shook her head. "That is why the will has still not been read although it will be in a few days. However, as I understand it, his previous will remains in effect which, as I said, leaves me his only heir." She slanted him an odd look. "If the motive for killing my husband is his legacy, I alone stand to gain. Had I not been in the country, I daresay I would be at the top of the list of potential murderers."

He stared.

"Goodness, my lord, did you think I killed him?" A hint of genuine amusement shone in her eyes.

He cleared his throat. "No, of course not. The thought never occurred to me."

"It had occurred to me," she said under her breath. "However, I did not kill him; nor did I arrange for his death. My limited allowance does not allow for extravagances like hiring an assassin."

"Which means the party responsible is still free, and you may well be at risk."

"I am quite capable of ensuring my own safety." Her jaw tightened.

"Still, I would recommend —"

"Your recommendations are of no interest to me, my lord." A hard note sounded in her voice. "You have expressed my father's concerns. I have assured you that I will take precautions. If there is nothing else?"

"But you didn't."

She frowned in confusion. "I didn't what?"

"Assure me you will take precautions."

"Very well then." She heaved a long-suffering sigh as if he were a hapless child she was appeasing. "I assure you I will take precautions."

"What kind of precautions?"

"I don't know." Her delicate brows drew together. "I shall alert the servants although most of them are new, and I would hate to frighten them unnecessarily."

"I would consider a threat to your life necessary."

She waved off his comment. "There has been no threat."

"Nothing you know of. Your servants should be warned and aware of anything unusual." He nodded. "What else?"

"I shall ask Giddings to check all the locks

to ascertain that they are in good order and make certain all doors and windows are locked at night."

"Excellent. And?"

"And?" She stared at him. "Isn't that enough?"

"No." He paused. "I would feel more confident if you allowed me to speak to your butler."

"Will it make you leave?" she snapped.

"Yes."

"Very well then."

"And?"

"And . . ." She clenched her teeth. "I shall keep a revolver on the table at my bedside in the event I am accosted in the middle of the night. Are you satisfied now?"

"No." It wasn't nearly enough. "But it will have to do, I suppose."

"Yes, it will." She drew a deep breath. "I think this vague threat may well only exist in my father's mind. Therefore, I think your concern is both unwarranted and an intrusion. However, I do appreciate it." She started toward the door. "I shall send Giddings in to speak with you. As he and the housekeeper are interviewing servants within the hour, I would appreciate your being as succinct and quick as possible."

"I have no desire to linger. I know my

presence is not welcome."

"No, my lord, it isn't." She reached the door and glanced back at him over her shoulder. "Did you expect me to be frightened?"

He shrugged. "I didn't know what to expect."

"Any danger I have been in passed with my husband's death. In ten years, I have neither felt so safe nor been as safe as I am now." Her firm gaze met his. "And I refuse ever to be frightened again."

Olivia stepped out of the parlor and sagged against the wall beside the door. *Dear Lord.* She was shaking. How absurd. Certainly, this was the first time she had spoken to Sterling in ten years, but any feelings she once had for him had long since vanished. Now, there was only one thing she wanted from him, and when that was accomplished, she would have nothing more to do with him for the rest of her days.

Still, she was rather pleased with herself. In spite of the betrayal of her body, the shaking of her hands and odd weakness in her knees, she was confident he hadn't had so much of a glimpse of anything but a woman in complete command of her faculties. A woman who did not need his assistance in any way.

The years had not changed him. He was as tall, his shoulders as broad, his hair and eyes as brown and rich as they had been a decade ago. If perhaps those eyes now carried a shadow of the losses he had known, if the broad stretch of his shoulders seemed somewhat straighter in an effort to carry the responsibilities he now bore, it did not make him seem older so much as stronger, solid, trustworthy. He appeared to be the kind of man one could turn to in times of crisis. She, of course, knew better.

She drew a calming breath, then another. If one looked with an unbiased, strictly rational eye, one might well understand Sterling's actions — or more accurately lack of action — all those years ago. Her father had told her then what he had said to Sterling. That it was her desire to marry Rathbourne and that she wished never to see him again. Her father had further assured her that a man with Sterling's pride would never pursue a woman who didn't want him. Even now, it was hard to accept that he had believed her father at all and harder still to realize that he had let her go without so much as a murmur of protest. He hadn't even responded to her letters. The first, telling him everything and begging him to rescue her, sent before she'd realized that his interference would be at the risk of his life. But he'd obviously chosen to believe her father's words over her own. Then, some months later, he'd failed to answer two more letters, those of a woman terrified and desperate who had not yet learned the lengths her husband would go to to protect his possessions.

Not that any of it mattered anymore. She'd just rid herself of one arrogant man who had ruled her life. While she was confident Sterling and her husband had nothing whatsoever in common overall, she was also sure the Earl of Wyldewood was every bit as certain that he and he alone knew what was best for anyone who might venture into his world. She had no intention of lingering in the earl's world.

Still, for an arrogant man, he had appeared somewhat ill at ease. Guilt perhaps? She drew her brows together and thought for a moment. What else would have prompted him to come to see her? Perhaps her father had at last told Sterling the truth as to why she'd married Rathbourne. Perhaps, after ten years, he finally knew everything. Not that it mattered really. It didn't change anything at all. She had only one desire when it came to the Earl of Wyldewood, and it certainly wasn't to begin anew where they'd left off.

Giddings politely cleared his throat.

She did like how Giddings did that, subtly announcing his presence without overt intrusion. The previous butler, indeed the entire staff, while professional and efficient, had always seemed to carry as well the faintest hint of disdain. As if, in spite of their position as servants, they were somehow superior to her. Well, they were gone.

She straightened and nodded at the butler. "Lord Wyldewood would like to have a word with you."

Concern flashed in the man's eyes. "Have I done something to displease you, my lady?"

"Absolutely not. I am most happy with the way you have taken charge of the household. And Giddings, if I am ever unhappy with you, I shall tell you myself." She cast him a reassuring smile, then sobered. "Are you aware of the nature of my late husband's death?"

Giddings paused.

"Please, feel free to be candid."

"I daresay everyone in London is aware of the nature of Lord Rathbourne's demise."

"It was rather juicy," she murmured. "Lord Wyldewood, prompted by my father,

47

has gotten it into his head that there is some threat to my security. It's ridiculous, of course. Yet I suspect it will be easier to appease him than to argue with him. If you would be so good as to assure him that you, and the rest of the staff, will take every precaution, I would be most appreciative."

Giddings nodded. "As you wish."

"And then escort Lord Wyldewood to the door."

"Of course, my lady." Giddings nodded again and stepped into the parlor.

Olivia resisted the urge to listen at the door and headed back to her library. The whole idea of any danger was absurd. She'd never been as safe as she was now.

Even though it was rather, well, nice of him to have come to see her, it wasn't at all significant. She had long thought of her life as being divided into three parts defined by Sterling: the time before she had loved him, the brief time she'd loved him, and the time after she had loved him. Now, she was embarking on a fourth part. And he would have nothing whatsoever to do with it.

Nor would love.

THREE

Share the bed of Sterling Harrington.
From the secret list of desires of
Olivia Rathbourne

Olivia distinctly remembered when she was a girl visiting her great-aunt Wilomena's grand London house. She had been told in no uncertain terms she was not to pay any notice whatsoever to the scandalous painting of Great-aunt Wilomena that hung prominently on a wall in the back parlor. But the very moment she was told not to look, she found she could look at nothing else. She felt precisely the same way now.

Regardless of how ridiculous she considered Sterling's concerns, each night since his visit she'd slept fitfully. Aware of every creak on the stair, every servant footfall, every noise made by a large house of indeterminate age that was scarcely noticed during daylight but took on frightening propor-

49

tions in the black of the night. The day of his visit, she hadn't given his comments more than a second thought until she'd retired for the night. Then it seemed she could hear nothing save mysterious, threatening sounds. In spite of her best intentions, she had allowed them to grow in significance until she had been compelled to investigate. And compelled too to rouse her newly hired lady's maid to accompany her. There was, of course, nothing to be seen.

The second night she had again heard noises but thought it absurd to disturb anyone else's rest. She'd crept downstairs wielding a heavy candlestick to find nothing out of order save a maid in the back hallway dallying with a footman. She'd been so relieved, she hadn't made her presence known but had spoken to Giddings the next morning about the necessity of pointing out to the younger female servants that the possible consequences of such activities went far beyond dismissal. She had discarded the idea of a pistol beside her bed almost the moment it was out of her mouth and was glad. She would hate to shoot a servant inadvertently.

The third night, noises again drew her downstairs, much as she tried to tell herself there was nothing to worry about save an overly active imagination. And now, even as she slipped on her wrapper to investigate once again, she was more annoyed at her own vague sense of unease than anything substantial. And annoyed as well at the Earl of Wyldewood. The blame for her lack of rest these past nights could be placed squarely on his broad shoulders.

Even more annoying than her awareness of sounds in the night was her renewed awareness of him. She could no more stop thinking about Sterling than she could keep her gaze from drifting inevitably to the painting of Great-aunt Wilomena. Just like that scandalous painting, his presence claimed her attention whether she wished it to or not. Although, if truth were told, even in all this time, he had never entirely left her thoughts.

She'd cared enough about Sterling to mourn for him when his father had died and again when his wife had lost her life unexpectedly to a brief but fatal illness. While she'd tried, through the years, not to think of him at all, he'd intruded in her thoughts more often than she wished. Memories were triggered by nothing more significant than chance. The notes of a song brought a recollection of dancing in his arms. The scent of lilacs in the spring recalled walks in a garden. The sound of an unknown man's laughter at a ball brought sharp, painful remembrances of his laugh, a sound that having once taken up residence remained stubbornly buried deep in her soul. She'd thought she'd become hardened to such unwelcome reminiscences, indeed the moment such an intrusion occurred, she would viciously cast it aside. Still, regardless of her resolve, he had lingered in the back of her mind. And no doubt always would until she had crossed him off her list once and for all.

She stepped out of her room and headed down the hall to the stairs. There was a lamp lit in the upstairs hall, just as there would be on the ground floor. A nod to security Giddings had said, pointing out that intruders would be less likely in a house that was at least partially lit. Every night she'd been grateful that at least she didn't have to stumble along in complete darkness. She started down the stairs.

That Sterling's intrusion now was in the flesh brought to mind more unwanted memories that she tried and failed to ignore. The look in his eyes when his gaze would meet hers, the way his dark brow would quirk in amusement at something she'd said, the feel of his lips claiming hers. And worse were the questions that haunted the back of her mind. What if things had been different? What if he had fought for her?

What if she had fought harder?

No, that really wasn't a question at all. She knew the answer. Sterling would be dead, and she would still have had to marry Rathbourne.

She reached the ground floor and paused. Someone had forgotten to light the lamp. She sighed in annoyance. It scarcely mattered, she supposed. As much as she'd never liked the house, she knew it well enough to find her way around in the dark. She stepped into the parlor and listened for a moment. There was obviously no one there. She moved back into the center hall and turned toward the library, only then noticing a faint hint of light showing from under the closed door. She had been in the library earlier in the evening. Obviously, Giddings or another servant had failed to extinguish the lamp. That was the problem with new servants still learning the ways of a household. She sighed again and stepped to the door. She pushed it open, and at once the light died.

What on earth —

A large hand clamped over her mouth, and she was jerked back against a hard body. Her heart leapt to her throat and terror twisted her stomach. God help her, Sterling was right! She struggled futilely against whoever held her in his grip. The callused hand over her mouth smelled vaguely of garlic and onions. Fear surged through her, and she fought harder, but her arms were pinned. She flailed her legs, trying to kick at her captor, and was rewarded with a grunt and a muttered curse. Across the room a male voice muttered something in a heavy accent that she didn't catch. In some part of her mind not overcome with terror, it struck her as odd that a heavily accented voice could be indecipherable even if one understood both the speaker's native tongue and the one he was attempting.

Her captor dragged her a few feet and thrust her down onto a chair. The moment his hand slipped from her mouth, she sucked in a deep breath and screamed. Another curse rang out. A hard blow landed against the back of her head. Blinding pain shot through her.

And nothing.

"Lady Rathbourne?"

It was the strangest sensation, as if she were underwater, swimming upward toward the surface. Not that Olivia had had much experience with swimming beyond a few occasions as a girl in a lake on her father's estate. Still, she had rather enjoyed it, and it was on her list. Yes, toward the top: swim in warm seas, preferably naked. Odd, though, that she would be swimming in the dark. And it was extremely dark. Where on earth was she?

A sharp, pungent smell assailed her nostrils.

"Not smelling salts, you bloody idiot," a man said sharply. "She's been hit, she hasn't fainted."

Her eyes snapped open, and she jerked upright. Pain stabbed through her head. She groaned and clapped a hand to the back of her head. "Good God . . . what . . ."

She was reclined on the sofa. Giddings knelt beside her. Two of the newly hired footman and her new maid — what was her name? Ah yes — Mariah — stood surrounding her, concern in their eyes.

She felt a knot at the back of her head and winced. The last thing she remembered . . . She drew her brows together and tried to gather her thoughts. "I heard voices. Someone grabbed me . . ." She sucked in a hard breath. "What happened?"

"We heard you scream, my lady," Giddings said, and nodded toward the two footman. "They came to your assistance at once and scared the intruders off. Unfortunately, the brigands managed to make their escape."

"We are sorry, my lady," the taller footman said. "We were unable to catch them."

"We were investigating a disturbance in the garden," the other said quickly.

"What kind of disturbance?" Olivia asked, a dozen dire possibilities running through her head.

"Lord help us all," Mariah muttered under her breath.

The footmen exchanged glances. The taller one, Terrance, if she recalled his name correctly, looked somewhat abashed. "We heard dogs from the next garden and thought there might be intruders."

"I gather you found nothing?" she said.

"No, my lady." The other footman, Joseph, shook his head.

"I see." She studied the footmen. She'd thought when she'd met them they were rather large and burly for footman, but now she was grateful. The terror she had felt had abated, but knowing that there were two men in her household more than capable of pursuing villains in the night further eased her mind. She glanced at Giddings. "I thought there was a third new footman?"

"Yes, my lady, Thomas," Giddings said slowly. "He has gone —"

"To fetch me." A firm, familiar voice sounded from the doorway.

Olivia's jaw clenched. Sterling strode into the room, Thomas a few steps behind. Olivia started to get to her feet, but her head throbbed, and she sank back down on the sofa. "What are you doing here?" She looked at Giddings. "Why did you send for Lord Wyldewood?"

Giddings drew himself up indignantly. "I did nothing of the sort, Lady Rathbourne. I sent for a physician."

"I don't need a physician." She waved off his comment. "Aside from an aching head, I'm perfectly all right. Then who sent —"

"They were under orders to let me know if anything happened." Sterling knelt beside her, his gaze searched hers. "You're not the least bit all right. You've had a nasty knock on the head."

"I'm fine." She glared at him. "Why would footmen in my employ fetch you?"

"Because they're in my employ as well." Sterling straightened, nodded at the trio, and they started toward the door.

"Stay right where you are," Olivia said sharply, and the men stopped short. "I insist on an explanation. Giddings?"

"Lord Wyldewood recommended the footmen and gave them excellent references." Giddings aimed an indignant look at the footmen. The butler was far too well trained to regard the earl in that manner. "Given Lord Wyldewood's concerns, it seemed an excellent idea to hire footmen more substantial in nature than might usually be expected."

"Yes, of course." It did make a great deal of sense. Still, it was most annoying. She glanced at Giddings. "Were you aware when you hired them that they were in the earl's employ?"

Giddings huffed. "Absolutely not, my lady. I would never have condoned such a thing. Had I so much as suspected, I would have come to you at once."

She nodded and turned her attention to Terrance. "So, I am paying your wages as well as Lord Wyldewood?"

He nodded. "Yes, my lady."

"Do you wish to continue in my employ?"

Terrance glanced at Sterling.

"They were to remain here for as long as it was deemed necessary," Sterling said smoothly.

"For as long as you deemed it necessary, you mean."

Sterling's eyes narrowed slightly. "Yes."

"I see." Given tonight's disturbance, she would prefer the men stayed on, at least for the immediate future. "If the three of you are to remain in my household, I would expect that first and foremost you would answer to me and me alone. If that is acceptable to all of you, I will discuss with Giddings raising your wages to compensate for whatever Lord Wyldewood has been paying you." Her gaze slid to Sterling. "Such payment is to desist at once. I can well afford to pay my own servants."

"They're not exactly servants," Sterling said in an offhand manner. "Their training is more in the line of . . . protection, shall we say, rather than the duties of footmen."

"Imagine my surprise." She considered the trio. She should have realized at once that they were not ordinary footmen. In addition to their appearance, they weren't very good footmen. "Regardless, especially in light of tonight's events, I should like you to stay on."

Almost as one, the men's gazes shifted to Sterling. He gave them a barely perceptible nod. Olivia clenched her jaw.

"Thank you, my lady," Terrance said.

"Now, if you would all take your leave, I should like to have a few words with Lord Wyldewood."

"Yes, my lady," Giddings said. "When the physician —"

"When he arrives, tell him I am perfectly all right and send him on his way."

Giddings glanced at the earl. Blast it all, if one more man looked to Sterling for approval of her orders, she would discharge each and every one of them.

Sterling raised a brow.

She blew a resigned breath. "Tell him if I feel unwell in the morning, I shall send for him."

"Yes, my lady." Giddings nodded and shepherded the others out of the room, closing the door behind them.

"I don't recall your being so stubborn," Sterling said mildly.

"I don't recall your being so arrogant and overbearing," she snapped.

He shrugged. "It seems we have both changed through the years."

She got to her feet, anger sweeping aside the ache in her head. "You had no right to place your . . . your *bodyguards* in my household."

He nodded. "Perhaps not."

"Perhaps?" She glared at him. *"Perhaps?"*

"Perhaps." He studied her calmly. "I didn't think you took this threat seriously.

60

Nor did I think you would take any precautions."

"I took precautions!"

"Oh?" His brow rose again in a superior manner that made her want to throw something at him. "What might those have been?"

"I instructed Giddings to make certain the house was locked and a light was left on during the night and . . ." It did sound rather unsubstantial even to her ears. "And . . ." She gestured aimlessly. "And other things."

"And they were apparently most effective."

"They were adequate."

"Did you put a pistol by the side of your bed?"

"That was absurd, and you well know it. I could have easily shot a servant or . . ." She smirked. "An unwanted earl."

"Or prevented someone from bashing you over the head."

She ignored him and narrowed her gaze. "This is none of your concern."

"Oh, but it is. Your father made it my concern when he came to me. My responsibility as it were. As I was confident you would not do what was necessary to provide for your protection, I took it upon myself to see to your safety."

She stared in disbelief. "My God, you are arrogant!"

His gaze met hers directly. "I am the Earl of Wyldewood. I take my responsibilities seriously."

"I am not your responsibility!"

"When your father —"

"Regardless of what you think of as your responsibility, I am perfectly capable of taking care of myself."

"Yes, I can see that." He paused. "And how is your head?"

"Fine!" Her fists clenched, and she made a concerted effort to relax her hands. She hadn't kept her emotions under control for ten years, hadn't survived one arrogant man for a decade, to allow another to waltz back into her life and commandeer it. She forced a measure of calm to her voice. "I do not mean to appear ungrateful for your assistance."

The hint of a smile touched the corners of his mouth. "And yet you do."

"My apologies, my lord. I can only attribute my rude behavior to the lateness of the hour and the ache in my head."

"As well as the fact that you would prefer never to lay eyes on me again."

She shrugged. "I thought that was understood. However, I am most appreciative, and you have my heartfelt thanks. I shudder to think . . ." At once the terror of being grabbed by a strange man in the night in her own home swept through her, and she shivered. "What might have happened if your men had not been here." She drew a deep breath. "Indeed, I am most grateful."

He nodded. "I am glad I could be of assistance."

"Now." Her gaze narrowed. "If you would be so good as to get out."

"So much for gratitude," he murmured.

"What do you want from me, my lord?" At once the tenuous hold she had on her temper shattered. "I have thanked you. Perhaps not as graciously as I should have, but, given the circumstances, even you can see that is understandable." She straightened her shoulders. "I don't need you, or my father, to come to my aid. I am not a fair maiden in a children's story in need of rescue. Once, perhaps, I might have needed assistance, but you're entirely right when you say we have both changed. I have changed a great deal. I am not the girl you once knew."

"No," he said slowly. "I can see that."

"Don't look at me as if it's a great shame that I am not the same."

"I think it might be," he said quietly.

"We all change, my lord." She crossed her arms over her chest. "Time and events mold us, form us, shape us."

"Certainly. It's just that I remember —"

"The memories of one's youth are no more than illusions. Reality bends and shapes us with the passage of years and the experiences of life. I daresay neither of us is as the other remembers; nor would we probably wish to be. Illusions are as insubstantial as dreams in the night, with no more significance."

"Still, it is rather disheartening to see your illusions shattered."

"There are all sorts of illusions in this world. Most deserve to be shattered. It is far less painful to face the reality of a situation than to cherish what is, in truth, only imaginary." She met his gaze. "Reality is difficult enough to accept, but accept it one must. One cannot survive this world by placing one's faith in illusion, in things that don't exist."

He stared at her for a long silent moment, and for the briefest fraction of a second, regret, stark and powerful and unyielding, ripped through her.

"I apologize for my intrusion, Lady Rathbourne," he said coolly. "I shall not bother you again."

"Thank you, my lord." She paused. "And again, you have my gratitude for your foresight."

He started to go, then hesitated. "If you need further assistance —"

"I won't," she said firmly.

"And I suspect I am the last person you would accept it from at any rate."

She stared at him for a long moment, a dozen comments running through her head. Things she had wanted to say to him for years. Words she had practiced and rehearsed in her mind, late in the night, when the dark had eased the reins she held on her thoughts and emotions and desires. She forced a tight smile. "You're right, my lord, as always."

He nodded and took his leave.

Her heart twisted in spite of her resolve. Why oh why had he insinuated himself back into her life? And why did the very sight of him, the sound of his voice, the look in his eye resurrect memories she'd long thought were buried as deep as her husband? Memories that carried with them the pale suggestion of feelings long ago set aside.

At least he wouldn't be back. She had no doubt on that score. One thing about Sterling obviously hadn't changed. His pride would never allow him to pursue a woman who didn't want him. Her father had used that to his advantage, now it was her turn. She had made it perfectly clear she had no interest in seeing him again, ever. It would be best for her, best as well for him.

And if that meant she couldn't cross him off her list, so be it. It was just a list after all. Not the least bit important anymore. Not now when the entire world was open to her.

Now, she was free.

Sterling poured his second glass of brandy or possibly his third, he wasn't sure, and replaced the decanter on the side table. Even from across the library, he could see the three letters laid out on his desk. Not that he needed to see them to know they were there, waiting to at last be opened. As they had waited for a decade.

It had been remarkably easy to locate them. Indeed, he knew exactly where they were. Most of his correspondence was appropriately filed by his secretary, Edward Dennison. But the letters from Olivia had been pushed to the back of one of his shirt drawers, much as thoughts of her had been pushed to the back of his mind. Still, just as with his memories, he knew they were there.

He'd been tempted on occasion to open the letters; but as time went on, it seemed less and less important to do so. So they had remained in the back of the drawer. Neither forgotten nor acknowledged. Odd, that he'd never seriously considered throwing them in the fire.

Now, they sat on his desk and beckoned to him. It was absurd not to open them. It had been ten years since Olivia had written the letters. Whatever they said scarcely mattered. Life had gone on, hers and his. Regardless of what she'd written, there was nothing to be done about it.

Without realizing he had taken so much as a step, he found himself beside the desk, the brandy in his glass half-gone, staring at the letters. He had arranged them precisely, side by side as if neatness made a difference. They were addressed to him in her fine hand. A bit bolder than was appropriate for a female perhaps yet still entirely feminine. He sank down in his chair, his gaze never leaving the letters. He had always thought her notes were in the form of an apology, a request for forgiveness he'd had no desire to grant. Looking at them now, he thought his name appeared written in haste. Or perhaps desperation.

He'd heard the rumors about Rathbourne through the years. The viscount had been known to be ruthless in the pursuit of those artifacts or priceless pieces of art or antiquities he collected. And ruthless as well in his protection of that which he considered his. The man didn't even display his acquisitions as other collectors did but kept them hidden away in a treasure room for his enjoyment alone. Had Olivia been another treasure for him? Nothing more than a possession? A perfect specimen? A perfect wife?

He reached for the first letter, but his hand hesitated over it. Was it guilt that stilled his hand? Or was it fear? He'd never thought of himself as being afraid of anything. But this . . . He'd always believed she had abandoned him, that he had been the injured party. Now, it appeared he was wrong. No wonder she wanted nothing to do with him. Hadn't he felt the same before her father had confessed his misdeeds?

If these letters were a cry for help, unheeded and ignored, then he did indeed owe her far more than mere protection against those who had killed her husband. He owed her a debt he could never repay. He owed her a life.

Sterling drew a deep breath and picked up the first of the three letters.

FOUR

Disregard convention.
From the secret list of desires of
Olivia Rathbourne

Olivia resisted the need to scream in frustration. And resisted as well the desire to wrap her fingers around the neck of her late husband's solicitor and squeeze the very life out of him just as she now felt her dead husband's hands reaching out from the grave to squeeze the life out of her. Still, she would not reveal so much as a hint of her turmoil to the wretched man who had worked — who still apparently worked — for the late, unlamented, Viscount Rathbourne.

She drew a calming breath. "As I'm certain you can understand, Mr. Hollis, the specifics of my husband's will come as something of a surprise. And, as it strikes me as somewhat complicated, would you be

69

so good as to repeat your explanation?" What she truly needed was a moment to gather her wits, to maintain her composure. She forced a polite smile. "I am but a woman in mourning after all."

"I had hoped to see your father here for the reading of his lordship's will." Mr. Hollis's brows drew together in a disapproving manner. "It is customary, in circumstances such as these, to have a male relation in attendance for guidance."

Still, it would be lovely to hear Mr. Hollis gasp for breath as his face turned red then purple. "My father and I are estranged, Mr. Hollis. Nor was he especially close to my husband." She shrugged in her best helpless-female manner. "I fear you shall have to deal with me alone."

"Very well." Mr. Hollis folded his hands on top of the papers on her husband's — her — desk and considered her as if trying to decide how simplistic and childlike to make his explanation. "As you know, Viscount Rathbourne was an avid collector. Upon his death, there were still several of his collections he considered incomplete. The terms of his will are in regard to three such collections. My understanding is that through the years, he was unable to acquire the items required to complete those collections. Until such time as you are able to complete the collections, the monies and property that comprise his lordship's estate will remain under the administration of myself and this firm." He paused. "Furthermore, it is stipulated that said collections bear his name regardless of whether you retain ownership, sell, or donate the collections."

"So," she said slowly, "in order to receive the inheritance that is rightfully mine, my late husband has decreed I should go on some sort of hunt for treasure?"

Mr. Hollis chuckled. "I would not have put it in quite that manner, but essentially, yes."

She drew her brows together. "Forgive me for asking, Mr. Hollis, but is this legal?"

Indignation furrowed the solicitor's brow. "The terms of his lordship's will were drawn up under the guidance of this firm. I assure you all aspects are entirely legal." He frowned. "You have by no means been left destitute, Lady Rathbourne. In such a case the validity of the will could certainly be challenged. As it stands, you will be provided with a suitable allowance for household expenditures that exceed the household accounts currently administered by this office and, of course, personal necessities. You will also be permitted to live in this house as well as the one in the country for however long you desire. If you will address your attention to the papers we prepared for you, you will see the amounts allocated are more than adequate."

She glanced at the papers in her hand. Adequate was something of an overstatement. Minimal was a better description.

"In many respects, Lady Rathbourne, your circumstances shall remain remarkably similar to those you experienced before the death of Lord Rathbourne."

"I see." She chose her words with care, ignoring the way her stomach clenched with Mr. Hollis's pronouncement although she had already realized much the same thing. "And if I complete the *Rathbourne collections?*"

"Then all properties and monies become yours and yours alone." Mr. Hollis cast her a condescending smile. "Should that be the case, it is my hope that you would continue to allow this firm to be of service in the manner in which it has well served Lord Rathbourne for many years."

"Of course," she murmured although it would be a very cold day in the fires of Hell before she so much as considered putting her affairs in the hands of anyone even remotely connected to this man or his firm or her husband. Not that she would tell him that. It would not be wise to alienate the solicitor as long as he controlled her finances. "Tell me, Mr. Hollis, I assume these items are not easy to acquire?"

"No, indeed. It is my understanding Lord Rathbourne had tried for years to locate, then purchase the items in question."

"And what, precisely, are they?"

"My apologies, Lady Rathbourne." For a moment, what might have been genuine regret flickered in the solicitor's eyes. "According to your husband's instructions, if you decide to pursue the articles, you will be given the information regarding the first item only. Once that has been acquired, you will receive information regarding the second and so forth."

She smiled in a wry manner. "And you said it was not a treasure hunt."

Mr. Hollis had the good grace to look slightly abashed. "I am only carrying out his lordship's wishes, my lady." He paused. "I confess, Lord Rathbourne's stipulations have put this firm in an awkward position, but there is nothing that can be done about it." He drew a deep breath. "As my responsibility is now to you and your best interest, I should tell you I did advise against this course. However, his lordship would not be swayed."

"He rarely could." She thought for a moment. "Is there a deadline? A time limit for completing the collections?"

"Not as such." Mr. Hollis shook his head in a decidedly relieved manner. "You may take as long as is necessary."

She raised a brow. "The rest of my life even?"

"Well, yes, I suppose —"

"Very well then." She rose to her feet. "If you would be so good as to return tomorrow, I shall tell you of my decision."

Mr. Hollis stood. "Your decision? I fear you have me at a loss, my lady. What decision?"

"Why, whether or not I will pick up the gauntlet my late husband has thrown down."

"As I said, there is no particular hurry. I would strongly recommend you wait until a suitable period of mourning has passed to so much as consider —"

"On the contrary, Mr. Hollis, there is a very great hurry." She forced a pleasant smile. "Indeed, I feel that completing my husband's collections and thus acquiescing to his last wishes to be a matter of great urgency and very much my duty."

74

"These items are not to be found in London," he warned.

"I did not for a moment assume they were. That would be entirely too easy."

"Procuring them will require significant travel as well as substantial funding." He frowned. "Might I point out, you do not have the financial means this venture requires."

"There is no need to point that out, I am well aware of it. Regardless, this is something I must at least consider. For my late husband. For his memory." She adopted an indignant note. "Surely you understand?"

"Forgive me, Lady Rathbourne, I did not mean to imply —"

"Of course not, Mr. Hollis. I am certain neither you nor my late husband imagined I would think for even a moment of undertaking this task he has set. But I shall give it a great deal of thought." She shrugged. "And if I fail, I shall be no worse off than I am right now."

He nodded. "Aside from the regrettable passing of your husband, your life can continue on in the same manner in which it always has."

"I am a widow, Mr. Hollis. A woman alone. My life cannot possibly continue on in the manner it always has."

"I suppose not." He studied her for a moment, then sighed and collected his papers. "As you wish, Lady Rathbourne. I shall return tomorrow." He started toward the door, then paused. "I suspect Lord Rathbourne may have underestimated you."

"Good day, Mr. Hollis."

"Good day, my lady." He nodded and took his leave.

The moment the door closed behind him, Olivia's smile vanished. *Damn him and the dead man he served.* She wrung her hands together and paced the room.

She should have expected something like this. Her late husband had never relinquished an article he acquired, never given up a possession that belonged to him. She should have known even death would not change that. Should have known he would find a way to keep her in his grasp even from the grave. Rathbourne had made certain she would not have the resources to start her life anew. Mr. Hollis was right. Her life could go on exactly as it always had. Even as her late husband had breathed his last breath, he no doubt had some satisfaction in the knowledge that he had arranged for her to continue to live under his complete control. In his clutches until she grew old, alone in this house, where everywhere she turned were reminders of the man who had owned her body but never her heart, never her soul. Trapped for the rest of her days.

Not bloody likely. Her jaw clenched. She had not survived her husband's life only to be defeated by him in death. She would find whatever it was that the viscount had been unable to acquire and complete his collections. After all, she had far more to gain than he ever had. Still, it would be a costly venture and her minimal allowance would not allow for either travel or purchase. Nor was there anyone she could turn to for help. He'd known she would never go to her father, and she couldn't name a single friend. Those friendships she'd had before marriage had vanished with her isolation. It seemed there was only one option left to her. And if pride made it a difficult choice to make, so be it.

She would never give up the chance to be free of the Viscount Rathbourne, free to at last live her life. She drew a deep breath and sent a quick prayer heavenward for help, vowing in return to donate a goodly portion of her inheritance to those less fortunate. Perhaps orphans or widows whose husbands had left them with nothing save bad memories.

But Mr. Hollis was right. Viscount Rathbourne had underestimated his wife. His perfect possession. As much a part of his collections as the antiquities and art he kept hidden from prying eyes. His late lordship had indeed underestimated Lady Olivia Rathbourne.

And the lengths to which she would go.

"I must confess, after our last encounter, I was surprised to receive your note asking me here this evening." Sterling swirled the brandy in his glass and eyed Olivia thoughtfully. "Surprised" was something of an understatement. She'd made it clear that she wished nothing more to do with him. Only a complete idiot would fail to understand why.

"Upon reflection, I realized my behavior last night was reprehensible. In your own way, you were simply trying to help." She smiled in a polite manner, and his heart twisted. Good God, she still took his breath away. She sat on the sofa in her parlor, adjacent to the chair he occupied. Close enough that with little effort he could reach out and pull her into his arms, should he ever again have the courage to do so.

"I do hope you can forgive me."

"That goes without saying. My own behavior was, as you pointed out, somewhat overbearing." Still, of all the regrets he had, that was not among them. And the events of last night had proved him right. "How is your head?"

"I have a nasty knot." She felt the back of her head and winced, and he wondered if her hair would still feel like silk against his fingers. He ignored the thought. "But I am quite fine." Amusement gleamed in her eye. "As it only hurts when I touch it, I endeavor not to touch it."

"Why did you ask me here?" he said abruptly.

"I wished to apologize for my behavior."

"You did so last night."

"But I was not particularly gracious." She sipped her brandy, her gaze meeting his over the rim of the glass. "Indeed, I was quite rude."

"You could have simply sent a note," he said without thinking and at once wished the words back. She'd sent him notes before.

He'd sat at his desk for long hours, well past dawn, reading and rereading her letters. It was as if once he had picked them up, he could not put them down. He had read and regretted and wondered what if he hadn't been such a fool all those years ago.

What if he had read the first note when she had sent it? The one telling him she loved him, that she was being forced to marry Rathbourne. How different their lives might have been.

"I did send a note, my lord. I —"

"Sterling," he said at once, then hesitated. "My apologies. That was most presumptuous of me."

"Not at all." She smiled and again his heart shifted. "We have known each other most of our lives. It seems silly not to call one another by our given names. Besides, I find it rather difficult to call you by your title as I have always thought of you as Sterling. And I did send a note, requesting you to call on me."

"Yes, of course." He paused. "What I don't understand is why."

"Other than offering my continued apology you mean?"

He nodded.

"You're very perceptive, Sterling. I don't recall your being quite so discerning."

"I don't believe I was the least bit perceptive in my younger days. Rather, I was proud and stubborn and concerned only with myself." He smiled in a wry manner. "One can only hope the changes wrought by the years and responsibility have tempered that."

"One can hope." She sipped her brandy, her gaze considering. "I have given a great deal of thought to something you said last night."

"Oh?"

"You offered me your assistance."

"And you refused. I believe you agreed that I was the last person you would ever accept help from."

"Indeed I did. However it now appears . . ." She shrugged. "I was wrong."

"You were wrong," he said slowly.

"I was." She reached for the brandy decanter and refilled his glass.

He raised a brow. "Will I need this?"

"Probably." She smiled.

He studied her for a moment. Beneath her cool exterior, he suspected she was more than a little apprehensive. "Very well then. How may be I of service?"

"It seems even in death my late husband is determined to maintain his grip on my life." She paused to choose her words. "The terms of his will are such that I will not inherit what is rightfully mine unless I undertake what can only be called a hunt for treasure."

He stared. "Unless you what?"

"I am sure you are aware of Viscount Rathbourne's passion for collecting art, artifacts, and any number of other valuable items."

"I daresay there are few members of the Antiquities Society who are not aware of it." He sipped his brandy. "While his collections were not displayed, I understand they are extensive and quite extraordinary."

"No doubt." She waved off the comment as if she had little interest or knowledge about her late husband's collections. How very odd. "There were apparently three such collections he considered incomplete. Until I acquire the items necessary to complete them, I am to have nothing save a minimal allowance." She blew a frustrated breath. "My life now has come down to two choices. I may continue to live as I always have, or I can attempt to locate these items." She met his gaze directly. "I do not intend to spend the rest of my days under my late husband's thumb."

"What are the items in question?"

"I don't know." She huffed in annoyance. "It's ridiculous, and dictated by my late husband's instructions, but I will be given that information only if I decide to seek them."

"You're not serious."

"If I were not serious, you would not be here," she said sharply. "I hadn't realized my late husband was quite so fond of games, but apparently he was. It's distressing and annoying and . . ." She drew a calming breath. "Forgive me."

He shook his head. "No apology is necessary. I can well understand your frustration at the circumstances you find yourself in."

"Frustration is the mildest of my feelings. Beyond that . . ." She took a bracing sip of her brandy. "I find turning to you to be rather more difficult than I had thought."

He leaned forward and met her gaze directly, her green eyes dark with hope or reluctance or both. "How can I help you, Olivia?"

She considered him for a moment, then shook her head. "This is absurd. It will never work." She jumped to her feet and paced the room. "I don't know what I was thinking. I was mad even to consider asking for your help."

Sterling rose to his feet. "You have no one else."

She pulled up short and stared at him. "Thank you for being so gracious as to point that out."

"I don't mean to be cruel. I merely think it's practical to face the reality of the situation. Olivia —"

"Don't," she snapped. "Do not take that kindly tone with me. I do not want your sympathy." She paused to regain her composure. "You're right of course, there is no one else I might turn to. No family save my father, and I would rot in this house for the rest of my days before I would ask him for so much as a kind word. I have no friends. His lordship saw to that." The words were said without undue emotion. Olivia was obviously a woman used to keeping her own feelings firmly in hand.

"You have me," he said simply.

She ignored him. "This is insane." She shook her head and resumed pacing. He suspected that a hundred conflicting thoughts filled her mind. She paused and looked at him. "You understand what I'm asking of you?"

"You wish me to help you find the items needed to fulfill the terms of the will."

"You realize this will likely be a costly venture. It will no doubt require a considerable expenditure."

He shrugged. "My finances are sound, my fortune extensive. That is not a particular problem."

"I intend to reimburse you for every penny."

"I have no doubt of that."

"I am certain as well these items are not to be found easily. I have been told they are not in London." She narrowed her eyes. "Travel will undoubtedly be necessary."

He nodded. "I have not traveled for many years. I shall look forward to it."

"With me?"

"I should like nothing better," he said staunchly.

"I intend for this to be an impersonal arrangement."

He raised a brow. "Impersonal?"

"I do not foresee resuming the relationship we once shared. Nor do I wish for us to do so." She shook her head. "Too much time has passed for that, and we are in agreement that we are not the same people we once were. We shall be partners in this endeavor in a most businesslike manner. However . . ." Her brow furrowed as if she were reaching a decision. "I see no reason why we cannot be friends."

He nodded solemnly. "Nor do I. After all, we will be spending a great deal of time together, and I would much prefer to spend that time with someone who considers me a friend rather than someone who detests the very ground beneath my feet."

Her eyes widened with surprise. "I have

never detested the ground beneath your feet." A reluctant smile curved her lips. "The ground is blameless." She sobered. "Which brings up another point. I suggest we start our *friendship* anew. As if we had just met. And put what once passed between us firmly in the past, where it belongs."

He drew his brows together. "That is what you want?"

She squared her shoulders. "I think it's best."

"And yet it's because of the past that you have turned to me."

"Yes, well, as you pointed out, I have no one else."

"Not all of the past was bad," he murmured.

"Regardless, I don't think we shall accomplish anything if we continue to drag what happened long ago behind us like the chains of Marley's ghost. I think it's best to start fresh." She set her chin firmly. "As friends."

He smiled. "One can never have too many friends."

"Excellent." She nodded. "Now then, as I cannot expect you to do this simply out of the goodness of your heart, I propose to offer you compensation."

"Compensation?" He drew his brows

together. "Absolutely not. I owe you my help. This is the least I can do. I consider this a debt long overdue. An obligation I am only too pleased to meet."

"Nonetheless, you should receive something for your trouble."

"I absolutely will not hear of —"

"You don't think I was offering to pay for your help did you?" Amusement danced in her eyes. He ignored it.

"I did think something like that," he said under his breath.

"You needn't look so insulted."

"It did sound suspiciously like an insult."

"Nonsense. You completely misunderstood. I know you would never accept any sort of payment, and, frankly, if I had the funds to do so, I would not have to undertake this quest at all." She met his gaze. "Once I have my inheritance, I plan to donate or sell each and every one of my late husband's collections and give a sizable percentage to charitable endeavors. I propose that fully half of those donations will be made in your family's name. Does that sound fair to you?"

He nodded slowly. "It's not necessary, but yes, it sounds more than fair."

"Very well then, we are agreed."

"As to terms yes but what of specifics?"

"I have asked my late husband's solicitor to call on me tomorrow. I intend to tell him that I will pursue the items necessary to fulfill the terms of the will. I anticipate he will then present me with information as to the first object. I would appreciate your presence at that meeting." She thought for a moment. "Would it be possible for Nathanial and Miss Montini to accompany you as well? As she has spent some time with the collections, her expertise might be beneficial in determining where we might find the article in question."

He nodded. "Excellent idea."

"Very well then, I shall see you tomorrow," she said, obviously dismissing him. "I do appreciate your willingness to help me in this matter, Sterling. I hope you do not regret it." She extended her hand to him.

He took her hand to shake it but instead held it, warm and soft and small within his. "Of all the regrets I may have, I cannot imagine this being one of them."

She raised a brow. "There is that arrogance again."

"I suspect arrogance is a beneficial quality in an endeavor such as this. One wouldn't want anything less than complete confidence in a partner." He raised her hand to his lips, his gaze never leaving hers. "Or a friend."

"And as you say, one can never have too many friends." She smiled. "Do keep in mind I am most serious about the limits of that friendship." She pulled her hand from his. "I want — I expect — nothing more from you than your assistance."

"And I shall offer nothing more," he said smoothly, and smiled. "I shall return tomorrow then." He turned and started toward the door.

"Oh and Sterling."

He turned back to her. "Yes?"

"When I insult you . . ." She grinned and it struck him as genuine and rarely used. "There will not be a doubt in your mind."

He laughed, nodded, and took his leave.

A few minutes later he was settled in his carriage, headed for home. This evening had not been at all what he'd expected even if he'd had few expectations upon his arrival. He'd had no idea why she'd asked him to call, but he had never imagined this.

She'd turned to him for help. His heart lightened. She'd turned to him once before, and he'd failed her. He would not fail her now. And in the process, somehow, they would find again what they'd once had.

He wasn't sure when it had happened but

somewhere, in the course of their conversation or perhaps it was simply being with her again, he'd accepted what he'd been fighting from the moment he had learned the truth from her father. Everything was different, yet nothing had changed. He had never put Olivia — Livy — behind him. Never truly gone on with his life. Oh, certainly he had been an excellent husband to Alice and would be still if she hadn't died. He had cared deeply for her, but the affection he had felt for his wife paled in comparison with what he had felt — still felt — for Livy.

Now he had a second chance, not that he deserved it. He had been a fool. But he'd also been young and proud and far too inexperienced to know that there are some things in life worth fighting for. Some things that are rare and valuable and only come once. Some things a man would — should — be willing to give his very life for.

Right now, she was only offering friendship, but it was an excellent place to start. He smiled to himself. Yes, friendship was a first step, and he had time. Who knew long it might take to find the items to complete the late viscount's collections?

Not that it would be easy to recapture what they'd lost. He had no illusions on that score. In spite of her words about starting anew, there were too many betrayals on his part for her to forget easily or forgive. He would still have to earn her forgiveness, then he would win her heart. And this time, he would not give up.

He couldn't change the past, but the future was in his hands. Olivia Rathbourne was the one true love of his life, and he would do whatever was necessary to make certain she stayed in his life for the rest of their days.

She needed him, and for the moment it was enough. But he now realized he needed her as well. He always had. Resolve throbbed in his blood. He would win her back. And he would do everything in his power to help her find the items needed to gain the inheritance that should, by rights, already be hers.

And he absolutely refused to consider what might happen when they succeeded. When she no longer needed him.

FIVE

Follow my heart.
From the secret list of desires of
Olivia Rathbourne

"In many ways, Lady Rathbourne." Mr. Hollis peered at her in a disapproving manner. "While your decision does not come as a complete surprise, the haste with which you have reached it is distressing. I had hoped for a somewhat more considered response from you."

"I have given this a great deal of consideration, Mr. Hollis. Indeed, I have thought of little else," Olivia said coolly, addressing the solicitor, who was seated in front of her desk. Olivia had taken the chair behind the desk before Hollis could do so. She refused to be in the subservient position she'd had at their last meeting. Sterling stood close at hand near the fireplace, and even if she did not wish to admit it aloud, his very presence strengthened her resolve and bolstered her courage. Nathanial and Gabriella sat discreetly at the far end of the library along with a young man Mr. Hollis had introduced as Josiah Cadwallender, another solicitor, silent witnesses to the discussion. "It is nothing less than my duty to comply with my late husband's wishes."

"And yet I cannot imagine the late viscount, or any rational husband, truly expecting you to do so."

"Then he should not have placed such stipulations in his will." She cast the solicitor a serene smile. The man really did deserve to be strangled or perhaps simply whipped thoroughly. Each was a delightful thought. "And perhaps you should have done more to dissuade him."

Mr. Hollis ignored her. "And for you to attempt to complete his collections with assistance" — his gaze slid to Sterling then back to her — "from a gentleman who is not a relation is nothing short of scandalous."

"I am a longtime friend of Lady Rathbourne's family," Sterling said smoothly.

"Who has graciously offered his assistance in this endeavor." Olivia shrugged. "The appearance of scandal does not concern me. My concern is only to fulfill my late husband's final request. As any dutiful wife would," she added in a prim manner.

Sterling coughed, then smiled apologetically.

"Even so, Lady Rathbourne." The solicitor's brow furrowed, and he again glanced at Sterling. "This is most improper, and I cannot approve."

Sterling glanced at her. "Is his approval necessary?"

"Not to my knowledge." She fixed Mr. Hollis with a firm look. "Is there something in the will regarding the manner in which I acquire these items? Something prohibiting me from accepting help?"

"No." Mr. Hollis sputtered. "Still, it is most improper."

"Propriety is no more a concern than scandal." She narrowed her eyes. "You cannot have it both ways, Mr. Hollis. You cannot bemoan the fact, as you did at our last meeting, that I had no male present for guidance, and now complain that the gentleman in attendance is unsuitable."

Sterling's brow rose. "I can't recall ever being regarded as unsuitable."

A faint snort of laughter sounded from the back of the room, obviously from Sterling's brother. Mr. Cadwallender had scarce said a word other than a polite murmured greeting.

"Oh no, my lord, I mean nothing of the sort," Mr. Hollis said quickly, obviously aware of the implications of insulting the Earl of Wyldewood. The earl was a man of power and wealth who could engage Mr. Hollis's firm in the future. Or ruin it. Mr. Hollis turned to Sterling. "My apologies, my lord. I mean no insult."

Sterling nodded.

"It is simply my responsibility to ensure that Lord — Lady Rathbourne's interests are protected. As well as the interests of the estate." Mr. Hollis raised his chin. "Surely you can understand my concern?"

"Absolutely, and your concern is commendable," Sterling said in what could only be called his best Earl of Wyldewood manner. It was most impressive. "You may rest assured on that score. I fully intend to make certain *Lady* Rathbourne's interests are indeed protected. And Lady Rathbourne is your client now, is she not?"

"Yes, of course, my lord. As she is, I would advise strongly against this undertaking." He turned his attention to Olivia. "Lady Rathbourne, as I said yesterday, your life can continue in the comfortable manner it always has. There is no need —"

"There is every need, Mr. Hollis," she said

in a calm tone that belied the frustration churning within her. "I have no desire to continue my life in the manner I have lived it thus far. I am now a widow and still young enough to wish to have more out of the rest of my days than a comfortable existence. My late husband has set me a challenge, and I shall rise to it."

"Very well then." Mr. Hollis stood and gathered his papers. "I shall take my leave. Mr. Cadwallender will remain to inform you of the first item to be acquired. In addition, he will accompany you in your pursuit of the items."

"He will what?" Olivia rose and leveled an annoyed look at the solicitor. "Why? To what purpose?"

"To ensure that your interests and the interests of the estate are protected," Mr. Hollis said.

"As well as the interests of your firm," Sterling pointed out.

"Without question, my lord." Mr. Hollis met the earl's gaze directly. "Lord Rathbourne's estate is sizable."

"As is the income you derive from its administration no doubt." Sterling smiled a noncommittal sort of smile that nonetheless spoke volumes.

"Quite right, my lord." Mr. Hollis squared

his shoulders. "And I would be remiss in my responsibilities to my firm, as well as to his late lordship's estate, if I failed to provide a witness and documentation as to Lady Rathbourne's efforts. While there is nothing regarding how she acquires these items, it clearly states in the will that the administrators of the estate are to make certain in whatever manner they deem necessary that there will be a concise accounting of the methods employed to complete the collections." He glanced at Olivia. "As I am certain her ladyship noted in her perusal of the copy of that document and the others I left for her yesterday."

"Yes, of course," Olive said blithely. She'd been far too busy coming up with a way to meet the terms of the blasted will to do more than skim it. "It simply slipped my mind."

"His expenses, within reason, will be paid by the firm. In addition he will be able to provide legal counsel should it be required. He is unmarried and unencumbered and, in spite of his youth, has a good head on his shoulders. He will represent the interests of the firm well. Good day, my lord." Mr. Hollis nodded at Sterling, then at Olivia. "Lady Rathbourne. I do hope, should you be successful that you continue to allow this firm to be of service —"

"Yes, yes." She tried and failed to hide the impatience in her voice. "In the manner in which you served Lord Rathbourne."

"And, I might add, served him well," Mr. Hollis pointed out. "Good day, Lady Rathbourne." With that, the solicitor took his leave.

Sterling chuckled softly. "The man has no idea does he?"

"I don't know what you're talking about," Olivia said in a lofty manner.

Sterling leaned closer, and said under his breath, "I'm talking about the fact that, should we succeed, it would take the power of heaven itself to convince you to retain his firm."

"It scarcely matters at the moment as I am not in a position to employ or dismiss him." Still, Sterling was right, and it was most annoying. She stared at him. "Do not think you know me, Sterling Harrington. I am not the same girl I was."

He smiled a slow knowing smile, and she resisted the urge to smack him. "Some things never change, my dear."

She ignored him and turned to the trio at the back of the library. "Mr. Cadwallender, Nathanial, Gabriella would you join us?"

Sterling's brother and his fiancée approached the desk. The solicitor was a step behind, well-worn valise in hand.

"Mr. Cadwallender," Olivia began, "no doubt you heard the bulk of the conversation."

"Not at all, my lady. I tried very hard not to hear a word," the young man said stiffly. *Dear Lord.* In spite of his handsome face and admirable form, the solicitor was following in the footsteps of the eminently stuffy Mr. Hollis.

"I heard." Nathanial grinned. "Not everything but enough to know what's going on."

"Sterling acquainted us with the details of the viscount's will." Gabriella's gaze met Olivia's. Gabriella's work cataloguing Olivia's late husband's antiquities would have led to her appointment as curator of a museum of the viscount's collections. Olivia knew nothing of his plan until after his death. Nor did she care. She had never seen his treasures and had no interest in them. "How can we be of help?"

"I don't know that you can, yet." Olivia looked at Mr. Cadwallender. "It all depends on what Mr. Cadwallender has to say."

"Yes, of course." Mr. Cadwallender drew out an envelope from his valise, presenting it to Olivia with a vague hint of a flourish. Perhaps there was hope for the young man after all.

Olivia tore open the envelope, unfolded the single page, and stared at the few lines of precise writing. Her stomach lurched slightly at the recognition of her late husband's hand. "I have no idea what this is."

She passed the page to Sterling, who glanced at it and handed it to his brother. Nathanial read it and exhaled a long breath. "Well, this will not be easy. The first item is the canopic jar of Aashet bearing the head of Imsety."

Olivia frowned. "A what?"

"Ancient Egyptians placed the organs of a body in canopic jars during mummification," Nathanial said. "There were usually four jars, each often with a stopper carved in the shape of a different head. A human, a baboon, a jackal, and a falcon, representing protective spirits if you will. The jar with the human head represented Imsety."

"Dare I ask what that jar would have held?" Sterling winced.

"The liver, I think." Nathanial looked at Gabriella for confirmation, and she nodded.

"Aashet was believed to have been a concubine or perhaps a lesser wife of Tuthmosis III, ruling, oh, more than three thousand years ago," Gabriella said.

100

"I see." Olivia thought for a moment. "Well, if we need one jar to complete a collection presumably, my late husband had the other three."

All eyes turned to Gabriella. "I really can't say," she said in an apologetic manner. "There is a great deal here that remains to be catalogued. I suggest we look."

"That's a bit of a problem." Olivia blew an annoyed breath. "As you know, the viscount kept his collections in a specially built room." She turned toward Sterling. "A vault really, but he referred to it as a treasure room." She glanced around the library. "I know the entrance is in here, but as I have never seen it, I neither know exactly where it is nor do I know how it's opened. I assumed I would have the walls demolished to reach it." And indeed, had relished the idea of destroying the house wall by wall.

"We know where it is." Nathanial stepped to a book shelf, pulled off a handful of volumes to reveal a lever mounted on the back wall of the shelf. "The viscount showed us on Gabriella's first visit. This opens the door to the room. The lever is released by a combination lock."

Sterling raised a brow. "And that is located where?"

Gabriella shook her head. "I don't know. The few times I was here . . ." Gabriella's gaze strayed to the French doors that opened to a small garden. No doubt the poor girl was remembering the day when she had found Olivia's late husband propped on a garden seat in a pool of blood. "Lord Rathbourne always dialed the combination before my arrival."

"I believe I can help." Cadwallender rummaged in his valise and pulled out a sheaf of papers. "Mr. Hollis provided me with copies of everything he left for you." His gaze shifted to Olivia, without so much as a glimmer of chastisement in his eyes. "The combination lock is behind a three-volume set of Mr. Dickens's *Great Expectations.*"

At once, the group turned toward the bookshelves. "Here." Sterling pulled out the books to reveal a combination lock resembling that on a fair-sized safe. "I assume, Cadwallender, you have the combination as well."

Cadwallender paused as if debating the wisdom of handing over the information, then passed a paper to Sterling. "Sir."

Olivia smiled to herself. Yes, the boy definitely had promise. Sterling twirled the combination, then nodded at his brother.

Nathanial grinned at Olivia. "Watch this."

He flipped the lever, and a wall of shelves slid to the side, revealing a large opening and utter darkness beyond. Nathanial stepped into the black. Olivia shivered.

Gabriella cast her a reassuring smile. "There are gas sconces on either side of the door."

A moment later light flared, illuminating the windowless room. Gabriella followed her fiancé; Sterling and Cadwallender waited for Olivia. She couldn't quite seem to take that first step. As if, in stepping over the threshold, she would, in truth, become what she'd been for the last decade. Yet another possession to hide away from prying eyes, from the world. From life.

"Olivia?" Sterling nodded at the room. "After you."

"Yes of course." She drew a deep breath and moved into the treasure room, Sterling and Cadwallender a step behind.

It was larger than it had at first appeared. Opposite the door, the wall consisted of narrow, footwide panels stretching from the floor to a few inches below the ceiling. A brass knob was positioned in the same center spot on each panel.

"I think this is what we need." Gabriella grabbed a knob on a panel toward the left side of center and pulled. The panel slid outward into the room. It was the end piece of a long, glass display case. Rows of narrow shelves were wedged between the glass, each shelf filled to overflowing with what, even to Olivia's untrained eye, appeared to be Egyptian antiquities.

"Good God." Sterling stared.

"These are just some of the Egyptian artifacts." Gabriella nodded. "There are also Greek, Roman, Etruscan items. These collections rival any museum and, as far as I was able to determine, represent very nearly every significant age of ancient man." She looked at Olivia. "There is also a case filled with gems both cut and uncut."

"The artifacts alone are priceless but the gems . . ." Nathanial blew a low whistle. "There's a fortune in jewels, Olivia."

"Excellent." Her late husband's fortune and property was enough to fund her needs a thousand times over. His treasures should be put to better use. "And when they are mine to do with as I please, they shall go to fund a worthy cause." As her husband had not had a charitable bone in his body, he would have hated the idea.

Nathanial grinned, Gabriella smiled, Sterling nodded approvingly, and even Cadwallender looked impressed.

"First, however" — Olivia's gaze skimmed

over the items created by long-dead hands — "I suppose we need to determine which of the collections we are to complete."

Sterling shrugged. "I don't see why." He glanced at the solicitor. "Mr. Cadwallender, is there anything in the will or the accompanying documents that specifies which collection we are to complete?"

Cadwallender shook his head. "No, my lord."

"It's purposely vague. No doubt to make it more difficult." She should have known her late husband would make even determining exactly what collections were involved next to impossible. "I am to complete the collection but we don't know if we are to complete a collection of twenty canopic jars bearing the head of whatever his name was —"

"Imsety," Nathanial said helpfully.

"— or a collection of the jars of that king's wives or . . ."

"I should think that determination could be made by Mr. Cadwallender," Sterling said mildly.

The young man stared at Sterling, then nodded. "Since the exact collection is not named, I would think that any collection that could be considered complete by the item in question would fulfill the terms of the will."

"Excellent." Sterling nodded. "As Nathanial and Gabriella are the experts on such things, I suggest we leave them to search in here, and we determine where the jar we are to acquire is currently located."

"I have that information, my lord." Cadwallender led the way back into the library. "In drawing up his will, Viscount Rathbourne provided us with copies of the letters he wrote to the current owners of the items Lady Rathbourne is to collect as well as their responses. She, of course, has copies of these as well."

Sterling glanced at her. If she had taken the time to go through all the papers Mr. Hollis had left for her, she would already know this. Sterling didn't say it aloud, but his thoughts were obvious.

Mr. Cadwallender pulled a paper from his bag and read it. "The item in question is in the possession of one Sir Lawrence Willoughby."

"You are a treasure, Mr. Cadwallender." Olivia cast him her brightest smile.

"However . . ." Mr. Cadwallender frowned at the letter. "He currently resides in Cairo."

Sterling's brows drew together. "Egypt?"

Olivia brightened. "I have always wanted to see the pyramids." Indeed, travel to exotic places was very nearly at the top of her list. *Walk in the shadow of the gods.* "How exciting."

"How inconvenient," Sterling muttered.

"Your first trip to Egypt, Olivia?" Nathanial strolled into the library. "I envy you. I remember my first —"

"Here they are," Gabriella called from the treasure room, then joined her fiancé. She brushed back an errant strand of dark hair and grinned. "That was remarkably easy. The three other jars of Aashet were in the third cabinet I opened."

"Wonderful." Olivia grinned. "Now, it's on to Egypt."

Gabriella's smile faded, and she shook her head. "I daresay the easy part is at an end. Sir Lawrence is as passionate a collector as your late husband. I have never heard of him parting with any of his artifacts."

Nathanial drew his brows together. "He's something of an academic too, I believe. Studies . . ."

"Ancient Egyptian funerary customs and mummification," Gabriella supplied. "He occasionally comes to London for the meeting of the Antiquities Society. I met him once if I recall." She wrinkled her nose. "A rather unpleasant sort."

Olivia waved off the assessment. "He

could be an ogre for all I care. I am only interested in his canopic jar."

"Lady Rathbourne, I regret having to point this out, but according to this" — Mr. Cadwallender waved the letter — "Sir Lawrence had, on more than one occasion, refused to sell the jar to your husband."

"It works out beautifully then, Mr. Cadwallender, as I have no money with which to buy it." She beamed at the young man. "Still, I am certain I can convince Sir Lawrence to turn the object over to me."

"I don't see how." Mr. Cadwallender shook his head.

"Mr. Cadwallender," she said firmly, "if we are to be traveling companions —"

"Traveling companions?" Cadwallender's eyes widened.

Sterling's eyes narrowed. "Traveling companions?"

"— then you simply must have a more optimistic outlook. I have no idea how we shall obtain the jar, but obtain it we shall." She grinned. "There isn't a single doubt in my mind, and I would much prefer there not be a doubt in yours either."

Cadwallender nodded. "Yes, Lady Rathbourne."

"Oh, and when we are in private, do call me Olivia, and I shall call you Josiah." She nodded toward Sterling. "You may call the earl by his given name as well."

Sterling smiled reluctantly, and Olivia bit back a laugh. Sterling was certainly far stuffier than he had once been.

Cadwallender — Josiah — shook his head. "I don't think that would be at all proper."

Olivia heaved a resigned sigh. "Josiah, I don't believe you were listening after all. Propriety is no longer a concern of mine. Indeed, I intend to be as improper as I wish from this moment forward."

Josiah stared.

"Now then, off with you. I'm certain you have your own affairs to settle, especially as I have no idea how long we shall be gone." The most remarkable sense of excitement and anticipation swept through her. She'd almost forgotten such feelings were possible. "We should leave for Egypt as soon as arrangements can be made."

She looked at the earl. His vaguely stunned expression matched the solicitor's.

"Sterling's secretary can be of assistance with that," Nathanial said in an overly innocent manner. No doubt he too had noticed the look on his brother's face.

Sterling nodded. "Yes, certainly he can but —"

"And I have matters to attend to as well.

Goodness, there is a great deal to do." She drew a deep breath. "I fully intend to leave within the next few days."

"As you wish." Josiah smiled weakly, then bid them a good day and took his leave, followed almost at once by Gabriella and Nathanial.

The moment the door closed behind them, Olivia turned to Sterling. "Think of it, Sterling, Egypt! Land of pharaohs and Cleopatra and ancient wonders. Oh, it will be glorious, simply glorious." She had the irresistible urge to pirouette around the room. "I can scarcely wait!"

He stared at her as if she'd lost her mind, and indeed perhaps she had. She certainly hadn't felt like this in longer than she could remember. Her life was starting anew, and, regardless of the circumstances, this . . . well, *adventure* was the only word for it. This adventure was the perfect way to begin.

"Don't be absurd." Sterling's brows drew together. "I have no intention of going to Egypt."

Six

Livy stared at him as though he had just grown an additional head. "What do you mean you 'have no intention of going to Egypt'?"

"Exactly what I said." Sterling shook his head. "I have no intention of going to Egypt, nor have I ever had any intention of going to Egypt."

She crossed her arms over her chest. "Why on earth not?"

He was not about to tell her why the mere thought of so much as stepping foot upon the sands of that exotic land struck fear into his very soul. His reasons were absurd, and he well knew it. Still, they were his reasons, they were private, and there was no need to share them with her. Or anyone else for that matter.

"Aside from the minor fact of a war only recently concluded?" He strode across the room to a decanter of whisky, poured a healthy draft into a glass, and drained nearly half of it in one swallow.

"The war doesn't seemed to have deterred anyone else."

"Regardless, I have my reasons."

She narrowed her eyes. "What are they?"

"They are none of your concern, and they have nothing whatsoever to do with the matter at hand."

"They have everything to do with the matter at hand. I need to go to Egypt. You said you'd help me. I warned you there might be travel involved."

"When you said travel, I assumed perhaps Scotland or maybe France even possibly Greece."

"Why on earth would you think Scotland?"

"I don't know," he snapped. "I just did." He met her gaze firmly. "But I never imagined Egypt. Egypt is an uncivilized, dangerous place, and no one in his right mind would go there willingly."

She ignored him. "You said you had not traveled for many years, and you would look forward to it."

"I would look forward to it if it were Scotland or France or Greece." He blew a long breath. "And in truth, my traveling experience is limited to a tour of the capitals of Europe with my family when I was a boy." He had once planned a grand tour as a wedding trip when he had planned to marry Livy. But his father had fallen ill, he had married Alice, and any plans for extended trips were out of the question. He had taken over some of his father's duties then, and when he had inherited his title and the myriad responsibilities that accompanied it, he'd had no time for visits to foreign lands. "If I recall correctly, it was a great deal of trouble, most inconvenient, and often tedious."

"I have to go to Egypt," she said in a hard tone.

"No, you don't. I can send an emissary to negotiate with this Sir Lawrence and obtain the jar."

"Perhaps you weren't listening?" She glared at him. "If Sir Lawrence would not sell the jar to my late husband for what was no doubt an extraordinary sum, what makes you think he would hand it over to you?"

"I am the Earl of Wyldewood," Sterling said in what sounded even to him like an overly pompous manner. "I am also on the board of the London Antiquities Society. I have resources Viscount Rathbourne did not."

"I doubt that." She rolled her gaze toward

the ceiling. "Very well then. Don't go to Egypt." She crossed the room and poured her own glass. "You may render your assistance in terms of providing funding for my travel. Mr. Cadwallender — *Josiah* — and I will simply go without you."

"You're not going anywhere with that . . . that boy."

She sniffed. "He's scarcely a boy. A bit young perhaps, but that might be best. He's not so old as to be afraid of a little inconvenience. Afraid of the unknown. Of danger perhaps and adventure."

Sterling sucked in a sharp breath. "I am not the least bit afraid of adventure!"

"Hah!" She snorted in disdain. "Then tell me of your adventures, Sterling. Tell me of an adventure the Earl of Wyldewood has had."

" 'Adventure' is rather a vague term, is it not?"

"I don't think so. I think it's quite specific."

"The Earls of Wyldewood have had all sorts of adventures." At least previous earls had. Sterling couldn't imagine when they had found the time. And the world was a far different place now than when his ancestors had held the title. In 1885, the opportunity for adventures for a respectable

British lord struck him as extremely limited.

"I'm not talking about any Earl of Wylde-wood other than you." She sipped her whisky. "Do tell, Sterling. Surely you have had one adventure."

"Most certainly." He scoffed as if the idea that his experience with adventure was minimal was absurd. "I simply can't think . . . at the moment . . . so many to choose from . . ."

"Come now. One adventure, no matter how insignificant."

"I'm trying to recall . . ."

"Perhaps something of an amorous nature then?"

He raised a brow. "I would certainly not be inclined to reveal details of an amorous adventure with you." Not that he'd had anything that could even remotely be called an adventure. Indeed, his dalliances with women through the years had been sadly very few and quite far between.

"Perhaps because you haven't had one?"

He cast her the kind of knowing smile he'd seen his brother Quinton employ with women. Of course, Quinton had had any number of adventures, amorous and other-wise.

She considered him for a moment, as if to determine whether his adoption of Quinton's smile was genuine. Sterling wondered if she cared about any amorous adventures he might have had.

"My apologies, Sterling, that was altogether too personal and, well, intimate I suppose. I had no right to ask you about your exploits with women. I do hope I did not offend you."

"Not at all, Olivia," he said in a gracious manner that belied his relief.

"Still . . ." She swirled the liquor in her glass and studied him thoughtfully. "Has there never been one instance when you did something completely unexpected? When you forgot for a moment that you were the stiff, stodgy, dull Earl of Wyldewood."

"I am neither stiff nor stodgy." Indignation colored his words although an annoying voice in the back of his mind pointed out he might be the tiniest bit stiff, but surely he wasn't stodgy or dull. "And no one has ever referred to me as dull."

"Perhaps not to your face," she murmured.

He ignored her. "Besides, I don't think something like that would be considered an adventure."

"Admittedly, I am stretching the definition somewhat to accommodate you. The thought that you have had no adventures whatsoever is most disheartening. I should think doing something out of the ordinary, a single unexpected, unplanned, unprepared act would constitute adventure of at least a mild sort. Anything that makes your blood rush through your veins and a buoyant feeling rise in your soul." She took a thoughtful sip. "At this point, I would think you would be willing to grasp at any straw that might be considered an adventure. If only to ease my assessment of you as stiff, stodgy, and dull."

He clenched his jaw. "I am not stodgy."

"And if it's disheartening for me, it must be most disappointing for you to realize you have reached the ripe old age of . . . How old are you now?"

"Thirty."

"Ah yes, thirty. The ripe old age of thirty without a single adventure."

"I've had adventures." He ground out the lie through clenched teeth.

"Simply none significant enough to come to mind." She shook her head and sighed. "It's possible, I suppose, that your brothers got all the adventurous bones in your family."

"My brothers do not bear the responsibilities I do. And it's been my experience that adventures rarely end well."

"Perhaps it would be best if I had Nathanial accompany me to Egypt."

"Nathanial is about to be married."

"Yes, of course, although I suspect Gabriella would be more than amenable to a trip to Egypt as well." She thought for a moment. "Quinton then. Quinton is an adventurous sort, and I daresay he would be a stimulating traveling companion."

"I cannot begin to imagine what dangers might befall you with Quinton by your side." Aside from Quinton's penchant for the seduction of whatever woman might catch his eye, he had the most alarming tendency to find trouble wherever it might lurk. "I will not allow Quinton to accompany you."

" 'Allow'?" Her voice rose. "You don't have the right to allow or forbid me to do anything."

His voice matched hers. "I am if I am funding this quest of yours."

"Then I shall find the funds elsewhere."

"You have nowhere else to turn!" He winced at the stricken look that flashed through her eyes. "I am sorry, Olivia, I should not —"

"No apology is necessary." She shrugged in an offhand manner. "You were simply stating a fact."

"Still, I should not have . . ." He drew a deep breath. "At least allow me to investigate the possibility of procuring this jar without travel to Egypt."

She raised her chin defiantly. "I have to do this myself."

"It doesn't specify that in the will. It simply says you must complete the collections." He paused. "But, of course, we don't know everything that is in the will as you have not seen fit to read it."

"I will read it."

"And unless it specifically requires you to personally acquire this item, there's no need for you to —"

"I have to go!"

"No, you don't!"

"Yes, I do!"

"Why?" He glared at her. "Tell me why!"

"Because . . ."

"Why?"

"Because I can't breathe here!" She flung the words at him, downed the whisky in her glass, slapped the glass onto a table, and paced the room. "I cannot breathe, and I long for air! I feel as though I have worn a corset entirely too small for the last ten years. And finally, *finally,* the stays were loosened for a brief moment until I learned the terms of that bloody will, and now they have tightened around me again. And I cannot breathe!"

He stared at her.

"I have been as much a part of my late husband's collections as if I were enclosed in one of those glass cases in his treasure room. The only difference between me and one of his artifacts is that I, on occasion, when he wished it, have been taken out to display in public. My life has not been my own, and I want it returned to me. I have earned it!" She turned on her heel, away from him, her shoulders rising and falling again as if she struggled to regain control. At last she drew a deep breath and turned back to him. "The only thing that sustained me, sustained my soul if you will, through the years of my marriage was a list I kept in secret of the things I would do when I was free. Without the inheritance that is rightfully mine, I cannot accomplish any of them. I can only continue to live the life I have lived. Without hope." She met his gaze directly. "Without breath." Her hands curled into fists by her sides. "With or without you, I will not live the rest of my days that way."

His heart twisted. "Olivia."

"I have asked for your help once again." Her voice was cold. "It was not an easy request to make. Obviously, I was wrong to think I could depend on you. I should have learned my lesson. You failed me —"

"Very well then." He made the decision the moment the words left his mouth. He started toward the door. "I'll make the arrangements at once."

She scoffed. "I scarcely think —"

He turned back to her. "Know this, Olivia, dull or not, the Earl of Wyldewood does not fail in his responsibilities. As for adventures . . ." Without thinking he moved to her, pulled her into his arms, and stared into her startled green eyes. "The only adventure of my life was you." His gaze slipped to her lips, then back to her eyes. He ached to kiss her with a longing suppressed for a decade. But now was not the time. "And it did not end well."

Abruptly, he released her, turned, and strode from the room. And wondered even as the door snapped shut behind him what was on her list and what he had gotten himself into.

And realized as well that whatever the cost would be worth it.

Olivia stared at the closed door. *Good God what just happened?* She crossed the room and refilled her glass with a shaky hand. It was entirely too early in the day for spirits. Regardless, she took a long swallow.

He had almost kissed her! The look, the desire, in his eyes was unmistakable. It had been a very long time since she had been kissed. It had been a very long time since she'd been touched. Not that she wasn't eternally grateful.

She had learned quickly after her marriage that her husband was only interested in the more intimate aspects of wedlock if she resisted his embraces. It took less than six months for her to understand that resistance to his advances was futile and only flamed his desire. He liked nothing better than to force her submission. To take what he wanted using whatever means he wished. And dare she ever forget, she had the scars to remind her. Once she had become complacent and accepting of her fate, he no longer wanted her in his bed. She had often wondered if he realized that was her victory.

In the beginning, she had hoped telling him she was not the virginal perfection he had thought would dissuade him from marriage altogether. But it had done nothing save enrage him, and he had beaten her for the first time on the night of their wedding.

Sterling was, in truth, the only man who had ever really kissed her. Her late husband's tastes did not lie in that direction, and for that too she had been grateful. Long after Sterling had ignored her pleas for help, the memory of his lips on hers, or the touch of his hand, or the love in his eyes had provided a secret source of strength. Until those memories had faded and, with them, the feelings she'd had for him. By then, she'd found her own strength within herself, and it was no longer necessary to cling to her memories of him.

Even so, there had been moments, through the years, when she had lain awake at night and wondered if she would have enjoyed the relations between a man and a woman if she'd been with a man who considered her more then merely his property. If she had been with someone she loved, someone who loved her. If she had been with Sterling. After all, it had been somewhat pleasurable — or at least one could tell there was a great deal of potential for pleasure — if a bit awkward, the lone time she had shared his bed. When she had thought she'd spend every night for the rest of her life lying in his arms.

Indeed, wasn't sharing his bed at the top of her list? She sipped her whisky thoughtfully. She had no intention of losing her heart to him again. She'd done so once, and once was quite enough. That door was closed forever. But sharing his bed, feeling the warmth of his naked body wrapped around hers, the intimacy of his breath mingling with hers, their bodies joined as one . . . She shook her head to clear it. No doubt the thoughts filling her head were at least in part attributable to the whisky. As was the fact that she'd told him about her list. She groaned to herself. She wasn't sure why she'd blurted that out. She'd never planned to tell him, never planned to tell anyone. It had been her secret for so long. Very nearly the only thing that was hers and hers alone.

At least he had agreed to accompany her to Egypt. Time enough to consider his seduction later. Or, given the look in his eye, hers. Perhaps when they had completed all three collections . . . Regardless, it would be her decision and hers alone.

Still, restraint might be rather more difficult than she thought. If Sterling had kissed her today, she was fairly certain she would have kissed him back.

Sterling drummed his fingers on his desk and stared out the nearest window at the pleasant day beyond the glass.

Egypt. Of all the places in the world, why

Egypt? He would do damn near anything for Livy. Give up his fortune. Lay down his life. Even, apparently, he grimaced at the thought, travel to Egypt.

His fears were absurd. He was well aware of that. They were the fears of a small child. Still, when he so much as considered a trip to Egypt, he felt rather like a small child. For the Earl of Wyldewood, it was not an acceptable feeling. He should have faced those fears long ago, but then there had been no need to. It hadn't been the least bit difficult to avoid travel to Egypt.

He knew very well when it had started. His father had had a passion for the study of artifacts and ancient man. Indeed, Sterling's seat on the Antiquities Society Board had been his father's before him. While everyone in the family had always suspected that Charles Harrington had a secret longing for the type of adventures two of his sons would grow up to engage in, he had never truly had the opportunity. Sterling's father's position as the only heir to the title, then his duties once he had inherited, had prohibited him from dashing off to seek ancient treasure in the farthest reaches of the world as his sons, Quint and Nate had done. However much he would have wished otherwise, Father had been a responsible sort. As was his eldest son.

The previous earl had lived his adventures vicariously through the guests who frequented the family's dinner table. Often, those were men engaged in the pursuit of artifacts, the bits and pieces left behind by long-lost civilizations. Sterling distinctly remembered one such gentleman. He could not recall either the man's face or his name, but his hand played a prominent role in Sterling's nightmares for years. Or rather what was left of his hand.

Even though children of the household rarely dined with the adults otherwise, his father firmly believed these antiquities hunters, as well as explorers and adventurers, provided the sort of firsthand education that could be found neither in books nor at the hands of whatever governess was in residence. He had insisted on his children's attendance from an early age. In hindsight, Sterling believed it was a scheme on the part of his father to develop in his sons the same love of the ancient that he had. It had certainly proved successful with Sterling's brothers.

While Sterling could not remember his exact age, surely no more than seven or eight, young enough that his brothers were still not of an age to attend the dinner, every other detail remained as distinct in his mind as though it were yesterday. The guest on this particular night was not especially remarkable, aside from his hand. Indeed, there had been any number of others far more colorful in manner and appearance. But perhaps it was because he had struck Sterling as not the least bit out of the ordinary that his story had had such a profound effect. Regardless, when one has a treasure hunter with only two fingers on one hand to dinner, and one discusses his many and varied adventures, inevitably the question of how said fingers were lost tends to surface.

While on an expedition in Egypt, the gentleman had reached into his baggage to grab, not whatever it was he had wanted, but instead had pulled out a small, venomous snake — an asp or viper or something of the sort. The man was annoyingly vague on that point, not that it really mattered. Regardless the creature had promptly bitten him between the first and second fingers of his hand.

The adventurer had obviously told this story many times, for he embellished it with dramatic pauses and grand theatrical gestures. An accomplished storyteller, he held the gathering around the table in the palm of his good hand. He explained that he knew his life was in mortal danger if he did not act quickly. As he would rather lose several fingers than breathe his last, he immediately grabbed a conveniently close knife that he kept for protection against thieves, although it apparently did not deter snakes. Without so much as a second thought, he chopped off half his hand diagonally, losing two fingers and his thumb. This account was accompanied by a slashing gesture and an unexpected thud on the table with his fisted whole hand so hard as to rattle the glasses. Mother uttered an inadvertent scream, Father gasped, and Sterling's heart lodged firmly in his throat.

Worse, the snake made a complete escape and slithered off into the desert, no doubt to spread the word among his fellow reptiles as to the tasty nature of Englishmen.

The adventurer had joked that he was grateful it had been his left hand as he favored his right. Still, watching him maneuver his flatware, one was not convinced. Dinner continued on uneventfully after that, but Sterling never forgot either the story or the hand.

From that point on, the future earl was convinced Egypt was teeming with snakes lying in wait for the next unsuspecting visitor. And everything he saw or read about Egypt only confirmed that suspicion. It seemed that nearly every Egyptian artifact had snakes depicted in some manner in golden armbands or headpieces or carved on sarcophagi. And didn't Plutarch write that Cleopatra tested the venom of any number of deadly Egyptian snakes on condemned prisoners before selecting the type of asp she would employ for her own death? Sterling had tried to overcome this absurd fear with knowledge, occasionally perusing a volume on Egyptian native species, but even as he had grown older, it had not helped. Nor did it matter. He had no need to visit Egypt. But even at the age of thirty, he could not rid himself of the irrational conviction that Egypt was a land filled with snakes that were not to be trusted.

Fortunately, no one else was aware of this childhood fear. The Earl of Wyldewood was not expected to be afraid of anything. And the topic of Egyptian snakes did not often come up in polite conversation. His brothers would have delighted in it, as it seemed very nearly every time they had related a tale of their adventures in Egypt, a snake had made an appearance. Either curled in a shoe or hidden in a pot or slithering across their path.

"My lord?"

Oddly enough, while he was not fond of snakes in general, they did not strike him with the same ridiculous terror he experienced in regard to Egyptian snakes. Why, he had encountered snakes on walks in the country, but even the venomous adder, while known to be deadly on occasion, was still a proper British snake.

"Lord Wyldewood?"

Sterling jerked his attention to his secretary, standing patiently in front of his desk. "Yes?"

"My apologies, my lord," Edward said. "You asked to see this accounting from the estate manager when it arrived."

"Yes, of course." Sterling took the papers and scanned them. At first glance, they appeared in order. He would study them more thoroughly later. It was simply part and parcel of the myriad of responsibilities that demanded his attention each and every day.

"If there is nothing else . . ."

"Unfortunately . . ." Certainly information had not eased his fears in the past. Still, he was the Earl of Wyldewood now and whether he wished to or not, he was going to Egypt. Land of snakes. "I know there are several books on the shelves here somewhere that detail the fauna of Egypt. If you would locate those for me."

"At once, sir." Edward hesitated. "Did you wish for information as to flora as well?"

"No, that will not be necessary. To be more precise, I am interested in creatures of a reptilian nature." He winced to himself. "Specifically snakes."

"I see." Edward paused. "Did you wish for information on crocodiles as well, sir?"

"Crocodiles?" Sterling drew his brows together. "Why on earth would I be interested in crocodiles?"

"I have no idea, sir, but then I don't know why you have an interest in snakes either. And as crocodiles are reptiles as well to be found in Egypt, I simply thought perhaps —"

"Quite right." Sterling sighed. Life might have been easier for the son of a devoted antiquities scholar if that long-ago dinner guest had lost a hand to a crocodile. At least crocodiles didn't lurk unexpectedly in one's shoes. "No, just snakes, Edward." He blew a long breath. "It seems I am to be traveling to Egypt as soon as arrangements can be made. I need you to investigate the most expedient means of getting there. We need to travel to Egypt and return as quickly as possible." He thought for a moment. "I need as well to know where to find a Sir

Lawrence Willoughby, reported to be living in Cairo. I expect the Antiquities Society can provide an address."

"At once, sir." Edward turned away, then turned back. "First the snakes, sir?"

"Yes, first the snakes." Sterling thought for a moment. "And if you would also inform my brothers and Lady Wyldewood that I should like to meet with them here in the library before dinner."

"And Lady Regina as well?"

His sister, Reggie, was eighteen and enjoying the festivities of her first London season. As his trip would not inconvenience her, he doubted she would be at all interested. Besides, no one especially appreciated being called to the earl's library for a family meeting as it usually involved chastisement of some kind. Still, she would be annoyed not to be included. "You may tell her she is invited but add that the matter does not especially concern her. No doubt she will be delighted at the reprieve."

"No doubt, sir." Edward smiled and moved to the nearest bookshelf to begin his search.

Edward Dennison was extremely competent and most efficient. And no one knew the affairs of the Earl of Wyldewood better than he. Sterling could rest easy knowing that while he was away, Edward would still be at his post. Although he had more on his mind these days than the business of his employer.

When Gabriella had entered their lives, so too had her companion, Miss Florence Henry. While the report of their first encounter did not seem to indicate romance, romance had indeed blossomed between them. She and Edward planned to marry as soon as possible after Gabriella and Nate wed. Love at Harrington House was certainly in the air. Perhaps, it was a good sign.

"How is Miss Henry, Edward?"

Edward looked away from the shelves he'd been perusing and grinned. "Quite well, thank you, sir."

"And the plans for your wedding?"

"They have been eclipsed somewhat by the plans for Miss Montini's." Edward shrugged in a good-natured manner. Edward's demeanor overall had mellowed since he had lost his heart to Miss Henry, who was, from all accounts, apparently his equal in terms of competence and efficiency. It was a match made in heaven, as they said. Still, Miss Henry's charms obviously extended well beyond her capable nature as evidenced by the look in Edward's eyes whenever he spoke of her. "Which is as it should be, sir. Besides, it will not be more than a few months, and I have always thought a long engagement to be beneficial, in a strictly sensible sense."

"Really?" Sterling studied the older man who was, in many ways, as much a friend as employee. "I didn't think sensibility had anything to do with matters of the heart."

"Yes, well, I did not say it was easy. Merely sensible." Edward grinned. "One should indeed be careful what one wishes for, sir."

Sterling laughed. And what did he wish for? What had he always wished for, in the back of his mind, in the long-locked recesses of his heart? The opportunity to redeem himself? To prove to Livy he could be depended upon? A second chance to rescue the fair damsel and win her heart?

"Yes, indeed, Edward." Even if said rescue meant facing the nightmares of his childhood. "Be careful what you wish for."

SEVEN

"And as that is the situation . . ." Sterling's gaze slid from his mother, to Nate to Quint. Reggie had, not surprisingly, chosen to forgo the meeting. "I shall be leaving for Cairo as soon as arrangements can be made."

Something more than surprise and less than shock showed on the faces of both his mother and Quint. Nate smiled in a vaguely smug manner. It was not often that the youngest brother knew something before the rest of the family. "And while I am gone" — Sterling fixed Quint with a no-nonsense look — "you will assume my duties."

Quint laughed. "Not bloody likely."

"Quinton." Mother cast him a chastising frown.

"My mind is made up." Sterling shrugged. "You have no choice in the matter."

"Of course I have a choice." Quint scoffed.

"I'm not the earl. I don't want to be the earl. And I have no desire to assume the duties of the earl."

"Nonetheless, you should be prepared, and this is the perfect opportunity. I shall be away for four to six weeks, possibly more. I cannot leave our affairs in any hands save that of a family member." Sterling pinned his younger brother with a stern look. "Have you ever considered that, as I have no children, you could inherit the title at any time? Why, I could step out into the street today and be run over by a carriage. Have you thought about that?"

"No, I haven't." Quint glared. "But at the moment the idea is oddly appealing."

"I don't know why you think Quinton should be prepared. I'm the one who may well be next in line should anything happen to you." Nate shrugged. "Quint is much more likely to perish unexpectedly. Destined, no doubt, to be shot by an outraged husband."

"That's enough," Mother said in the exact same tone she had used when they were boys.

"Nate's right, you know," Quint continued, as if she hadn't said a word. "Not about the jealous husband —"

Nate snorted.

"— but my life is . . ." Quint slanted a quick glance at his mother ". . . one of uncertainty. And travel. Yes that's it. To places that are often less than civilized, where very nearly anything can happen. Although . . ." He cast his mother a reassuring smile. "I am nothing if not cautious."

"Excellent." Sterling stifled a grin. Everyone in the room knew Quint was the least cautious person ever born. "Then you are no more likely to perish unexpectedly than I. Particularly while you are here in London."

"But I had planned to leave. Very soon," Quint said quickly. He and Nate had already been in London for nearly a month. Their visits home rarely lasted much longer. Still, now that Nate was to be married and would no longer travel the world searching for treasures with his brother, it was possible Quint would linger in London. Possible but not probable. Quint had always chafed under the yoke of civilization.

"And now your plans have changed," Sterling said in a pleasant yet firm tone.

"But . . ." Something that might well have been panic shone in Quint's eyes. "I'm not the least bit responsible. Why, I am renowned for my irresponsible behavior, part and parcel of my irresponsible nature. Oh no." Quint shook his head mournfully. "I am not to be trusted."

"Nonsense, Quinton," Mother said in a straightforward manner. "It has been my observation that you have become quite responsible in recent years. I have been most impressed."

Quint stared at his mother. "Well, you're wrong. It was an act designed to ease your fears. I haven't changed a bit." He cast a pleading look at his younger brother. "Go on. You tell them how very irresponsible I am."

"Unfortunately . . ." Nate heaved a reluctant sigh. "I'm afraid I have to agree with Mother. You do what you say you are going to do. You live up to your obligations. And you have a distinct, if not overly developed, sense of honor."

Quint's eyes narrowed. "You give me too much credit, dear brother."

Nate grinned.

"You will have Mr. Dennison to guide and assist you." Sterling nodded at his youngest brother. "As well as Nathanial."

Nate's eyes widened. "I have wedding plans to attend to."

"Nonsense, darling." Mother waved off his objection. "The groom has little to do save appear at the appropriate time. Besides, we shall be back well before the wedding."

"We?" Sterling's brows drew together.

Quint stared. "We?"

Nate studied his mother with a barely suppressed grin. "I suspect you need to define 'we.' "

Mother continued as if no one had said a word. "I shall have to ask your aunt Elise to come stay with Reggie to guide her through the remainder of the season. There's nothing more enjoyable than shepherding a young woman through her first social season. It quite recalls the days of one's youth. Now, as for —"

" 'We'?" Sterling glared at his mother.

"Yes, Mr. Cadwallender, you, Olivia, and myself, of course." Mother's smile didn't change, but it struck Sterling as far less serene and far more determined than a moment ago. "That would be *we.*' "

"What do you mean 'that would be we'?" Sterling stared at his mother.

She stared back. "Goodness, Sterling, I should think you could understand something as simple as 'we.' It's a very simple word."

"You're not going to Egypt!" *Land of snakes.*

"I most certainly am." Her smile didn't

139

change, but the look in her eye was unmistakable. "Olivia cannot go traipsing around the world accompanied by two handsome, unmarried men." Her gaze shifted between Sterling and Nate. "I assume Mr. Cadwallender is unmarried and handsome as well?"

Nate nodded.

"Excellent. Traveling with two dashing gentleman by my side will quite add to the adventure." Mother beamed, then turned her attention back to Sterling. "It would be most improper for you and Mr. Cadwallender to accompany Olivia without benefit of chaperone."

"Olivia doesn't care about propriety, Mother," Nate said.

"I do," Mother said firmly. "And not simply when it comes to Olivia's reputation but Sterling's as well." She fixed her oldest son with a stern look. "You are the Earl of Wyldewood and as such are held to higher standards."

Sterling clenched his jaw. "I am not concerned, and if Olivia is not —"

"Someone needs to be, and apparently that would be me. Me, Sterling. A word very similar to 'we,' only singular. Do you understand 'me'?"

"You're not going to Egypt," Sterling said again in a hard tone.

"Oh but I am. For your sake and Olivia's," Mother added. "Besides, I alone among all of you have spoken to Olivia through the years of her marriage. You" — she cast her son an annoyed glance — "have studiously avoided her. Admittedly, I have only crossed her path rarely, but I have observed her often enough to know that the young widow we called on after her husband's demise was more the Olivia we once knew than the cool, remote Viscountess Rathbourne she has appeared this past decade."

Mother's brows drew together in a forbidding frown. "One never knows what transpires in the privacy of a marriage. But there were more than enough rumors and accounts regarding the nature of Viscount Rathbourne's character . . ." She narrowed her eyes. "Someone should have dispatched that man years ago."

Quint raised a brow. "Surely you're not condoning murder, Mother?"

Mother paused as if she were considering just that. "No, of course not. And whoever is responsible should certainly burn in the fires of Hell for his sin. Where he will no doubt encounter the viscount once again," she added under her breath.

Sterling struggled to keep his voice level.

"Olivia's past is neither here nor there at the moment."

"No, dearest, I am simply explaining her demeanor. The life she has led either destroys or strengthens. Given what you've said of Olivia's determination, I should think the latter. One cannot fault her for wishing to experience excitement. Nor can one blame her for not caring how the rest of the world will view her actions. However, I do care."

"Egypt is a dangerous place, Mother," Sterling said pointedly. "And we have been at war with Egypt."

"Pish posh." She waved away his objection. "We are always at war with someone. And aside from your need for a chaperone . . ." She paused for a moment. "Your father always wanted to go to Egypt, as have I. This is the perfect opportunity."

"Nonetheless, Mother, this is not a trek for carefree tourists. I intend to travel as quickly as possible, and I have no intentions of lingering at the pyramids or whatever else you might wish to see. As much as I appreciate your concern as to my reputation" — he met his mother's gaze directly — "you are not coming. The matter is settled."

"Indeed, it is." Mother leaned closer to the desk and lowered her voice. "Make no mistake, Sterling, either I accompany you, or I will be right at your heels. Traveling alone if need be." Her tone softened. "You have never been one to accept defeat graciously. However, I would suggest you attempt a modicum of good humor now, as you have indeed lost."

He stared at her and realized further debate was pointless. Damnation! He was headed to the land of snakes with the lost love of his life, an overly handsome youngster, and his mother.

She straightened and smiled. "Now then, I should send word to Elise at once."

Sterling blew a resigned breath. This was another battle he wouldn't win. "Does it have to be Aunt Elise?"

"Elise is your father's sister." Mother's tone defied any of them to object. "I trust her implicitly."

"As did her three husbands, no doubt." Nate grinned.

"When one marries men substantially older, one is prone to losing them," Mother said in a lofty manner.

Lady Elise Quartermain was not exactly a figure of scandal even though her exploits were, at least within the family, considered to be perilously close to scandalous. Choosing her to chaperone Reggie was tantamount to giving Reggie free rein to do exactly as she pleased.

"Still," Sterling began. "I don't —"

"She has a certain freedom of spirit and perhaps her behavior, on occasion, could be considered, well, unconventional —"

Quint choked.

"But the rumors of her adventures are greatly exaggerated. And those that I know to be accurate are not nearly as improper as they may sound." Mother huffed. "Furthermore, I must confess that I have quite envied her through the years as I have had no adventures at all."

Sterling tried again. "Mother, you should really —"

"Nor have you," she said pointedly. "Goodness, Sterling, perhaps if you'd had an adventure or two, you wouldn't be so condemning of others. Nor would you be quite so . . . stuffy."

Sterling gasped. "I am not stuffy." He looked at his brothers. "Am I?"

"I'm not sure I would say 'stuffy,' " Nate began in a diplomatic manner.

Quint snorted.

"Thank you," Sterling said, slightly mollified.

"Stiff, perhaps," Nate murmured.

"Pompous, I would say," Quint suggested.

Sterling glared. "I am not —"

"You're really quite staid, darling, some might even call you dull." Mother shook her head. "It's not at all becoming."

"I am not dull," Sterling said through clenched teeth.

"It's past time you had some adventure in your life." Mother leveled him a stern look.

"I have agreed to go on this *adventure*. I have accepted that you are going." He drew his brows together. "What more do you want from me?"

"Nothing really, dear." Mother smiled. "I simply want you to enjoy it."

Olivia stared at the lady perched on her sofa in an eminently prim manner, belying the words coming out of her mouth.

". . . and so it is in everyone's best interests that I accompany you." Lady Wyldewood cast her a pleasant smile. "Besides, I have always wanted to see Cairo, all of Egypt really, and this may well be my only opportunity."

"I see," Olivia said in a cautious manner. "And your son has agreed to this?"

The older woman laughed. "Agreed is perhaps not as accurate a word as accepted. I gave him no choice."

"I see," Olivia said again, trying and failing to hide a smile.

Lady Wyldewood grinned. "It was quite amusing. Sterling is not at all used to not having his own way and not getting exactly what he wants. I cannot recall the last time such a thing happened. Oh yes." Sterling's mother fixed her with a firm look. "It was when he lost you."

Olivia's stomach twisted.

"My dear, I am a firm believer in clearing the air, as it were." Lady Wyldewood met her gaze directly. "I have been consumed with curiosity regarding the severing of your relationship with Sterling since the moment it happened. You should know that whether it was out of honor or pride, he never fully confided in me. It was most annoying. However, as I regarded you as I would a daughter, I never believed you were at fault. Furthermore, knowing the nature of your father and the reputation of Lord Rathbourne I long ago concluded, for whatever reason, you had no choice."

Olivia swallowed the lump that had lodged in her throat. One of the best parts about once planning to marry Sterling had been that this woman, who had indeed always treated her like a daughter, would be the mother Olivia had never known. "No, I didn't."

Lady Wyldewood nodded with satisfaction. "Nor do I know the circumstances of your marriage to Viscount Rathbourne. Suffice it to say, that the Olivia Rathbourne I have encountered rarely through the years was not the same girl I knew." She paused for a long moment. "I will confess that the opportunity to resume our acquaintance was yet another reason why I decided to accompany you. Aside from the appearance of propriety of course."

"Of course," Olivia murmured.

The older woman raised a brow. "Have I stunned you into silence?"

"No." Olivia shook her head. "Well, yes, I am rather shocked." She smiled. "But pleased. I can think of no other better traveling companion."

Lady Wyldewood studied her. "And this doesn't disrupt your plans regarding my son?"

"I have no plans regarding your son," Olivia said slowly. "He offered his assistance and I accepted his offer."

"And?"

"And . . ." Olivia shrugged. "And there's nothing more to it than that."

"No, of course not." Lady Wyldewood sighed. "I never thought there was."

Olivia drew a deep breath. "As we seem

147

to be confessing all, you should know, I have no intentions of resuming our previous relationship. I only want my freedom, my independence. I have no designs on your son."

"Are you sure?"

"Yes," Olivia said firmly.

"What a very great pity." Lady Wyldewood smiled and rose to her feet. "Mr. Dennison is making our travel arrangements. The details should be delivered to you tomorrow. It is Sterling's hope that we can be off the day after that."

Olivia stood and narrowed her eyes. "What did you mean by that?"

"I mean the day after tomorrow."

"No. What did you mean when you said it was a great pity."

The older woman smiled. "Just musing to myself. It was nothing of significance."

"Lady Wyldewood." Olivia drew a deep breath. "If your true purpose on accompanying us is to encourage a match between Sterling and myself I am quite serious when I say that is not my intention. Nor is it my desire." She shook her head. "Some things are best left in the past. My future does not include your son."

Lady Wyldewood's eyes widened indignantly. "My dear child, I thought nothing of

148

the sort. I am not the kind of mother who interferes in the affairs of her children. My primary purpose in accompanying you is to save both you and Sterling from the ill-effects of gossip and scandal. And, as I have admitted, I do wish to renew our friend-ship. But I assure you I have no hidden ulterior motive regarding you and my son. Now." She swept toward the door. "I have a great deal of packing to do." She paused and glanced at Olivia. "I assume you're bringing along at least one maid."

"I thought it might be easier and more ef-ficient to travel with as few people as pos-sible."

Lady Wyldewood's brow furrowed. "I do recall reading somewhere an account of travel in Egypt. The writer said it was most unfair to drag servants along as conditions were far less civilized than they are ac-customed to." She heaved a resigned sigh. "I suppose we should forgo maids then. Very well." She squared her shoulders. "It will simply make it more of an adventure."

"Your son considers this more of a chore than an adventure." Olivia shrugged. "And he seems exceptionally fond of pointing out that this is not a pleasure trip. I suspect the man won't allow me — us — to see anything of interest that does not relate directly to our purpose. Which means we probably will not be given the opportunity to walk in the shadows of the pyramids unless they have been moved to the center of Cairo." She set her jaw. "But I will one day."

"And one never knows. One day may be far closer than anyone expects." Sterling's mother cast her a conspiratorial smile. "I, for one, have no intention of traveling to Egypt without seeing something of merit."

Olivia shook her head. "Sterling wishes to spend as little time as possible on this excursion. And, as he is paying my expenses, I am hard pressed to argue with him."

"Oh my dear girl." Lady Wyldewood scoffed. "You should most certainly argue with him. No one else does. It will only do him good." She nodded, again headed for the door and again paused. "Oh, and about that nonsense regarding the resumption of your previous relationship. You may well tell yourself that, you may fool yourself into believing it. However, I do not. I require proof." She beamed at the younger woman. "Good day, Olivia."

"Good day." Olivia stared after the lady. Proof? What possible kind of proof could Olivia offer that would convince Lady Wyldewood that there was no future to be had with her son?

They had both changed too much to go back. They would be traveling companions, partners, even friends after a fashion but nothing more. He had broken her heart once and only a fool would trust her heart again to the same man. As for Lady Wylde-wood's comment that Olivia was only fool-ing herself, why that was absurd.

Still, even as her mind turned to the myriad of details she had to attend to in preparation for travel, she couldn't entirely ignore the older lady's charge. Just as her gaze could never resist straying to the paint-ing of Great-aunt Wilomena, the idea that she harbored any hope of a life with Sterling lingered in her thoughts.

Apparently, Olivia too would require proof.

EIGHT

Swim naked in a warm sea.
From the secret list of desires of
Olivia Rathbourne

It was not difficult to understand why Sterling had described travel as tedious. It did seem endless. Still, Olivia thought every moment exciting and invigorating. At long last, she was going somewhere. She was doing something. No matter how eager she was to reach their destination, the journey itself was an adventure.

Sterling had chosen to travel almost entirely by sea, and they were in their third day aboard a packet steamer they'd taken from London. Four more days, and they'd arrive in Marseilles, where they would board another ship that would take five days to transport them to Egypt. Sterling had admitted that traveling from London to Dover, crossing the Channel, taking a train to Paris and another train to Marseilles would have been a bit faster but not, he had said, as efficient. Apparently, he had found the idea of transferring two ladies with their assorted baggage from one mode of transport to another somewhat daunting. Olivia further suspected he feared, once in Paris, it would be difficult, or impossible, to keep his mother from lingering in the French capital. On that point, Olivia had to agree. She too would be hard-pressed to simply transfer from one train to another without experiencing some of the sights of Paris.

She'd never been to Paris, but then again, she'd never been anywhere. Her mother had died when she was so young that she did not remember her at all. Her upbringing had been delegated first to her father's spinster sister, who had died when Olivia was ten, then to a series of governesses. All of whom, upon reflection, were quite nice and even affectionate in their own ways. And each and every one had instilled in Olivia the desire to one day see as much of the world as possible.

Her marriage had put an end to any hope of travel beyond the daylong carriage ride from the manor in the country, where Olivia preferred to spend her solitary days, to the London house whenever her late husband had required the presence of a perfect wife. But even as she was a prisoner in her own life, her mind had been unencumbered by the restraints imposed on her. In the years of her marriage, Olivia had devoured books about travel and foreign lands. She'd read of the history of countries both familiar and unknown, in Europe and Asia and Africa and the Americas. She'd learned of strange exotic customs and fascinating peoples who lived in places both civilized and savage. And through the years, the desire to see what she'd only read about moved closer to the top of her list. And comforted her soul.

She leaned on the railing of the ship and gazed at the water rushing by. It didn't bother her in the least that she would not see Paris on this trip. She was as eager as Sterling to be done with this trek. The sooner she acquired the items necessary to meet the terms of her late husband's will, the sooner she would have her inheritance and be free to do whatever she wished. Then she would see Paris and Vienna and Rome. Then she would travel to America and Morocco and India. Then she would live and breathe.

And perhaps she would have a scandalous affair with a French count or allow herself to be seduced at a Venetian masked ball by a stranger or swim naked in the Aegean with a Greek god. Once she was a woman of independent means, she might never reside in London again. After all, there was nothing to keep her there.

"I thought I would never be alone with you again." Sterling's chuckle sounded beside her.

She straightened and glanced at him. The breeze ruffled his dark hair, and in spite of the eminently proper nature of his attire, he looked more relaxed and at ease than she had seen him since she had first asked for his help. But then she couldn't recall when she had last felt so calm and serene. Still, she suspected the Earl of Wyldewood was seldom relaxed and at ease.

"I see the sea air agrees with you."

He rested his forearms on the railing and gazed out at the horizon. "Apparently." He smiled. "I cannot remember the last time I had nothing to occupy every minute of my day. There is something to be said for enforced idleness."

She studied his profile, strong and resolute and far too familiar from the dreams of a decade. "Perhaps you should experience travel more often."

He shook his head. "I haven't the time. I have far too many responsibilities to abandon them. Nor do I have the desire to do so." He slanted her a quick grin. "It is perhaps what makes me so dull."

She bit back a smile. "Yes, I imagine that's why."

He laughed. "I like being on the sea though. The water stretches endlessly, and one can only wonder what adventures lie ahead."

"Adventures?" She raised a brow. "From the staid, proper Earl of Wyldewood? Do take care, Sterling, or you shall lose your dull reputation altogether."

"I very much doubt that will happen." He paused for a moment. "Being aboard a ship reminds me of things I have never done. Roads not taken if you will. When we were children, my brothers and I would talk of becoming adventurers and explorers. And play at being pirates and smugglers in the attic."

"Pirates and smugglers? You?"

"We had an ancestor who was engaged in smuggling. Adventure must run in our blood, or at least in my brothers' blood." He glanced at her. "Don't mention it to my mother. She's quite proud of our ancestry, and I don't think she knows."

"From what I know of your mother, I daresay she'd find a smuggler in the family exciting." Indeed, Lady Wyldewood — or rather Millicent as she'd insisted Olivia call her as they were to be friends — seemed to find every step of their journey so far an adventure.

Olivia had discovered it was surprisingly nice to have the older woman along, not that she had opposed her accompanying them in the first place. If for no other reason than to provide a shield between her and Sterling. But Olivia hadn't had a friend for so very long and had quite forgotten how delightful it was to exchange confidences and gossip with another female. Olivia was certain that, by the time they returned to London, Millicent would have acquainted her with every scandalous tidbit of the last ten years. Millicent Harrington did seem to know everything there was to know about everyone worth knowing.

Certainly Millicent's presence had meant changing Olivia's plans somewhat. For one thing, she had found herself bringing a great deal more luggage than she had anticipated. Millicent had insisted they each bring along eveningwear because one never knew when one might be invited to an unexpected social event even in Egypt and one should be properly prepared. And, of course, between the older lady and Josiah, she and

Sterling were very rarely alone.

"I imagine you were an excellent smuggler."

He shook his head. "I was never the smuggler. I was the intrepid Earl of Wyldewood, agent of the crown. I was the courageous hunter of smugglers and other nefarious brigands." He cast her a wicked grin. "And I was the rescuer of fair maidens."

She laughed. "And have you rescued many fair maidens?"

"You are my first." His grin faded. "I should have rescued you long ago."

"Yes, well, that's neither here nor there at the moment," she said brusquely in an effort to forestall this particular subject. She had no desire to reexamine their past. If truth were told, she was grateful to Millicent for her constant presence. There had been no real opportunity to speak privately with Sterling. No opportunity for him to pull her into his arms and gaze at her as if she were the answers to his prayers. And no opportunity whatsoever for her resolve to soften, for her heart to melt. Again. Precisely as she wanted it. "Tell me, was the intrepid earl successful in his pursuit of smugglers and pirates?"

He considered her for a moment. "Always. The intrepid earl never fails in the pursuit of what he wants. Nor does he give up."

"Then no doubt your arrogance is well earned."

"In a dull and respectable sort of way." He smiled and resumed staring at the sea. Or at something far in the distance she couldn't see. The past perhaps. "I had once thought that I would spend at least some of my life in exploration and the search for adventure."

She remembered long-ago discussions with him about dreams and desires. Things he wished to see, places he wanted to go. No, places they would go together. "Why didn't you?"

"Primarily because my father died far sooner than anyone imagined. He had always enjoyed good health, so his demise was unexpected. And I then inherited the title with all the responsibilities that entails. There was no choice. My brothers became the adventurers, and I became the earl." His tone was matter-of-fact. "I have watched them through the years go off in their search for antiquities to parts of the world I will never see. I have to admit, if I have envied them, it was only for a moment or two."

But, of course, he wouldn't envy his brothers. He was the responsible one. Even in those days when she had thought she knew him well, when he had spoken of seeking adventure, it was a desire limited by the realities of his future position.

"This is the first time I have traveled beyond British borders since that trip in my boyhood."

"And you must admit you are enjoying it thus far."

"Thus far," he agreed, and continued, "I have heard Quinton and Nathanial tell their stories of danger and intrigue and the most hazardous thing I do is an early-morning ride in the park every day." He cast her a quick smile. "There is the ever-present possibility of contracting a head cold, you know."

She smiled. "Always a concern."

"Yet my life, as dull as you may consider it, has not been uneventful. I am, for the most part, content. I have the family's financial affairs to oversee and the country estate as well as my seat in Parliament. In truth, I rarely have time to consider that my days are not filled with the kind of adventure and excitement my brothers relish. But this is my lot in life. I have known it since birth. It could not have been otherwise; nor would I wish it to be."

"Then you have no regrets," she said without thinking.

"I have one." His gaze met hers, and the look in his eyes caught at her breath.

She shook her head. "Now is not the right time —"

"When is the right time?" He straightened, and for a moment she thought he was going to drag her into his arms again. The oddest ache washed through her. "We have a great deal to talk about. A great deal to resolve."

"No, we don't." She took a step back.

"There are things you need to know. Things I need to tell you."

"To what end, Sterling?" She stared up at him. "Will it change anything? Will the past be any different? Will the years that have gone by at once vanish as if they had never happened? The past is the past and cannot be undone."

He stepped toward her. "Livy —"

"Don't." She moved back. Hearing him call her that tore at a heart she long thought impervious to him. She would not pin her hopes on anything with this man. She would not make that mistake again. "We have agreed to be friends, and I think it's wise not to dwell on what is over and best forgotten."

"I have not forgotten." He shook his head. "I have never forgotten you. Not for a day, not for a moment." His intense gaze met

161

hers. "Have you forgotten?"

"Yes," she lied, and squared her shoulders. "I have had ten years to forget, and I have done so. Today and tomorrow and the rest of my life are my only concern now."

"And have you forgiven as well as forgotten?" His dark gaze bored into hers.

She stared at him for a long moment. "No."

"Of course not." At once the Sterling who had spoken of playing pirate and had laughed at the dangerous nature of his life vanished, replaced by the proper Earl of Wyldewood. "I shall not speak of the past again."

Without warning, the urge to throw herself into his arms seized her. To smooth his troubled brow with her fingers, to press her lips to his. She ignored the impulse and drew a deep breath. "My apologies if I have offended you."

"You have nothing to apologize for," he said coolly. "As you said, the past is the past. And there is nothing that can be done about it. I have agreed to be friends, and I shall endeavor not to cross the bounds of that friendship again."

"Yes, well, I . . ."

"There you are." Millicent bustled up to them, parasol in hand, a bright smile on her face. "Are you discussing the accommodations? Quite good if you ask me. All in all, I'm finding this most delightful. I can't think why I so much as hesitated to come along."

Sterling raised a brow. "Odd, I don't recall your hesitating."

"Then you should be more observant." She sniffed. "What a glorious day this is. Olivia, have you ever seen a sky that blue?"

"It is lovely." Olivia struggled to keep her voice level. Nothing at all had really happened between her and Sterling, yet her stomach was decidedly uneasy, and there was a definite ache in her throat. It was absurd, and such feelings were to be avoided from this point on. Which obviously meant avoiding any discussion of the past.

Millicent studied her curiously. "You look quite pale, my dear. Are you all right? Not suffering from mal de mer I hope. That would be simply dreadful given we are very nearly at the beginning of almost a fortnight of traveling by sea."

"No, I'm fine, thank you." Olivia smiled. She wasn't the least bit fine and wouldn't be as long as Sterling's brown eyes studied her with an intensity that twisted something deep inside her. And made her wish . . . "But the glare on the water has made my head ache, so I think I shall retire to my cabin for a bit." She summoned her brightest smile. "Good day, Millicent. Sterling." She nodded and turned quickly but not before she noted the considering look in his eye.

She hurried back to the cabin she shared with Millicent, more than a little annoyed. With him for bringing up the past but more with herself. Why had she ever thought she could spend time with him without feelings she had long since put aside recurring? In hindsight, it was the height of foolishness. She paced the small cabin. Apparently, now that the man had returned to her life, he was in her blood as much as adventure ran in the veins of his brothers. The question now was what could be done about it.

There was no possibility of finding again what they had once had. She hadn't forgiven him, she wasn't sure she ever could. The pain of his betrayal had dimmed, and indeed she had thought it vanquished altogether. Now, she realized it had never been entirely forgotten. Even when he had invaded her dreams, it had lingered, a vague shadow of despair. Beyond that, they had each changed too much to go back. No, she wouldn't trust her heart to him again. She couldn't. She'd survived heartbreak at his hands once, she could never survive it again.

It was absurd as well to have sharing his bed on her list. It was akin to standing before a rising river and daring it not to flood. Still . . . She paused in midstep. Perhaps that was the answer. Perhaps once she had crossed that item off her list, she could go on with her life and put him in the past, where he belonged. In the same manner in which overindulging in a treat one craved ended the desire for the treat ever again.

There's was nothing to be done for it then. She was going to have to seduce the Earl of Wyldewood. And seduce him as soon as possible.

Sterling stared after her for a moment, then clenched his teeth and directed his gaze back toward the sea. She was perhaps the most infuriating creature he had ever met. He wanted to resolve the past and move on. She wouldn't even discuss it. Worse, she made him feel helpless. He did not like it.

"I do hope she is all right," his mother murmured. "I had the distinct impression I was interrupting something important."

He drew a deep breath. "No, nothing important at all."

"Oh, darling, you're such a terrible liar.

You always have been." She sighed in resignation. "And you have never been one for revealing your feelings. Or for talking about them. Perhaps it's time you did so."

"I have nothing to say." That was, of course, another lie.

"Then I shall have to do all the talking." She paused, and he hoped she intended to prattle on about the fine day or the better-than-expected accommodations. "You have never told me precisely what transpired between you and Olivia before she married."

So much for that hope. "There is little to tell. Her father told me she was to marry Rathbourne. And that she wished never to see me again."

"And?"

"And . . ." He blew a long breath. "It was a lie. She was forced by her father to marry Rathbourne."

"I see," she said under her breath. "I have long suspected as much."

He cast her a sharp glance. "Why didn't you say anything?"

"Goodness, Sterling." Her brows drew together in an annoyed frown. "What was I supposed to say? That you should fight for the girl? That you should refuse to allow her to walk out of your life? That you should follow where your heart led?"

"Something like that," he muttered.

"How could I? You did not confide in me." She huffed. "And, as I recall, you gave me no opportunity to say much of anything. You were entirely too proud."

He snorted in disdain. "I was a fool."

"No doubt. Besides, she was married within days, and you were engaged to Alice and wed nearly as quickly. It seemed to me it was best to keep my opinions to myself. After all, what was done was done." She paused. "And I did like Alice very much although I never thought she made you truly happy."

He stared at her. "I was happy."

"No, Sterling, you were content. There is an enormous difference." Her voice softened. "When your father and I were first married, we couldn't bear to be apart from one another. You and Alice . . ."

He narrowed his gaze. "Yes?"

"You and she behaved much as though you'd been married forever rather than newly wed."

"If I recall correctly . . ." Annoyance sounded in his clipped words. "Father was ill, and I had other things on my mind."

"I'm not faulting you. If Alice had lived, I have no doubt you would have had a long and good life together." She met his gaze firmly. "However, I never once saw you look at her the way you looked at Olivia. And when Alice died . . ."

"Yes?" he snapped.

"When she died, it did not break your heart."

Sterling stared. "I was most distraught."

"Yes, you were. You had lost a great friend." She shook her head. "Not a great love."

"I cared deeply for Alice."

She studied him.

"I did," he said again firmly, as if trying to convince himself as much as her. He'd had a great deal of affection for Alice. If the love he'd felt for his wife had not been the same as his feelings for Livy, well, wasn't that to be expected? Livy had been the great love of his life. Alice was . . . he cringed to himself. He had never admitted it even in his own mind, but Alice was second. His mother might not think he lied well, but he seemed to do an excellent job of lying to himself. "I never intended —"

"No, you didn't," his mother said quickly. "You are not that sort of man."

"Do you think she knew?" The idea that Alice might have realized that he'd never really put Livy behind him tore at his heart.

He wouldn't have hurt her for the world.

Mother hesitated as if searching for the right words. "I am sorry, darling, of course she knew. A woman always knows."

"She never said a word," he said staunchly.

"Nor would she. She had loved you for much of her life." She laid her hand on his arm. "Don't think for a moment that Alice wasn't happy. She was, very much so."

"I did try," he said, more to himself than to her. And indeed, hadn't he put all thought of Livy aside when he married Alice? Hadn't he ignored her letters?

"Now what do you intend to do?"

"I intend to help Olivia meet the terms of her husband's will, acquire her well-earned inheritance, and become independent."

"Oh dear." Mother shook her head. "I had rather hoped . . ."

"Don't."

"Don't what?"

"Don't say what you were going to say."

"Don't say that she is free now and as she has turned to you for help, it seems an excellent beginning?"

"She had no one else."

"Regardless, the simple fact is that she did turn to you." Mother narrowed her gaze. "And when this is over and done with, then what?"

"Then I shall resume my life exactly as I left off." That too was a lie. His life had changed forever the night her father had told him the truth.

"And Olivia?"

"Olivia will be able to breathe," he said softly.

"So you are giving up any hope of a future together?"

He cast her an annoyed glare. "You are an exasperating female, Mother."

"I always have been, dear." She smiled. "It is not like you to give up."

"I am facing the reality of the situation." He shook his head. "She has not forgiven me."

"Your primary fault was in believing her father." She shook her head. "In truth, who could blame you? You had no idea —"

"She wrote to me, Mother. She sent me three letters." Perhaps he did need to talk to someone after all. "The first before she married Rathbourne telling me the truth of the matter. I assumed it was an apology." He glanced at her. "I never opened it." He drew a deep breath. "The next two came after she married, when Father was ill. They went unopened as well. In those, she again asked for help." Even now, the words in her letters twisted something inside him and carried with them guilt and remorse. And anger. At Rathbourne and more at himself. "There were not a lot of details; I suspect she was too afraid for that. But he treated her abominably, and she feared for her life. She begged me to help her escape him."

"Good Lord." Shock rang in his mother's voice. "I never imagined. But you said you didn't open them."

"I didn't." He shrugged. "Recently, Lord Newbury came to me and told me the truth. He thought she might be in danger because of the nature of her husband's death. I took it upon myself to pay a call on her." He smiled in a wry manner. "She was not pleased to see me."

"I can understand why."

"There was an incident after that, but suffice it to say, I at last read her letters." He met his mother's gaze directly. "She has not forgiven me. I can't say that I blame her."

"Nor can I."

"She won't even let me talk to her about it. Tell me, Mother, what am I to do?"

His mother raised a brow. "I have not been able to tell you what to do since you were a very small boy."

He snorted with disbelief. "You have never stopped attempting to tell me exactly what to do on all manner of subjects."

"Yes, well, you have never listened to me." She paused for a long moment. "You shall have to make amends, you know."

He scoffed. "I'm funding her quest for her inheritance. I'm accompanying her to Egypt. What more can I do?"

"I don't know." Mother chose her words with care. "But, it seems to me, you can be her friend. Prove to her that you can be trusted with her friendship, and, perhaps, eventually she will trust you again with her heart."

He shook his head. "I don't —"

"Furthermore, you must control that tendency of yours toward impatience. It is not an endearing trait," she said firmly. "You have only recently learned the truth, and it's to be expected that you would want to act at once. But Olivia has had a decade to consider your actions or lack thereof. And apparently those years have been most unpleasant."

"My fault." A heavy weight settled in his stomach. "I should have helped her. If only —"

"If only what?" Mother narrowed her eyes in irritation. "Would you have left your wife?"

"No, of course not." But he never would have married Alice. "If I had opened her first letter —"

"But you didn't, and that cannot be undone. Now, you have the future ahead of you. Much in life has come easily to you, but you have never been one to give up what you have wanted. Do not make that mistake now. Sterling." She leaned closer to him. "You have never stopped loving this woman. I failed to tell you once to follow your heart. I do not hesitate to do so now."

He stared at her. "You're right, Mother."

"I usually am." She frowned. "About which part?"

"I don't know what I was thinking."

"Nor do I. What were you thinking?" she said cautiously.

"I have never given up on what I have wanted. I have never accepted defeat, and I am not about to do so now."

"Thank goodness." She smiled.

It wouldn't be easy, and it would require patience, never his strongest quality. His spirits lightened. He had won her heart once before. He was older and, hopefully, wiser, and he was determined. They couldn't pick up where they had left off, but they could go forward from here. He grinned. "Don't plan a wedding just yet, Mother."

"Oh, I wouldn't think —"

"And do not interfere."

"I would never —"

He raised a brow.

She cast him a weak smile. "Very well, I shall try . . ."

"You shall do more than try."

"Trying is all anyone can do. You cannot ask for more than my wholehearted attempt to keep at bay a mother's natural instinct to help her child," she said in a lofty manner.

He fixed her with a firm look.

"I do promise to keep myself from assisting my son." She heaved a long-suffering sigh. "However, I do retain the right to lend my assistance should you request it."

He laughed, leaned forward, and kissed her cheek. "That is most appreciated."

"As well it should be." She sniffed and shifted her parasol. "Oh, that nice Mr. Cadwallender has come out on deck." She studied the young man for a moment. "He's not nearly as stodgy as most solicitors of my acquaintance. Of course, he is quite young, and perhaps stodginess comes with age and experience in that profession. Still, it does seem to me that he has a great deal of potential. He is quite dashing, with all that blond hair and those dark blue eyes.

"I thought it was most interesting to learn he is related to the publishing Cadwallenders. I believe the last book I read was printed by Cadwallender. For the life of me, I cannot recall the title, but I did like it rather a lot. Oh, not so much as the latest offering from . . ."

His mother continued, unaware that her conversation was entirely one-sided. It was surprisingly refreshing to have bared his soul. To have spoken his thoughts aloud. He wondered why he didn't do so more often.

He had become accustomed through the years to keeping his own counsel. In truth, he'd had no one to share his thoughts with. There had only been one person in his life he'd ever been completely open with.

He nodded in agreement to something his mother said and smiled to himself. She was right, and whether or not he took her advice again in the future, he would do so now.

He would curb his impatience and bide his time. He'd be bloody charming, the perfect traveling companion. He would be friendly, gracious, carefree, and enjoy every blasted moment of this so-called adventure. After all, he had no family finances to administer, no political questions to occupy his mind, no issues regarding the estate to concern himself with. He had left it all behind in London. Why, he was very nearly free of all of his usual responsibilities.

The thought struck him that he'd be the

man he once was, before he'd become the Earl of Wyldewood. Before the responsibilities and the tragedies and the heartaches of his life had sobered him, before he learned that he had failed her. Abruptly, he realized that since Olivia had come back into his life, he'd been grim and morose and far too serious. That was about to change. And by God, even if it killed him, he would indeed earn Livy's friendship.

And then he would claim her heart.

NINE

Dance with a prince in the moonlight.
From the secret list of desires of
Olivia Rathbourne

The docks at Marseilles teemed with the life of a thriving seaport. Pity they were only here for a few hours.

Olivia rested her forearms on the railing of the packet and drank in the intoxicating foreign scene laid out before her. There was little else for her to do at the moment. Josiah was arranging the transfer of their baggage to the ship that would take them to Egypt. Or, to be more accurate, Josiah was manfully trying to wrest control of the transfer of their things from Millicent, who was confident she knew better than the solicitor how to efficiently accomplish moving the baggage. Although, with an odd sort of tug-of-war going on between the two, "efficiently" was perhaps not as accurate as

177

"haphazardly." Olivia did hope Sterling's mother and the young man did not come to verbal blows although she wouldn't put it past Millicent to box his ears.

In the five days of their journey thus far, Millicent had adopted the solicitor as one of her own. Josiah did not seem particularly averse to said adoption even as he struggled to maintain a professional manner.

He had also taken on the position of Sterling's secretary for the duration of their travels for what Olivia assumed was handsome compensation. He was therefore in charge of making certain they progressed from one point to the next. Josiah had pointed out that he really had nothing else to do and did wish to be useful. All in all, he was a very nice and thoroughly competent young man.

Olivia was grateful that the details of transferring their party and their belongings and the sundry and assorted details of travel were out of her hands. She was left free to contemplate the exotic scene laid out before her. Marseilles was the shipping portal to the Mediterranean and lands to the east. The setting of the port in the French town was an intriguing mix of old and new. Ancient fortresses and castles stood watch over the harbor where modern steamships rested, iron beasts straining to break their bonds and rush toward the freedom of the open sea. A forests of masts from steamships and sailing vessels alike reached upward toward the brilliant blue sky as if they too yearned to break free and soar through the heavens. She wondered how the masses of ships managed to avoid one another in a harbor that appeared huge yet still did not seem big enough to support the number of vessels crowding the water.

The scene on the docks was every bit as crowded. Cargo masters and sailors and fishwives bustled about their daily chores with voices raised in a cacophony of foreign tongues and languages both lyrical and coarse. The business of commerce and the transport of products and people mingled with a chaos Olivia suspected was confusing only to the unfamiliar eye. Carts and wagons laden with cargo made their way through the throngs of workers and passengers, exotic and ordinary. Cargo in giant nets was lifted onto ships by cranes cranked by burly men with sweat-glistened skin.

Those traveling for pleasure were easy to spot. They stood on the docks in groups of various sizes. Large fashionable hats and delicate parasols separated the ladies from their maids, expressions of inconvenience differentiated the gentlemen from their valets. Which of them might be joining them on their voyage to Egypt? She did hope their fellow passengers would be a carefree lot. She wished to enjoy the rest of the voyage, and convivial companions would certainly help in that respect.

Not that she hadn't enjoyed their travels to this point. Millicent was most amusing. After the first few days, when he was obviously trying to maintain his position as official overseer, Josiah had proven to be a pleasant traveling companion as well, as interested as she in what excitement might lie ahead. Sterling, however, remained an enigma although she had to confess, she was enjoying his company.

She had thought to avoid him, then discarded the idea as both impractical and annoying. This was *her* adventure, after all, and she refused to spend it hiding in her cabin. But he had apparently taken her desire not to discuss their past to heart and had not brought up the subject again. Admittedly, he had had no opportunity as they were very rarely alone. He had been charming and attentive, the epitome of polite and gentlemanly behavior, and hadn't seemed the least bit interested in being anything other than her friend. Exactly as she wanted it. Then why did she find his perfect, gentlemanly manner so annoying?

As for the matter of his seduction . . . she sighed at the thought. She'd been sharing a cabin with his mother, Sterling had been quartered with Josiah, so there had been no opportunity for that either. She'd tried to be as flirtatious as possible once she had decided on his seduction. But even to her own ears her flirting had struck her as somewhat forced and unnatural. Apparently, flirtation was indeed an art, and she was long out of practice. Coupled with Sterling's proper behavior, well, it was all most frustrating. Still, she would have her own cabin on the next, much larger, ship.

She turned her attention back to the sights on the docks. The kaleidoscope of images and sounds was mesmerizing, and she found herself wondering if a teetering stack of crates was cargo bound for someplace exciting and exotic. Or if a well-dressed young woman, who even at a distance had an air of uncertainty about her, was traveling to join a husband or a fiancé for a new life in a new land. Still, in spite of the thoroughly up-to-date steamships and the fashionable clothing of the more well-to-do passengers, Olivia imagined that the scene was the same as it had been for hundreds of years.

"It's new, you know." Sterling came up beside her.

She started at his voice. "What's new?"

"The port. Well, fairly new as these things go."

She narrowed her gaze. "Were you reading my mind?"

"Yes." He grinned. "Admittedly, it was not at all difficult to guess at what someone like you would be thinking."

She raised a brow. "Someone like me?"

He laughed. "You needn't look offended. It was an observation, not a criticism."

"Very well." She paused. "What did you mean then by someone like me?"

"I meant someone who hasn't traveled or seen the sights beyond the boundaries of her own life but has always wanted to." He leaned toward her in a conspiratorial manner. "I have to confess, I am finding this all as fascinating as you do."

She started to protest that he no longer knew her that well, then caught herself. "You're enjoying this then?"

He grinned. "You're surprised, aren't you?"

"You seem to be full of surprises," she said under her breath.

"Ah, you expected me to maintain my surly demeanor all the way to Egypt and back." It was a comment more than a question.

Heat washed up her face. "Well . . ." She cast him a reluctant smile. "Yes."

He laughed, the carefree laugh she remembered from so long ago, and it settled in her heart. She ignored it.

"I had fully intended to remain inconvenienced for the duration of our journey, but I admit, the, well excitement of it all has worked its way past my resistance." He braced his hands on the railing and drew a deep breath. "In spite of myself, I find this intoxicating. The lure of the sea, the call of foreign lands, the mystery of what may lie just out of sight."

She widened her eyes and stared.

"You needn't look so shocked." He grinned a boyish sort of smile, probably unused for years. "It has been my experience with dull, staid, stodgy sorts such as myself, that we either become most difficult to live with when taken out of our natural surroundings or we adapt. I have decided to adapt."

"Oh." She struggled to find the right words. "How very accommodating of you."

"Not at all." He laughed "I can either

resent every moment of every day, or I can embrace the adventure of it all. I have chosen to embrace and enjoy."

Perhaps there was some of the Sterling she once knew left after all.

"And in the spirit of the adventure, I have taken it upon myself to read something of the place we now find ourselves. My mother has brought along a number of guidebooks." He shook his head. "It's a shame there is no time to see the city itself. It's quite old, you know. It has been a seaport for nearly two thousand years."

"Yes, I know," she murmured.

"The Greeks were here first, then the Romans. But the docks where we are now were only built about forty years ago, to accommodate the kind of steamship we will soon be boarding."

"How clever of them."

"Very farsighted really." He paused. "Do you know the legend of the founding of Marseilles?"

She bit back a smile. She wasn't sure what had possessed him but she was grateful for it. This new Sterling was much more like the man she had once loved than the earl who had agreed to help her. Not that it mattered. "No. Do you?"

He smiled in a smug manner. "When the

Greeks first arrived here, their leader was a man named Protis. He was strong and handsome, an excellent leader and prone to adventures. Very much in the manner that oh, say, an earl, whose name I think we both know, would be today."

"Leader of men? Strong, handsome, and adventurous?"

"Under the appropriate circumstances."

She laughed. "Goodness, Sterling. What utter nonsense."

He gasped with indignation. "Are you saying I could not lead men if necessary?"

"No, not at all," she said quickly. "I'm certain you would be an excellent leader of men."

"Then you are saying I am not strong?" Before she could protest, he swept her into his arms and lifted her off the deck.

"Sterling!" She huffed. "Put me down this instant!"

"Only if you admit I could easily carry two of you."

"Yes, yes, I admit it." He set her down and released her without holding her even a moment longer than necessary. It was surprisingly annoying. "Fortunately for you, there is only one of me."

"Fortunately for us all." He flashed her a wicked grin. "And as for handsome —"

"Yes, yes, you are one of the handsomest men I have ever seen." She smoothed her dress. "I suspect you are also a bit mad. What has gotten into you?"

"Adventure, my dear. Now, may I continue my story?"

She cast him a suspicious look. "With or without your own embellishments?"

"I am simply making a good story better in the nature of all good storytellers," he said in a superior manner. "When you tell a story, you may tell it in your own way. This is the story as I see it." He cleared his throat. "When Protis arrived, he went to meet with the local people. As fate would have it, that was the very day the king's daughter, Gyptis, was to be married. Well, she took one look at our hero, the strong handsome earl —"

"I believe you mean Greek."

"Yes, of course. I can't imagine what I was thinking." Amusement twinkled in his eye. "Gyptis took one look at Protis, decided she couldn't possibly live without him, threw over all her other suitors, and gave him her heart. And together" — he waved in a grand gesture at the shore — "they founded all this."

She raised a brow. "All this?"

"Well, what would become all this." He

186

leaned toward her. "It's an excellent story, don't you think?"

She laughed. "Yes it is. And only made better by the telling."

"I thought so." He gazed at the city. "Marseilles has endured the Greeks, the Romans, plague, war, and revolution. And through all that, it has remained an excellent seaport."

"One would expect no less of a city founded on a love story."

"My sentiments exactly." He paused for a moment. "Pity we have no time to appreciate it. We have barely two hours before we sail."

"Oh dear, then we should go." She glanced around. "Have you seen your mother and Josiah?"

"They said they would meet us aboard." He offered his arm. "Might I have the honor of escorting you off this ship and onto the next?"

"You may." She took his arm, and a delightful chill shivered through her. He hadn't done more than offer her a polite hand to assist her in or out of a carriage since the day he had told her she had been his only adventure. It was oddly pleasant to be on his arm. To feel the strength of his muscles beneath his coat and the warmth of his body brushing against hers.

He escorted her off the ship and along the docks, pointing out ancient fortresses overlooking the harbor and a cathedral in the distance.

"You have become quite an accomplished tour guide."

He flashed her a quick grin. "Just one of my many hidden talents."

"Along with being a leader of men?"

He laughed. "Don't forget strong and handsome."

"Oh, I could never forget that." She fluttered her lashes at him. "I am most impressed."

He tucked her hand close against him. "And you are flirting with me."

She gasped in mock dismay. "Don't be absurd."

"You need practice." He paused. "At least with me."

"Whatever do you mean?"

"When you flirt with me it seems an effort." He smiled down at her. "However, when you flirt with Josiah, it is completely natural."

She stopped in midstep and stared at him. "I do not flirt with Josiah."

He snorted. "You most certainly do."

She pulled her brows together in indignation. "I most certainly do not. Aside from any number of other considerations, he's merely a boy."

"Scarcely." He tucked her hand back into the crook of his arm and started off again. "He is twenty-two years of age, and is furthermore a competent responsible man with a serious profession."

"Regardless, I do not flirt with him."

"Oh, Josiah." He adopted a high-pitched voice and heaved a heartfelt sigh. "You are so good at taking care of every little detail. Why I don't know what we would do without you."

She gasped. "I never said anything of the sort!"

He cast her a skeptical glance.

"Admittedly, I may have complimented him on his efficiency, but I never . . ."

Sterling bit back a grin.

"Well . . . perhaps, but I certainly didn't intend to." She huffed. "Why, I wouldn't think of . . ."

"He is smitten with you, you know."

"Nonsense," she lied. "It's your mother he adores."

"Perhaps, but only as a mother." He sighed again in a dramatic manner. "Would that you would flirt so easily with me."

"I am out of practice," she said under her breath.

"Then we should do something about that." He smiled. "You are an eminently eligible widow now, and you may wish to marry again one day."

"I have no desire ever to marry again."

He ignored her. "Flirting is a skill that will serve you well. And I am willing to suffer your attempts to improve."

She stared. "How very gracious of you."

"It's the least I can do for a friend." He patted her hand. "And we did agree to be friends, did we not?"

"Yes we did, but —"

"By the time we return to London, you will be prepared to charm even the most reluctant of suitors."

They reached the gangway of their new ship and started up. The packet they'd taken to Marseilles was considerably smaller than the ship they now boarded.

Sterling inclined his head toward her. "I understand this ship has a grand dining room and dancing in the evening."

"What? No more whist?" Their party had played whist on very nearly every evening thus far. And while it had been enjoyable, it was beginning to tire.

"Oh, we shall certainly play whist, and

charades as well." He grinned. "And we shall dance." He paused. "I haven't danced for some time. I quite look forward to it."

"As do I." Even as the words were out of her mouth, she realized she did very much wish to dance again in Sterling's arms.

Once on board, they were directed to their cabins. Sterling escorted her to her door.

She paused before her cabin and drew a deep breath. "Would you care to come in and see my accommodations?"

"That would be most improper." He smiled. "Even for a friend."

The vaguest hint of disappointment stabbed her. "Of course."

"However." He took her hand and raised it to his lips. "I shall be on deck when we pull out of port if you wish to join me." He released her hand, and, again, a sense of disappointment washed through her. "I want to see the Ile d'If as we pass by. Somehow, I missed it on our approach."

"The what?"

"The island in the harbor."

She thought for a moment. "The one with the castle?"

He nodded. "Fortress really, built to provide protection against invaders. But it soon became a prison. It still is, I think. Its most famous prisoner never actually resided there."

She narrowed her gaze. "This is some sort of trick isn't it?"

He laughed. "Not at all. The island is where Edmond Dantès was imprisoned for fourteen years."

"Yes, of course." She rolled her gaze heavenward. She had loved *The Count of Monte Cristo* as a girl. As an adult, she hadn't found the story of the man falsely imprisoned and kept from the woman he loved to her liking. "I can't believe I didn't remember that. Although he wasn't really imprisoned there as he was fictional."

"Ah, but I'm told." He glanced one way then the other down the corridor, and lowered his voice in a confidential manner. "The hole where he made his escape can still be seen."

She stared at him for a moment, then laughed. "You can't see the place where a prisoner who never existed escaped. It is no doubt nothing more than a lure for romantic, unsuspecting tourists."

"And I" — he swept a dramatic bow — "can be quite romantic." He grinned. "In a literary sense, that is."

She laughed. "I shall join you on deck in an hour or so then."

"I shall look forward to it." He nodded and strolled down the corridor, a jaunty spring to his step. *Jaunty?* Sterling?

What had gotten into the man? She opened her door and stepped into her cabin, barely noting the stylish furnishings. In recent days, Sterling had become an entirely new person. He did indeed seem to be enjoying their journey. And she was enjoying him. Why the man was even willing to play parlor games.

She sank down on her bed. This wasn't the same Sterling who had insisted her father's concerns had made her his responsibility. Who had placed guards in her household. Who had initially refused to go to Egypt. He was neither stiff nor stodgy, and certainly not dull. Why, almost overnight he had become an entirely new man.

Good God! He wasn't a new man at all. This was the Sterling she had once fallen in love with. The Sterling she had given her heart to. The Sterling who had haunted her dreams. And nothing was as dangerous as that.

She could resist the sober, proper Earl of Wyldewood, who carried the weight of his responsibilities on his shoulders. Could she resist the carefree Sterling Harrington, whose eyes twinkled with amusement and smile settled in her heart so easily?

Worse, with every day spent in his company, would she reach a point where she no longer wished to resist?

TEN

*Converse with natives
on the American frontier.*
From the secret list of desires of
Olivia Rathbourne

Sterling was as good as his word. The man had become bloody charming and damn near irresistible.

Olivia watched him dance with a young American passenger — a Miss Johnson she thought — and tried very hard to ignore how irritating she found the scene before her. The girl — the very pretty girl — was obviously flirting with him, and he was obviously enjoying it. She clenched her jaw. Not that she cared. He could flirt his way from Marseilles to Egypt and back for all she cared. Even so, he could be enjoying himself a bit less.

The room set aside for dancing and card playing and other activities of amusement

195

was not overly large but was nicely ap-
pointed and well suited for the numbers of
first-class passengers it served. The ship
itself was fairly new, and Olivia had been
told that it rivaled anything sailing the
North Atlantic between Europe and
America. How exciting it would be to be on
a ship sailing that route. Someday, she
vowed, she would be.

Sterling had become quite a sought-after
dancing partner and, no doubt, the handful
of eligible women on the ship saw him as
potentially something much more perma-
nent. In the three days they'd been on the
ship, Olivia had not had the opportunity to
share more than a dance or two each
evening with him. Certainly there were
other men aboard although the majority did
seem to be considerably older, which suited
Millicent. She too appeared to be having an
excellent time. Not that Olivia had any lack
of eager partners, and she scarcely ever sat
out a dance. Why there was that nice Aus-
trian gentleman, and the French count, and
the American ambassador to somewhere or
other. They were all quite pleasant although,
admittedly, Sterling was an excellent dancer
and considerably more handsome and dashing. And annoying.

"Lady Rathbourne, would you care to

dance," Josiah said with a hopeful smile on his face. No matter what she said, the young man refused to address her by her given name.

She cast him a grateful smile. "I should like nothing better."

The small orchestra was playing a waltz. Josiah escorted Olivia onto the floor and he took her in his arms in a most proper and correct manner. Ever since Sterling had made his absurd assertion that Josiah harbored feelings of affection for her, Olivia had gone out of her way to treat the young man with a certain amount of reserve. And there had been no flirting whatsoever, at least so far as she could tell. As she hadn't thought she'd been flirting with him in the first place, she couldn't be sure. But she certainly did not want to encourage him in anything more than a good sound friendship.

Still, she did enjoy dancing, and it had been years since she'd danced at all. Even then it was only with partners selected by her late husband. When she had appeared at public events with the viscount, he had made certain she had known with which partners it would be in his best interest for her to dance. Very early in her married life, she had decided not to dance at all rather than with gentlemen who might prove useful to her late husband. There was a time when she had lived in fear that having bartered her hand on the dance floor, he might barter her in other ways to further his own ends. She needn't have worried. He was far too possessive to share this particular possession.

Josiah executed a turn, and she followed him rather well considering that she was as out of practice at dancing as she was at flirtation. Coupled with the fact that Josiah's dancing was more enthusiastic than skilled, she was forced to concentrate on her own movements to avoid his feet stepping on hers, which had happened more than once on previous nights.

Josiah gazed down at her. "You seem rather preoccupied tonight, Lady Rathbourne."

"Do I?" She smiled up at him. She would never offend him by an honest assessment of his proficiency on the dance floor. "No doubt it's simply because we are drawing ever closer to Egypt, and I have no idea what will transpire there."

His brows drew together in concern. "Are you apprehensive then?"

"Not apprehensive exactly." She thought for a moment. "Oddly enough, I am rather optimistic. But, then, I have never had an adventure before, and I find everything to be most exciting." She smiled. "And I have come this far after all. Against all probability, I suspect."

He chuckled. "Admittedly, Mr. Hollis never imagined you would choose to attempt to meet the terms of the will."

She laughed. "I daresay he must have had some choice words to say about it in the privacy of your offices."

A blush washed up the young man's face. "He did express, shall we say, surprise at your decision after the meeting in your library. He fully expected you to be quite content with the allowance provided you by the estate and more than happy to continue your life as you had when your husband was alive." He paused. "I must confess, I have never seen his face quite so red or heard him use language even remotely as colorful."

"And what of you, Josiah? Were you surprised?"

"Not after I had met you," he said without pause, then winced. "My apologies, that sounded rather presumptuous of me."

"Not at all, I thought it sounded honest."

The solicitor's expression relaxed.

"Do tell me why you weren't surprised

once we had met."

He thought for a moment as if choosing his words. "I would prefer not to offend you."

"I am not easily offended."

"I thought your late husband was a beast of a man," Josiah blurted. "Not that I had many direct dealings with him. But he struck me as cold and unfeeling and, well, cruel. Although I have nothing really to base that on save my knowledge of his business affairs and the occasional meeting. I imagined his wife to be . . . not at all like you."

She raised a brow. "Not like me?"

"I thought the Viscountess Rathbourne would be a timid sort of creature, well used to obeying the commands of her husband without question. Even in death. I expected the viscount to have a wife he had chosen for the benefits of an alliance with her family or for her fortune and therefore not to be the least bit lovely and charming and gracious." He grimaced. "Again, my apologies. I should not be so forthright. Do forgive me."

"There is nothing to forgive. I appreciate your candor." She had nothing to hide and no one to protect from the truth save herself. She did not wish to be pitied. The viscount was thankfully dead and buried and, in spite of his best efforts, she had emerged from her marriage strong and whole. She drew a deep breath. "And I applaud as well your perception. My late husband was not of my choosing. He was indeed a vile sort, and I have lived the years of my marriage waiting for the moment I would be free of him." She studied him coolly. "Have I shocked you?"

"I might have been quite shocked before meeting you or spending the last week in your company." He grinned. "But I am not the least bit shocked. Indeed, I am most impressed by your determination and courage."

"Courage?"

"To have endured a life with such a man and now to be endeavoring to improve your fate." He fell silent for a few moments, hopefully concentrating on the movement of his feet. "Tell me, what are your plans if you are not successful in meeting the terms of the will?"

"I have no plans, as the idea of failure is not something I wish to think about," she said with a smile. "Which is not merely optimistic but probably quite foolish. After all, we are going to attempt to convince men who could not be swayed by my late husband's considerable wealth to hand me objects they cherish. It would seem an impossible task."

"Only for one without determination and courage," he said staunchly.

She laughed.

"But if you do not succeed?"

"I really have no idea." Her tone hardened. "But I shall not return to the life I have lived. Perhaps I will take that which is determined to belong to me and me alone, sell whatever that may be, and use the proceeds to begin anew."

"You could marry again," he said in a casual manner.

"I have experienced marriage once, thank you, I have no desire to do so again. Besides, there are no doubt dozens of impoverished widows scouring London society even as we speak in hopes of finding someone suitable to wed."

"None like you." He squeezed her hand.

"That's very kind of you, Josiah, but —"

"My living is not overly substantial at the moment, but it will be someday." He gazed earnestly into her eyes. "One day I intend to have my own firm, and I have no doubt I shall be quite successful. My prospects are excellent. Lord Wyldewood has already indicated he may be interested in my services in the future. But even now, I could support a wife. My family has money as well, and I stand to inherit an impressive sum." His brows pulled together. "Admittedly, that is rather far in the future. My father is extraordinarily robust, and I would have it no other way but someday . . ."

"Josiah." *Good Lord!* "Surely you're not —"

"I would be an excellent husband, thoughtful and considerate. I would worship the very ground you walked upon." He pulled her slightly closer than was proper and gazed into her eyes. "I already do. Marry me, La— Olivia."

"You don't even know me."

"I know enough. If you don't get what you want, want me. I would spend the rest of my days making you happy."

"Josiah." She shook her head. "I am deeply flattered, but I am not looking for a husband."

"But if you do not succeed —"

"Then I shall cross that road when I come to it. But I don't think —"

"We would suit well together."

"I am entirely too old for you."

"Nonsense." He scoffed. "Age is immaterial when one has found the woman one wishes to spend the rest of one's life with."

"Josiah." She choose her words with care.

203

"You haven't found the woman you wish to spend the rest of your life with."

"I may be younger than you, Olivia, but I know my own heart."

"And your heart is too valuable to give to someone who . . ."

"I have already given you my heart," he said staunchly.

She ignored him. "Someone who loves you as she would a brother. A younger brother."

His brow furrowed. "I have no desire to be your brother. I want to be your —"

"You are a dear, sweet wonderful bo—man. Any woman would be thrilled to hear you say those words. But you deserve better."

"You're everything I have ever dreamed of. I don't want better, I want you." His eyes widened. "Forgive me, I didn't mean —"

"You only think you want me." She shook her head. "But you don't want a woman who only marries you because she has no other choice. You deserve a woman who loves you with her whole heart and soul. Who would do anything for you. Who would worship the very ground *you* walk upon." She smiled up at him. "I will never forget what you have offered. It has been a very long time since I have experienced such kindness. It means a great deal to me."

"It would mean more if you accepted," he muttered.

"And you will always have a place in my heart."

"As a brother."

"As a *beloved* brother." She adopted a teasing note. "I have never had a brother and have always wanted one."

He blew a long breath. "I have five brothers and two sisters. I do not need another sister."

"And yet you now have one more."

His gaze searched hers. "If you change your mind . . ."

"I won't," she said firmly.

His brow furrowed. "I am not a man to give up easily."

"And I rarely change my mind."

"Will you at least grant me one favor then?"

She smiled with relief. "Yes, of course. What is it?"

He drew a deep breath. "I would ask only that you refrain from giving me your answer —"

"I believe I have already given you my answer."

"Your final answer."

She sighed. "Josiah —"

"Until such time as you have either succeeded in your quest, or you have failed." His gaze bored into hers, his blue eyes dark with emotion. "I will not accept your answer as final until then."

"It will be no different," she warned.

"One never knows what may happen tomorrow." He grinned. "And I am nothing if not optimistic."

She cast him a weak smile. Mercifully, the music drew to a close, and their dance ended.

"I was hoping we could have another —"

Before he could finish, Olivia spotted Sterling off to one side of the dance floor speaking with Miss Johnson. Excellent. He wished to rescue maidens, and Olivia was in dire need of rescue. "Forgive me, Josiah, but I promised Lord Wyldewood the next dance."

"Very well," he said with a wistful smile. "Perhaps we can have another dance later in the evening?"

"That would be lovely." She smiled and started to make her way around the room.

What a dreadful, awkward thing that was. To dash a man's hopes and attempt do so in a manner that was both kind and firm. She did hope she had managed to convince him of the futility of pursuing her. They would be traveling together for some time yet, and she didn't want to have to watch every word she said for fear he would misconstrue it. Nor did she wish to lose the comfortable companionship they had shared.

Although — a reluctant smile curved her lips — it was most flattering. It had been a very long time since she had been the object of a young man's affections. To have caught the eye of a handsome man, even if a little too young, was something she had not considered. Her mirror told her she was still lovely, and certainly she had realized there was a possibility of romance somewhere in the future, but so much had transpired since she had become a widow that it had never occurred to her that someday might be now. Besides, if one were paying attention to such things, one would consider her in deep mourning even if she had no intention of mourning Viscount Rathbourne. She had refused to acquire more than one new black gown and she hadn't brought it with her.

She drew closer to Sterling and realized he wasn't merely speaking to Miss Johnson, he was flirting. And judging by the manner in which she inclined her head toward him and fluttered her fan, the cheeky American was flirting right back. Didn't the man know there was such a thing as being too charming?

Sterling glanced in her direction, and her gaze caught his. She smiled in what she hoped was a fetching manner and nodded slightly toward the dancers. He grinned and turned back to the young woman to hopefully make his apologies. If not, Olivia would have no difficulty dragging him onto the dance floor if necessary. She'd used Sterling as an excuse to avoid further entanglement with Josiah, and she had no intention of allowing the young man to know she had lied.

Sterling took the American's hand and lifted it to his lips, his gaze never leaving the girl's. Hmph. Was that a technique he had learned from Quinton? Surely he didn't think it was effective. Still, given the look on the young woman's face, she was ready to fling herself into his arms and damn the consequences. Nonsense. She was entirely too young for Sterling. Oh, indeed, men tended to prefer women considerably younger than they, but a man like Sterling needed a woman who was more of a challenge than an untried girl could ever be. He would be bored with an insipid miss like this one in no time at all. Admittedly, he didn't look bored at the moment, and the girl appeared positively entranced.

Sterling released the girl's hand, bowed in a polite manner and started toward Olivia, meeting her halfway.

"I gather you wish to dance?" He offered his arm.

"Yes." An annoyingly grateful note sounded in her voice. She cleared her throat. "As we haven't danced more than once tonight, and the evening . . ."

"And you wished to dance once more before the evening is at end." He led her onto the floor, took her in his arms, and favored her with a knowing smile. "With me."

"Yes." She huffed and glared up at him. "With you."

He chuckled. "You do realize I am only allowing you to order me about because I wished to dance with you as well."

"Imagine my delight." She smiled sweetly. In spite of her words, his declaration was nice to hear. It had been somewhat distressing to realize that she danced with Sterling as easily as they once had. As if they had never been apart. As if they had spent the last ten years dancing in each other's arms every day. As if they were still made one for the other. It was an excellent reason to avoid dancing with him at all, and yet she couldn't resist. She'd nearly forgotten how much she loved to dance and thought it best to ignore altogether how much she had missed dancing with him.

"So." He grinned down at her. "Has Josiah declared his undying affection?"

"Why on earth would you ask that?" she said in a lofty manner.

"The two of you appeared to be having a conversation far too serious to be conducted on the dance floor."

She raised a brow. "Were you watching us?"

"No more so than you were watching me," he said smoothly.

"I wasn't . . ." She surrendered and heaved a resigned sigh. "She's entirely too young for you, you know."

"Really? I thought she seemed just the right age."

"If that's what you want, certainly." She shrugged. "I simply assumed that you would prefer a woman more . . . accomplished. Sophisticated. Worldly."

"Older, you mean."

"Not necessarily." She paused. "However, a girl of that age —"

"I believe she is eighteen." He grinned. "Which is considered more than old enough to wed."

"Nonsense." She scoffed. "A girl of eighteen scarcely even knows her own mind. When I was eighteen . . ."

"Yes?" He raised a brow. "When you were eighteen?"

When I was eighteen, I found the love of my life. She pushed the thought away.

"When I was eighteen, I was flighty and overly romantic," she said in a lofty manner.

"When you were eighteen, you were lovely." He grinned. "You still are."

"How very kind of you to say," she murmured. He might well have been the love of her life once, but he definitely wasn't anymore. Why the thought had popped into her head at all was bothersome. Sterling was now her friend and could never be anything more.

"You also giggled a great deal."

"I did not. I never giggled." She stared at him. "Nor do I do so now."

"Perhaps not now, but you used to." He executed a complicated turn, and she followed him without hesitation or difficulty. Which was the difference between dancing with an accomplished partner and one unsure of himself. And had nothing at all to do with the familiarity of dancing in this particular partner's arms. "I remember it distinctly."

"I did not giggle. I may have laughed in a thoroughly lighthearted manner, but I did not giggle."

He laughed. "Very well then, it was some other young woman whose giggle lingers still in my memory."

"No doubt." She paused. "A giggle is an odd thing to remember."

"Perhaps I recall it because it was so rare. Most of the time she — whichever she I am thinking of — laughed. A fine laugh full of joy and promise." He smiled. "She only giggled when she was embarrassed or unsure of herself."

"Well, it wasn't I," she said knowing full well it was. "One would think a giggle would be most annoying and not at all memorable."

"It wasn't the least bit annoying then. It was delightful. Although, I will admit, I do not find Miss Johnson's giggle quite so charming."

"Eighteen-year-old girls do tend to giggle," she said. "Perhaps you do not find it charming because you are no longer twenty yourself."

"That's probably it." He heaved a heartfelt sigh. "Pity."

She raised a brow. "What? That you are

no longer in your youth or that you do not appreciate pretty eighteen-year-old girls?"

"Both. But I do appreciate pretty eighteen-year-old girls." He grinned. "I'm just not sure I could live with one."

She smiled but held her tongue.

"And you did not answer my question."

"Which question was that?"

"Did Josiah declare himself?"

"Yes, you were right. I don't know why I didn't see it myself." She sighed. "It was quite awkward, telling him I do not share his feelings without breaking his heart."

"He's a fine young man."

"He is indeed, but I have no desire to marry him."

"He asked you to marry him?" Surprise sounded in Sterling's voice.

"If I do not meet the terms of the will and have nowhere else to turn." She shook her head. "It was very kind of him."

"Kindness has nothing to do with it," Sterling said firmly. "You are an exquisite woman, Olivia. More so now than ever. Beautiful and charming as well as clever and determined. It is not difficult to see why a young man's head would be turned by you. Or any man's head, for that matter."

She tilted her head and met his gaze. "Even yours?"

"You're flirting again, Livy," he said, deftly changing the subject. "And you still don't have the knack for it."

"Nonsense, I wasn't flirting." A blush washed up her face. Perhaps she was.

He chuckled. "Very well then. The tilt of your head, the look in your eye, the tone in your voice weren't attempts at flirting at all."

"No, they were not. Besides, I didn't do any of that. Not deliberately at any rate." She paused. "But if I had been attempting to flirt, what was wrong with the tilt of my head or the look in my eye or the tone of my voice?"

"First of all." He gazed down at her and turned flawlessly in rhythm with the music, and again she followed him without effort. "You tilted your head too much to one side. It should be subtle, as if you were trying to ascertain my thoughts by the study of my face."

"Like this?" She tilted her head just a fraction.

"Much better." He nodded. "And the tone of your voice should be lighter, as if what you're saying isn't the least bit important on the surface but carries all sorts of hidden meanings and suggestions and promises."

"I see," she murmured, not knowing at all

214

how to accomplish saying one thing and meaning much more. Surely she had known how once.

"As for the look in your eyes." His gaze trapped hers. "It needs to hold the tiniest hint, the merest suggestion of what might be. Of something wonderful." Did his hand tighten around hers, or did she just imagine it? "When you flirt with a man, when you gaze into his eyes, he needs to wonder what might happen when next you meet or dance or walk together in the moonlight."

"Next?" The word was scarcely more than a sigh.

"Flirtation is not really a promise as much as it is a possibility." He gazed into her eyes. "The possibility that this is merely the beginning of what he has always desired, always dreamed of. That he has at last found what he has long wanted but never realized until now. And then . . ."

"Then?" She raised her head slightly.

"Then, should he be so caught in the web of flirtation you have spun, and should you be so inclined, he will more than likely kiss you." His gaze slipped to her lips and back to her eyes. "It should be the merest hint of a kiss, the soft brush of his lips against yours. A tease, a suggestion, and, yes, now a promise of what might be. Of what could be."

"A kiss is all that?" Would he kiss her now? Here?

"And more." He stared into her eyes. "Much more." He drew a deep breath. "The music has ended, Olivia." She hadn't even noticed that they'd stopped dancing and were simply standing in one another's arms. He released her and stepped back with a smile. "And I for one, find I am ready to retire for the evening."

She struggled to catch her breath. The blasted man wasn't going to kiss her after all. Not that she wanted him to. Still, the evening wasn't quite over yet. "As am I." She smiled and ignored the urge to tilt her head and perhaps even flutter her lashes. "Could I trouble you to escort me to my cabin?"

"As it is only a few doors from mine, it will be no trouble at all." He offered her his arm, and they walked off the dance floor. He glanced around. "I don't see my mother, so I assume she has already retired." They started for the corridor. "Josiah, however, doesn't look at all pleased to see us leaving together."

"We should bid him good evening. I wouldn't want him to think . . ."

"To think what?"

"Anything he shouldn't," she said quickly.

They approached the young man. "Josiah, I fear I am quite done in, so I shall take my leave and retire for the night."

"Yes, of course." Josiah's considering gaze slipped from her to Sterling and back.

"Lord Wyldewood has been good enough to offer to escort me to my cabin," she said in an offhand manner as if there was nothing out of the ordinary about Sterling accompanying her to her cabin, After all, it wasn't the first time he had done so. Why then did she have the oddest tremulous feeling in the pit of her stomach?

"I think I shall remain here a bit longer," the solicitor said coolly. And why wouldn't he be cool toward her? She had turned down his proposal and was now leaving with another man.

"I shall see you tomorrow then." Olivia cast him a friendly, but not too friendly, smile.

Sterling leaned toward the younger man and lowered his voice. "I believe Miss Johnson might be amenable to a dance."

Josiah's gaze flicked to the pretty American, and his expression brightened. "Yes, well, perhaps she would."

They bid him good evening and started toward their cabins.

"That was very nice of you," she said. "I

do hope he likes Miss Johnson."

"There's nothing not to like." Sterling smiled. "If one is only twenty-two." He paused. "Did you consider his proposal at all?"

"Don't be absurd." She scoffed. "He's scarcely more than a boy."

"Would you have considered it if he were older then?"

"No," she said firmly. "I do not plan to marry again."

"But if we are not successful . . ."

"We will succeed. There isn't a doubt in my mind," she lied. There were a great many doubts about their eventual success or failure, she simply preferred not to think about them. They reached her door, and he released her arm.

"I see." He studied her for a long moment. "I would not want to dash your hopes by being too practical, but the fact of the matter is —"

"I know full well the facts of the matter." She shrugged. "It does me no good to consider the possibility of failure; therefore, I prefer not to do so."

"You're right of course." He smiled. "It's best not to get ahead of ourselves. We shall take every step as it presents itself."

She drew a deep breath. "The steward

leaves a small decanter of sherry in my cabin every night. Would you care to join me for a glass?"

"I should like nothing better." He took her hand and raised it to his lips. "But I fear I have kept you entirely too long already."

"Oh." She ignored yet another twinge of disappointment. Good Lord, she would never seduce him if he insisted on being so blasted thoughtful. Although he still held her hand, which seemed a good sign.

"Besides, the steward leaves a decanter of brandy in my cabin." He grinned. "And I have to admit while I have never been overly fond of sherry, I do appreciate a good brandy."

"Perhaps I should join you then," she said boldly.

"I would like nothing better," he said, but released her hand. "But I fear that would be most improper."

She lifted her shoulder in a casual shrug. "I am not concerned with propriety."

"Then one of us should be." He chuckled. "Good evening, Olivia." He turned to leave.

She sighed. "Good evening, Sterling."

"Oh, by the way." He glanced back at her. "The look in your eye a moment ago?" He grinned. "Most flirtatious." His grin widened, he nodded and headed down the corridor.

She quickly slipped into her room. The last thing she wanted was for him to catch her staring after him like . . . like . . . like a smitten eighteen-year-old girl. Which she wasn't. Perhaps once, but no longer. She had changed too much to let a few moments that might have recalled long-dead feelings mean anything. She wanted him in her bed, and that was all. Once that had been accomplished, that would be the end of it, and she would have crossed off one item on her list. And he would be out of her blood, and hopefully her dreams, once and for all.

Seducing him was obviously going to be more difficult than she had expected. Sterling was living up to his promise to be her friend and nothing more. But since then, he had become so much the man she remembered, the man she had loved. Damnation, he was maddening and so bloody charming she wanted to wring his neck. And it was most irritating that she was not the only woman on board who had noticed his charm. Not that it mattered to her. Not at all.

Still, she couldn't help but wonder what might encourage Miss Johnson to turn her attentions away from a dashing earl and toward a handsome young solicitor closer to her own age, with excellent prospects.

ELEVEN

It was all going remarkably well. Sterling puffed a cigar on the terrace of Shepheard's Hotel in Cairo and resisted to urge to smirk. It wasn't easy. But by the time they returned to London, Livy would once again be his. Forever. Reason enough to smirk with satisfaction.

Since that day on the packet when he had vowed to be patient and pleasant, charming and a perfect traveling companion he had done exactly that and had succeeded admirably. It had been easier than he had expected. After all, he had nothing else to occupy his time. No demands on his attention, no correspondence needing a response, no problems to resolve. While initially he had experienced a certain restlessness at his unaccustomed idleness, it had passed quickly.

He knew any number of men who lived lives dedicated to nothing but idle pleasure, able because of wealth and family position to do little of any consequence save enjoy themselves. He'd always viewed them with a certain disdain and seen himself as superior in a moral sense. For the first time he could appreciate the merits of a life dedicated to nothing but fun and frolic. Not that he had any intention of adopting this carefree existence permanently, but, for the moment, he could not merely bear it but take pleasure in it. Oddly enough, he was finding the more he accepted and enjoyed his enforced holiday, the easier it was to enjoy.

Not that some portions of their journey hadn't presented a challenge to his newfound determination to appreciate this adventure. Their ship had docked in Alexandria and from there they had taken the train to Cairo. Hot, dusty, and crowded, even with first-class passage, the accommodations were nowhere near pleasant. Still, a certain amount of discomfort was no doubt part and parcel of adventure.

As were new experiences. He surveyed the street that stretched before the hotel and chuckled. He never would have imagined himself here. Cairo was an intriguing blend of old and ancient. In the distance, one could even faintly see the pyramids, everpresent specters of another time. Shepheard's was reputed to be the best hotel in Egypt, and from its terrace, one could watch the lifeblood of the city flow by. The streets of Cairo were crowded with natives, tourists, merchants, military officers, and Europeans here to represent their own countries in some manner. And filled as well with entertainers: musicians and dancers, jugglers and storytellers, and God help him, snake charmers. He had not seen one perform, nor did he wish to. But he had noted the reptile handlers making their way through the streets carrying their distinctive round baskets. He knew full well what those baskets contained, and whenever he caught sight of a snake charmer, Sterling kept his gaze firmly on the man's basket. As a precaution in the event of a snake escape. It seemed only wise and prudent to do so.

Still, Sterling refused to allow the ever-present threat of snake encounters to dissuade him from his new determination to enjoy whatever came his way. He blew a perfect smoke ring out into the street. Would that his brothers could see him now. Stiff and staid and dull. Hah! If nothing else came of this, he would at least understand them somewhat better.

Livy seemed both appreciative of his manner and skeptical. On more than one occasion he caught her studying him as if he were a puzzle she was trying to solve. He grinned. He liked that. Often, Livy's assessment came the morning after he had had politely refused to join her in her room for one reason or another. Either he was invited to join her for a sherry or to look at the train schedule or one of his mother's tourist guides. He had come up with one perfectly proper excuse after another even though he would like nothing better than to be alone with her behind closed doors. He reminded himself that patience was a virtue even if it felt more like a vise squeezing the very life out of him. He was not a patient man. Nor was he about to let her know that every time he said good night quite properly at her door, each moment when she gazed into his eyes as if she did indeed wish to be kissed, and he restrained himself, he ached for her. In his body and his soul.

Regardless, it didn't seem wise to be completely alone and in compromising circumstances with a woman who might well have been plotting revenge for a decade. Not that he truly thought she had, but they had both been changed by years and circumstances, and he could not be entirely certain. After all, she had admitted she had never forgiven him, which was an obstacle he did not yet know how to overcome. But he would.

She was determined to get him into her room, and he didn't know why. With any other woman, he might assume she wished to ravage him. He grinned at the thought. He wouldn't at all mind being ravaged, especially by Livy, although it had been some time since he'd been ravaged by anyone at all. When he considered it, while celibate would not be an entirely accurate description of his life, it would not be far from wrong either. There had been the occasional actress or dancer or widow at a house party he'd been forced into attending as a social necessity. Indeed, any social event not deemed prudent to attend by his mother was to be avoided. Now he wondered why. When had he become so, well, dull? He distinctly recalled once having loved balls and soirees and masquerades. When had he changed?

Still, he wasn't the same man he had been at the beginning of this venture. And it seemed the more he became the man he used to be, the more she became be the girl she once was. She was as much unlike the woman who had told him to get out of her life as he was the man who had installed his own men in her household. He wondered who they would ultimately be once this adventure had ended.

Josiah stepped out onto the terrace from the hotel and Sterling signaled to the young man to join him at his table. Josiah was doing an excellent job managing the details of their travel. He handled the passports, tickets, and, when the hotel had tried to give them inferior lodgings, had taken care of that as well.

Josiah took a chair at Sterling's table, hesitated, then accepted the cigar Sterling offered and lit it.

"So, did you receive a response from Sir Lawrence?" Almost immediately upon their arrival at the hotel, Sterling had sent Josiah to Sir Lawrence's residence with a note requesting a meeting regarding an artifact in his possession.

"Indeed I did, sir." Josiah pulled a folded note from his coat pocket and passed it to Sterling. "He read your letter while I was present and seemed, well, amused."

" 'Amused'?" Sterling raised a brow. "Not exactly the reaction I expected." He unfolded the note and scanned it. "He has invited our party to join him for dinner." He addressed his words to the solicitor but continued to read. "Apparently, he knew my father. Which, I suppose, is not surprising given Father's lifelong interest in ancient artifacts and his involvement in the Antiquities Society."

Josiah puffed on his cigar. "Do you think that will help our cause, sir?"

Sterling smiled to himself. It was most interesting that Livy's quest had now become *our cause.* "That depends on whether he liked my father or not, although most of the scholars and antiquity hunters he befriended did appear to like him." He finished the note and set it on the table. "We shall find out soon enough."

"Do you think he'll give us the jar?"

"I don't think he'll *give* us anything save an interesting evening." Sterling considered the question. "I am still not sure how to approach him about relinquishing the jar, but I suspect Lady Rathbourne has some ideas on that score. It is, after all, her quest. The rest of us are here simply to provide assistance, legal counsel, the appearance of propriety, and, in my case" — he chuckled — "funding."

Josiah tapped his cigar thoughtfully. "You do realize if we fail here, her attempts to meet the stipulations of her husband's will are at an end."

Sterling nodded.

"I think I should warn you, sir." The

young solicitor squared his shoulders. "I fully intend to pursue Lady Rathbourne's affections."

"Do you now?"

"I do indeed." He paused. "I have already offered to marry her if her efforts prove unsuccessful."

"And did she accept?"

"Not exactly. But she did agree not to give me a final answer until this is at an end," he added quickly.

"I see."

Josiah studied him cautiously. "Doesn't that concern you?"

Sterling blew a long stream of smoke. "Why should that concern me?"

"I've seen the way you look at her."

"I look at her in the same manner I do any beautiful woman."

"Do you, sir?" A skeptical note sounded in the young man's voice.

"You must admit, she is a very desirable woman."

"Yes, sir, very desirable. She is beautiful and kind as well." A dreamy look appeared in the younger man's eyes. "And intelligent and clever and amusing and determined. I don't think I've ever met anyone with the strength of character that she has."

Damnation. It was worse than he had

thought. Josiah was clearly head over heels for Livy. Sterling chose his words with care. "Do you think a woman like that would be willing to marry simply because she has no other choice?"

"I can't say, sir." He heaved a heartfelt sigh. "I only know I would not have a chance with her otherwise."

"Have you considered that you might be somewhat young for her?"

"I don't think age is a concern when it comes to affection," Josiah said staunchly.

"I see." He studied the younger man. "Then you are in love with her."

Josiah nodded. "I am."

"And does she return your feelings?"

"Not yet." A reluctant note sounded in his voice. "But I am determined to change that."

"As are we all, Mr. Cadwallender." Sterling drew on his cigar. "Tell me, Josiah, do you know anything of her life with Rathbourne?"

"No, sir." He shook his head. "But I have my suspicions."

"Based on?"

"Nothing more really than my assessment of the man himself. She has not seen fit to confide in me." His eyes darkened with suppressed anger. "I can only hope my suspicions of her treatment at his hands are false."

"I daresay my suspicions are similar." Sterling paused for a long moment. "It's my fault she married him you know."

Josiah's eyes widened. "Your fault? I don't understand."

"Olivia and I were to be married when her father informed me she had decided to marry Rathbourne, and she wished not to have anything further to do with me." Sterling forced a casual note to his voice. "It was a lie."

"Good Lord. How did you find out?"

"Her father told me the truth after Rathbourne died." He drew a deep breath. "She thought I had abandoned her, failed her. She has not forgiven me." Even now, the truth was hard to admit. This was no misunderstanding on her part. Nothing that could be swept away with a simple explanation. He had indeed abandoned and failed her. He tapped his cigar into a conveniently placed saucer. "I will not fail her again."

Josiah's jaw hardened with resolve. "Nor shall I."

"There's something else you should know. You're correct in your assessment of my feelings regarding Lady Rathbourne." He leaned forward and met the younger man's

231

gaze. "And I have no intention of losing her again. She agreed to marry me once, and she will do so again."

Josiah's eyes narrowed. "You said she has not forgiven you."

"She hasn't, but she will eventually." He settled back in his chair and smiled. "Her ultimate purpose is to gain her rightful inheritance and with that her independence. Whether or not she is successful remains to be seen. Regardless, *my* ultimate purpose is to win back her heart. And there is no question as to my success."

"I see." Josiah puffed his cigar thoughtfully. "At this point am I to graciously set aside my own intentions and allow you a clear field?"

Sterling grinned. "That would be most appreciated."

"You are a very powerful man, my lord," Josiah said slowly. "Your influence and patronage could make a significant difference in my future. I would be a fool to cross you."

"Probably," Sterling said coolly.

"However . . ." He met Sterling's gaze directly. "I would be a bigger fool to give up Lady Rathbourne without a fight."

"Don't let your heart be broken in a game you cannot win."

"I might give you the same advice, sir."

"I like you, Josiah. For the most part you have a good head on your shoulders. One cannot fault you too much for letting your heart lead your head." Sterling chuckled. "It happens to us all."

"Even to you?"

"No, not to me, and therein lay the biggest mistake of my life." He shook his head. "I did not listen to my heart when I should have, and I have paid for that. As has she. I shall not make that mistake again."

"I shall continue to pursue Lady Rathbourne," Josiah warned.

"Excellent. I have always enjoyed a certain amount of competition." Sterling grinned. "Perhaps a small wager would make it more interesting."

"A wager, sir?" Josiah studied him suspiciously. "I have nothing to wager with."

"You have a great deal. Let us say if you win her affections, I shall give some of my business to your firm so that you may be able to support her properly."

"And if you win her affections?"

"Then you shall come to work for me in a manner to be determined later." Sterling puffed on his cigar. "Perhaps a firm of your own. With my patronage, you could do very well."

Josiah narrowed his eyes. "It seems it would be in the best interests of my future to lose."

Sterling shrugged. "It all depends on what you truly want."

"I want Lady Rathbourne," he said without hesitation.

"As do I."

"I am determined to win her heart."

"As am I."

"It further seems to me that, win or lose, I stand to benefit."

"As I said, it all depends on what you truly want."

"For what shall it profit a man, if he shall gain the whole world, and lose his own soul?" Josiah said under his breath.

Sterling resisted the urge to roll his gaze toward the sky. God help him, the boy was not only overly romantic but quoted the Bible as well. He leaned toward the solicitor and lowered his voice. "Josiah, allow me to give you one piece of well-considered advice."

"Yes, sir?"

"While it is admirable to set your sights high, it is also wise to understand the limits of possibility."

Josiah shook his head. "I don't understand."

"Regardless of your efforts, this is a wager you cannot win. Because I would have to be dead and buried to concede defeat. And I have no intention of dying anytime soon. Furthermore . . ." He puffed on his cigar and blew another perfect smoke ring. "Olivia is not your soul, she is mine."

"Is something wrong?" Sterling looked down at Olivia, his brow furrowed.

"No, it's quite lovely." She glanced around the foyer of Sir Lawrence's home. On the inside it looked very much like it did on the outside, the type of grand house one might see on any square in London. She shouldn't be surprised. She had read how, with the construction of the Suez Canal some twenty years ago, and even before, there was a significant European presence and a subsequent influence on buildings in this century in Cairo and Alexandria. Even today, one out of every four people one passed on the street was not a native Egyptian. Still . . . "I confess I am disappointed. I had expected something more, well, exotic. More Egyptian."

"Tomb paintings on the walls and such? Perhaps a mummy propped in the corner?" A tall older gentleman stepped into the foyer. Distinguished in appearance, Lawrence Willoughby didn't look at all like a scholar but rather an elder statesmen. "When one spends one's days studying ancient writings in tombs well below-ground, haunted by the ghosts of the ancients, in a land far from one's own, one wishes to surround oneself when at rest with the accoutrements of home. As well as modern comforts."

"Quite understandable." She cast him her brightest smile. "Thank you for inviting us to your home."

"You must be Lady Rathbourne." Sir Lawrence took her hand and raised it to his lips. "How lovely you are. What a delightful surprise."

"And you are most gallant. I too am surprised."

Sterling cleared his throat.

"My reputation precedes me then." Sir Lawrence chuckled. "I confess I am not always as charming as I appear. But I have had an excellent day, and Lord Wyldewood's note has piqued my curiosity. You are interested in one of my canopic jars I understand."

She nodded.

"I should tell you your late husband and I corresponded about that very item. I met the man once." The older man's eyes narrowed. "I can't say I cared much for him."

She smiled and met his gaze firmly. "Few people did. My late husband was not a man to inspire affection."

Sir Lawrence stared at her for a moment, then laughed. "But I do like you."

"Sir Lawrence." Sterling stepped forward.

"Ah yes, the young Lord Wyldewood." Sir Lawrence shook Sterling's hand, studying him with an assessing gaze. "You look a great deal like your father."

Sterling smiled. "I had no idea that you knew my father until I read your invitation."

"You should have. It's always best to know exactly with whom one is dealing. Gives you the upper hand." He turned to Olivia. "I spent many nights, on those rare occasions when I was in London, far too long ago to say exactly when now, as a guest at Lord Wyldewood's home. Quite pleasant evenings too as I recall." He glanced at Sterling. "I even remember you. Never did understand why your father insisted on having children at the table."

"He thought his guests would have a good influence on us, sir," Sterling said with a smile.

"And did we?"

Sterling paused, a brief image of a man with only two fingers flashing through his head. "For the most part, I believe you did."

"Influenced your brothers, no doubt. I hear all sorts of interesting things about them. Mostly good." He narrowed his eyes. "Some bad."

Sterling smiled weakly.

"Still, that's neither here nor there at the moment. You have all grown somewhat." He chuckled. "I have simply aged. You can thank your father's hospitality for my agreeing to see you although I wouldn't have hesitated if I had known how lovely Lady Rathbourne is." Sir Lawrence craned his neck to peer around them. "Is the rest of your party here?"

"My mother encountered people she met aboard ship," Sterling said smoothly. "She joined them for tea and promised to meet us here. Mr. Cadwallender will accompany her."

"I see. That changes things somewhat." He frowned. "Although perhaps it's for the best. We can discuss the business at hand before the others arrive. Lady Rathbourne." He offered her his arm and escorted her into a parlor.

The room was high-ceilinged and filled with light from long windows. Tall French doors were open to a courtyard. The house may have been influenced by European architecture, but she couldn't recall ever having been in a parlor in London that was so bright and airy.

Olivia and Sterling settled on a sofa, Sir Lawrence took a chair and signaled to a servant for refreshments.

"Now then," Sir Lawrence began. "Your note said Lady Rathbourne wished to acquire the canopic jar in my collection that is apparently from the tomb of Aashet, although the tomb itself has never been found. I have the jar that bears the head of Imsety; her husband had the remaining three. Which of course is why he wanted mine."

Olivia nodded. "We do know that, Sir Lawrence."

"I assume you want my jar so that the collection is complete in some sort of misplaced homage to his memory." He pinned Olivia with a narrowed gaze.

"Not at all, Sir Lawrence," Olivia said lightly as if the matter were of no importance. "I have no desire to honor my late husband's memory in any manner whatsoever. If I could erase his name from the face of the earth, I would do so without hesitation."

The older man glanced from Olivia to

Sterling and back. "Then you had best explain."

"It's really quite simple and, as you have met my late husband, you will no doubt find it easy to understand." Olivia drew a steadying breath. "I am the only heir to my husband's estate. However, in order to inherit, I must complete three of his collections. Your jar would complete the first."

Sir Lawrence studied her. "He left you with nothing?"

She shrugged. "I have a minimal allowance."

"You." His gaze shifted to Sterling. "What is your part in all this?"

"Lady Wyldewood is a very old friend of my family," Sterling said smoothly. "She needed assistance in this endeavor, and I am grateful I was able to help."

"If you could see your way clear to sell us the jar," Olivia began.

"I never sell my artifacts," Sir Lawrence said in a matter-of-fact manner. "Never have, never will."

"But surely, given the situation you would at least consider —"

"Would you trade for the jar?" Sterling asked casually.

Sir Lawrence narrowed his eyes. "Trade for what?"

"Oh, I don't know." Sterling thought for a moment although Olivia suspected he already had something in mind. "A mummy of the twentieth dynasty perhaps."

Olivia stared. "You have a mummy?"

"My father was not as accomplished a collector as your late husband or as Sir Lawrence" — he nodded to the older man — "but he did accumulate an assortment of artifacts. Whatever struck his fancy at the moment, I think. Our house is filled with odd and unusual items. Including" — his gaze fastened on Sir Lawrence — "a mummy of the twentieth dynasty."

Sir Lawrence laughed. "Not interested, my boy. I gave that mummy to your father."

"Did you?" Sterling's brow furrowed thoughtfully. "I thought it was the other one."

"What other one?" Suspicion sounded in the older man's voice.

"My father had two mummies, one from the twentieth dynasty, one from the eighteenth. I assumed the older one was the one you gave my father."

"No," Sir Lawrence said thoughtfully. "Eighteenth you say?"

"That is my understanding." He nodded at Olivia. "While my father's collections are somewhat haphazard, he did make certain everything was catalogued accurately."

"Do you recall what it looked like?" Sir Lawrence asked.

"No." Sterling shook his head. "But I did bring along a photograph and notes regarding the mummy."

"I see." Sir Lawrence considered him thoughtfully. "Perhaps we can do business after all." He looked at Olivia. "Would you excuse me for a moment?"

She smiled. "Yes, of course."

Sir Lawrence stood and walked briskly from the room.

She turned to Sterling. "I thought you didn't know him?"

Sterling shrugged. "I don't. Nor do I remember his visits."

"Then how did you know he had given a mummy to your father?"

"I didn't." He grinned. "But after he said he had given one mummy to my father, I hoped that while I knew we have two mummies in the attic, he did not."

She cast him an admiring glance. "Why, Sterling, I am most impressed."

"You should be." He flashed her a grin. "I can be most impressive."

"You planned this all along, didn't you?"

"Given Sir Lawrence's reputation, I did not think your plight or your charm alone would be enough to convince him to hand over the jar." His grin widened. "But I thought a mummy that I certainly have no use for might do the trick."

"How very clever of you."

"I can be very clever when the need arises. When it comes to something I want."

She studied him for a moment, wondering if his words had more than one meaning. But his expression gave nothing away. "Given your reluctance to accompany me at all, I must say, I am both surprised and pleased."

He chuckled. "Surprising, and pleasing, you is an unexpected bonus." A serious note sounded in his voice. "I said I would do all I could to help you, and I intend to live up to that obligation."

"And I am most appreciative." She forced a smile to her face. She wasn't at all sure she liked being his obligation.

"There now, that's taken care of." Sir Lawrence stepped back into the room. "It has occurred to me . . ." Voices sounded in the corridor, and Sir Lawrence's gaze slipped to the arched doorway. A smile of genuine pleasure stretched across his face, and at once the man appeared twenty years younger. "Millicent."

"Lawrence Willoughby." Lady Wyldewood

stood in the doorway, Josiah a step behind. Her smile matched the older man's. "What a delightful surprise."

"The delight, my dear lady" — the older man's smile widened — "is entirely mine."

Twelve

At once, Sir Lawrence crossed the room to Lady Wyldewood, took her hand in his, and raised it to his lips. "You are as beautiful as ever, Millicent."

Millicent? Sterling rose to his feet.

"And you, Lawrence, are as charming as I remember."

Lawrence? It was all Sterling could do to keep his mouth from dropping open in shock.

Mother tilted her head and smiled, a thoroughly flirtatious sort of smile. What was the woman doing? "It has been a very long time."

"Twenty-three years, four months and some-odd days by my count." Sir Lawrence gazed into her eyes. "Which would make it twenty-three years, four months and some-odd days entirely too long."

His mother laughed. A girlish sort of sound, young and fresh and, had she not been his mother, intoxicating. Where had she learned to do that?

"I thought I would hear from you after Charles died," she said lightly.

Sir Lawrence grimaced. "I did send my condolences."

"And they were most appreciated. Still, I had rather thought . . . once I was out of mourning . . . Surely, you have been in London in the past decade?"

What on earth did she mean by that?

Sir Lawrence nodded. "I have but, well, I was not certain of the reception I would receive. I did not wish to be forward."

And what did he mean by that?

Sir Lawrence bent closer and said something into his mother's ear, and she laughed again. Behind the couple, Josiah looked as if he didn't know whether he should remind the gathering of his presence or keep silent. He wisely chose to say nothing.

Livy stood and nudged Sterling with her elbow, her voice low. "You should stop staring."

His mother was gazing at Sir Lawrence with a look he could not recall ever having seen on her face before. "I am not staring."

"You're right. You're glaring, and you should stop it at once." She slanted him a chastising look. "It's not at all becoming."

And Sir Lawrence was returning the very same look! "But that's my mother!"

"Indeed it is. And that . . ." Livy grinned. ". . . is apparently an old and *very* good friend."

"I had no idea." Sterling was hard-pressed to tear his gaze from the older couple. Fortunately, his mother remembered poor Josiah and turned to reintroduce the young man to Sir Lawrence.

"It's always best to know exactly with whom one is dealing, you know." A teasing note sounded in Livy's voice. "It gives you the upper hand."

"This is not amusing," Sir Lawrence said through gritted teeth.

"Odd, as I find it most amusing." Livy grinned.

Sterling cleared his throat and caught his mother's attention.

She cast a reluctant smile at Sir Lawrence, almost as if she did not wish to leave his side, which was absurd, and moved farther into the room. "Darling, you didn't tell me the gentleman we were coming to see was Lawrence Willoughby."

"I am certain I mentioned it," Sterling said, trying and failing to keep disapproval from sounding in his voice. Livy elbowed him hard.

"No, I would have remembered. Imagine." Her gaze again settled on Sir Lawrence. "My dear friend, Lawrence, is going to be the one to help rescue our darling Olivia."

Livy tensed beside him. "Millicent, rescue is not at all accur—"

It was his turn to elbow her. He lowered his voice for her ears alone. "If the man wishes to rescue you, which means giving you what you need, let him."

Her brows drew together. "I do not need to be rescued."

"Of course not, my dear." Millicent smiled. "We are modern women and have no need of something as old-fashioned as rescue." She directed her smile toward Sir Lawrence. "She is a tower of courage, Lawrence. I couldn't be prouder of her than if she were my own daughter. It was her decision to come here in person. Sterling thought it would be more expedient to send an emissary."

"Expedient perhaps, but not successful." Sir Lawrence cast Livy a smile so charming even Sterling was impressed. Hadn't Gabriella described him as unpleasant? This was the least unpleasant man he had ever met. At least when it came to the female members of their party. And if the man didn't stop staring at his mother as if she were a plum pudding and he a man long deprived of sweets, Sterling would have to . . . well, he'd have to do something.

"I have taken it upon myself to arrange for your baggage to be brought here. I do hope you will accept my hospitality while you are in Cairo." He addressed the gathering, but his gaze remained on Sterling's mother. "Nothing would make me happier than to have you stay in my home." He glanced at the others. "All of you."

"I don't think —" Sterling began.

"Of course, if you prefer to stay at Shepheard's, I will certainly understand." His gaze met Sterling's, and there was the slightest hint of a warning in his tone. "I simply thought staying here would give you the opportunity to convince me of the wisdom of the trade you have proposed."

"We would be delighted, Sir Lawrence," Livy said quickly. "Your offer is quite gracious and most appreciated."

"Yes, Lawrence." Did he imagine it, or was his mother's voice just a shade lower than before. Almost, God help him, sultry? Good lord, his mother was a tart! "Most appreciated."

"I believe, Sterling," Livy said softly for his ears alone, "that is a shining example of the art of flirtation."

He shot her an annoyed glare, and she bit back a grin. Blasted woman was enjoying this.

"Now, as that's settled." Sir Lawrence nodded. "And as dinner has not yet been announced, perhaps you would allow me to show you my gardens?"

"I should like that very much." His mother gazed into the older man's eyes.

"As would we all," Sterling said with a forced smile.

Sir Lawrence cast him an exasperated look. "I did mean to show all of you." He offered his arm to Sterling's mother. "Millicent."

Sterling stepped forward. "If you don't mind, I have a few items to discuss with my mother regarding our move from the hotel. Why don't you and the others go ahead, and we shall join you in a minute or two."

"Of course." Sir Lawrence smiled reluctantly at Sterling's mother, then turned to Livy and offered his arm. "Shall we, my dear?"

Livy cast him her brightest smile and took his arm. "I've never seen an Egyptian garden."

"You'll find it an interesting blend of native flora as well as plants brought here by Europeans." They started for the door, and the older man glanced back. "Are you coming, Mr. Cadwallender?"

"Yes, of course," the solicitor murmured, and trailed after them.

"I suspect, Lady Rathbourne, you may be quite surprised at some of what I have here." They stepped through the door, the older man's voice fading with each step. "Did you know the ancient Egyptians were especially fond of roses? They say that . . ."

Sterling turned and glared at his mother. "Well?"

"Well, isn't this the most wonderful coincidence." She beamed. "But you should have told me that Sir Lawrence is the gentleman we were coming to see."

"I thought I had."

"No, you didn't," she said firmly. "Although this is a lovely turn of events as I had planned on calling on him while were here."

"You had planned . . ." He sucked in a sharp breath. "That's why you wanted to come to Cairo!"

"Not entirely," she murmured.

"I demand to know what your involvement is with this man!"

She raised a brow. "I do not take well to demands from my son. Particularly not in that tone of voice."

"My apologies, Mother. You're right, of course." He drew a steadying breath. "Now, would you be so kind as to explain your . . . your relationship with Sir Lawrence."

"There really is no relationship as of yet." She shrugged. "Sir Lawrence is simply a very old friend of mine and your father's."

"He seems considerably more than a mere friend to me."

She ignored him. "I met Lawrence about the same time I met your father. They were very good friends then but drifted apart. The passage of time will do that you know."

"Go on."

"Patience, Sterling, I am going on." She sighed. "After your father and I married, he was often a guest in our home. A welcome guest I might add."

"And?"

"And you might say we carried on something of a flirtation through the years."

Sterling gasped. "A flirtation?"

"You needn't look so appalled." She cast her son a chastising glance. "Surely you don't think anything untoward occurred between us?"

"The thought had occurred to me," he snapped. "Given the last few minutes."

"If you were younger and shorter, I would box your ears for even suggesting such a thing." She sniffed in indignation. "If not for your father, who thoroughly owned my heart, I might well have married Lawrence. But from the moment I met your father, there has never been another man in my life or in my affections."

"You just said you carried on a flirtation —"

"And that is all it ever was," she said firmly. "The man has never done more than kiss my hand. Nor would I have allowed him to do so in the past." She paused. "Now, however . . ."

"Mother!"

"I should very much like to see what might transpire between us now."

Sterling groaned. "I cannot believe this."

"Why?" She frowned and studied him. "Because I am too old to have such thoughts?"

"No," he said quickly. "Not at all. I simply meant . . . well, you're my mother."

"Indeed I am." She nodded. "But you are grown, as are Quinton and Nathanial, and Reggie will have her own family one day soon no doubt. I would prefer not to spend the rest of my life alone."

"What about Father?"

"Your father is dead, and, while I would give anything to still have him with us, that is a fact that cannot be changed. And he would wish me to be happy."

"But you are happy."

"In many ways, yes. I am content I would say. For the most part." She paused. "When one has shared a great love, as I did with your father, and it is taken away, one cannot help but long to share that again."

Sterling widened his eyes. "You are in love with Sir Lawrence?"

"Good Lord, Sterling." Mother laughed. "You do jump to the most absurd conclusions. Might I remind you he and I have not seen each other for twenty-three years."

"But you just said —"

"I wish you would stop reminding me of what I have just said." She huffed. "I said I would like to know love again. Whether that is to be found with Lawrence remains to be seen." She grinned in an altogether-too-wicked manner for anyone's mother, let alone his. "But I should like to find out."

He winced. "Dear God."

"Sterling." Her voice sobered. "Your father has been dead for ten years. Ten years is a very long time to be alone." She pinned him with a firm look. "You of all people should understand that."

He stared at her for a moment, then nodded. "I suppose I do."

"Then allow me to have my flirtation, preferably without your glaring at me as if I were doing something terribly wrong."

He blew a long breath. "Very well."

"And if something more comes of it . . ." She met his gaze directly. "I expect you to respect my decisions."

"I shall . . . try."

"You shall do more than try."

"I shall try," he said again. "Trying is all anyone can do."

"And I do hate it when you throw my own words back at me. You are a very stubborn man and very much like your father." She sighed. "But that will have to do for the moment, I suppose. Now, shall we join the others in the garden?"

He forced a smile. She took his arm, and they started toward the door. "Besides, it seems to me you should spend less time concerned with my intentions and more concerned with your own."

He frowned. "What do you mean?"

"Why, your efforts to win Olivia back of course." She smiled. "Apparently you have a rival."

"Josiah?" He scoffed. "He thinks so."

She chuckled. "It might be wise not to be overly confident."

"In truth, Mother, I am not as confident

as I am hopeful." He grinned. "And optimistic."

"Patience, Sterling. Patience is a virtue. All things come to him who waits you know."

"I am trying, Mother." He heaved a frustrated sigh. "But it is one virtue I have never possessed, and I have waited a very long time."

"As have we all, darling." She patted his arm. "As have we all."

Patience, Sterling gritted his teeth, and said it to himself again for the tenth or perhaps the hundredth time since their arrival at Sir Lawrence's home yesterday.

Not that Sir Lawrence wasn't indeed a gracious host. In spite of himself, Sterling had enjoyed last night's dinner. The food, a mix of Egyptian and European dishes, had been excellent and the conversation around the table lively. Both Olivia and his mother had been in high spirits; Josiah had been more talkative than usual; and Sir Lawrence proved to be both informative and interesting. In many ways, he reminded Sterling of his father. It was most disconcerting.

The rooms they'd been provided were spacious and well-appointed. While primarily European in style, there were influences throughout the house of that part of the world outside the front gates. Lanterns of brass and brightly colored glass hung from the ceilings. Rugs from local craftsmen covered the floors. Small ancient figurines were displayed in niches.

They had spent much of the day seeing the sights of Cairo, including the mosque of Sultan Hassan, said to be one of the largest buildings of its kind in the world and built in part with stones from the Great Pyramid. That, of course, had prompted his mother to bring up yet again the matter of seeing the pyramids. As they could be reached with a drive of less than two hours, wouldn't it be a shame to have come all this way and not see them? Sterling had pointed out even from Cairo they could already be seen far off in the distance, and as time was an issue . . . Regardless, Sir Lawrence had then offered to arrange an excursion for tomorrow, delighting the other members of his party but adding yet another day to their stay.

Still, Olivia had pointed out that the more Sir Lawrence enjoyed their company, the more likely he would be to relinquish the jar. And wasn't that, after all, the purpose of their trip?

The ladies were resting after the exertion

of the long hot day, and Josiah had wandered off to a bazaar to purchase gifts for his family. Sterling sat at a table in the courtyard with a glass of lemonade, one of Sir Lawrence's excellent cigars, and his own thoughts.

"You should keep an eye open for snakes," Sir Lawrence said behind him.

Sterling jumped to his feet. "Where?"

"None that I see at the moment." Sir Lawrence settled in the chair opposite Sterling's and selected a cigar from the box on the table. "But we have them in the garden."

Sterling cast a suspicious look at the lush foliage bordering the courtyard, then cautiously sat back down. "I shall keep my eyes open."

Sir Lawrence raised a brow. "Dislike snakes, do we?"

"I'm not especially fond of them." Sterling shrugged in an offhand manner.

"One gets used to them. There are more than twenty species of snakes in Egypt. The bites of any of them are dangerous, but only three or so will actually kill you."

"Good to know," Sterling muttered.

"I keep a pistol by the side of my bed just in case one wanders into my room unannounced." He paused. "Besides, this area has been plagued of late by intruders. Thieves in the night looking for jewels or artifacts, small items that can be quickly sold. They are far more dangerous than snakes and usually armed with daggers, sharp and deadly. They can slit a man's throat before he can so much as cry out."

"I see." At once the thought of how close Livy came to serious injury when intruders invaded her house sprang to mind. Surely she was safe here. Still, one should be prepared.

"I've shot at more than one intruder in this house in recent months. Frowned on by the local authorities." He trimmed his cigar. "I don't think I hit anyone, but I can't be sure. Between snakes and thieves, it's a bloody good idea to have a pistol by the bed."

"No doubt," Sterling said coolly. Indeed, it sounded like an excellent idea. Especially for the snakes.

"There will be one in the drawer in the table by your bed tonight."

"Oh, I don't think . . ." Sterling paused, then nodded. "That would be most appreciated."

Sir Lawrence lit his cigar and puffed on it thoughtfully. "I have a proposition for you, my boy."

"Oh?"

Sir Lawrence nodded. "I have been giving Lady Rathbourne's predicament a great deal of consideration. Helped by your mother." He chuckled. "She can be very persuasive."

"She always has been."

"And persistent."

Sterling smiled wryly. "You've noticed that."

"Hard to miss." He puffed on his cigar. "I have come to a decision."

"Excellent." Sterling leaned forward. "Then you will trade us the jar for the mummy?"

Sir Lawrence shook his head. "Not exactly."

"What do you mean by 'not exactly'?"

"Oh, I'll take your mummy. After all, you have no use for it."

Sterling settled back in his chair and puffed on his cigar. "True enough."

"But you have something far more valuable to trade."

"And that would be . . ." Sterling said slowly.

"I have been talking to your mother."

Indeed, it seemed to Sterling that Sir Lawrence had barely left her side since their arrival. "And?"

"And I know you are eager to return home."

"I am." Obviously Sterling was one topic of their conversation.

"I know as well that you weren't eager to come to Egypt at all."

"No, I was not." With any luck, his mother talked about his brothers or anything other than Sterling.

"And I further know that you would like nothing better than to continue this journey with Lady Rathbourne without the charming yet intrusive presence of your mother."

Sterling arched a brow. "Did she tell you that as well?"

"Some things are obvious." The older man gestured with his cigar. "The way you look at her. The way young Cadwallender looks at her. The way she looks at you."

"How does she look at me?"

Sir Lawrence chuckled. "If you don't know, you're not as clever as your mother says."

Sterling forced a smile. "You were saying?"

"I was saying that I could arrange for you and Lady Rathbourne to leave Egypt with the jar. If you would encourage . . ." He tapped his ashes into a saucer. "Your mother to remain here."

Sterling narrowed his eyes. "I shall not

barter my mother for a mere artifact."

"Nonsense, boy. It's not as if you're selling her into a harem. And you're not bartering her for a mere artifact." He leaned forward. "All I ask is that you help me convince her to stay in Egypt for a time. A few weeks, possibly months, if I am very lucky. A minor thing really that would enable you to help Lady Rathbourne achieve her purpose." He settled back in his chair. "Seems little enough for you to do to me."

"I have already done a great deal." Indignation rang in Sterling's voice.

"Not according to your mother."

"What more does she think I could have done?" He rose to his feet and paced the courtyard. "Olivia insisted on going to Egypt, and here I am in Egypt. She doesn't want to talk about the past, so I don't talk about the past. She wants friendship, so I have done everything possible to be the best *friend* anyone could ever have. I have been more than pleasant. I have made an effort to enjoy every moment of this never-ending adventure. And I have done everything in my power to be anything other than staid, stodgy, and dull!"

Sit Lawrence gazed at him in silence and puffed his cigar. "So you will encourage your mother to stay here?"

Sterling glared. "I will do nothing of the sort."

Sir Lawrence shrugged. "I should tell you, I have already asked her to stay."

"And?"

"And she is considering it which is why I need someone, ideally you, but I suspect Lady Rathbourne might do as well, to help me convince her."

"Aside from acquiring the jar for Olivia, why on earth would I wish to do that?"

"Because you are a good son who loves his mother," Sir Lawrence said idly. "And because I can make her happy."

"She is happy," Sterling said in a staunch manner, ignoring that she had explained only yesterday that she wasn't especially happy but merely content.

The older man shrugged.

Sterling clenched his jaw. "Do you intend to marry her?"

Sir Lawrence's gaze met Sterling's. "If she will have me."

"That's absurd. You haven't seen her for more than twenty years. You've probably changed a great deal through the years, and I know she has. Why, you can't possibly be the same people you once were."

"No, we're not." Sir Lawrence drew on his cigar and gazed into the past. "A very long time ago, a young man met a lovely lady who captured his heart although he was too stupid to realize it at the time. The lady then fell in love and married his best friend, and the young man went off to hunt for treasures and artifacts and immerse himself in the remains of kings and queens and lovely ladies and foolish young men who had long ago turned to dust." He glanced at Sterling. "Do you understand?"

Sterling sank back down in his chair. He chose his words with care. "May I ask why you didn't call on her after my father died?"

Sir Lawrence considered the question for a long moment. "It seemed somehow a betrayal of your father to do so. He was my friend, after all, and I had always felt somewhat guilty for feeling the way I did about his wife." His gaze met Sterling's directly. "Although I never acted on my feelings, never declared myself, and never let either your mother or your father know. I would never have done that to Charles; nor would I ever have embroiled Millicent in an awkward situation.

"But the moment I saw her again . . ." He smiled. "I should never have waited this long. But I have been given a second chance. An opportunity to atone for the greatest mistake of my life. Can you understand that?"

"Atoning for one's mistake?" Sterling nodded. "Yes, I can well understand."

"I should warn you as well. Should Millicent decide not to stay here, I fully intend to follow her back to England." The older man's tone hardened. "I will not lose her again."

Sterling studied him for a long moment. Would that Sterling had someone to help him regain Livy's affections. He blew a resigned breath. "Very well then, I will speak to her."

"Excellent." Sir Lawrence snuffed out his cigar and stood. "I have arrangements to make for this evening. I have invited a few people I thought your mother might like to meet to join us tonight. We shall have dinner followed by an evening of traditional entertainment. Native dancers and . . ." an altogether-wicked look gleamed in his eye, "a snake charmer."

"I look forward to it," Sterling said with a weak smile, knowing full well that, even with a pistol by his side, he would get no sleep in this house tonight.

THIRTEEN

Walk in the shadows of the gods.
From the secret list of desires of
Olivia Rathbourne

"How lovely," Olivia murmured, watching the brightly colored troupe of dancers in the courtyard of Sir Lawrence's home.

Sir Lawrence had invited thirty or so others to join them for the evening. Most of the gathering was European, primarily British, and there were nearly as many ladies as gentlemen. They stood or sat at tables arranged along the edges of the courtyard. The female dancers performing were clothed in baggy trousers and sheer veils, embellished with gold-colored coins. Off to one side, sitting on the floor, a small group of musicians accompanied them with flutes and drums and a type of lute. While the gyrations of their hips and the graceful, erotic movements of their limbs might well prove shocking to another woman, Olivia found it all quite extraordinary. The rhythm of the music was intoxicating, reaching into one's very soul.

"I wonder how difficult it might be to learn such a dance." She glanced at Sterling, sitting beside her, who didn't appear to be watching the dancers at all although how any man could fail to do so was beyond her. Indeed, Sterling looked as if he were anywhere but here, anywhere, no doubt, but Egypt. "I think it's quite wonderful, don't you?"

"Very entertaining," he said in a clipped tone.

She raised a brow. "You're not enjoying this?"

"It's rather, well, improper don't you think?"

"Welcome back, my lord," she said wryly.

"What?" His gaze jumped to hers and abruptly realization dawned on his face. He ran a hand through his hair. "My apologies." He smiled a rather halfhearted smile. "Is this better?"

"If one likes the pretense of a smile, it's still no more than adequate." She studied him curiously. "You have been as tense as a wound spring all evening. Whatever is the matter?"

"Nothing," he said quickly. "I am impatient to be on our way. And I do wish Sir Lawrence would make up his mind. There's nothing more to it than that."

"I realize you have no desire to linger here; however, it seems to me, that if Sir Lawrence wishes for us to stay, it would be in our best interests to stay. My fate is very much in his hands, you know. Besides, as I have never been to Egypt, I am finding everything quite fascinating and most enjoyable. As, I believe, is your mother." She bit back a grin. Enjoyable was something of an understatement when it came to Millicent. She was as fascinating to watch as the native dancers.

"Yes, of course," Sterling murmured.

Odd he didn't bat an eye at the mention of his mother's enjoyment of their stay in Egypt. Or rather her enjoyment of their host.

"It was most thoughtful of Sir Lawrence to provide entertainment for this evening, don't you agree?"

"Yes, of course," Sterling said again.

She studied him curiously. She had no idea what was on his mind, but it certainly wasn't her conversation or the entertainment. "I'd say he was a very thoughtful man."

"Quite," Sterling said under his breath.

"And something of a catch as well."

"No doubt."

"Your mother could do far worse."

"Certainly."

Why, she'd wager he wasn't paying attention to a single word she said. "Did she mention that she intended to purchase a camel and bring it back to London?"

"Fine idea," he said absently.

"She thought your garden would be an excellent place to keep a camel."

"Excellent."

Olivia tried not to grin. "Although she insists that if one has a camel at hand, one should use it on occasion. For rides and the like."

"Indeed."

"In the park."

"Where else?" he murmured.

What on earth was wrong with the man? She followed his gaze. He appeared to be keeping a cautious eye on the other side of the courtyard, where his mother sat beside Sir Lawrence, obviously enjoying herself. Off to one side, a wizened turbaned man waited patiently, a large, round, cloth-covered basket at his feet. A snake charmer if she wasn't mistaken. How delightful. She glanced at Sterling. Although he didn't seem the least bit delighted by anything.

She tried again. "Dressed as an Egyptian dancer."

"Cer—" His gaze snapped to hers, his brow furrowed. "What did you say?"

"I said your mother was going to ride through the streets of London on a camel practically naked."

He stared without comprehension, as if she were speaking a language he had never heard of. "When did she decide that?"

She burst into laughter, noted the disapproving frowns of those guests closest to them, and lowered her voice. "What in the world is the matter with you?"

His gaze slid to his mother and back to her. "Nothing. Really. Not a thing."

"That was the most unconvincing answer I have ever heard." She frowned at him. "Has something happened I should know about?"

Sterling hesitated. "No."

"I don't believe you."

"Nonetheless . . ." Sterling's gaze slipped away again.

"I insist on knowing . . ." She gasped. "Good Lord. You're afraid —"

He jumped to his feet, grabbed her hand, and fairly dragged her into the house, ignoring more than a few curious glances cast in their direction. He didn't slow down until they had reached a side parlor. At last he released her hand.

"First of all, I am not afraid of snakes. They simply make me uneasy." He paced the room. "Not snakes in general, mind you. Admittedly, there is something about Egyptian snakes . . ." He ran his hand through his hair. "Given Cleopatra and the gentleman with two fingers and the preponderance of snakes in Egyptian antiquities and, well, one could certainly see how a small boy . . ." He stopped in midstep and glared at her. "There now, you know. Are you happy?"

She stared at him. "You're afraid of snakes?"

"*Egyptian* snakes," he corrected. "And 'afraid' is not the right word. Cautious in regards to the vile creatures perhaps, but not afraid."

"I didn't think there was anything you were afraid of."

He gritted his teeth. "I am not afraid."

She ignored him. "Only Egyptian snakes?"

"I am cautious about any number of things, but yes, Egyptian snakes in particular do elicit a heightened sense of caution. Rightfully so, I might add. And now, thanks to you, here I am in Egypt, land of snakes, a country I have thus far managed to avoid.

With snakes in the garden, the possibility of snakes in my room, and a man with snakes in a basket right outside those very doors!"

She snorted back a laugh.

He narrowed his eyes. "This is not funny."

"No, of course not." She tried and failed to keep her amusement in check. "Tell me, Sterling, have you ever encountered an Egyptian snake?"

"Not yet!" he snapped. "But apparently I shall do so shortly when this" — he gestured at the courtyard — "*entertainment* continues."

"I see." She nodded. "It's the snake charmer you were staring at then, not your mother."

"Why would I be staring at my mother?"

"Because she is paying far and away too much attention to Sir Lawrence. When I said you were afraid —"

"I am not afraid!"

"I thought you feared your mother's growing attachment to Sir Lawrence."

"Yes, well, as annoying as that is . . ." He again ran his hand through his hair. "She is perfectly capable of making her own decisions."

"Did you know you only do that when you're upset?"

"I am not upset. I simply am not fond of

feeling as if . . . as if . . . everything — life if you will — is out of my hands. I am the Earl of Wyldewood. It's my responsibility to make certain things go as they should." He paused. "Do what?"

"Run your fingers through your hair."

"I do not . . ." He hesitated, his hand halfway to his head, and huffed. "Habit, I suppose. I am only vaguely aware of it."

She considered him for a long moment. It was obvious, at least to her, that he was indeed afraid of snakes. She wasn't overly fond of them herself although she had no idea why he specified Egyptian snakes. "I've found the best way to conquer one's fears is to face them."

"Have you indeed?" He met her gaze directly. "And have you done so? Faced your fears?"

"You're trying to change the subject, Sterling. We're not talking about me."

"Perhaps we should. Have you faced your fears?"

"In the past, yes," she said firmly. "And I learned to do what was necessary."

"What about now? What about this very minute? Have you faced your fears?"

She shrugged. "At the moment, my only fear is failing to meet the stipulations of my late husband's will. Of not getting the inheritance that is rightfully mine. And I admit, I have not faced that because I have no intention of failing."

"Is that truly your only fear?" His gaze bored into hers, as if he were looking for an answer to a question he hadn't asked.

She stared back at him. *No.* "Yes, of course. What other fear might I have?"

"None, I suppose." He shook his head in what might have been mild disgust, but she couldn't be sure. "As for your one and only fear . . ." He blew a long breath. "Sir Lawrence has agreed to give you the jar if I agree to convince my mother to extend her stay here."

"I see." She shook her head. "Given how you feel about your mother and Sir Lawrence —"

"I have changed my mind."

"Have you?" she said slowly.

"Not that I wish to see my mother involved with the man, but, other than the fact that I did not like his overly friendly manner with her, he is not as objectionable as he might otherwise be." He closed his eyes briefly as if praying for strength. "They have both spoken to me."

"Oh?" She raised a brow.

"My mother wishes to . . ." He paused. "She pointed out that my father has been dead for ten years, a very long time to be alone."

She caught her breath. "A lifetime."

He heaved a resigned sigh. "I see no reason not to encourage my mother to do something she more than likely is inclined to do anyway."

"You're willing to leave her here?"

"It's not what I want, but if that's what she wants." He shrugged. "She sees a . . . a possibility, if you will. One she wishes to explore further. I cannot deny her that. She has lived much of her life for her family. If she now chooses to live for herself, it seems the least I can do is ease her path."

She nodded. "By encouraging her to stay."

"By encouraging her to follow her heart." He smiled. "As she has always encouraged me."

"You are a good son, Sterling Harrington."

"Yes, I am," he said in a dismissive tone. "Now, shall we return to the festivities?"

"I see no need to do so." She shrugged. "I really have no desire to see the snake charmer."

"Are you sure?"

"Absolutely." She nodded. "In truth, it sounds rather unnerving to me."

"And you don't think a snake charmer is one of those sights of Egypt one must see?"

"Not at all." She scoffed.

"Nonetheless." His eyes narrowed. "We shall see this one."

"Sterling, it's really not necessary —"

"Oh, but it is." He offered her his arm. "Shall we."

Regardless of his fears, the man was determined. She smiled and hooked her arm through his. "If you insist."

"And I do," he said firmly, and escorted her back to the courtyard.

The dancers had finished, and they were able to take a seat close to the entertainment although she thought it might be a tad too close for his comfort or hers.

The snake charmer uncovered his basket, lifted the lid, and began something between a song and a chant, gesturing with a wand as a conductor might direct an orchestra. The snake rose from the basket as if mesmerized, swaying to the rhythm of the man's chant.

Certainly there was no real hazard. The snake charmer had no doubt been practicing his art most of his life. Still, even to one not especially terrified of snakes, there was an element of perceived danger. Obviously part of the appeal of this type of entertainment. One couldn't help but wonder if the tenuous connection between man and reptile might break at any moment and the snake strike out at the nearest warm body. She was right. It was decidedly unnerving. While the rest of the gathering watched the snake and its master, she kept her gaze locked on Sterling.

A casual observer would have said the earl appeared to be enjoying the dance of man and serpent. Aside from a certain tension around his eyes that would only be noted by someone paying close attention, she would have wagered her entire inheritance not another soul would so much as suspect the Earl of Wyldewood was afraid of any-thing, let alone snakes. But, of course, that was his nature, part and parcel of who and what he was. Even long ago, when his life was simpler and his responsibilities few, he had never really shown his feelings. Except to her, and even then not fully.

Still, his demeanor was admirable and in many ways courageous. It might seem a silly thing. That a man like Sterling would be afraid of snakes — Egyptian snakes she amended. It was as well strangely endear-ing, knowing there was an irrational chink in this man's cool collected façade. To watch him sit there and fight that fear twisted her heart, and she wanted nothing more than to lay a comforting hand on his arm. Not that he would acknowledge that comfort. After all, the man wasn't scared, he was simply cautious. In spite of his words, fear, even if absurd, was a crippling emotion.

And who knew better than she? Olivia hadn't been entirely truthful when she'd said she'd faced her fears in the past. She'd done no more than accept the terror her late husband provoked as a part of her life and did what was necessary to avoid annoying him. She'd learned quickly that defying the man, pitting her will against his, was futile. Fear for her life kept her from overt defiance. She made her list of desires and dreamed of what she would do when she was free, but she'd never truly faced them or him. And eventually, she had triumphed because she was here and whole and sound. She was free, and he was dead.

Now, her only fear was that she would fail to finish her late husband's collections. Fail to achieve her independence and the means to start her life anew. Scarcely worth considering as she had no intention of failing.

She continued to study Sterling, and the oddest thought occurred to her. Soon, they would be one-third of the way to success, which should have made her happy rather than pensive. Now, staring at the earl's composed, handsome face, she couldn't help but wonder if perhaps her greatest fear wasn't that she would fail but perhaps that she would succeed.

Even the pistol Sir Lawrence had indeed placed in Sterling's bedside table wasn't enough to ease his mind. He tossed and turned restlessly through the long night, and when he did sleep, his dreams were filled with snakes. Serpents rising out of hampers and crawling across floors and curled in shoes waiting to strike. Snakes surrounding Livy, advancing on her. Her calling to him for help. Begging for him to save her. Asking for his assistance again.

He stared at her, in the midst of a floor so solidly covered with reptiles it moved as if alive. But he was unable to take so much as a single step toward her. Frozen with the kind of fear that lodged in his throat and knotted his heart and held him helpless in its grip. He struggled to break free as the creatures slithered inevitably closer to her. He knew what he had to do. He could not fail her again. And he would not allow all the snakes in Egypt to keep him from her. Finally, he burst free of the invisible hands that held him and raced toward her.

And her scream ripped through the predawn silence.

FOURTEEN

Sterling bolted upright in bed.

Livy!

That was no dream! He leapt out of bed, yanked the table drawer open, grabbed the pistol, and sprinted for the door. He jerked it open, grateful that it was nearly dawn and while still dark, it was not the black of night, and raced down the hallway toward her room. Snakes no doubt. He had overcome his fear in his dream to save her, and he would not fail to so now.

He flung open her door, expecting to see snakes covering the floor. Instead a shadowy figure stood frozen midway between the bed and the window. At once, he remembered the intruders in her house and her father's words of warning. His jaw tightened. In the dim predawn light, he could make out Livy's form against the headboard. "Livy!"

"Sterling!" Terror sounded in her voice.

The figure leapt for the window.

"You there, stop at once." Sterling's command resounded in the room.

The figure didn't pause.

"Stop I say. Make no mistake, I will shoot." Still, he hesitated. The thought flashed through his mind that this could be a house servant who had stumbled into Livy's room inadvertently. Regardless, he had been warned. Sterling raised the pistol and fired well above the shadow's head.

The shot reverberated through the house. The figure froze, and nothing at all happened for a second or a lifetime then a crash sounded. A huge chuck of ceiling collapsed, burying the intruder. Dust choked Sterling's throat and stung his eyes, blinding him for a moment.

"Sterling!"

He heard Livy scramble off the bed and in less than a heartbeat she was in his arms.

"Good God, Livy." He held her close. "Are you all right. Did he —"

"No, no, I'm fine." She clung to him. "I woke up and there was someone . . . All I could think was that whoever had broken into my house had followed us here. Dear Lord, Sterling, if you hadn't —"

"I know." His arms tightened around her. "The thought occurred to me as well."

"What in the name of all that's holy . . ."

Sir Lawrence stepped into the room, tightening the belt of his robe around him. A servant, a step behind, handed the older man a lamp and the light illuminated the scene.

A large section of the ceiling had crashed to the floor, pinning the intruder, or what could be seen of him, under the plaster.

"Bloody hell." Sir Lawrence surveyed the room, then looked at Livy. "Are you hurt?"

She shook her head. "No. Just . . . no."

Sterling reluctantly released her, handed the pistol to Sir Lawrence and stepped toward the pile of debris and man. "We should see if he's hurt."

"I think hurt is the least of his problems." Sir Lawrence set the lamp on a table, kept the pistol in his hand, and followed.

Sterling bent down, grabbed a large piece of plaster, far heavier than it looked, and moved it off the fallen intruder to uncover the man's head. His eyes gazed unseeing and blood trickled from the corner of his mouth. Sir Lawrence bent down beside him to feel for a pulse, then looked up at Sterling. "He's dead."

Sterling's stomach twisted into a heavy knot. "I didn't want to shoot him. I thought shooting over his head would stop him. I didn't intend . . ."

"That's obvious." Sir Lawrence stood and glanced up at the ruined ceiling. Nearly a third of it had fallen. "That will have to be repaired."

"What about him?" Sterling nodded toward the body, struggling to keep his tone level. "Is he one of your servants? Do you know him?"

Sir Lawrence shook his head. "I've never seen him before. Probably a common thief."

"What are we to do?" Livy stood by the door where he had left her, her eyes wide with shock.

"What is going on here?" Sterling's mother appeared in the doorway. Her gaze slid around the room, from the man half-covered with debris on the floor, to the remains of the ceiling, to Livy, then to her son. "Good Lord, is everyone all right?"

"He isn't." Sir Lawrence nodded at the dead man. "Lady Rathbourne and your son are damn lucky they weren't felled by the ceiling as well."

"But what happened?" Mother's eyes were wide.

"An intruder, Mother." Sterling started to run his hand through his hair then caught himself. "I heard her scream and rushed in here to find this man. I fired over his head but apparently hit the ceiling, which then collapsed."

Mother stared in shocked disbelief.

"Millicent, take them down to the parlor," Sir Lawrence said in a voice that did not allow for argument. "I believe your son and Lady Rathbourne too, from the looks of her, could use some brandy. She might want this as well." He plucked Livy's robe from the foot of her bed and tossed it at her. "I shall follow in a minute."

"Yes, of course." Millicent helped Livy with her robe, then put her arm around the younger woman and steered her away from her room. She glanced over her shoulder at her son. "Are you coming?"

Sterling looked at Sir Lawrence.

"Nothing you can do here," Sir Lawrence said. "And brandy is the best thing for you at the moment."

Sterling nodded and followed the ladies down the hall. His mother paused by his room. "You do realize you're clothed in nothing but your nightshirt?"

"There wasn't time to dress," he said in a sharper tone than intended, stepped into his room, and grabbed his dressing gown.

He pulled it on and trailed after them to the parlor. A servant appeared almost at once with a decanter and glasses and set them on a table. It appeared the noise of the gunshot and the collapsing ceiling had roused most of the household. His mother waved the servant out of the room, then filled the glasses and handed them around. Livy sank down on a sofa in exhaustion, his mother followed suit. No one said a word. Silence hung in the room like an accusation. God help him, he'd killed a man. It scarcely mattered whether he had intended to do so or not. He had taken a life.

"The authorities shall have to be informed at once," Sterling said at last.

"Leave that to me." Sir Lawrence stepped into the room, crossed the floor to the decanter and poured his own glass, downing nearly half of it in one swallow. "I have awakened Mr. Cadwallender and apprised him of the situation. He should be down shortly."

"What's going to happen now?" Livy said in a hollow voice. Bloody hell, she sounded as bad as he felt.

"There will be repercussions, I imagine," Sterling said slowly, wondering about the state of Egyptian prisons. "Even in Egypt, I suspect one can't go around killing people without consequences."

"You didn't kill him," Sir Lawrence said firmly. "The ceiling did."

"But I shot —"

"This was an accident. The ceiling was already in need of repair, damaged through the years by a leak in the roof. I'm not sure if the shot hit the ceiling or the reverberation alone caused the collapse. This was regrettable, yes, but this intruder was in the act of committing a crime. I shall take care of the authorities." Sir Lawrence chose his words with care. "However, I think it would be in your best interest to leave Egypt at once."

Sterling narrowed his gaze. "I do not mean to sound unappreciative, but this death is my fault. I can't possibly leave until this matter is resolved."

"I shall resolve it." Sir Lawrence's gaze pinned Sterling's. "Believe me when I say it would be best for all concerned if your involvement goes unnoticed."

"Regardless, I cannot flee the country like a common criminal. I am to blame for a man's death, and I cannot go on as if nothing has happened." He looked at Livy. "Surely, you can understand that?"

"What I understand," she said slowly, "is that you came to my assistance. I called you, and you came." Her gaze met his. "And now you need my help as well as Sir Lawrence's." She drew a deep breath and turned to the older man. "What about your servants?"

"My staff is very loyal. They are as protective of this household as I am." Sir Lawrence shook his head. "They will not cause any difficulty."

"Nonetheless," Sterling began.

"I am not without a certain amount of influence here. You are nothing more than a visitor, and whether you wish to acknowledge your part in this or not is of no significance. Ultimately, the man was killed by a falling ceiling. You did not shoot him; nor did you intend his death." Sir Lawrence swirled the brandy in his glass. "Coming from me, the explanation of the circumstances surrounding this incident will not be questioned. If you remain here however . . ." He shrugged.

"Then there is no choice." Livy rose to her feet. "We must leave Egypt as quickly as possible."

"There is a morning train to Alexandria in a few hours," Sir Lawrence said. "You should have no trouble booking passage on a ship, and I would advise taking the first ship scheduled to leave port. Regardless of where it's going."

"Italy." Josiah stood in the doorway. The young solicitor appeared calm and collected, as if he were frequently roused from his bed by tales of murder and flight. "We should travel to Italy. Venice to be exact. It's where the next item stipulated in Lord Rathbourne's will is to be found." He look at Livy. "My apologies Lady — Olivia. I was instructed to present you with the note regarding the second item only after you had acquired the first. However, when I heard Sir Lawrence say we should take the first ship, and as I assume . . ."

"Thank you, Josiah." She cast the young man a grateful smile, then turned to Sir Lawrence. "In regard to the first item —"

"The jar is yours," Sir Lawrence said with a wave of his hand.

"Lawrence." Sterling's mother beamed. "I knew you would give it to her."

"Well, I am getting a mummy," he said under his breath.

Mother stood. "Come now, Olivia, I shall help you pack your things. We must hurry if you are to make the train. Oh dear." She winced. "It might be best to have a servant pack your things as your room is . . . well . . . occupied."

"I'll instruct a servant to do so at once." Sir Lawrence nodded.

"And have them bring her traveling clothes to my room. Olivia, you can dress in there. And Sterling." She looked at her son, a determined gleam in her eye. "I shall not be accompanying you. I intend to remain in Egypt for a few more days. I have no intention of leaving this country without visiting the pyramids, and I think I should like to see the ruins at Memphis as well. Besides, there is much yet to be seen here in Cairo."

Sterling studied his mother. "And what of propriety? Isn't that why you insisted on accompanying us in the first place?"

"I am confident you will behave in a manner expected of you." Mother squared her shoulders. "As will I."

"I see." Sterling's gaze slid from his mother to Sir Lawrence. The older man and Sterling's mother traded glances. The way he looked at her, as if she were a rare treasure, was at once irritating and reassuring. "Sir Lawrence?"

"I would be delighted to have your mother's company for as long as she desires to stay," he said smoothly, as if he and Sterling hadn't spoken of this very thing. And hadn't discussed extending her visit with his mother as well. "And when she wishes to return to London, I shall be happy to accompany her."

"Then I have . . ." it was difficult to say the words, "no objections."

His mother arched a brow.

"Sir." Josiah directed his attention to

Sterling. "We have only a few hours."

"Yes, of course," he murmured. This was all happening entirely too quickly. As if he were caught in a rapid whirlpool, buffeted by currents, and could not break free. He was not used to doing anything without first giving it a great deal of consideration. Now, there was no time for thought. Sir Lawrence was probably right about the need for Sterling to leave Egypt without hesitation. Still, it did not sit well.

"Go now and get your things together," Mother said. "Olivia, I need to have a few words with Sir Lawrence. I shall join you in a moment."

Livy smiled weakly, and the three travelers headed back to their rooms. Sterling walked Livy to his mother's door.

"This is the right thing to do, you know," she said softly.

He shook his head. "Then why does it feel entirely wrong?"

"Because you are a good and honorable man."

"Honorable?" He scoffed. "Wouldn't an honorable man stay here and face the authorities?"

"And say what, Sterling?" She laid a hand on his arm. "This man's death was not your fault. If you stayed here, inevitably it would all become much more complicated than necessary. You are a foreigner, and your presence would only muddy the waters. We would be delayed here for who knows how long." She stared into his eyes. "Sir Lawrence is not a fool. He would not advise us to leave if he did not think it was the appropriate action to take."

"Still . . ." He shook his head. "I have never been responsible for the taking of a life."

She paused for a long moment. "It has a certain biblical quality you know. Fleeing from Egypt."

"I suppose it does." He forced a resigned smile. "Moses too fled after he killed a man."

"My apologies." She winced. "I had forgotten that part."

He ran his hand through his hair. "I shall never forget."

"Nor would I expect you to. But it could have been worse." She cast him a weak smile.

"I know." He drew a weary breath. "You could have been injured, again. He could have hurt you. The ceiling could have killed you as well."

"Or you," she said pointedly, "but that's not what I was thinking."

Fifteen

Frolic in a fountain and fly in a balloon.
From the secret list of desires of
Olivia Rathbourne

Olivia drew a deep breath. She did so love traveling by sea and vowed to do it as much as possible as soon as she had the means to do so. There was something about standing on the deck of a ship, with the constant breeze and fresh air, that was somehow freeing. Indeed, this was freedom at its best. She leaned over the railing and watched the water flow past the ship. If one could spread one's arms and fly, she suspected that the feeling would be very similar to this. And wouldn't that be delightful?

Sir Lawrence's canopic jar was wrapped and carefully packed in her trunk. Only two objects were left to acquire, and she would receive her inheritance. And true freedom.

Which should have put her in better spirits

and would have if not for Sterling. He had been quiet and pensive and, well, brooding in the best manner of Heathcliff on the moors ever since they'd left Sir Lawrence's house. It was most disturbing. Particularly as it seemed there was nothing she could do to help ease his mind.

They had taken the morning train to Alexandria and managed to get passage on a ship bound for Italy thanks to Josiah. The young man was most efficient and thoroughly capable. He continued to earn Sterling's respect and her friendship although she did wish he would stop staring at her like a love-struck puppy.

They had all spent the first day of the voyage ensconced in their own cabins. It was shocking how exhausting fleeing could be. Yesterday, she and Josiah had spent much of the day on deck, enjoying the blue skies and bluer seas, speaking about nothing in particular. Fortunately, the young man did not bring up his feelings although even a blind man could see them. Sterling had failed to make any appearance at all, taking his meals alone in his cabin. She had toyed with the idea of confronting him directly but discarded it after due consideration. The man probably needed to be alone with his thoughts and his guilt, as absurd as she considered it.

Today, however, was another matter. Her jaw tightened with resolve. Today, she would not allow Sterling to brood. She realized he saw what she thought of as *the incident* as his fault. But in truth, wasn't it the intruder's? Or even hers? If she hadn't turned to him, if she hadn't challenged him to come to Egypt in the first place . . . She blew a frustrated breath. Beyond all else, she shouldn't have been so weak. Didn't she pride herself on not needing anyone to save her? Still, the fear she'd felt when she'd awakened to find a stranger in the dark by her bed had been crippling, and only one thought had come to mind. Sterling. Sterling would rescue her. Perhaps she had forgiven him after all. Or perhaps she had changed enough to acknowledge her own weaknesses and needs and possibly even desires that were not on her list.

She had slipped a note under his door a few hours ago requesting his presence and had asked Josiah to join them. It was past time to learn what the second item stipulated in the will was. In truth, she was surprised at her lack of curiosity. Josiah had been good enough to tell them where it was. What it was scarcely mattered. Still, if anything could draw Sterling out of his self-imposed prison, it was their quest. At least she hoped it was. Odd, she smiled to herself, when had it become their quest instead of hers?

"Good day." Sterling stepped up beside her.

"Good day." She studied him carefully. Tiny lines of tension marked the corners of his eyes, but his expression had eased. She couldn't help but wonder if this was the Sterling who had arrogantly placed watchdogs in her household or the carefree traveler he had become on the way to Egypt or the tortured earl who had caused the death of another man. Or some new incarnation altogether. "Are you . . . well?"

"The sea air agrees with me," he said wryly, then drew a deep breath. "I am . . ." he thought for a moment, "realistic. Sir Lawrence was right. It would have done no good for us to linger in Cairo. As much as I regard what happened as my fault, when all is said and done, it was indeed an unfortunate accident. I did not intend for it to happen. Had I known the tentative nature of the ceiling and the possible consequences of my firing the pistol, I might have acted differently." He shrugged. "Or not. My concern at that moment was not for him but for you. Should you be in danger again, my actions might very well be the same."

"Oh." She stared at him, and her heart fluttered.

"So yes, in answer to your question. I am fine." He smiled. "And eager to find out what awaits us in Venice."

"I have always wanted to see Venice."

"Is it on your list?" He had not mentioned her list before, and she'd thought he had forgotten about it.

"Not specifically although much of what is listed involves travel," she said, and changed the subject. "Have you been to Venice?"

"For some reason, we did not travel to Venice when I was a boy. Rome and Florence, but not Venice. I hear it's quite extraordinary. And I have come to a decision."

"Have you?" She raised a brow. "Dare I ask regarding what?"

"I was not eager to spend any time in Egypt. Part of that was expediency and my hope that we could accomplish our purpose as quickly as possible and return to London."

"And, of course, your cautious attitude regarding Egyptian snakes." She resisted the urge to grin.

"Yes, well, there was that." He cleared his

throat. "Nonetheless, for all those reasons I had no interest in seeing those sights I might never have the chance to see again. I would imagine seeing the pyramids is on your list, so I must apologize for denying you that."

"It's not necessary. And again, the pyramids are not specifically listed." Although *walk in the shadows of the gods* certainly applied to the pyramids as well as the Parthenon and the Coliseum. "I did see them from a distance, and one day I shall return to Egypt."

"Nonetheless, it was foolish of me to not take advantage of the opportunity presented us."

"Is the Earl of Wyldewood admitting he might possibly have been wrong?"

"Possibly." He smiled. "I do not intend to make that mistake in Venice. I propose that regardless of what the item is we are to seek in Venice, we take the time to see all there is to see. No matter how long it may extend our visit. *Carpe diem.* From this moment forward, I intend to seize the day."

"Seize the day." She stared in disbelief. "Who are you?"

He chuckled but ignored the question. "Josiah is awaiting us in the forward lounge. Are you ready to learn what is next on this adventure of ours?"

This adventure of ours? His words, even as casually said as they were, warmed her heart. The thought struck her that with him by her side, she could well meet the challenge laid down by her late husband. Indeed, she might be able to accomplish anything. Or rather, *they* could accomplish anything.

It was an absurd notion, and she pushed it aside. Once they had fulfilled the terms of her late husband's will, there would be no *they.* She was an obligation to him. A debt as yet unpaid. Nothing more than that. Nor did she wish to be more.

She summoned her brightest smile. "I am indeed."

A few minutes later they met Josiah in the lounge. Once they had taken their seats, he pulled an envelope from his ever-present valise and offered it to Olivia.

She hesitated for a moment, then accepted it.

"Before you open that, there are a few things I feel you should know," Josiah said. "When I received this assignment from Mr. Hollis, I was given only two of Lord Rathbourne's envelopes. As I was not given that third envelope, I can only assume that means the final item is to be located in

London. I furthermore suspect —"

"That the last item will be almost impossible to acquire," Sterling finished the sentence. He and Josiah exchanged glances. "As no doubt was Lord Rathbourne's intent."

"No doubt," she said under her breath.

Saving the most difficult quest for the last was exactly the sort of thing her late husband would do. He would have relished the idea that just when she thought victory was in sight, it would be yanked from her hands. She knew his nature far better than he had known, or had cared to know, hers. It had been one of the tiny triumphs of her marriage to keep her emotions and concerns and character to herself. Along with her list of desires.

"Gentlemen, it's far too early to concern ourselves with item number three, as number two has not yet been acquired," she said firmly. "Furthermore, neither Mr. Hollis nor my late husband, I imagine, expected me actually to undertake this challenge in the first place. As I have done so, and we have thus far been successful, I see no need to worry about the end of this odyssey at this point since we are scarcely in the middle."

Josiah nodded.

Sterling flashed her an admiring look.

"Well said, Olivia."

She smiled, braced herself for the sight of her late husband's handwriting, and tore open the envelope. She studied the words for a moment. "I'm not sure I understand this. It says the next item is a copy of one of Bellini's works depicting the history of the Venetian Wars with the Holy Roman Emperor, painted by Titian."

"Giovanni Bellini produced a series of six or seven paintings depicting the Venetian war with the emperor. They hung in the Doge's Palace in Venice. Little is known about them except that they were reputed to be the artist's greatest works. Unfortunately . . ." Sterling grimaced. "They were destroyed by fire in the late 1500s, I believe."

She stared at him. "How did you know that?"

"I know a great many things you would not suspect," he said in a lofty manner. "I have had an excellent education, and I have always been fond of art."

"Then do you understand what this refers to?"

"I know Titian was a student of Giovanni Bellini — not to be confused with Gentile Bellini, his brother, or Jacopo, his father. Also artists." Sterling grinned. "As for what we are looking for now" — he shrugged — "I have no idea."

"I believe I can explain," Josiah said. "In preparation for this trip, I examined Lord Rathbourne's correspondence regarding this painting and his attempts to purchase it." He pulled out several papers from his valise and shuffled through them. "According to letters written between Lord Rathbourne and an Italian nobleman" — he glanced down at the paper in his hand — "the Conte de Sarafini, copies were made of Bellini's" — he nodded at Sterling — "Giovanni Bellini that is, of his most impressive work up to that time by several of his students including Tiziano Vecellio."

"Titian," Sterling said to her in a superior manner.

She ignored him. "Go on."

"According to these letters, while there could be as many copies by Titian's hand as there were original works, only two have ever come to light. One of which was owned by the viscount, now Lady Rathbourne, and the other by the Conte de Sarafini."

"If I understand what you're saying correctly . . ." She drew her brows together. "Then the collection I am to complete consists of only two paintings?"

Josiah nodded. "That would be my assessment, yes."

"Do the letters explain why the conte refused to sell the painting?" Sterling asked.

"Yes and no." Josiah shrugged. "It appears the viscount and the conte went back and forth for years, each man trying to acquire the painting the other had. Neither willing to sell."

Sterling frowned in confusion. "Was this a cordial correspondence?"

"It does appear to have become quite heated now and then." Josiah paged through the letters. "On one occasion Lord Rathbourne referred to the conte as an ignorant jackal who could not appreciate the nuances of a master work because his sense of taste did not extend beyond his mouth. Whereupon the Italian gentleman responded by suggesting the viscount was an uncultured barbarian whose ancestors were mucking about in the mud while his were building structures to last through eternity and further questioned his lordship's parentage."

Sterling nodded. "Cordial then."

"As cordial as my late husband ever was," Olivia said under her breath.

"In spite of instances of obvious dislike, overall the tone of the correspondence is polite and well mannered," Josiah said. "I suspect each man wanted the other's painting far too much to sever all communication between them even if one was an ignorant jackal and the other an uncultured barbarian. Regardless, all correspondence appears to have ceased a little over two years ago unless there are letters Lord Rathbourne did not bring to the firm's attention."

"Do you think that's important?" She looked at Sterling.

"It could mean any number of things. One of them could have abandoned his desire for the other's painting and simply stopped writing." He paused. "Correct me if I'm mistaken, but I don't recall seeing any paintings at all in the treasure room."

"The paintings are in a room similar to the treasure room on the floor directly above it." She shrugged. "I've never been in that room either."

"I see. We can assume the viscount's painting is still there, but the jackal could have given his to a museum or as a gift to a friend."

"A very good friend, I would think," Josiah murmured.

"Or, the painting itself could have been destroyed as Bellini's original works were," Sterling said.

"If the painting no longer exists . . ." A heavy weight settled in the pit of Olivia's stomach. If the second item was impossible to get, her quest would end in Venice. And her hopes.

"I would suggest we not borrow trouble by speculating." Sterling shook his head. "Rather wait until we find this Conte de Sarafini and speak to him for ourselves."

"Very well." Olivia drew a deep breath. Sterling was right. There was no need to fret over why correspondence between the men had ceased. Her time would be better spent trying to come up with a plan to convince the conte to part with his rare painting than by dwelling on what would happen to her if she failed. That alone should be enough to keep her mind occupied through the remainder of the voyage to Venice. That and renewing her attempts to seduce Sterling.

"In the meantime, I suggest we spend our time making a list of the sights we wish to see in Venice." Sterling's smug smile returned. "My steward was good enough to leave a guidebook in my cabin, which I have been reading since we boarded."

She raised a brow.

"And you thought I was simply brooding." Amusement shown in his eyes.

"Something like that."

"I should like to ride in a gondola," Josiah said. "Beyond what everyone knows about Venice, that it is an ancient city built on islands with canals instead of streets, I know nothing about the place. I never dreamed I would see it, and I find the prospect most exciting." Eagerness sounded in the young man's voice. "But then I never imagined I would travel to Egypt either." He put his papers back in his valise, then grinned at Olivia. "And I have you to thank."

She shook her head. "None of this was my idea."

"If you hadn't had the courage to pick up the gauntlet your late husband cast down, I should at this very minute be trapped in my dreary offices, trying to come up with a solution to a client's no doubt dull problem. Instead . . ." He grinned. "I am on my way to sunny Italy to bargain for a centuries-old masterpiece. Life is certainly filled with unexpected turns."

"Indeed it is." Sterling chuckled. "*Carpe Diem,* my boy. 'Rejoice while you are alive, enjoy the day, live life to the fullest, make the most of what you have. It is later than you think.' " He nodded at Olivia. "Horace."

She stared.

"In addition to ancient classic writing, I am also familiar with more contemporary literary references appropriate to our travels such as Ruskin's *Stones of Venice*." Sterling grinned. "I am exceptionally well-read."

"You are full of surprises," she said under her breath.

"And I have just begun. Now then." He thought for a moment. "According to Baedeker's *Guide to Northern Italy* there are guides who may be hired to show us the sights who can be found in the Piazza of St. Mark. However, the guide also recommends with the book in hand one can dispense with a hired guide altogether and strike out on one's own. Which I suggest we do. We shall explore and wander and perhaps lose our way. It will make our visit much more of an" — his grin widened — "adventure."

Josiah's grin matched the earl's.

"Much of Venice is unchanged from the glory days of the doges and seafaring supremacy and" — he flashed her a wicked glance — "the adventures of Casanova."

"Giacomo, I assume," she said wryly. "As opposed to another member of the Casanova family."

"None of whom are worth mentioning in contrast to Bellini's brother and father, both of whom are of note in their own right." He heaved an overly dramatic sigh. "Giacomo was the only member of the Casanova family to have truly made his mark on the world."

"Or rather the women of the world," Olivia pointed out.

"He was most successful in that respect, at least according to his account of his life. Although admittedly, a biography a man writes about himself may not be as accurate as one written by an unbiased observer. Regardless, I suggest we follow his advice in seeing the city of his birth as well as that of Baedeker."

Josiah's eyes widened. "My lord, I scarcely think —"

"Casanova said his system of living was to glide away unconcernedly on the stream of life, trusting to the wind wherever it led." Sterling swept an exaggerated bow. "What say you, Olivia? While in Venice, shall we follow the advice of one of its best-known, if not its most infamous, sons and trust to the wind?"

She stared. "This is not at all like you."

"It is now," he said firmly. "Now then, there are a number of hotels Baedeker suggests. Josiah, I suggest you see if we can get accommodations at the Grand Hotel Royal Danieli. It is situated on the Grand Canal and comes highly recommended. Once we are settled . . ."

Olivia nodded her approval when her companions looked her way, but her mind was too distracted by Sterling's manner to pay close attention to his words. He appeared to be a changed man although she suspected anyone who considered himself at fault for another's death would indeed be changed in some manner. But *carpe diem?* Even the man she had loved so long ago would never have suggested trusting to the wind. He was a mystery, albeit not an unpleasant one, and became more so with every step of their journey. Who would he be at the end?

The thought stuck her that this Sterling was a dangerous man. Oh, not because of the death he had inadvertently caused, but because of how he now seemed to be seizing life as it were. No, this Sterling was a man to guard against. This Sterling was a man who could again claim her heart.

Sixteen

Remarkable. It was the only word Sterling could think of to describe the scene spread out before him.

He stood on the balcony off his rooms in the Grand Hotel Royal Danieli. Behind him, a hotel valet was seeing to his baggage and unpacking his things. In front of him lay the Venetian lagoon, filled with boats of various and assorted sizes, most looking more like craft from a fairy story than anything seaworthy. Across the lagoon, the church of San Giorgio Maggiore gleamed in the midday sun, its campanile rising toward the heavens.

Josiah had been dispatched to the home of the Conte de Sarafini and had already been gone for several hours. While they had an address and the hotel had provided directions, Sterling wasn't entirely confident the young man would be successful in finding the right house. Still, he had been eager to explore the twisting, turning passageways of Venice on his own. Although Sterling suspected that if Livy had volunteered her assistance, the young solicitor would have been only too glad of her company. Sterling grinned. The boy had already lost their wager even if neither he nor Livy yet realized it.

He could thank that poor devil in Cairo for his newfound attitude. Not that he would ever forget the man's lifeless eyes staring toward eternity. Nor could he ever put from his mind the devastating knowledge that he, no matter how accidentally, had caused a death. But in the days following the incident, he had come to grips with what had happened. He had also realized, with an odd sort of sudden clarity, that life was uncertain and fragile. Regardless of what plans one might make for the future, despite one's expectations that life would continue in the manner it always had, nothing was assured. Nothing in this life could be depended upon save, perhaps, love.

Livy had loved him once, and she would again. Not because he had come to her rescue in Egypt or because he was helping her achieve what was rightfully hers or because he loved her and always had. But because they belonged together, and life was entirely too short to let mistakes, no matter how devastating the consequences, ruin any chance for true happiness. One way or another, he would make her realize that as well.

"It's glorious, isn't it?" Livy joined him on the balcony.

"It's quite remarkable." He smiled.

"The valet let me in," she said apologetically. "Although are you aware there is a door connecting your room to mine? Locked on my side, of course."

"I was indeed aware of both the door and the lock. Apparently, as we are traveling together, there were certain assumptions made." He shrugged. "We can change rooms if you like."

"No need." She paused. "I do hope I am not intruding."

"You are never an intrusion." He took her hand and raised it to his lips. "It's said Venice is the most romantic city in the world, you know."

She laughed but didn't pull away. "Said by Casanova no doubt."

"No doubt."

"I thought perhaps we could stroll for a bit. I know we told Josiah we would wait for him before seeing Venice, but I find I am too restless to delay much longer."

He nodded. "My sentiments exactly. Perhaps we could have an ice at the Caffé Florian?"

She raised a brow. "You have been studying your guidebook."

"Indeed I have."

"An ice would be lovely." She studied him curiously. "This has been good for you, I think. Not all of it," she added quickly. "But for the most part, you are not the same man who called on me at my father's request."

"And is that good?"

She smiled the very smile that had lived for years in his dreams. "Very good."

"And how have I changed?" He smiled into her eyes. She still did not pull her hand away, and he did not release it.

"When we first set out, you were somber and quite serious and carried the weight of the world on your shoulders."

"I see." He nodded in a sober manner. "The very definition of stiff, stodgy, and dull. Or rather, the very definition of the Earl of Wyldewood."

"And arrogant. You shouldn't forget arrogant."

He winced. "I could never forget arrogant."

"Although" — she grinned — "I suspect that has not changed."

He laughed. "Probably not."

"Then on the ship to Cairo, you . . ." She drew her brows together. "I'm not sure how to describe it."

"Really?" He brought her hand back to his lips. "I tried very hard to be the perfect traveling companion."

"And you succeeded admirably. Very nearly every woman on the ship thought so."

"And you?" He gazed into her green eyes. "Did you think so as well?"

"I enjoyed your company. You were quite charming." The vaguest hint of uncertainty showed in her eyes. Still, she had not pulled away. Would she protest if he drew her into his arms? "You were very much like the Sterling I once knew."

"I see." He turned her hand over and kissed her palm. "Was he charming as well?"

"The Sterling I once knew?"

He nodded and stepped into his room, noting with satisfaction that the valet had left, and pulled her slowly into his arms.

She caught her breath. "Very charming. He was . . . quite wonderful."

"I see." He stared down at her. Would she stop him now if he kissed her?

"And then in Egypt . . ." She swallowed hard.

"Yes?" He bent his head and brushed his

314

lips against the side of her neck. "In Egypt?"

"Egypt . . ." She leaned slightly toward him. "In Egypt, you were . . ."

He kissed a spot right blow the lobe of her ear. "I was what?"

"Preoccupied . . ." She made the tiniest moaning sound, so faint he wouldn't have heard it if his lips hadn't been trailing over her lovely throat. "It was Sir Lawrence and your mother and . . . oh my . . . the snakes, I think."

He murmured against the base of her throat. Her scent, the merest hint of spring, wrapped around him and drifted into his soul. She tasted of what he remembered. Of summer and passion and awe. And faintly of sweet and spice. "Now you know my secret."

"Yes . . ." The word was barely more than a sigh. "That you are . . . cautious about snakes."

"Egyptian snakes," he corrected. God how had he ever lost her? He pulled her closer and feathered light kisses along the line of her jaw.

"Of course," she said faintly.

"I have other secrets." He brushed his lips over hers.

"Do you?" Her hands clenched by her sides as if she wanted to put her arms around him but wouldn't allow herself to do so.

"Um-hmm."

"Yes . . . well . . . we all do . . ."

"Ah yes . . . your list."

She sighed and nodded. He pulled her tighter against him, nuzzling her ear. "What are your secrets, Livy? What is on that list of your desires?"

"Travel and adventures and . . ." She moaned softly, and her arms at last slid around him. "You . . ."

"You wanted me?" He smiled against the warm flesh of her neck.

Her eyes drifted closed, and she nodded. "Wanted . . . you . . . in your bed . . ."

He kissed her softly. "And?"

"And . . ." She sighed. "That would end it . . ."

He paused. "End what?"

"Mmmm . . . you and me."

"What?" He drew back and stared at her. "What do you mean end you and me? I didn't know there was a you and me. I didn't know you thought there could be a you and me."

She looked at him in confusion for a moment, then her expression cleared. "Oh."

He drew his brows together. " 'Oh'? I daresay a statement like that deserves more than a mere 'oh' in response."

"Yes, well, my apologies," she said lightly. "Oh is all that comes to mind at the moment."

"You intended to share my bed? Like a common trollop?"

She huffed. "Hopefully *not* like a common trollop."

"This is on that blasted list of yours?"

She crossed her arms over her chest. "Yes."

"And then what?"

"Then . . ." She shrugged. "Then nothing."

He narrowed his eyes. "Nothing?"

"That's what I said."

At once the truth struck him. "You intended to leave me, didn't you? Never see me again?"

She lifted her chin. "That was the plan, yes."

He clenched his jaw. "Break my heart as I broke yours?"

"I hadn't thought of it that way." She paused. "I never dreamed your heart would be involved."

"Fine," he said sharply, reached out, and yanked her into his arms. If all she wanted was to share his bed, so be it. For now. "Then my heart is no longer involved, and we can cross this item off your list."

For a moment she stared into his eyes, then her arms slid around his neck, and she angled her face toward his.

His lips met hers, and his anger vanished with the taste of her. As did any good intentions that might have raised their ugly heads. She opened her mouth to his, and his tongue dueled with hers. An ache of longing so powerful swept through him that he thought surely she could feel it as well.

Her body was tight next to his, so close he could feel the rise and fall of her chest with every breath. So close the heat of her body warmed him through her clothes and his. So close his growing arousal pressed hard against her. His hand caressed the small of her back and drifted lower. He wanted her and he loved her and for now that was enough.

A knock sounded at the door, and he raised his head.

"Yes?" he barked.

"It's Josiah Cadwallender, sir," the voice from the other side of the door called.

At once Livy wrenched free of his embrace and moved away as if grateful for the interruption. She smoothed her skirts and refused to meet his gaze.

"I imagine you don't want him to see you in the arms of another man," he said sharply.

"Indeed, that would be rude," she snapped.

He took a moment to compose himself, then stepped to the door and yanked it open.

"Sir." Josiah stood beaming in the doorway.

Sterling moved aside and waved him in.

"This is a remarkable place." Josiah stepped into the room, and Sterling closed the door behind him. "The streets, or what passes for streets, twist and turn, and around every corner there is a new and interesting sight to see. The buildings are like something concocted out of spun sugar and magic. Quite fanciful and . . ." He caught sight of Livy and paused. "Olivia." His gaze slipped to Sterling. "I do hope this is not an inopportune time."

"Not at all," Sterling said smoothly. "We were just discussing —"

"Venice," Livy said quickly. "We were considering a walk in the piazza while we waited for your return."

"I am sorry about the delay." Josiah shook his head. "Even with the hotel's instructions, it's remarkably easy to lose one's bearings here. Fortunately, eventually, one ends up at the Grand Canal regardless of what wrong turns one takes."

"But you did find the conte's house?"

"Palace," Josiah corrected. "Very grand. I've never seen anything quite like it."

"And?" Sterling prompted. He did wish the solicitor would get on with it.

"And I delivered your note, but I was unable to speak with the conte directly, only with his secretary." Josiah pulled two large envelopes from his coat pocket. "These are for you." He handed one to Sterling and another to Livy. "I waited while the conte's secretary took your note to him. He would be happy to meet with you. However, he is hosting a gala tonight in honor of an exhibition of his family's collection of art. He hopes you will accept his invitation."

"An exhibition?" Sterling murmured. "How interesting."

Livy opened the envelope and drew out a stiff, formal invitation then glanced at Josiah. "Only two?"

"As much as we have become somewhat lax about such things during the course of our journey the fact remains that you are Viscountess Rathbourne and he is the Earl of Wyldewood. As such, the pleasure of your company is requested at the ball of an Italian count." Josiah shrugged. "I am a lowly solicitor without a drop of noble blood. My exclusion is to be expected." He grinned.

"However, I am confident I will find something to amuse myself while you enjoy the conte's hospitality."

Sterling smiled in spite of his mood. The young man's enthusiasm was annoyingly contagious.

"And now, if you will forgive me, I have not yet unpacked."

Sterling nodded, thanked Josiah for his efforts, and a moment later, the solicitor took his leave.

"I should be going as well." Livy moved toward the door.

Sterling stepped to block her path. "I don't think so. We have a few things yet to discuss."

"Nothing I can think of," she said coolly.

"I want to know more about this list of yours."

"It's really none of your business."

He gritted his teeth. "Everything about you is my business."

"I was right." Her eyes narrowed. "The arrogance remains."

He ignored her. "Where precisely am I on this list?"

"It scarcely matters."

"It matters to me!"

"Very well then." She glared. "You are the first item on my list!"

"The first?" He stared. In the back of his head, a voice noted that being at the top of a list that had helped her survive years of unhappiness was not necessarily bad. He ignored it. "So I am the first item you wish to check off so that you may go on with your life?"

"I wasn't going in any particular order." She scoffed. "I had rather thought to cross items off in a random, even haphazard, manner. As they presented themselves, as it were."

At once clarity slammed into him, and he gasped. "On the ship on the way to Egypt, all those nights you tried to get me into your room. You were trying to seduce me!"

"Not very successfully if you recall. One would have thought it would be easier." She rolled her gaze toward the ceiling. "And you needn't sound so appalled. A few minutes ago you had no objections to seduction, be it mine or yours."

"That was different."

"Why? Because it was your idea?"

"Yes! No!" He shook his head to clear it, to think rationally. "Because it wasn't planned. It wasn't part of a scheme to allow me to get you out of my blood."

She paled. "I never said that."

"You didn't have to say it. Your intentions

were obvious. Once you had shared my bed, you could put me behind you and go on with your life."

"I *have* put you behind me. I did so long ago. And even if I hadn't, you needn't say that as if there was something wrong with it."

"There is something wrong with it!"

"I don't see why," she said in a lofty manner.

"For one thing, it's highly improper —"

"I don't care."

"For another, it's quite scandalous."

"Good!"

"And beyond that, it's . . . it's immoral!"

"Oh, I see. Planning to seduce you is immoral. Your seducing me without prior planning is not."

He clenched his teeth. "That's not what I meant."

"That's what it sounded like." She raised her chin defiantly. "I have earned the right to do what I wish with my life. Be it improper, scandalous, or immoral."

He shook his head. "Not with me."

"With you above all else! Who better than with you? Besides, once you have finished with your . . . your penance for the past, you will have no part in my life. In my future."

He stared at her for a long tense moment. "Are there other men on your list?"

She shrugged. "Not by name."

"What then? By title? By occupation? By social standing?"

"For the most part" — she met his gaze directly — "by possibility for adventure."

"I see. Then a dull, stuffy, responsible earl is only on your list by virtue of what?" He narrowed his eyes. "A desire for revenge?"

"Don't be absurd." She huffed.

"You said you have never forgiven me."

Her jaw clenched. "Nonetheless, I never thought of you in terms of revenge. Indeed." Her eyes hardened. "I never thought of you at all."

He considered her for a long moment, then drew a deep breath. "You're lying."

"You'll never know!"

"Oh, but I do know," he said coolly. "You put me on your list. The top of your list. The list that sustained you through the years. I daresay, you thought about me quite a lot."

"You are an arrogant beast!" She moved toward the door, and this time he did not stop her. She reached the door, opened it, and turned toward him. Her voice was level. "You were on the list because you were a . . . a book whose ending had not yet been read. I simply wished to finish it."

His heart lurched. "Then, my dear Lady Rathbourne." He swept an exaggerated bow. "Anytime you wish to cross this particular item off your list, I should be happy to be of service."

She started to say something, then paused and cast him a brilliant smile. "I shall keep that in mind, my lord. However, if I were you, I would say your chances were better of sharing a bed with an Egyptian snake than with me." She nodded, stepped through the door, and shut it hard behind her.

He stared after her.

He was on her list. Her damnable, bloody list! He meant no more to her than a line drawn through a sentence! Which was no more than he deserved. Still, hadn't he done everything in his power to atone for his mistakes? Perhaps not entirely yet but at least a little?

She was the one who didn't want to talk about the past. But she was obviously the one who hadn't put it in the past. And he was the one doing his best to win her heart. She was planning all along to have her way with him, then toss him aside as if he were expendable.

Not in this lifetime.

And it was past time he stopped being so damn charming and amenable all the time. If he didn't want to smile, he would no longer do so. Although, in truth, he had enjoyed their adventure thus far when he wasn't trading his mother for ancient Egyptian jars. Or committing murder by ceiling. Or trying his best to make up for a mistake he made a decade ago. And hadn't it been working? Hadn't she begun to at least like him again?

He was on her list! Damnation. He meant no more to her . . .

Good God. He smacked his palm against his forehead. He was on her list! What a fool he was. He'd said it just a minute ago and apparently had paid no attention to his own words. She'd clung to that list through the years. And he was on it! He should have known. She'd always been a dreadful liar.

She had thought about him. She hadn't forgotten what they'd had. And being on her list meant she wanted to be with him as badly as he wanted to be with her.

A grin broke on his face.

Wasn't that an interesting development? Still . . . his grin faded. She was not going to admit that easily. Why the blasted woman might even try to prove some sort of absurd point by attempting to cross off the items on her list. Items that included other men.

Not bloody likely.

As for having no part in her future, he *was* her future. As she was his. And long before they finished this quest, he would make her realize it as well.

But if she wanted to share his bed and cross him off her list, his smile returned, she'd have to marry him to do it.

Seventeen

Be seduced by a handsome stranger.
From the secret list of desires of
Olivia Rathbourne

If one weren't twenty-eight years of age and a widow and eminently practical as well, one might have considered oneself an enchanted princess from the pages of a children's story given one's surroundings. At least for a moment. Olivia glanced around the ballroom, with its soaring frescoed ceilings and carvings picked out in gleaming gold. It was indeed a setting fit for enchantment.

They had arrived at the conte's palace by boat, gliding along the silent canals, passing from light cast by lamps along the canals to mysterious shadows, from one pool of illumination to the next, under a sky lit by a thousand stars. An evening like this wasn't on her list, but it should have been.

The hotel had supplied someone to dress her hair, and now, wearing the best gown she had brought, a lovely blue-green confection that reminded her of the waters of Venice, the mirror told her she looked her best. As did the look in Sterling's eyes. Not that he had said so, or indeed had said much of anything on the ride here. Of course, neither had she.

A gentleman approached them and bowed. "Lady Rathbourne and Lord Wyldewood, I presume?"

Sterling nodded. "Good evening."

"Good evening, my lord. I am Giuseppe Montalvado, secretary to the Conte de Sarafini."

Olivia smiled. "And the conte?"

"He regrets he was unable to greet you upon your arrival as he was otherwise engaged," the secretary said smoothly.

"We have only just arrived," Sterling said.

"The conte would like to welcome you personally to his home and to his city. He awaits you in the drawing room. If you would be so good as to follow me."

"Excellent." Sterling nodded.

They made their way through the crowd, the elegance of which rivaled, or possibly surpassed, anything she had ever seen in London. She would have to remember to thank Millicent for advising her to save her grandest gown for an occasion worthy of it. Heads turned as they passed, and she noted with satisfaction the admiring glances of the gentlemen. And noted as well, with admittedly less satisfaction, the equally admiring looks directed at Sterling by the ladies of the gathering. Tall and dashing and handsome, in his evening attire he was nothing short of magnificent. Enough to make any woman's heart flutter in her chest. Even, perhaps, hers.

She had never intended to tell him he was on her list. And certainly not at the top of it. But she'd lost her head when his lips had caressed her neck, and his body had pressed close to hers. The words had come without thinking. Indeed, at that moment, she been unable to think of anything at all save his touch. Not that her admission wasn't true. She had planned to share his bed and never see him again. But since their heated words this afternoon, she could not ignore the fact that just possibly that was no longer her plan. Nor could she ignore that since the moment his lips had touched hers, she could not think of anything but his kiss, his arms around her, his body next to hers. Yet another thing she did not intend to tell him.

They reached the far side of the ballroom

and stepped into a corridor, the décor there only a little less ornate than the room they had just left.

She was still angry although admittedly she wasn't sure why. She conceded that Sterling had every right to be irate. If he had intended to seduce her, then never see her again, she would certainly be furious. Perhaps her lingering anger was due to nothing more than the truth at last spoken aloud and the fact that he knew her far better after all these years than she had ever expected. Nonetheless, she was not about to fall into his arms or, at this point, his bed. And definitely not his life. He had indeed changed through the course of their journey and through the years as well, and no doubt was as trustworthy a man as anyone could hope to meet. Regardless, the question remained of whether or not she could trust him with her heart. Whether her own fears would allow her to do so. One fear she had admittedly not faced. She wished to start her life anew. How could she do so with him?

The secretary pushed open tall, carved, painted doors and gestured for them to enter. Olivia stepped into a room somewhat less ornate than any they'd passed through yet still elegant and most impressive.

"Lady Rathbourne." A tall, handsome, dark-haired gentleman stepped forward and took her hand. "Allow me to introduce myself. I am the Conte de Sarafini." He raised her hand to his lips, his gaze never leaving hers. She realized with surprise that he was fairly young, probably no older than Sterling. And shockingly attractive. "And I am at your service."

She smiled into his dark eyes. "It was most gracious of you to invite us to join you this evening. Your home is magnificent."

"Enhanced only by your presence." His gaze still locked with hers. "It is but a meager setting for a jewel such as you. You must allow me to show you the rest of the house and perhaps some of the city as well." His English was very good, made intriguing and even seductive by his accent as well as the look in his eyes. In truth, this was a man worthy of being put on any woman's list of desires. "The Palazzo de Sarafini has been in my family for twelve generations. But its beauty pales in comparison with yours."

She laughed. "You are a charming devil, aren't you?"

"When it comes to women of remarkable beauty." He flashed her a wicked grin. "Indeed, I am."

Sterling cleared his throat, and the conte

released her hand.

"My apologies, Lord Wyldewood. Your delightful companion has distracted me from my duties."

"No apologies necessary. Lady Rathbourne can be quite distracting," Sterling said with a pleasant smile.

She glanced at him sharply, but his expression was cool and nothing more than polite.

"I was most intrigued by your note." The conte studied Sterling curiously. "I assume there is more to this story than the mere acquisition of a painting."

Sterling nodded. "Indeed there is."

"Then I shall wish to hear all about it. But not tonight." He turned his attention back to Olivia. "Tonight is for dancing and enjoying the company of a beautiful stranger who, it is my most fervent hope, will soon no longer be a stranger but a friend."

She tilted her head and considered him. "One can never have too many friends."

"That's what I always say," Sterling said in an overly jovial manner. "One can never have too many friends. No, indeed."

The conte cast him an acknowledging smile. It was obvious, at least to her, that friendship with Sterling was not exactly what the Venetian had in mind.

"Allow me to escort you back to the

ballroom." He offered his arm. "And then I hope you will do me the honor of a dance."

She cast him her most flirtatious smile, the very one she'd practiced after Sterling had informed her of her lack of skill at flirtation. Judging by the look on the conte's face, or perhaps in his eye, she had at least mastered the smile. "I should like nothing better."

They started off, Sterling a step behind.

The conte leaned closer and lowered his voice in a conspiratorial manner. "It is something of a coincidence that brings you here on this particular night, Lady Rathbourne."

"Really? Why is that, my lord?"

"Tonight's festivities mark my announcement that my family's collection of art will soon be on display for all to see." He chuckled. "The cornerstone of the exhibition is the Titian."

She raised a brow. "The one I am interested in?"

He chuckled. "Indeed, my lovely Lady Rathbourne. The Titian you want that I have."

Good Lord. He made a simple transaction sound quite, well, seductive. She laughed lightly, belying a twinge of concern. The Titian's importance in this exhibit was a twist that could well make the painting impossible to acquire. Or, the vaguest beginning of an idea formed in the back of her mind, it could make it much, much easier.

"Tomorrow, perhaps, you will allow me to show it to you."

"I look forward to seeing it."

The moment they crossed the threshold into the ballroom, the conte's secretary approached and spoke quietly into his ear. He nodded and turned to Olivia. "Do forgive me, there is a matter requiring my attention. I shall not be long." He again kissed her hand. "Do not forget we are to dance."

"I should never forget that." Her voice was low, filled with unspoken promise and decidedly seductive. She was quite pleased with herself.

"Nicely done," Sterling said behind her.

Her gaze stayed on the conte as he made his way around the room. "What was nicely done?"

"Your flirtation, of course." A grim note sounded in his voice. "You have certainly learned quickly."

She shrugged. "I suspect it's like riding a horse. Even if one hasn't done it for many, many years, given a bit of practice, it all comes back."

"What was he saying to you? No doubt charming nonsense designed to turn your head."

"Oh, he was simply saying those sorts of things a man says to a woman whom he hopes to entice into his bed." She wasn't quite ready to share the information about the painting the conte had just imparted. Sterling had come up with a plan to acquire the jar. It was time to do her part. After all, it was her future that hung in the balance. "Not that it's any of your concern."

"Oh, but it is my concern, just as you are my concern. And will continue to be my concern until we have achieved what we set out to do."

"I refuse to argue the point with you at the moment," she said in a lofty manner.

"Nonetheless," Sterling continued, "you are aware that gentlemen like the conte are not to be trusted when it comes to the fairer sex."

"You needn't lecture me like I was an unruly child. I am a widow and well aware of the ways of the world."

"I doubt that," he muttered.

She glanced at him. "And what do you mean — 'gentlemen like the conte'? You just met the man. You can't possibly have formed an accurate opinion."

"I know his type. He has a certain air about him," Sterling said in a superior tone. "He reminds me of Quinton."

"Well, he is charming and handsome."

"Too charming, I'd say. There is something not to be trusted about a man who is too charming. Besides, the man is a foreigner."

"We are the foreigners, Sterling." She directed her gaze back to the conte. "I suspect there are those here who might say the same things about you."

"That I am not to be trusted because I am too charming and handsome?"

"You are handsome . . ."

"Don't forget charming."

"That remains to be seen."

He adjusted his cuffs and surveyed the room. "I daresay there are any number of ladies here who would find me quite irresistible."

She ignored him. "I think you're jealous."

"Jealous?" He scoffed. "Why would I be jealous?"

"Because I am flirting with him and not with you."

"Yes, but you fight with me," he said under his breath.

She glanced at him. "What does that mean?"

He smiled an enigmatic sort of smile, as if he knew all sorts of things she did not. He glanced past her and nodded. "Your conquest is returning."

She turned and watched the conte approach. "I suspect he is an excellent dancer, among other things."

He snorted. "No doubt."

"You're rather smug tonight."

"Well, I am on your list."

The conte drew closer, and she favored him with her brightest smile. She leaned toward Sterling and spoke softly for his ears alone. "Dallying with a handsome Italian count is also on my list."

"I am not as concerned with your list tonight," Sterling said smoothly, "as I am with his."

"You needn't be. I can take care of myself. I have for a very long time. After all," she added without thinking, "I had no one else."

"You do now."

She cast him a sharp glance, but a polite smile curved his lips, his expression was composed and cool. It was most unnerving.

The conte stopped before her and nodded a bow. "Lady Rathbourne, I believe this is our dance."

"Indeed it is, my lord."

He took her hand and led her toward the

other dancers. She glanced back at Sterling, who didn't look even the tiniest bit concerned or responsible. But rather annoyingly smug.

The conte took her in his arms, and she was right. He was an excellent dancer. "Are you enjoying Venice, Lady Rathbourne?"

"We only arrived this morning, so we have seen little thus far." She smiled. "It is a beautiful place."

"Venice, La Serenissima." He chuckled. "The most serene."

"And is it? Serene, that is?"

"In many ways, yes. But we have a long past, much of which is not the least bit serene." He led her through a complicated turn. "We are, and have always been, a city of light and love."

"And art?"

"Art is part of the fabric of existence here. It surrounds us and is as much a part of Venetian life as the very air we breathe. The frescoes on this ceiling were painted by Tiepolo in the last century." He smiled. "As such things go in Venice, they are considered fairly new."

"But the Titian —"

"Is not considered new." He chuckled. "But the last thing I wish to do with a beautiful woman in my arms is discuss business or even the great art of La Serenissima. Unless, of course, it is the art of love."

She laughed. "Very well then. What shall we discuss?"

"You." He smiled. "You grace the room with your presence."

"You shall quite turn my head, my lord."

"Ah yes, it is a beginning I think." He grinned. "You are a widow for how long?"

"The viscount's death was a little over a month ago."

He narrowed his eyes. "And yet you do not wear the clothes of mourning."

She lifted her chin. "No, I do not."

He studied her curiously. "You do not regret his death?"

"I regret only that it did not come sooner."

He stared at her for a moment, then smiled. "Are you certain you are English and not Italian? There is a touch of the Medici about you."

She raised a brow. "I did not kill him."

"Nor would I expect you to confess such a thing if you had." He grinned. "Still, your candor is refreshing and unique among the women of my acquaintance."

"I see no reason to be evasive about my late husband. One of the joys of my life is being able to call him 'my late husband.' "

"The Medici women were prone to poison

you know."

"My husband's throat was cut."

"Most certainly not a woman's weapon." He winced. "From his correspondence, I gathered he was not a . . . a nice man?"

"No, he was not a nice man."

"I see." He paused. "And the earl. Is he a nice man?"

She nodded. "Quite nice."

"You are his mistress?"

"His mistress?" She nearly missed a step. "Why on earth would you think that?"

"You are not married, and yet you travel together . . ." He shrugged. "It seems obvious to me."

"Well you are mistaken. Lord Wyldewood is simply a very old friend who is assisting me as a means of paying off a debt of sorts that be believes he owes me."

"And does he?"

She thought for a moment. "Yes."

"I see." He considered her thoughtfully. "He does not look at you as though you were an obligation."

"Nonetheless —"

"He looks at you as if you were . . ." He pulled her a bit closer and spoke low into her ear. "His."

"Nonsense." She paused. "Does he?"

He chuckled. "He does indeed."

"Well, I am certainly not . . . *his.*"

"Excellent," he murmured, and steered her through another turn. Surely the conte was mistaken about how Sterling looked at her. Admittedly, given what had nearly happened between them today, he wanted her in his bed although God knew he had resisted all her efforts to accomplish just that on the ship to Egypt. Yes, they had forged a friendship in these past weeks. And indeed, he was protective of her, which was part and parcel of what he saw as his responsibility. But as for more . . .

"Where are you, Lady Rathbourne?"

"Where?" Her attention jerked back to him. "My apologies, my lord. I am sorry. I did not intend to offend you."

"The fault is entirely mine." He heaved a heartfelt sigh, but his eyes twinkled with amusement. "I should know better than to bring up the feelings of another man toward a lady when that lady is in my arms. I should instead be telling her that her eyes are the color of the rarest emerald, and the fire that burns within the stone burns as well in her eyes and sears my soul."

"Indeed you should." She laughed. "It's most effective."

"Alas though." He considered her. "You are not the least bit affected."

342

"But I am most flattered and quite charmed."

"It is a very great pity then."

"What is?"

"That the fire that burns in your eyes does not burn for me." He smiled in a regretful manner. "But for him."

"Utter nonsense." She scoffed. She had no feelings for Sterling save gratitude and friendly affection. Certainly, when he had kissed her today, she had felt desire, but that was to be expected. It had been a very long time since she had been kissed at all let alone by him. And yes, the thought had occurred to her since he had come back into her life that she might possibly feel more than friendship for him. And admittedly, in those unguarded moments, the idea had flitted through her mind that perhaps it was not completely out of the question that he and she might . . . possibly . . .

The music drew to a close, and the conte escorted her off the floor. "Will you do me the honor of joining me for luncheon tomorrow? We can discuss the question of the painting then."

"I assume your invitation includes Lord Wyldewood?"

"Unhappily, yes," he said with a smile. "If I cannot have you all to myself."

She laughed. "Then we shall be delighted."

"I must attend to my other guests." He took her hand and raised it to his lips. "Regretfully."

"Tomorrow then."

"Tomorrow." He paused. "But you should know the Titian has been in my family's possession for generations. I am not inclined to give it up at any price."

"But you are still willing to discuss it?"

"With you, I would discuss anything." He stopped a passing waiter and selected a glass of wine, then presented it to her. "Have you tasted our Prosecco yet? It is our champagne but much better."

She accepted the glass and took a sip. It was very much like champagne and quite refreshing. "It's very good."

"It has been produced here since Roman times. We are as proud of our wine as we are of our art. It is all part of our heritage." His brows pulled together. "I should warn you, Lady Rathbourne, I am aware that your late husband tried for many years to acquire the Titian from my father without success."

"Your father?"

"Yes, of course." He stared at her for a moment, then his expression cleared. "Oh, I see, you thought . . . It was not I who corresponded with Viscount Rathbourne but my father. He has been dead these past two years."

"My condolences." She shook her head. "I simply assumed that you . . . Are you a collector of art as well then?"

"Not with the passion of my father. I am a guardian, as it were, of my family's heritage. And I am no more inclined to part with the painting than my father was. Still . . ." His gaze slid over her in a most improper manner that was not so much offensive as it was flattering. An action that would have made her hand twitch to slap the face of another man, from this man was most amusing. He was just so, well, his intentions were obvious. "My great weakness has always been beautiful women. I may be persuaded to change my mind."

She sipped the wine and met his gaze. "Under the right circumstances?"

He chuckled. "I look forward to discussing it further with you."

She flashed him a brilliant smile. "As do I."

He bowed and took his leave. Olivia sipped the wine thoughtfully and glanced around for Sterling. She spotted him almost at once, dancing with a lovely woman who gazed at him as if he were the moon and the stars. It was very well done. Obviously, flirtation was as highly developed here as the wine and the art.

Did he really look at her as if she were his? And did she look at him with fire in her eyes? Regardless, she would never be any man's possession again. As for anything else, that would have to wait until she'd won her inheritance. Until she'd beaten her late husband at his own game. Until she was independent and could base her decisions on desire rather then need. She sipped the wine and watched him dance. Now was not the time to dwell on what might or might not happen.

Sterling had offered to trade a mummy to Sir Lawrence for the canopic jar although he had, in effect, traded his mother as well. Perhaps, a similar offer would be successful with the Conte de Sarafini.

Surely she had something he wanted? Something she could offer him that no one else could? Something . . . unique. She sipped the Prosecco and smiled.

And she knew exactly what that something might be.

EIGHTEEN

"You dance divinely, my lord." The lady in his arms gazed up at him.

"I have an excellent partner." Sterling smiled down at her. With dark hair and darker eyes, and a figure to melt the resistance of even the strongest man, she was one of the loveliest women in the room. Precisely why he had asked her to dance.

"Is your stay in Venice to be a long one?"

"I doubt it, but my plans are uncertain at the moment." At least his plans regarding Venice. For the first time since her father had told him the truth, Sterling had a plan of sorts fueled by his own resolve and the knowledge that no matter what Livy might say, he had always been in her thoughts. And, with any luck, her heart.

"Perhaps" — she looked at him through lowered lashes — "I can convince you to extend your visit."

"Perhaps." He chuckled.

Granted, it was nothing more than a loosely formed plan at the moment. The vaguest of ideas that somehow he could use Livy's list to his own advantage. Surely she had brought it with her. It would be to his benefit to know exactly what else was on it. But as important as that list was to her, he didn't think simply demanding marriage in exchange for crossing him off would be successful. Besides, she had no interest in marriage. At least not yet. And until she had completed meeting the terms of her husband's will, she would never consider marrying anyone, let alone him.

"Ah me." His partner sighed. "It is the way with you Englishmen is it not?"

"My apologies." He drew his brows together. "I'm afraid I don't know what you mean."

"You are preoccupied, my lord." She shook her head in a chastising manner. "And I fear very much that your head is not filled with thoughts of me."

"Then I am a fool," he said firmly. "You are delightful."

"Yes, I am." She considered him thoughtfully. "And yet it is not enough to capture your attention completely."

He stared into her eyes and lied. "You have my complete attention."

She laughed. "You do not lie well, my lord." She paused. "It is the fair-haired lady, your companion, who fills your thoughts, is it not?"

"She is not my companion." His gaze slipped to where Livy stood sipping a glass of wine and watching . . . him? Surely, he was mistaken. Still, if he wasn't, the least he could do was give her something to watch. He turned his gaze back to his partner.

The lady raised a brow. "She is not your mistress then?"

"My mistress?" He stared at her in surprise. Was that what everyone here thought? That Livy was his mistress? "Why on earth would you think that?"

She shrugged. "You have come to Venice together, and she is not your wife." She smiled knowingly. "Therefore, she must be your mistress."

"She is most certainly not." He huffed.

"But you wish her to be."

"Not at all." Although it was an intriguing idea.

She laughed softly. "You do not lie well even to yourself."

He grinned. "I lie better to myself than to anyone else."

"Perhaps." Curiosity shone in her eyes.

"Why have you not told her of your feelings?"

"What makes you think I have feelings?"

"Come now, my lord." She looked at him as if she could not believe the stupidity of men in general and him in particular. "We have only just met, and yet I can see you look at the lady with longing as well as determination."

"She wants nothing that I want."

"Ah well, then that explains it."

"Explains what?"

"Why she cannot seem to tear her eyes from you. Surely you have noticed?"

He started to deny it, then smiled. "Perhaps."

She leaned closer and without missing a step spoke low into his ear. "You wish to make her jealous then, yes?"

"No," he said quickly. "Of course not. I would never . . ." He paused. Was it such a bad idea?

"And yet you do not dance with her but with me."

"And in that have earned the envy of every man in the room."

She laughed. "You are a charming creature, for an Englishman."

He grinned. "On behalf of Englishmen everywhere, you have my thanks."

"Pity your affections are otherwise engaged."

He studied her cautiously. "I don't know how to answer that."

"It was not a question but an observation." They danced silently for a few moments, then she nodded. "I will help you."

"Help me," he said slowly. "I don't need help."

"You are a . . . what is the word?" Her delicate brow furrowed. *"Ottuso? Stupido?"*

"Stupid?"

"Yes, that is it. You are a stupid man like every other man of my acquaintance. And I shall help you."

"I don't really think I need —"

"Which is what makes you stupid." Her smile took any sting out of her words. The music ended, and she took his arm. "Come into the garden and we shall talk about how I shall help you."

"I really don't think —"

"She is watching you, no?"

He glanced at Livy, who was engaged in conversation with a gentleman much shorter than she. Even as he looked, her gaze strayed to him. He nodded. "Yes."

"Then it will do her good to see you leave with another."

Why not? "Very well."

She led him to doors that opened onto a terrace. They stepped outside and moved to steps leading down into a garden far larger than he had anticipated. Lit with lanterns, what he could see was lush with thickly growing plants, overflowing with exotic blooms.

She tilted her head and smiled. "You thought we lived with only the water at our doors?"

He chuckled. "Possibly."

"It is something of a secret I think, the gardens of Venice. One does not expect them." She gazed over the gardens, a slight smile of pride curving her lips. "It has been my experience when one travels with a companion, that one is rarely left to one's own devices, no?"

He nodded.

"Then perhaps it would do good for you not to be where she expects you to be. Not to be at her . . ." She thought for a moment. "Beck and call is it?"

"Yes, but I'm not. Well, not entirely." He shook his head. "But I don't understand."

"Come, join me tomorrow here in the garden for a visit. Luncheon perhaps? Yes, that would be lovely."

"Here? In the conte's garden?" He frowned. "Won't that be awkward?"

"Not in the least." She cast him a curious glance. "I am often to be found in the gardens here."

"I see," he said slowly. "Then you and the conte are . . . companions?"

She laughed. "Of a sort, yes."

"And he won't mind your seeing another man."

"My dear Lord Wyldewood, it is a mere luncheon, not an assignation." Mischief twinkled in her eyes. "And if he finds it annoying . . ." She shrugged. "I would not mind it."

He narrowed his eyes. "You have me at a disadvantage. You seem to know my name but I do not know yours."

She smiled. "You failed to ask."

"My apologies. That was unforgivable."

"Not at all." She laughed. "It is a ball, my lord. You needn't ask the name of every woman with whom you dance. Part of the pleasure is the mystery. Who is the lady in your arms? Does she belong to another, or will she belong to you?"

"Yes, well . . ."

"I know your name because the conte's secretary, while the soul of discretion on many matters, can always be persuaded to tell me what he knows. I know as well that you sent a note to the conte requesting a meeting regarding a Titian copy of a lost Bellini painting that your Lady Rathbourne would like to acquire."

"The conte's secretary is certainly efficient," Sterling murmured. "Perhaps I should ask him who you are?"

"It is not necessary. I shall introduce myself." She extended her hand and he took it. "I am your hostess."

He took her hand and raised it to his lips. "Then you are . . ."

"Alessandra." She smiled. "Contessa de Sarafini."

Olivia paced the width of her room in the Grand Royal Hotel Danieli as she had since their return from the conte's more than an hour ago. She ignored the doors open to her balcony and the magical sight of the Venetian lagoon reflecting the stars overhead. After all, it was not a sight to be enjoyed alone but rather a sight meant to be shared by lovers.

Lovers? Hah! Whatever had made her think of such a thing? Certainly not the man even now in the very next room. The man whose own balcony overlooked the same scene hers did. The man who had once owned her heart and quite possibly still did.

It had been a grand and glorious evening.

Or would have been had Sterling not made such a spectacle of himself. Why the man had flirted outrageously and charmed and danced with very nearly every lady there. Except for her, which was most annoying. Not that she'd had any lack of partners and had indeed danced nearly every dance herself. And flirted as well. But she certainly hadn't left the ballroom with anyone as he had.

Admittedly, he had every right to flirt and do whatever it was he was inclined to do with other women. She had made it perfectly clear to him right from the start that there could never again be anything more between them than a certain cautious friendship. But something had changed, or perhaps she had changed. Or possibly nothing had changed at all.

Blast it, she was indeed jealous. Of the women dancing in his arms tonight. Of the ladies whose eyes he had gazed into as if they and they alone held the key to his heart. And definitely of the lovely creature he had left the ballroom with, even if they hadn't been gone for very long.

She and Sterling had scarcely exchanged more than a handful of words on the way back to the hotel. He had been lost in thought, as if something of importance was on his mind, probably a woman, which had only increased her annoyance.

Odd that after all they had been through together, it was something as simple as jealousy that now brought her to her senses. The thought struck her with blinding clarity. She did not want to lose him again.

She sank down on the bed. It was past time to face a truth that the conte had recognized, perhaps that even Millicent had seen, that everyone may well have noticed but Olivia. Past time to face her own feelings and her fears.

Yes, her list had sustained her spirit through the years, but was it so much the list itself as the fact that she had put him on it? Perhaps, if she had simply inherited her late husband's wealth, she wouldn't have given Sterling a second thought although she doubted it. He had always been there, in the shadows in the back of her mind, in her unguarded dreams, in the locked places in her heart. Why couldn't she admit it?

Was she still so hurt by his betrayal? Still so afraid that she would be hurt again? She prided herself on her strength. Strength forged in the last decade. Was she strong enough to face the truth about her feelings? Strong enough to risk losing him again? Not that she had him. After all, she was nothing more than an obligation to him. Yet another responsibility to be borne by the Earl of Wyldewood.

Still, hadn't he been there when she had needed him now? Hadn't he put his life aside to help her gain her inheritance? Hadn't he done everything anyone could possibly ask of him? Surely it was more than merely his desire to make amends for the past. And more than his sense of responsibility. Was it time, then, to put the past to rest and go on from here? With him? The man she had once loved. And God help her, the man she had always loved.

She'd been the one unwilling to discuss those dark days. But even ten years ago he was not the type of man to have abandoned her. Which only begged the question of why he had. Certainly she couldn't fault him for believing her father. But why hadn't he, at least in some cursory manner, acknowledged her letters?

Past time to get the answers and in doing so be able truly to leave the past behind. She stood, crossed the room, and stepped out on the balcony, craning her neck to see across his balcony. And past time as well to forgive. There was no light on in his room. Perhaps he was already in bed. No matter. Now that she had decided to face their past, she refused to do it alone. Besides, she hadn't told him about tomorrow's — no — today's meeting with the conte. And if being with him now led to something more, well, it wouldn't be simply to cross him off her list.

She moved to the door to his room, drew a deep breath, and knocked. Nothing. She tried again. Again there was no response. She tried once more and still he did not answer. Damnation, the man was a sound sleeper. There was nothing to be done then, she would have to wake him. She turned the key in the lock, pushed open the door, and stepped into his room.

"Sterling?"

The light from her own rooms illuminated his. The bed was empty, as was the room, and no light shone from the parlor beyond. Where was he?

And more to the point: Whom was he with?

"Well, this is awkward." Sterling drummed his fingers on the small table next to his chair in Josiah's room. "But there's no need to panic."

"No, of course not, sir." Josiah's voice lacked the conviction of his words. "Panic would not serve Lady Rathbourne well."

"Still, I am glad you sent for me." Sterling had been back in his room for less than an hour when a hotel porter had knocked on his door with a note from Josiah, requesting his presence on a matter of urgency.

Josiah nodded. "I thought it best to bring this to you first, sir." He paused. "Although I daresay she won't see it that way."

"No, she won't." The drumming of his fingers increased. "Why wasn't she told about this?"

"I don't know." Josiah shook his head. "I wasn't aware of it myself until tonight."

"And how did you discover it?"

"It has bothered me for some time that there was to be a concise accounting of the methods used to obtain the items. It seemed odd to me as there was nothing regarding how the items were obtained. Nothing that prohibited purchase for example. Yet I was instructed to note the place, date, and time of every acquisition."

"Why time?"

"Precisely what aroused my curiosity."

"I thought your Mr. Hollis told her there was no time limit or deadline."

"I'm not sure Mr. Hollis was aware of this."

Sterling raised a brow. "Someone must have been."

359

"No doubt. But, indeed, time is not a factor unless she undertakes to finish the collections before a suitable period of mourning."

"A year then?"

Josiah nodded.

"Good God." Sterling rubbed his hand over his eyes. "And if she does?"

"Then from the time she completes the first collection to the time she completes the last can be no greater than the length of time the viscount had been dead before the first object was acquired."

"Rathbourne died on the eighteenth of last month. We received the jar on the twenty-third of this month." Sterling furrowed his brow. "Thirty-six days?"

"By my accounting." Josiah nodded. "It has been seven days since we received the jar and left Egypt. Depending on the route and mode of transport, and any number of things we cannot control including weather, it will take at least six to return to London. Which means —"

"She has no more than twenty-three days left to meet the terms of the will." He narrowed his eyes. "Why didn't you know about this? I thought you were well versed in the details of the will."

"I was. I am," he said firmly. "I quite

thoroughly studied one copy of the will before my first meeting with Lady Rathbourne. I did not see this. However, in the papers I was given when we left London, I received a different copy of the will. The one I examined tonight. You must understand." He leaned forward. "In the last few days before his death, the viscount was changing his will to provide a trust for his own private museum. As he died before completing those arrangements, his original will was still in effect. However, there were several different members of the firm involved and a myriad of files. Which is why the will was not read until more than a fortnight after his death. It is distressing but not especially surprising that something would be misplaced. This particular clause was part of an addendum added several years ago."

"No doubt when the viscount realized his widow would want to be out from his control as soon as possible."

"Or simply to make her quest more difficult. This could have been a simple oversight, and certainly no one ever expected that she would accept the challenge. Still . . ." He shook his head. "I find it difficult to believe that Mr. Hollis did not know of this. And most disturbing that he said nothing."

"It is in your firm's best financial interest that Olivia fail."

"I am well aware of that." Josiah paused for a long moment. "I have always thought my employers to be men of honor and integrity." He met Sterling's gaze firmly. "I shall retain my position until Lady Rathbourne's fate is decided, but I will not remain with the firm after that."

Sterling nodded. "You'll need a new position if you still intend to support a wife."

Josiah cast him a wry smile. "It has become apparent to me, if not to her, or you either for that matter, that her affections are otherwise engaged. Even if she fails, she will not marry me to save herself."

"If she fails, she will not marry anyone. Her pride and her desire for independence will not permit her otherwise."

"Then it is up to us, sir, to make certain she does not fail."

Sterling smiled. "Are you conceding our wager then?"

"I am . . ." Josiah thought for a moment. "Accepting the inevitable."

Sterling studied him. "And I am the inevitable?"

"I believe there is much between you that remains to be resolved. But . . ." He shook his head. "I can only hope one day to have a woman look at me the way she looks at you. It is subtle and cautious, but it is unmistakable."

"Do you really think so?"

"I do although I suspect it is not obvious to anyone other than a close observer." He drew a deep breath. "Will you tell her about this tomorrow then, or rather today?"

"I don't know." Sterling's first impulse was not to say anything. To protect her from undue anxiety. "I'm not sure we should tell her at all."

"I don't think that would be wise, sir," Josiah said slowly. "She should know that time is now of the essence. Besides, she would not take your keeping this from her well."

"No, she wouldn't. It is possible she already knows. She has a copy of the will after all." They exchanged skeptical glances, neither of them needing to say what they both knew. Sterling blew a long breath. "Yes, of course, I'll tell her."

"As we do not know what the third item is, she needs to acquire the Titian as quickly as possible so that we may return to London."

"And needs to convince the conte to turn over a painting that has been in his family for generations. It will not be easy; nor, I suspect, accomplished quickly." Sterling thought for a moment. "But perhaps the conte is not the one to convince."

NINETEEN

Ignore inconvenient rules.
From the secret list of desires of
Olivia Rathbourne

Olivia was not about to wait for Sterling to make an appearance. Besides, the conte had sent a boat for them. As she was hoping to convince him to relinquish the painting through not much more than charm and persuasion, it did not seem wise to keep him waiting. She ignored any qualms she might have had about meeting the Venetian alone. After all, this was her quest, and she was more than capable of negotiating with the conte on her own. She wished to be independent; what better time to start? Still, where was the blasted man?

Olivia had refused to wait for his return last night, instead choosing to retire although "retire" was not entirely accurate. She had tossed and turned and risen from her bed more than once to press her ear against the adjoining door to determine if she could hear any sign of Sterling's presence. She reminded herself that the fact that she could not did not mean he was not in his bed but rather that the door was exceptionally sound. She unlocked the door to his room but even as she started to turn the handle, resisted the urge to see for herself if he had returned or not. If he hadn't, she wasn't entirely sure that she wanted to know.

Her gondola made its way toward the conte's palace, and the beauty of Venice slid by in an ever-changing panorama of places and people but her mind was anywhere but there. Her restless night had taken a toll. She slept far later than she had planned. When she had finally awakened and dressed for her luncheon with the conte, she had knocked on Sterling's door, again to no response. A passing maid said his lordship was not in his rooms, but she did not say if he had slept there, and Olivia did not ask.

Jealousy was certainly not a virtue; but in this case, nor was it a vice. If only because it made her realize what she wanted. She wanted her inheritance, she wanted her independence and the freedom to choose how she would live her life, and she wanted

Sterling. It was as simple as that, and she should have realized it sooner.

The conte's secretary greeted her and escorted her into the palace. He left her in a parlor smaller than the one she had seen last night but just as exquisite, with gilded, painted ceilings, an ornate fireplace, and tall doors thrown open to the terrace beyond. A fanciful glass chandelier of the kind she had seen only in Venice sparkled overhead. A chaise and two chairs in the rococo style graced one side of the room. In the center, a table was set for luncheon for two. Off to one side, an easel stood supporting a painting. The Titian no doubt.

She moved closer to study the work. She knew far less about art than Sterling apparently did, but this scene of battle was obviously the work of a master.

"It is amazing to me that the colors remain vivid even after nearly four hundred years." The conte stepped up behind her. "Bellini —"

"Giovanni?"

He chuckled. "Yes, Giovanni, was one of the first to recognize the depth and potential of oil instead of tempera, but Titian took his techniques to new heights."

"It's magnificent," she said with a smile, and turned toward the conte.

"Indeed it is." He moved to the table, poured a glass of wine, and handed it to her. "But its magnificence pales in your presence."

She arched a brow and accepted the glass. "Last night it was your palazzo that paled in comparison."

"Ah, you have caught me." He grinned. "I am less original than I am sincere."

She took a sip and nodded at the table. "You did not expect the earl to join us?"

"I had but hoped." He poured a glass for himself. "The table was set for three, but when my majordomo saw you arrive unaccompanied, the earl's place was removed. Has that eased your mind as to the honorable nature of my intentions?"

She grinned. "Not at all."

"Excellent." He sipped his wine. "I shall have to send your earl a note of gratitude."

"For being so rude as to fail to appear?"

"For being so kind as to allow me to have you all to myself."

"I should tell you, the earl was unaware of your invitation." She shrugged. "We seem to have missed each other this morning."

"And for that I am eternally grateful." He studied her for a moment. Whereas last night his perusal was amusing, today it was disconcerting. As if he were assessing her fitness for his bed and how best to get her there. "Perhaps you would like to eat first?"

"First?"

"Before you tell me the story."

She shook her head. "I'm afraid I don't understand."

"The story of why you want my Titian." He pulled out a chair. "Please, sit."

"Thank you," she said with a touch of relief. She had obviously misjudged him. She sat down, and he joined her. A moment later, a servant appeared with the first course.

"Tell me, Lady Rathbourne," the conte began. "What of my beautiful city do you wish to see?"

She thought for a moment. "Very nearly everything I think."

"Then you shall have to stay indefinitely," he said, with a smile. "Might I suggest you begin with a visit to San Marco . . ."

The conte's recommendations of what she must not miss in Venice were accompanied by a casual lesson in history and included any number of fascinating and amusing stories about natives and visitors alike. Galileo, Lord Byron, and Casanova had all at one time graced the cobbled streets of La Serenissima. The conte was as charming by day as he had been by night. Between the excellent food, the stimulating conversation, and far more wine than was probably wise, by the end of the meal Olivia was hard-pressed to keep her wits about her and was just a touch light-headed.

"Now, my dear." The conte leaned back in his chair, steepled his fingers, and considered her. "Tell me why you want my Titian. I suspect from your words last night, it is not to honor your husband's memory."

"No, it's not." She drew a deep breath. "In order to inherit what is rightfully mine, my late husband's will decrees that I complete three of his unfinished collections. One is the Titian copies of Bellini's lost histories of Venice. As the only known copies are yours and his, if I acquire yours, that particular collection will be considered complete."

"I see," he said thoughtfully. "I was right then. Your husband was not a nice man to have set you such a course."

"No."

"And if you do not complete these collections of his?"

"My life will continue as it did before his death," she said simply.

He narrowed his eyes. "And it was not a good life?"

She met his gaze directly. "No."

"Then you wish to purchase the painting?"

"I can, of course, if that's what you prefer." She rested her arms on the table, folded her hands together, and leaned toward him. "But I had something else in mind I think you might appreciate more than mere monetary compensation."

"Aside from the eternal gratitude of a beautiful woman?" A slow, knowing smile curved his lips. Dimly she noted something brushed against her foot under the table, so faintly she wasn't sure she felt anything at all. "I can think of any number of things I might appreciate more."

She shifted her foot away and returned his smile. "I have a proposition for you, conte."

"Pietro." He reached for her hand and brought it to his lips. "My name is Pietro. Say it."

She stared at him. "Pietro?"

"Ah, I knew it. It falls from your lips like the blossoms in the breeze."

She stared at him and again something brushed her foot. What on earth . . .

"And you, *cara mia?*" He turned her hand over and kissed her palm in a most *Italian* manner. "You are Olivia. Like the fruit. A gift from the gods."

371

"Oh," she said faintly.

His lips had progressed to her wrist. "They are most generous gods."

Gods or not, where did the man think he was going? And, good Lord, was that his foot nudging hers? She moved her foot and tugged at her hand. He stood and pulled her into his arms.

"Conte!" If she'd had less wine, she might have been a bit more indignant. As it was, he was, well, amusing. "Do you know how . . . expected this is?"

He paused. "What do you mean?"

"My dear Pietro, every Englishwoman in every novel I have ever read has been seduced by an Italian if she so much as dared to step foot in the country. I would have been quite shocked if you hadn't attempted it."

He flashed her a wicked grin. "And disappointed?"

"No. Insulted." She laughed. "Now unhand me."

"But you have a proposition for me."

"I do indeed. If you would release me."

He gazed into her eyes in a manner he no doubt thought was quite effective. "Perhaps I shall have to counter your proposition with one of my own."

"Perhaps. Now." Her voice hardened, and

she meet his gaze with an unflinching eye. "Unhand me."

He paused for a moment. "If you are certain."

"I am certain."

"But if you wish the painting . . ." The comment remained unfinished, but then there was no need to finish it.

"Then I should allow you to seduce me?" He smiled.

"Come now, Pietro." She cast him a chastising look. "I am not so foolish as to think simply because I join you in your bed you will give me a work of art that has been in your family for generations."

His eyes narrowed. "No?"

"Of course not."

"Excellent." He pulled her tighter against him. "Then you will not be disappointed."

"I shall not be anything." She pushed against him. "But I must say I am quite disappointed by your obvious dishonorable intentions."

"My intentions?" He bent his head to nibble on her neck. "And what are my intentions?"

"Yes, Pietro, what are your intentions?" a feminine voice asked from the doorway.

Pietro froze, and Olivia took the opportunity to break free of his embrace.

Sterling stood in the open doors to the terrace looking something less than amused. At his side was the dark-haired beauty who had obviously just spoken. The very same woman he had left the gala with last night. And had perhaps returned to later in the night?

Olivia drew her brows together and glared. "Who are you?"

The lady raised a patrician brow as if she couldn't believe the question. "You ask who am I? You? Who are you to ask such a thing? Who am I? Hah! Who are you?"

"Allow me to present Viscountess Rathbourne," Sterling said in a wry tone.

"I knew that." Sterling's companion huffed and turned her attention to the conte. "And you. You did not answer my question."

"Question?" The conte shrugged in an innocent manner. "What question, *amore mio?*"

The dark-haired woman narrowed her eyes in a menacing manner. "Your intentions, Pietro?"

"My intentions?" He gasped as if shocked by the implication in her tone. "My intentions were most honorable. It was she." He aimed an accusing finger at Olivia. "She wished to proposition me."

"I most certainly did not!" Olivia huffed. "I do have a proposition for him. But not the sort of proposition he is implying, and he well knows it."

"Hah! The man is a pig," the lady said with a toss of her head.

"I believe you're right." Olivia glared at the conte. "He is a pig."

"Olivia, may I present the pig's wife." Sterling moved to Olivia's side. "This is the Contessa de Sarafini."

Olivia winced. "Oh dear, I am sorry."

"That I am married to a pig?" the contessa shrugged. "One gets used to such things."

"I am not a pig." Indignation sounded in the conte's voice. "I am . . . a man. And perhaps weak. And look at her." He waved at Olivia. "She is lovely."

Maiale! The contessa fairly spit the word.

"Alessandra," the conte began.

Maiale! She crossed the room to her husband, spewing Italian and gestures all the while.

Sterling pulled Olivia off to one side of the room, which scarcely mattered, as the conte and his wife no longer seemed to notice they were there. Indeed, they had lapsed into Italian with ever louder voices and ever more dramatic gestures.

375

"I have no idea what they're saying," Olivia murmured.

Sterling snorted.

"Well, yes, of course I have a general idea." He sighed. "She continues to call him a pig, a stupid pig I believe, and he insists it's all your fault."

"How dare he! He is a pig." She paused. "You speak Italian?"

"Not enough to be really useful although I am fairly fluent in Latin." He furrowed his brow and studied her. "Olivia, are you inebriated?"

"No." She hesitated, then shook her head. "No, not at all." She raised her chin. "Although that was obviously the conte's plan. And where have you been?"

"The contessa invited me to see her gardens, and we had an errand to do first. But more to the point, why did you come here alone? Why didn't you wait for me?"

"I had no idea where you were, and I did not want to keep the conte waiting." She huffed. "And where were you last night? Were you seeing her gardens last night as well?"

"Are you jealous?" He stifled a smile.

"Not at all. You needn't look so smug. I am simply . . ." She groped for a word. "Curious. And you haven't answered my question."

"Because it doesn't deserve an answer. However, I didn't see the contessa after we left here last night until I met her today. And might I point out my assessment of the conte's character was accurate."

"You said he reminded you of your brother."

"And wasn't I right?"

"You don't always need to come to my rescue, you know." She sniffed. "I was perfectly capable of taking care of myself."

"Yes, that was apparent when we came in."

She ignored him. "You still haven't said where you were last night."

"I was meeting with Josiah."

"Without me?" She raised a brow. "About what?"

"Lady Rathbourne," the contessa interrupted. "What is your proposition?"

Olivia glanced at Sterling.

"Yes, my dear," Sterling said in an idle manner, "what is your proposition?"

"Well . . ." She drew a deep breath. "If you give me your Titian, when I am successful and have undisputed ownership of my late husband's collections, I shall not only return your painting to you, but I shall give you mine as well."

Sterling smiled.

The contessa eyed her suspiciously. "Why would you do such a thing?"

"Save for their role in gaining my inheritance . . ." Olivia shrugged. "The paintings mean nothing to me."

The conte muttered something in Italian she couldn't quite hear and thought it was probably for the best.

"It is an interesting suggestion." The contessa thought for a moment. "And if you are not successful?"

"Your painting will be returned to you at once. However . . ." Resolve sounded in Olivia's voice. "I do not intend to fail."

The contessa studied her closely. "Both works are beyond price."

"Not to me." She shook her head. "My late husband's collections are all considered extremely valuable. But when they are mine, I plan to donate them to museums or sell them and give the proceeds to charitable endeavors."

The contessa's brow rose. "You hated him that much?"

Olivia met her gaze directly. "Yes."

The contessa stared at her for a long moment, then a slow smile spread across her face. "I like you very much. You remind me of . . . me." She nodded once. "The painting is yours."

The conte gasped. "Have you lost your mind? What are you thinking? To give our heritage to an Englishwoman is bad enough, but to give it to an Englishwomen we do not know is —"

"Precisely why I arranged to meet the contessa a short time ago at the home of the British ambassador," Sterling said smoothly.

The contessa cast him an admiring glance. "He knew regardless of what arrangements might be made about the painting, we would need assurances that you and he were who you said you were." The contessa's gaze slid over Sterling as if she were assessing more than his identity. "He is very clever, no?"

The conte groaned.

"Apparently," Olivia said under her breath. So that was what he had been up to. She could scarcely fault him for thinking of a point that had completely escaped her. Still, she would have appreciated it far more if he had informed her. Although it was indeed very clever of him. She smiled at him. A smile she meant to be only one of gratitude.

His gaze meshed with hers, and her breath caught at the look in his eyes, deep and warm and forever.

Here was a man one could depend on. A man one could trust. With one's heart, with one's future.

"I shall have the painting wrapped and delivered to your hotel by the end of the day."

Olivia jerked her attention back to the contessa.

"There is one stipulation. My late husband wanted these collections to bear his name."

The contessa raised a brow. "A brass plaque perhaps, very small, very discreet? Is that acceptable?"

"More than acceptable," Olivia said with relief.

"But we have not given this due consideration," the conte protested.

"The second Titian returns to its home," the contessa said firmly. "That alone is sufficient reason to accept this proposal."

The conte huffed and crossed his arms over his chest. "Very well then, but this plaque should bear the name de Sarafini as well."

Olivia nodded. "I see no objection to that."

"Very good." The contessa smiled with satisfaction. "Then all is well for everyone. The earl has told me about Lady Rathbourne's quest. I find it remarkable and courageous. It is not easy for a woman in

380

this world to undertake such a challenge. Far easier to accept one's fate than to attempt to change it." She favored Olivia with a look of admiration and perhaps envy.

Olivia stared. "You have my eternal gratitude, contessa."

The conte snorted.

"Alessandra. And I have no doubt you will return the favor one day." The contessa smiled, and at once Olivia realized she might have made a friend. "There is one thing I ask."

"Anything."

"When it is time to bring to me both of my Titians, bring this Wyldewood as well." She leaned close and spoke low into Olivia's ear. "Perhaps by then you will be his mistress, yes?"

"Oh I don't . . ." Olivia paused then grinned. "Perhaps."

"Do not be a fool. He is rare, this one. And he wants you. You have his heart, I think."

"Do you?"

Alessandra nodded. "It is obvious to me even if not to you."

"Thank you." Olivia smiled. "And again you have my thanks for the painting."

"It is nothing. We are two alike, you and

I." She smiled. "Pietro is not my first husband."

Sterling cleared his throat. "We should be getting back to the hotel."

They said their farewells; the conte again kissed her hand. Even in the presence of his wife, there was a definite reluctance in his manner to let Olivia go. Sterling was again distant and thoughtful on the ride back to the hotel. He was obviously annoyed with her. At the door to his room, he opened it and waved her inside, stopping to pick up a note that had been slid under the door.

She swept past him. "If you are going to chastise me —"

"I have no intention of chastising you." He snapped the door closed behind him, unfolded the note, and read it. He rang for a porter, then strode to the desk, and quickly penned a response.

"You're not?"

"No." He folded the note. "I have no intention of chastising you for going to see the conte alone although I do think it was foolish."

She drew a deep breath. "Perhaps."

"Nor do I intend to chastise you for drinking too much wine. Although that too was foolish."

She squared her shoulders. "I am not inebriated."

"No, I can see that. But you admit you had more wine than was wise?"

"It was very good wine," she said under her breath.

"Nor am I going to chastise you for not telling me your plan." He paused. "I thought it was brilliant."

She bit back a pleased smile. "Did you?"

"I did indeed. But then for the most part, I have never questioned your intelligence." A knock sounded. He opened the door, stepped into the hall, and returned without the note.

"What was that?"

"A note to Josiah. The earliest ship does not depart until morning. I instructed him to book us passage."

She raised a brow. "I thought we were going to explore the city. Trust to the wind."

"That particular wind no longer blows."

She shook her head. "I don't understand."

"I shall explain later. Now, you and I have a discussion that is long overdue."

She swallowed hard. "Do we?"

"Yes, we do." He moved closer.

"About . . ."

"Everything. The past. As well as the future."

She stared up at him. "Oh?"

"First, as flattered as I am" — he pulled her into his arms — "I am no longer on your list."

TWENTY

Olivia scoffed. "You can't do that. It is not your list. You can't take yourself off."

"Nonetheless, I am." He stared into her eyes. She was in his arms exactly where she belonged. And where he planned to keep her for the rest of her days. But it would not be easy. "I refuse to be nothing more than an item to be scratched off." His lips met hers in a kiss hard and long and lingering. Until her body relaxed against his, and she met his passion with her own. At last he raised his head. "I had thought to allow you to cross me off your list only after I had married you, but I am an impatient man. And you are all that I want. All I have ever wanted."

"Very well," she said in a breathless voice.

He narrowed his gaze. "Very well what?"

"Very well, you are off my list."

"No argument?"

"No." The word was scarcely more than a

sigh. She reached up to press her lips to his, and he struggled to keep his wits about him. He drew his lips from hers and kissed a spot right below her ear. "What about marriage?"

"No." She sighed. "I will not marry a man because he feels an obligation to me."

"Obligation is not what I'm feeling." He let his lips drift down her neck.

She shivered. "I thought you wished to talk."

"We'll talk later," he murmured against her skin.

She tilted her head back and closed her eyes. "Are you seducing me?"

"I am trying."

She stilled and opened her eyes, her gaze caught his. "You should know I have not done this for a very long time."

"You needn't say —"

"No, I do." She grimaced. "I have not been with a man for more than nine years. My late husband —"

"Was a vile creature and a fool."

"No, that's not . . ." She shook her head and gently pushed out of his arms. "You should know . . ."

"There is nothing I need to know."

"Yes, you do." Apprehension flashed in her eyes.

"Livy." He reached out and took her

hands. "You can tell me anything."

She stared at him for a long moment, then nodded. "I am the one who has avoided talking about the past. It's time that I did."

"It's not —"

She ignored him, and continued. "I tried to escape marriage by telling him I was not . . . that is I had been . . ."

"With me." He nodded, ignoring a fresh wave of remorse. "Go on."

A myriad of emotions washed across her face. "The night you and I were together, so long ago now it feels like a dream, it was quite wonderful. With him . . ." She pulled her gaze from his, looking anywhere in the room but at him. "I did not want to be in his bed, and that was of no concern to him. I fought him at first. I fought him for a long time. He . . ."

He squeezed her hands. "You don't have to —"

"But I do. I have never told anyone." She paused as if searching for the right words. "He liked that I did not want him. He liked that I fought against him. He liked that he could use me as he wished. That he could take what he wanted. Because I was his possession as much as any of his artifacts." She met his gaze. "I learned that resistance was futile. That he enjoyed . . ."

"Livy."

"That, for him, causing me pain went hand in hand with his physical pleasure. If I did not protest, and he did not force me or beat me, he did not want the rest. So . . ." She closed her eyes as if praying for strength. ". . . I surrendered. I stopped fighting him. And he soon lost interest. I regret that, surrendering that is. I should have been stronger. But . . ." She raised her chin. "He is dead, and I have never been so alive."

She blew a long breath. "I want to be with you, Sterling. I want to be in your bed, and I want everything that means, but . . ."

He shook his head. "Therefore we shall wait."

"No." Her eyes widened and she pushed him backward. "Are you insane? I thought you wanted this. Wanted me."

"I do."

"Do you want to wait?" She pushed him back through the archway between the sitting room and the bedchamber.

"No," he said slowly, "but —"

"I have no desire to wait. We have waited far too long already." She stepped closer and pushed him again until he felt the bed behind his knees. "I want to feel again what I only dimly remember feeling. How it was to lie naked in your arms. With your body warm against mine and your heart beating in rhythm with my own." She threw her arms around him, and he lost his balance. Together, they tumbled backward onto the bed, and she kissed him without reservation. "I want everything you want. And I have wanted it for a very long time."

"Livy." He moaned and wrapped his arms around her, pulling her tighter against him. He would make it up to her. He would make it all up to her every day for the rest of her life.

Her mouth opened to his, and he drank of her, reveling in her taste. Of wine and what they had once and the promise of what they now had again.

She tore at his clothes and he struggled with hers and all the while their hands were on each other. He could not touch her enough, and she responded in kind. His mind fogged with lust and desire and love. Their movements grew more and more frantic, more and more desperate. He fumbled with the closures of her gown, and she tugged at his coat and pushed it off his shoulders. Her dress slid down around her waist and she wiggled out of it and kicked it aside. His lips met her lips, her neck, her shoulders. She pulled his cravat from his neck, and he drew his shirt over his head and tossed it away. He trailed kisses over her shoulders and lower to the swell of her breasts, revealed above her corset. He loosened her stays with fingers clumsy with need and pulled free her corset. She groped at the buttons of his trousers, and her hands slipped beneath the fabric to caress his naked flesh. He wasn't sure how it happened, but abruptly it seemed their clothes were scattered on the bed and the floor. And she lay naked beside him.

For a moment, he could do nothing but savor the look of her, her fair hair and warm skin colored in shades of peach and pink. Her breasts were full and firm, her hips shapely, her stomach softly rounded.

"Sterling." She reached out to him. "This is not a fear I have yet to face."

"Excellent," he murmured, and pulled her close, nuzzling that delightful spot where neck met shoulder. His hands roamed over her, lightly skimming along the side of her body, then sliding to the small of her back, gathering her close to press against him. Her breasts crushed against his chest. Her skin was exquisite, warm, and like fine silk beneath his fingers. His hand cupped her derriere, caressing and molding. He told himself to slow, to savor every intoxicating moment, to think of her pleasure, but she would have none of it and demanded more.

He cupped her breast and took the nipple gently between his teeth and flicked his tongue over the hard tip. She gasped and arched toward him. He toyed and teased and shifted his attention to her other breast, his fingers tracing light circles on her stomach and drifting lower to slip between her legs. She was slick with desire, and he slid his fingers between the soft folds of flesh and stroked her. She writhed beneath his touch, her hands grasping his shoulders.

He drew back and watched her face. Watched cautious enthusiasm melt to rapture. She was lost in the sensations he provoked, and he was lost in unbridled need.

He shifted to position himself between her legs, then guided himself slowly into her. She was tight and hot and wet with wanting him, and he slid into her with a moan of sheer pleasure. He stroked slowly, trying to resist the aching need for release at once tightening within him. She wrapped her legs around him, urging him on, deeper and faster.

He withdrew a bare fraction at a time until only the head of his cock touched her, then thrust hard into her. Her muscles tightened around him, and he throbbed within her.

Her moans surrounded him and mingled with his own. He pulled back and thrust again. She rocked her hips against his, matched his thrusts with hers, his passion with her own. Over and over he drove into her. Over and over she pulled him deeper. He lost himself in the exquisite feel of her, the pleasure of the joining of their flesh, the joy of the meshing of their souls. Until he could no longer fight the release that threatened to tear him part.

He slipped his hand between them and stroked her until he felt her tense around him. Her body shuddered against his. She called out his name and arched upward, her nails digging into this shoulders. And his own release exploded within him. His body jerked with spasm after spasm of sheer pleasure. He groaned and thrust again, then once more, his seed filling her, claiming her. Until at last he collapsed against her, savoring the feel of him inside her, of her body pressed to his. Joined. One. For now and for always.

They lay together entwined in each other's arms, her heart beating in tandem with his. Her breath was labored, and he struggled to catch his own. He stroked her hair and felt her sigh against him. A sigh of contentment and satisfaction and, surely, of love.

"Oh my." She giggled against him, the delightful girlish sound he had never forgotten tugged at his heart. He grinned although he felt rather like giggling himself.

" 'Oh my' indeed," he murmured.

She raised her head and stared into his eyes, her green eyes dark with passion. "Was that, well, normal?"

He laughed. " 'Normal'?"

"I mean is . . ." Her brows drew together. "Well, is that supposed to happen? That rush of . . . oh my. It's not odd or unusual?"

"Did you find it odd or unusual?"

"I found it extraordinary." She grinned in amazement. "Really quite . . . extraordinary. And wonderful."

He tightened his arm around her. "It happens when a man is as concerned with your pleasure as he is with own."

"I see. I had no idea . . . well, then you have my thanks."

"The pleasure" — he kissed the tip of her nose — "was mine."

She giggled again and curled against him. "Not entirely."

They lay together, spent, for a few moments more. The late-afternoon sun poured into the room, turning her fair hair to gold and gilding her skin. The woman fairly glowed, which Sterling decided was not at all attributable to the Venetian light that poets and artists praised but rather the spirit and the beauty of the woman herself. And she was his.

"Now." He kissed her lips, her nose, her forehead. "You shall have to marry me."

She laughed. "Don't be absurd."

"I'm not being the least bit absurd. You have ruined me, and now you have to marry me."

"I ruined you long ago."

"And now it's time to pay the piper."

"I have no intention of marrying again."

"And I intend to change your mind."

"Furthermore, I would never marry anyone who considers doing so an obligation."

"Neither would I." He grabbed her hand and pulled it to his lips.

"I will not marry because I have no other choice," she warned. "To save myself from genteel poverty."

He kissed her palm. "Josiah will be so disappointed."

"Therefore, if I do not win my inheritance, I will not marry."

"I knew that." He smiled into her eyes. "Which is why I will do whatever is required to help you succeed. Besides, it's always wise to marry a woman with money."

She laughed. "Or a man."

"It was the question of money, you know," he said slowly, "that should have made me realize your father was lying."

"Oh?"

"He said that you had decided to marry Rathbourne because his fortune was greater than mine." He smiled. "You were never especially concerned with wealth."

"Because I was never without it." She fell silent for a long moment. "When I sent you the first letter, the day after my father talked to you, before my marriage, I didn't know the lengths my late husband would go to, to keep me. He didn't know about the first letter, or the others, but he threatened to have you killed if I refused to marry him. If I so much as spoke to you. And I knew he would."

His breath caught. "You married him to save me?"

"It isn't as noble as it sounds. I didn't see another choice." She shrugged. "Your safety was the most important reason, but there was also my father to consider." Her expression hardened. "Although, if I had not feared for your life, I would have thrown him to the wolves. I was confident you and I could weather any scandal." She sat up, pulled up her knees, and wrapped her arms around her legs, resting her chin on her knees. "You should know it all now, I suppose."

He rolled onto his side and propped his head in his hand. "Know what?"

"The reason my father made me marry. Why he traded my life for his."

He studied her but didn't say a word.

"As perverse as my late husband's likes were . . ." She glanced at him. "Men are allowed to beat their wives, you know."

He nodded. "I find it appalling. A man who would hurt anyone weaker than he because he is allowed to do so is no man at all."

She cast him an absent smile, then turned her gaze toward the far wall and the past. "My father knew if his secret was made public, his life would be ruined. And mine as well, but I doubt that was a concern." She paused to choose her words. "As I said, while the viscount's preferences were unpleasant they were within his rights in regards to the law. My father . . ." She hesitated as if summoning her courage. "My father's tastes did not run to women. He preferred men. Young men."

"Good God!"

She shook her head. "I had no idea. The viscount took great pleasure in explaining to me in explicit detail my father's perversions."

"I am so sorry." He sat up and pulled her into his arms. "You're right though, we could have survived the scandal together."

"It scarcely matters now." She snuggled against him. "The threat to you and him is gone. And with any luck at all, I will soon have beaten my late husband at his own game."

"Damnation." He winced. "I had nearly forgotten although there is nothing we can do until morning."

She pulled away and looked at him. "What now?"

"Josiah discovered a clause in the will that had somehow been overlooked."

"A clause?" she said cautiously.

"Rather a nasty one too." He blew a long breath. "If you attempt to complete the collections before a suitable period of mourning, Josiah and I interpret that as a year, then your time to gather the articles needed is limited."

Her brows drew together. "How limited?"

"To the length of time from Rathbourne's death to your acquisition of the first item."

Her eyes widened. "Then that would be . . ."

"A total of thirty-six days. It has been

seven since we left Egypt and will take —"

"Twenty-eight days." She stared in disbelief. "Twenty-eight days?"

"By our estimate." He nodded. "But that includes time for travel. Given that it will probably take six days, we will have approximately twenty-two days once we arrive in England."

"We must to return to London at once." She started to leave the bed, but he grabbed her and pulled her back.

"We cannot leave until morning."

"Still, I need to get my things together." She shook off his hand, grabbed the coverlet, and wrapped it around her, then got to her feet. "Beyond that, we have assumed the final object is to be found in London. What if it's not? What if we have to cross another ocean to find it?" A touch of panic sounded in her voice. "What if —"

"What if we have as little difficulty acquiring the last item as we've had with the first two?"

She stared at him. "We cannot depend on that. My late husband was a very clever man, but he never anticipated that I would turn to you, or anyone, for help. If not for the fact that Sir Lawrence knew your parents, and the contessa understood my circumstances, we never would have succeeded. Indeed, I could never have come this far alone." She shook her head. "And we are certain the last item will be the most difficult to obtain."

"No doubt." He glanced around for his dressing gown, located it at the foot of the bed amidst their discarded clothes, and pulled it on as he climbed out of bed. "But he underestimated you as well."

"What if —"

"That's enough. 'What if' is a game we cannot afford to play."

She pressed her hand to her forehead. "You're probably right."

"There's nothing you can do now, and we are leaving in the morning." He smiled in his wickedest manner. "So I propose we put the time between now and then to good use."

She cast him a reluctant smile. "You are insatiable, aren't you?"

"We have a lot of time to make up for."

"And we shall have that time when this is at an end. But if we are leaving in the morning, I need to get my things together."

She bent to pick up some article of clothing, and the coverlet slipped to reveal her shapely derrière. He caught his breath, grabbed her waist with both hands, and stared at the small of her back. He had been too busy to notice before. His stomach turned.

She glanced at him over her shoulder. "What are you doing?"

He drew a deep breath. "Did you know you have scars across the small of your back?"

"No." Her voice was cool. "But I am not surprised. He took great pains not to mark any part of me that might be on public display."

"And I am to blame." Even when she'd spoken of the relations she'd had with Rathbourne, he had not imagined it to have been this bad. Guilt and regret washed through him. He pulled her close, her back pressed against his chest, and wrapped his arms around her. "I am so sorry. I didn't realize how bad . . ."

"You didn't?"

He shook his head. "No."

She chose her words with care. "But in my letters, I told you, or at least the implication was clear."

He paused for a long moment then drew a deep breath. "I never opened them."

"What?"

"I didn't open them until the night your house was broken into."

"You didn't look at my letters before then?

You didn't open them for ten years?"

"No." He shook his head. "I was too hurt to read the first. I assumed it was simply more of what your father had said, perhaps a bit kinder but . . ."

She wrenched free of his arms, moved away, then turned toward him. "The first letter, when I told you that I loved you and did not want to marry the viscount. When I told you I was being forced into the marriage. When I begged you —"

"Livy." He stepped toward her.

She backed away, shaking her head, stunned disbelief on her face. "I thought perhaps you were too hurt or too proud to respond. Or that you chose to believe my father over me. Or even that you hadn't received my letter, or you couldn't bear to open it until it was too late. I had a hundred different explanations for your silence. Then I realized it was for the best that you hadn't responded as I feared for your life. But I never imagined . . ." Her voice rose. "You never opened it?"

"No," he said quietly. "To my eternal regret."

"To your regret? *Your regret?*" Shock shone in her eyes. "Oh yes, your life has been quite dreadful these last ten years."

"You know nothing about my life."

401

Abruptly anger swept aside his guilt. "You broke my heart. I believed your father. I had no reason not to. And need I remind you, two days later you were wed? I had no desire to read your letter and absolutely no interest in anything you had to say." He narrowed his eyes. "Tell me, what would you have done if the situation had been reversed? If I were the one who had left you? Would you have read my letter?"

"Yes." She fairly spit the word. "Because I would never, never have believed such a thing until I heard it from your own lips. Because I would have trusted in you. In us."

"You could have found a way to come to me."

"I tried," she snapped. "And perhaps I should have tried harder, but I was watched and kept in my room, and I was afraid. Yes, there, I admit it. I was terrified. And I had no one to turn to except you. And turning to you might have cost your life."

"I am not a child. I can well take care of myself."

"Are you forgetting who we are talking about?" She scoffed. "My late husband was ruthless and cunning. He was found with his throat cut in his own garden. It is not the kind of death that happens to men who do not deserve it. Who do not give as good as they get."

"Still, you could have —"

"And you could have come to me! You could have demanded to hear from me what my father had said. You could have fought for me! Was it pain, Sterling, that kept you away, or was it merely pride?"

He hesitated for no more than a fraction of a second, but it was enough.

She cast him a disgusted look. "And the other letters? When I told you how frightened I was? That I feared for my life and my sanity? That I was a possession and a prisoner? And again I begged you to help me. You never opened those either?"

"They came when my father was ill, and my life was occupied with other matters." Even to his own ears, the excuse sounded feeble.

"Well, I would have hated to have inconvenienced you!" She stared at him. "Weren't you even curious? Didn't you wonder what could be so important that I, the woman you thought had treated you so badly, would write to you?"

"It was a difficult time."

"For both of us." She snatched up her clothes and started for the adjoining door.

"Livy." He stepped closer. "You must understand —"

"Oh, I understand, my lord. I understand a great deal." She paused before the door and glared at him. "I understand that you believed I had broken it off with you for a man with a larger fortune. I understand that you were too proud and hurt to read my first letter and too busy to read the others. I understand —"

"Livy, don't —"

"I understand everything." Her voice shook. "I understand that I never would have accepted that you did not want me until I had heard it from you." She drew a deep breath. "Through all the years, all the pain and fear and loneliness, the one thing I never doubted was what we had felt for one another. That no matter what had happened, the love that we had shared was real and true. Now I understand, for you, it was fleeting and meaningless and not worth fighting for."

"No, it wasn't like that at all." Anger sparred with desperation in his voice. "Never!"

She met his gaze, her expression hard, her voice cold. "It is now." She pulled open the door, stepped through, and closed it firmly behind her. Almost at once he heard the key turn in the lock.

Sterling stared at the closed door to her

room. What had just happened? Things had been going so well. Then he had admitted his failure to read her letters . . .

At once the answer struck him. It wasn't merely the letters that had angered her. These were feelings held in check for a decade, on her side and his. A flood of long-held-back emotion. Theirs was an argument ten years in the making.

She was right, and he knew it. Had known it for a long time. In the back of his mind, he might well have realized it years ago. He never should have taken her father's word for her feelings. He should have fought for her. But he was young and proud and stupid. And hurt. Reasons, perhaps, but inexcusable, nonetheless.

He ran a shaky hand through his hair. It was probably best to have it all out. All the recriminations and reproach. All the anger and the pain. The question was, now that they had faced the past, was there a future left to salvage?

Nothing had changed, at least not for him. But then he had known the full extent of his mistakes. He couldn't fault her for being hurt once again. His only revelation was the discovery of just how bad her life had been. And what she had sacrificed, rightly or wrongly, to save him.

He had asked her to put herself in his place. In hers, wouldn't he have done whatever he thought was necessary to save her life? There wasn't a doubt in his mind.

Still, he was not the same man he had been ten years ago. Not the boy, really, who couldn't see beyond his own heartbreak. He was older and hopefully wiser and the Earl of Wyldewood.

He had twenty-eight days to set things right between them. To prove to her he would never again fail her. Twenty-eight days to ease the pain of a decade and make amends for the past. And make her believe in him again.

And this time, he would fight for what he wanted.

TWENTY-ONE

Watch the sun set from an ancient place.
From the secret list of desires of
Olivia Rathbourne

Olivia leaned her back against the door to Sterling's room and struggled to regain some semblance of control. Her hands shook, and she couldn't quite seem to catch her breath. Her eyes fogged with tears and she angrily swiped them away. It had been years since she'd surrendered to tears. The last time was the moment before she had realized she could depend on no one to save her but herself. And she had vowed she would never cry again.

But then she'd vowed never to let anyone into her heart again either.

She pushed away from the door and crossed the room, noting that the painting, wrapped in paper, had been delivered in her absence. She pulled on her robe, stepped out on the balcony, and braced her hands on the railing. She drew a deep breath and stared out over the lagoon, the setting sun casting a glow of magic on the scene before her. She scarcely noticed.

He hadn't opened her letters. He hadn't trusted her enough to know that she would never betray him. She had long ago accepted that he had abandoned her to her fate. Until today, she had never suspected she still harbored any anger at all, let alone the rage that had swept through her. Why had this upset her so?

Because his revelation brought back the pain she thought she had long put behind her? Because she had allowed herself to think about the possibility of a future with him? Because once again, in spite of her best intentions, she had found herself loving him?

Sterling wasn't the same man he was ten years ago. He had been twenty years old, with his life stretching before him. He hadn't known the pain of losing people he loved, the burden of responsibility, or the duties of his position. Was it fair to continue to hold him accountable for actions that could never be undone? Was it right to hold the mistakes of the boy he was once against the man he had become?

Probably not. She blew a long breath. And, as much as she had never truly stopped loving him, it was the man he was now who held her heart. The man he'd become through the years and in these past weeks. The boy had failed her once, but the man was doing everything he could to help her now. He was strong and steady, and when she gazed into his eyes . . .

But was it enough to heal them both? To heal wounds she hadn't been aware she still had. She didn't know and was abruptly too weary to consider it further. Even she could see that she was in no state to make rational decisions. She needed to think. To sort out her feelings and emotions, her needs and desires and what she truly wanted. Now, however, she had more pressing matters to attend to. This newly discovered stipulation might well spell her defeat. Nonetheless, she — they — were not ready to give up yet. As for Sterling . . .

She shook her head. She still had time. Twenty-eight days until her quest was over one way or the other.

Twenty-eight days to complete the terms of the will. To decide her future, her fate. And this time, the decision was in her hands.

Polite disinterest. That was the term for it.

Sterling leaned on the rail of the ship and gazed unseeing at the water rushing by. Three days out from Venice, and he and Livy had shared little more than a handful of polite words. For the most part, she had stayed in her cabin, which was probably for the best. He had resisted the urge to pound on her door at least a dozen times. Try as he might, he couldn't think of anything he could say to make this right. It was best to leave her be. For now. It might well have been the hardest thing he had ever done.

"Fine day, my lord." Josiah stepped to the railing beside him and rested his forearms on the railing. "Excellent weather for sailing."

Sterling grunted in response. He was in no better mood than Livy apparently was.

"But they say we may be in for a storm."

"That would be a problem," Sterling muttered in a dismissive manner, and immediately regretted it. It wasn't the solicitor's fault that he and Livy weren't the most cordial of traveling companions. Josiah was caught in the middle. It was not a good place to be. He forced a pleasant note into his voice. "Thus far we are making excellent time."

"Indeed, we are." Relief sounded in the young man's voice. "Sir, might I ask you a question?"

"Go on."

"What did you do?"

He slanted the younger man a wry glance. "What? No initial pleasantries to ease into the discussion? No more talk of weather?"

"No, sir." Josiah paused. "I haven't said anything up to now because I didn't think it was my place. But I am a part of this effort, and it's quite obvious that you and Lady Rathbourne have had some sort of falling-out."

Sterling raised a brow. "And you assume I am to blame?"

"Since we left the hotel, in those rare moments when you and she have been together, I have noticed you cannot take your eyes off her." He shrugged. "Whereas she looks anywhere but at you."

"You're very observant."

"Thank you, sir." He paused. "What did you do?"

Sterling blew a long breath. "Nothing recently."

"I see."

"What do you see?"

"In Egypt, you told me that you had once failed and abandoned her."

"And?"

"Obviously your difficulties now stem

from that past situation. Unless I'm wrong?"

"No, you're not wrong."

"However, it seems to me," Josiah said slowly, "you have done more than anyone could expect of you in these past weeks to make up for that long-ago failure."

Sterling studied the younger man. "I do have a plan, you know."

"Excellent." Josiah nodded. "And that involves doing nothing?"

"Exactly."

"It seems to be working well," he said under his breath.

"Of course it's working," Sterling said with more conviction than he felt. "Olivia is a very intelligent and thoughtful woman. I am giving her time to come to her senses. To allow the sea air to refresh her spirits and put things in their proper perspective. Time to realize that no matter how I might have failed her in the past, I will not do so again. Admittedly, it might not appear to be working —"

"As she does seem to be quite pointedly ignoring you."

"These things move at their own pace. It's all part of the plan. Patience is a virtue, my boy." Sterling nodded, wondering whether he was trying to convince Josiah or himself. Still, even as he said the words, they made a certain amount of sense. "Once we arrive in London, she will have to acknowledge my existence if only because she cannot complete the final collection alone. I shall prove to her that, even though she may be angry with me, she can indeed depend upon me."

"I see."

"It would help matters if you said that with a modicum of conviction."

"My apologies, sir, but I really don't see." Josiah's brow furrowed. "Frankly, this plan of yours not to do anything at all seems rather, well, ill thought out."

"I have done nothing but think about it." *And think about her.* "I don't know what else to do at the moment."

"You could insist on speaking with her."

He shook his head. "There's nothing left to say."

"Perhaps a simple apology —"

"I have apologized." Although, now that he thought about it, perhaps he had never really told her how sorry he was. Perhaps he had never really admitted to her what a mistake he'd made. What a proud, foolish idiot he'd been. Was it possible that he had never done something as obvious as apologize?

"Then you have begged her forgiveness?"

"Of course." But he hadn't, not really.

"My older brothers, in situations such as this, would say a certain amount of groveling is in order."

"I do not grovel." Sterling sniffed. Still, he would crawl on his hands and knees if it came to that. Which was, no doubt, the very definition of groveling.

"Perhaps this particular situation calls for a certain amount of groveling." Josiah paused. "I care for her a lot, you know."

Sterling raised a brow. "I hope you don't think our estrangement will increase your chances."

Josiah shook his head. "I have lost her. Or rather, lost any chance with her if I ever had one. I know that. Regardless, I would not want to see her unhappy." He sighed. "And I think her happiness lies with you. Therefore" — he straightened his shoulders as if accepting the inevitable — "I shall assist you by whatever means necessary."

Sterling smiled. "Your offer is most appreciated, and I shall certainly call on you if need be. I think her happiness lies with me too. I know mine lies with her." Sterling directed his gaze back toward the water. "Now, I just have to make her realize it as well."

This was absurd.

During their last two voyages, Olivia had discovered just how much she loved being on the water. And she was not about to spend one more day alone in her cabin. If she ran into Sterling, so be it. She would be polite but distant. Pleasant but not especially friendly.

She left her cabin and made her way to the deck. Sterling was nowhere in sight. She breathed a sigh of relief and ignored the tiniest twinge of disappointment. As long as she could avoid him, she could avoid everything. The past as well as the future. And she certainly could not make rational decisions when every time she looked at him, she ached to be in his arms.

She leaned against the railing and gazed out at the sea. She simply didn't know what to do. The words they'd exchanged had made her think long and hard. Not merely about the past or how much they had both changed but about what she truly wanted now. Wanting the life she had once planned with Sterling seemed somehow a betrayal of what she had wanted for the last ten years. A betrayal of herself. Was she truly ready to go from being the possession of one man to being the possession of another? Not that Sterling was anything like her late husband. Still, regardless of the man in question, a wife in this world was little more than property. And hadn't she spent the last decade longing for freedom and independence? For control of her own life?

"I wondered if you were going to make an appearance again." Josiah joined her at the railing. "Or stay in your cabin for the duration of the voyage."

"If I didn't know better, I'd think you were lying in wait for me."

The young man chuckled. "I was." He paused, no doubt to gather his courage, then plunged ahead. "Are you still angry at Lord Wyldewood?"

"Are you hoping that might further your position?" She cast him a teasing smile to take any sting out of the words.

"Oh, no, absolutely not. I would never," he said staunchly. "Indeed, I have already conceded to Lord Wyldewood that I have lost our wager." His eyes widened in horror.

She arched a brow. "And what wager is that?"

"Nothing really," he said quickly. "It's of no significance. I shouldn't have mentioned it. I . . ." Sheer remorse colored his face.

"But as you have mentioned it."

"Um, well, I don't . . . that is . . ." The poor boy looked miserable.

"Go on."

"It was a wager as to who would win your hand." He winced.

"How interesting." She studied him curiously. "And you have conceded defeat?"

He nodded.

"Why?"

"Because it is obvious to me, even if not to you, that he has your heart."

"I see."

He considered her in a cautious manner. "You're not angry?"

"I should be, I suppose. To have been the subject of a wager like a piece of property."

"No, it wasn't like that at all! It was more . . ." He shrugged helplessly.

"It seems to me . . ." She chose her word with care. "Any woman who has two dashing men hoping to win her favor should be flattered rather than angry. After all, I was not the prize. The loser was not to hand me over to the winner. Was he?"

"No, no, it was nothing like that." He shook his head. "If you agreed to marry me, he was going to employ my firm to ensure me a better income." He glanced at her. "To better support you."

"How very generous of him," she murmured. "And if he won my hand?"

"Then he would offer me a position on

my own, perhaps help me establish my own firm."

She considered him thoughtfully. Regardless of whether Sterling won or lost, the arrangements were such that Josiah, and she, would be better off. It was . . . quite wonderful of him.

"He's a very generous man," Josiah said.

"And far too clever not to employ someone with your skills and intelligence."

"And I shall need employment." He blew a long breath. "I fully intend to resign my position when your estate is settled."

Surprise widened her eyes. "Do you?"

"Yes, I do. You should have been told about the stipulations regarding time before you decided to accept the viscount's challenge."

"As I recall, I asked Mr. Hollis about time constraints and was told there were none." Her tone hardened. She should have strangled the man when the thought first occurred to her. "He lied to me."

"I would prefer to think that, as he never expected you to take up this challenge at all, let alone so quickly, you took him unawares and the time clause slipped his mind." He blew a long breath. "But, in truth, I don't know, and it scarcely matters whether the omission was a mistake or deliberate. That you were not informed might well cost you everything. I cannot work for employers who are less than honorable. For men I cannot respect." He shook his head. "I could not respect myself if I did."

"You are a good man, Josiah Cadwallender. And I am honored to count you among my few friends." She took his hand and adopted a teasing tone. "So you have given up? On me that is?"

His expression brightened. "Not if there's hope?"

She favored him with an affectionate smile and withdrew her hand. "I'm afraid not."

"And you are not angry about the wager?"

"No."

"Then you should know, I have offered to help Lord Wyldewood in any manner he may need in his effort to win your hand."

She laughed. "He is a lucky man to have earned your loyalty."

"Are you still angry with him?"

She hesitated, then shook her head. "No."

"Yet you continue to avoid him."

"We still have the final collection left to complete. I think we should concentrate our thoughts on that rather than questions of a more personal nature. Avoiding him seems best at the moment." She shrugged. "Until all is resolved, and I know my own mind."

He smiled. "I thought you already did."

"Then I present a façade that is something less than accurate." She shook her head. "There is much for me to consider. My life, the future."

"As well as what you truly want." He was silent for a long moment. "And, I suppose, what you are willing to sacrifice to get it."

TWENTY-TWO

Breathe.
From the secret list of desires of
Olivia Rathbourne

The moment Olivia stepped over the threshold, into the house that had never been her home, her throat tightened.

It was not that she had forgotten how dark and oppressive it was. How even the bright late-afternoon sun scarcely penetrated the gloom. How the walls seemed to close in around her. Indeed, she hadn't given the house a second thought since she walked out and headed toward Egypt. She'd hated this house — this prison — from the first moment she'd entered it. If she was not successful, she would be in it for the rest of her days. Dependent on a minimal allowance, her finances controlled by her late husband's solicitors, unable to live. Unable to breathe.

She swayed slightly on her feet, and

Sterling grabbed her arm to steady her.

Concern creased his forehead. "Are you all right?"

"Yes, I think so." She cast him a grateful smile.

Somewhere between Italy and England, they had come to an unspoken understanding, a truce of sorts, about what could be discussed and what could not. They had managed to resume the companionship they'd had before the past had exploded between them. Still, it was Great-aunt Wilomena's portrait once again. Even when not looked at directly, it was always there. "I just . . . for a moment." She shuddered. "I have never liked this house."

Giddings and the rest of her staff assembled in the entry hall to greet them. He stepped forward. "Lady Rathbourne, I trust your journey was successful."

"Very much so." She had felt it necessary to explain to Giddings why she was going off with Sterling. After all, she hadn't wanted to shock a new butler with unexplained improper behavior. No doubt by now, the rest of the staff knew as well, and the story had probably spread to the servants of other houses and from them to their employers. She would be surprised if most of London didn't know about the quest her late husband had sent her on. Not that it mattered. She had no concern over what people might say about her behavior, and she didn't mind being considered eccentric. She had every intention of behaving precisely as she wished. She had earned the right to do so.

"Then all is well?" Giddings asked, a cautious note of optimism in his voice.

"Not yet, but it will be," she said firmly.

Giddings gestured to a footman, Terrance, or perhaps Joseph, she couldn't recall, to take her bags; but the moment the servant picked up her things the walls closed in on her again.

"No. Wait." She shook her head. "I can't stay here." She pulled a deep breath. "I shall go to a hotel for the time being. Claridge's perhaps, or —"

"Don't be absurd," Sterling said firmly. "You shall stay at Harrington House."

"I couldn't possibly —"

He raised a brow, and at once she realized what he hadn't said. He had paid all her expenses. She had no money for Claridge's or anywhere else.

She nodded. "Very well. Giddings." She turned to the butler. "A Mr. Josiah Cadwallender has been traveling with us and has been most helpful. He went to his offices while we came directly here, but he was to meet us here."

Giddings nodded. "I shall direct him to Harrington House, my lady."

"Excellent."

"Lady Rathbourne." The butler leaned closer and lowered his voice for her and Sterling's ears alone. "We are all praying for your success."

"Thank you, Giddings." The most remarkable feeling washed through her. These were all people she or Giddings had hired, and she barely knew any of them. But they were *her* people and were loyal to *her.* The number of servants in the house had never been excessive, so even if she failed, they would retain their positions. But the fact that they wished her well . . . a lump rose in her throat.

"Most appreciated, Giddings," Sterling said with genuine warmth. "Most appreciated."

The butler was too well trained to show undue emotion, but surprise flashed through his eyes. Obviously, he recognized that this was not the same Earl of Wyldewood he'd met previously.

A few minutes later, they were in a cab headed toward Sterling's house. A smiled quirked the corners of his mouth.

"What do you find so amusing?"

Sterling chuckled. "Your butler."

"He's a very good butler."

"No doubt." Sterling's smile widened. "He seemed surprised by my manner."

"You are not the same man who started out on this journey."

"No, I daresay I'm not."

She considered him thoughtfully. "Now that we are back, do you think you will become your old self?"

"Stiff, stodgy, and dull? Good God, I hope not." He grinned, then sobered. "No, I doubt I will ever be the same. I have tasted adventure, minor really compared to my brothers, but more than I've ever experienced. I have seen parts of the world I never thought I would and, in truth, never really cared to see. Travel has never appealed to me, Now . . ."

"Now?"

"Now, I wish to see more. I wish to do more. I fear I shall be too restless to resume my old ways, which might well make me a better man. If I am wise enough . . ." He fell silent for a long moment. "Since the death of my father, I have done little more than attend to my responsibilities. I have long prided myself that I have done so well or at least to the best of my abilities. But it's been years since I have had . . . dreams, I think, if that is the right word. Years since I opened myself to the possibilities presented by life. It was as though I was marking time, waiting for something to happen. Now I know life is too fleeting to waste. I feel, I don't know, different." He paused again. "Alive."

"So then you do not regret accompanying me?"

He met her gaze directly, and her breath caught. He took her hand. "I wouldn't have missed this for all the riches of the world."

Neither would I. The thought struck her abruptly. In spite of the stakes involved, what had brought them both to this point, all the questions and fears and concerns, and regardless of how it might end, neither would she.

And she did not pull her hand away.

A wave of nostalgia passed over her the moment she stepped through the door of Harrington House. This was how a house should feel. Warm, welcoming, and not entirely perfect. And full of life.

The family's butler greeted them. "My lord, we did not expect you today."

"The road is full of unexpected twists and turns, Andrews," Sterling said in a jovial manner.

The butler's eyes widened slightly as if he was afraid Sterling would slap him on the back at any minute. Olivia bit back a smile.

"Where is everyone, Andrews? My brothers, my sister, Aunt Elise?"

"I have sent Elise home." Millicent swept down the stairs, a welcoming smile on her face. "And where on earth have you been? We have already been back for several days. I thought we would find you here when we arrived."

She moved to her son and angled her face for a kiss on the cheek. Instead, he enfolded her in his arms and hugged her. When he released her, she eyed him curiously. "Are you all right?"

"I am excellent, Mother. In fact, I daresay I have never been more excellent."

"That is . . . excellent." She stared at him for another moment, then turned to Olivia, holding her hands out to the younger woman. "And how are you, my dear? How goes the quest?"

"Excellent as well." Olivia smiled and took her hands. "We have acquired the second item."

"That is . . ." Millicent beamed. "Excellent indeed. I wish to hear all about it."

"I thought you had planned to stay in

Egypt?" Olivia said.

"I preferred to return home." Millicent smiled. "I saw the pyramids, rode on a camel, and decided I had had quite enough of heat and sand fleas."

"Where is everyone, Mother?" Sterling glanced around as if expecting the rest of the family to flood into the entry at any moment and greet him. And looking a shade disappointed that no one did.

"Nathanial is with Gabriella and her family discussing wedding plans. Or perhaps they are somewhere avoiding the discussion of wedding plans. Possibly at a museum or . . ." She shook her head. "I really have no idea. Quinton escorted Reggie to Lady Williston's garden party."

"Quinton?" A skeptical note sounded in Sterling's voice. "My brother Quinton?"

"The very one. Acting in your stead, of course. I would have gone but . . ." Millicent forced a feeble cough. "I am feeling a bit under the weather."

Sterling laughed. "You just don't like Lady Williston."

She ignored him. "Quinton has taken his responsibilities as temporary head of the family quite seriously." Mother beamed. "I am very proud of him, but I never doubted that he would. And Sir Lawrence is visiting with some of his colleagues."

"Sir Lawrence is here?" Sterling's brow rose.

Millicent's eyes widened innocently. "Where else would he be?"

"I don't know. Egypt? A hotel?"

"Nonsense." She sniffed. "He extended the hospitality of his home to us in Cairo. We can do no less in London. Besides . . ." She directed a firm look at her son. "Although I have not yet made up my mind, I may well decide to marry him."

Olivia hugged the older woman. "How lovely for you."

"Well, I haven't decided yet. He has asked. Several times, in fact. Now that you are home, I suspect I will give him my answer soon. Well?" She narrowed her gaze and studied her son. "Don't you have a comment to make?"

"Frankly, Mother," he said slowly, "I'm rather surprised you're not already married."

She smiled in a decidedly mischievous manner. "So is Lawrence." She hooked her arm through Olivia's and started for the parlor. "I want to hear everything. Where did you go from Cairo?"

"Venice," Sterling said behind them.

"That's right. How lovely." She leaned

close to Olivia's ear and lowered her voice. "And how romantic."

"There were a few moments . . ." Olivia murmured.

"I don't know what you have done to him, my dear, but he is not the same man who left here." She squeezed Olivia's arm. "And I am most appreciative."

"I can hear you, Mother," Sterling said with a chuckle.

"You are supposed to, dear," Millicent said coolly.

Olivia and Millicent settled on the sofa. Sterling stood near the mantel, as though indeed he was too restless to sit, his gaze constantly drifting to the doorway. It struck Olivia that he was eager to see the rest of his family, and the tiniest prick of jealousy stabbed her.

They chatted for a good quarter of an hour, relating most of what had transpired in Venice, with Sterling's mother interrupting every few minutes to say how clever they had been. While Olivia thought they had been more fortunate than intelligent, it was still nice to hear.

Josiah arrived, and the look on his face immediately changed the mood.

"What is it now?" Olivia held her breath. "Do tell me it's not another stipulation we have not been informed of."

"Nothing like that." Josiah paused to chose his words. "The day after we left for Egypt . . . I'm not sure how to say this."

"Do get on with it, Josiah." She tried and failed to hide the impatience in her voice. "How bad could it possibly be?"

"It might well change everything." He drew a deep breath. "Lord Newbury passed away. Your father has died."

Olivia stared at the solicitor, his words echoing in her head. Sterling moved to stand behind her, resting a comforting hand on her shoulder.

"Oh dear," Millicent said under her breath. "How very unexpected."

"Not really, although I doubt it was public knowledge." Sterling said. "He told me he was ill."

"He had been dead for a long time, I think," Olivia said quietly. "I have not spoken to him since my marriage." She clasped her hands together and studied them, trying to dredge up some semblance of appropriate emotion. But there was noth-ing — not hate or resentment or regret. And certainly not love.

When she was a child, she had assumed her father had loved her if only because he was her father. As she'd grown older she'd understood that he would have much preferred a son to a daughter and attributed his disinterest to disappointment. When he'd traded her to save himself, she'd finally realized that she was not, nor had she ever been, anything but a commodity.

"My dear girl." Millicent laid her hand on Olivia's. "My condolences."

First Rathbourne was gone, and now her father. In an odd sort of way, she felt as if she'd been holding her breath for a very long time and had at last released it.

"You said this might change everything," Sterling said to Josiah. "What did you mean?"

"Lord Newbury left quite a substantial estate. Property as well as a significant fortune." The solicitor met her gaze. "You are his only heir."

Olivia passed a weary hand over her forehead. "And what do I have to do to earn that?"

Josiah shrugged as if he couldn't believe his own words. "Nothing at all."

Olivia stared at the young man, then shook her head slowly. "I don't want it."

"Don't be absurd." Millicent sniffed. "Of course you want it, it's your birthright."

"Nonetheless, I didn't want anything from him when he was alive." She raised her chin.

"I want nothing now that he's dead." She looked at Millicent. "I daresay you know any number of worthy charities that might benefit from my father's demise."

"Well yes, certainly but . . ." Millicent paused to chose her words. "Sometimes, we learn more about a person when he has passed on than we ever did when he lived. Your father could have made other arrangements for his fortune, but he obviously wanted you to have it."

"Olivia." Sterling stepped around the sofa and knelt before her. "You might need this."

"But I don't want it." Her voice rose in spite of her best intentions.

"Livy." The firm tone of Sterling's words matched the look in his eyes. "There is no need to make any decision now. You deserve this legacy every bit as much as you do Rathbourne's. More really. And if we are not successful —"

"We will be." Resolve rang in her voice.

"There's no need now to continue to meet the stipulations of your late husband's will," Josiah said. "The inheritance from your father, while not quite as large as Lord Rathbourne's, would enable you to have the life you want."

"Independence, Livy." Sterling stared into her eyes. "Your father has made that possible. He has at last freed you from Rathbourne."

For the briefest of moments, a wave of sadness washed over her. Not for anything lost but for what had never been.

"It changes nothing." She shook her head. "And I shall not begin a new life with failure. I shall not allow my late husband to have this last victory over me." She drew a calming breath. "But you're right. I shall make no decision now. In a practical sense, it would be foolish of me to act out of pride or . . . or anger."

"No." A hint of a smile touched Sterling's lips. "That would indeed be foolish." He rose and glanced at Josiah. "Do you have the information as to the last item?"

The younger man hesitated, then nodded. He set his valise on a chair, opened it, and withdrew the last envelope. He grimaced and handed it to her.

She took the envelope, tore it open without hesitation, and realized, for the first time, that the sight of her late husband's hand did not disturb her. It struck her that at the beginning of all of this, she'd had doubts even if she hadn't admitted them. Oh, not about the challenge set for her but about herself. About who and what she was and whether she did indeed have the strength to be who and what she wished to be. Regardless of whether she won or lost this game of her late husband's, he no longer had any power over her. Obviously, Sterling wasn't the only one who had been changed by their quest.

"The Ambropia seals," she read, then looked at Sterling. "This sounds familiar."

"And not surprising." A grim note sounded in Sterling's voice. "There is a set of three ancient cylinder seals that are believed to hold the key to the location of the lost city of Ambropia, commonly referred to as the Virgin's Secret."

Olivia raised a brow. "How on earth do you know that?"

"Gabriella's brother was in possession of one seal, but it was stolen from him."

"I remember." Olivia nodded. "She and Nathanial spoke me to about this before my late husband's death."

"In her efforts to recover her brother's seal, she learned Rathbourne had another, and the third was in the collection of the London Antiquities Society. When the seal was located, Gabriella gave it to the society, so both seals are now in its collections."

"So to complete my late husband's collection, we only need to acquire those two seals?" She glanced at Josiah for confirmation.

He nodded.

"Correct me if I'm wrong but Gabriella's seal . . ."

"Now known as the Montini seal," Sterling said.

"Was that recovered after my late husband's death?"

Sterling nodded. "Yes."

"Then he couldn't possibly know that the location of both seals would be known." She thought for a moment. "Which means, as far as he knew, there was no possible way for me to complete this collection."

"There is evidence to indicate that he had sought to acquire the Montini seal by less than legal means." Sterling paused as if reluctant to continue. "He admitted to Gabriella that he had hired someone to steal the seal. That effort, however, was unsuccessful. But, yes, as far as he knew, any attempt on your part to complete this last collection was fated to fail."

"I see." She smiled slowly. "Fate is certainly an interesting mistress and, at this point, I believe she is mine." Excitement rose within her. By her count she still had twenty-two days to meet the stipulations of the will. "But we do know where the final items are, and, best of all" — she met Sterling's gaze — "you are on the board of the Antiquities Society."

"I am." He and Josiah traded glances. "And in the eighty-some years of the society's existence, it has never relinquished an item in its collection."

Twenty-Three

Livy stared at him. "Never?"

Sterling shook his head. "Not that I am aware of."

"But surely, in this case —"

"The society is intractable about this issue. I believe it's stipulated in the bylaws, as I'm sure Rathbourne knew," Sterling said.

"There have been instances through the years where the society has been offered huge sums of money or valuable artifacts in exchange for an item in its collection, but to a man, the board has never seriously considered it."

"So this last collection is one I can't possibly complete," she said under her breath.

"Olivia," his mother interrupted. "Even without fulfilling the terms of the will, you have achieved victory. You have the means now to do as you wish."

"No." Livy shook her head firmly. "Victory has been handed to me through no effort of my own."

Mother cast her a sympathetic look. "If it's your pride —"

"It is pride to a certain extent, but it's more than that." She paused to pull her thoughts together. "If I give up now, my late husband has succeeded in continuing to own my life even from the grave. If I do not see this through to the very end . . ." She shook her head. "This will haunt me for the rest of my days and eat at my soul. I know myself well enough to know that. It will be a constant reminder, and I will never be free."

Livy's gaze met his, and at once he understood. In her place he would feel the same.

"I shall arrange for a meeting with the society's director for tomorrow morning," he said.

Livy smiled, and his heart ached. "Thank you."

Later that night, the entire family gathered for dinner, including Sir Lawrence, Gabriella, and Josiah, who could not keep his eyes off Reggie. His sister flirted with the young solicitor in a startlingly accomplished manner. It was a turn of events Sterling vowed to keep a close eye on. There was scarcely a quiet moment throughout the meal, with discussions leaping from Livy's final acquisition to Reggie's social activities to Quinton's handling of the family's affairs in his absence to Nathanial and Gabriella's wedding plans. All in all, it was a somewhat raucous affair.

Livy had the seat beside him, and he watched her more than he followed the conversation. Watched her study his family's reactions to one another and watched varying emotions flicker through her eyes. And watched her laugh. She did not laugh nearly enough. He would have to do something about that and ignored the thought that, until recently, neither did he.

During a particularly lively debate between Sir Lawrence, Gabriella, and his brothers as to the significance of a recent discovery of Asia Minor artifacts, he leaned close and spoke softly into her ear. "We can be a bit overwhelming. My family that is."

"Overwhelming?" She turned toward him, her eyes wide. "I don't find it the least bit overwhelming but rather quite delightful."

He raised a brow. "Do you?"

"I do indeed. Look at them." Her gaze swept the table. "Not one of them is afraid to say what he or she thinks even if they disagree with one another. In spite of the occasional heated nature of whatever the topic at hand, there is an undercurrent here

440

not merely of respect but of affection." She shook her head. "I have always envied you this."

He chuckled softly. "This?"

"It's a family, Sterling, with all of its quirks and foibles and even its disagreements." She smiled. "It's quite remarkable and most enjoyable. I am grateful to be a part of it, at least for tonight."

It was on the tip of his tongue to invite her to be a part of it forever, but he held back. She no longer needed to marry anyone out of necessity, not that she would have done so at any rate. But until her quest was resolved, he would refrain from pressing her for a future together. Given he had already waited for a decade, he could wait another twenty-two days.

Sir Lawrence cleared his throat and rose to his feet. "I should like to make an announcement or rather, I suppose ask a question. I should probably do this privately but as your entire family is gathered, this seems appropriate. I spent many hours around this very table in my younger days, but I did not have the right to do what I wish to do now." He met Sterling's gaze directly. "I should like your permission to ask for your mother's hand in marriage." His gaze traveled around the table. Not one face showed so much as

441

a hint of surprise. He smiled in a sheepish manner. "I see this is not unexpected."

"It was my understanding you had already asked my mother to marry you," Sterling said wryly.

"But she has not given me an answer, and I thought perhaps she was waiting for your approval." He turned to Sterling's mother. "So once again, Millicent, I have loved you for much of my life. Will you do me the honor of becoming my wife?"

"Goodness, Lawrence, you are persistent," Mother said with a sigh. "I thought you knew the answer."

The older man's brow furrowed. "Do I?"

"Of course you do." Mother favored him with a private sort of smile for him alone. "I should like nothing better than to marry you."

Sir Lawrence stared at her for a moment, then grinned. "Tomorrow then? Or the day after? Or as soon as it can be arranged?"

She laughed. "Not tomorrow or the day after. This family already has one wedding looming in less than a month. But perhaps the day after that."

He studied her. "I shall not allow you to change your mind, you know."

"Nor shall I allow you to change yours," Mother said in an offhand manner belying the affectionate look she cast at her newly betrothed.

Sir Lawrence sat down, and Josiah immediately cleared his throat and stood. "As we are requesting permissions, sir." He addressed his words to Sterling. "While my father has been knighted, my family holds no hereditary titles, so this is somewhat presumptuous of me but —"

"But you do have excellent prospects." Sterling smiled.

"Indeed, I do, sir." An eager note sounded in the young man's voice. "And I should like permission to call on your sister."

Reggie grinned at the solicitor, then turned an overly innocent gaze toward her brother. Even in the short time she'd been out in society, Reggie had already accumulated suitors with the avid dedication of a seasoned collector of art or antiquities. Sterling doubted anything would come of allowing Josiah to call on her. In spite of the solicitor's prospects, he currently had neither the means nor the position to truly appeal to his sister. And if, by some chance, affection did blossom between them, he was an honorable young man with a good head on his shoulders and a good future ahead of him. Reggie could do far worse.

Sterling nodded. "You have my permission."

"And best of luck to you." Quinton stifled a laugh.

"Thank you, sir." Josiah breathed a sigh of relief and resumed his seat. Beside him, Reggie tried and failed to hide a smug smile. Poor boy. Sterling did hope Reggie would not break his heart.

"What about you, brother?" Quinton said idly, his gaze sliding from Sterling to Livy and back. "Do you have permission to ask or an announcement to make?"

"Yes, Sterling," Nathanial added. "Surely you have something of that nature to share?"

"One would think, in the interests of propriety, given you have always been a stickler for such things and considering that you and Lady Rathbourne traveled a great deal together without benefit of chaperone . . ." Reggie pinned her brother with the kind of challenging look only an eighteen-year-old could assume. "That you should wish to do what is right."

"We were not entirely alone you know," Livy said in a casual manner. "Mr. Cadwallender was nearly always with us."

"And I saw no evidence of improper behavior," Josiah said staunchly.

"Nor did I," Mother said, adding under

444

her breath, "more's the pity."

Reggie ignored them and turned to Livy. "But surely you realize the appearance of impropriety is as damning to one's reputation as the actions themselves."

"This is neither the time nor the place for such a discussion," Sterling said in his best Earl-of-Wyldewood voice.

"My dear, Regina," Livy began. "I am not the least bit concerned about my reputation. However, it is not a position I advise, especially for someone of your age." She shrugged. "When one has experienced marriage, and travel and one's future has been the subject of a wager between men —"

Sterling shot a quick glance at Josiah, who winced.

"— one has earned the right to behave as one wishes, within reason, of course." Livy cast his sister a pleasant smile.

Reggie's gaze slide from Livy to Sterling. "What wager?"

"It's of no significance," Livy said lightly, and sipped her wine.

"It's not?" His gaze met Livy's over her wineglass.

"No." Amusement danced in her green eyes. "Not at all."

Quinton narrowed his eyes. "You never answered my question."

"The answer is no. I have nothing to ask; nor do I have anything to announce," Sterling said smoothly. Or rather, he should say, not yet. Not for another twenty-two days. If nothing else, he had at least learned patience.

"What a shame," his mother said under her breath.

A minute later the conversation thankfully shifted to another topic. He leaned toward Livy and spoke softly into her ear. "You're not angry then? About the wager?"

She shook her head. "Not at all."

He studied her carefully. "Why not?"

She smiled and turned to join in the discussion.

He directed his apparent attention toward the rest of the table, but his thoughts were on her. She wasn't angry about the wager, indeed, she didn't seem the least bit upset. Obviously, she knew that Josiah had conceded victory to him, yet she didn't seem at all bothered by it. At a minimum, he had expected comments about his arrogance. He chuckled to himself. This turn of events was most interesting and surely a good sign.

After dinner Livy pleaded weariness and retired to her rooms. Sterling joined his brothers on the terrace for brandy and cigars. They talked of the sorts of things brothers talk about long into the night. With his brothers' work taking them to the far reaches of the world, it was rare for the three of them to be together. And like anything rare, it was to be cherished. He wondered what it would be like to face the world without siblings, without family, as Livy had. Hopefully, one day soon, he could give her this.

And when at last he retired, he couldn't think of anything but her. And the past and the future. Until at last he rose from his bed and headed to the library. Work had always taken his mind off other matters. Admittedly, for nearly ten years, he had had nothing on his mind but work. He passed her room and resisted the urge, the need, to knock. Instead, he ran his hand through his hair and repeated what was fast becoming as much a motto to attempt to live by as *carpe diem.*

Patience was a virtue.

Olivia had no intention of retiring for the night after dinner. Instead, she did what she should have done long ago. She finally studied her late husband's will. She had glanced at it, of course. It would have been irresponsible not to. She had even taken it with her to Egypt and Italy with the very best of intentions but somehow could never quite bring herself to read it with the care she knew she should devote to it.

Now, she really had no choice. It was either study the will or think about Sterling. And thinking about Sterling clouded her mind with thoughts of the future and whether or not she could trust him with her heart. It was a silly debate really; she knew the answer. But was she ready to abandon her dreams of independence for the desires of her heart? Josiah's comment on the voyage from Italy lingered in the back of her mind. What did she really want, and what was she willing to sacrifice to get it?

Her bags had been unpacked, and the few guidebooks she had accumulated along with the will sat neatly stacked on the lady's desk in her rooms. She sat down, drew a deep breath, and began to read the document, ignoring the rush of anger that swept through her with every word. Anger would not serve her well. She needed to remain rational and keep her wits about her. Surely there was something in it that would help with the final challenge. Some minor point that might well spell victory.

She read the will thoroughly three times, then studied the section regarding the completion of his collections. Her heart sank. There was nothing unexpected. Still, she read until her eyes burned with weariness, and she was too tired to continue. Perhaps in the morning she would have Sterling look at it. He was far better versed in legal matters than she. At last she set the document aside and fell exhausted into bed, falling asleep almost at once. To dream of pages and pages of words all jumbled together, and dark brown eyes filled with desire and love, and ancient artifacts lost and found and something just out of reach . . .

Her eyes snapped open and at once she was fully awake. Good Lord, the answer was so simple, so very obvious. She should have seen it sooner. Or Sterling should have realized it or Josiah. Triumph flooded through her, and she leapt out of bed, pulled on her robe, grabbed the appropriate page of the will, and headed for Sterling's room. A light shone under his door. Excellent, he was awake. She knocked softly so as not to wake anyone else, then pushed the door open.

His bed was empty, although it had obviously been slept in. She heaved a frustrated sigh. Damnation, she was tired of not finding him in the bed he was expected to be in. There was no light in the adjoining parlor. Perhaps, he was in his library. It would be just like him to want to see exactly what had transpired in the management of the family's affairs in his absence. She hurried down the hall, nearly tripped in her haste down the stairs, and indeed there was a light showing under the library door.

She pushed open the door to find Sterling at his desk, in his nightclothes and dressing gown. His head jerked up at the interruption, and he stared at her wide-eyed as if she were a specter. "Livy?"

She laughed. "Of course. Whom did you expect?"

His brows pulled together. "Not you. What are you doing here at this hour?"

She approached his desk. "I might ask you the same question." She adopted a chastising tone. "Are you back to being the stiff and stodgy lord who has nothing but obligations and responsibilities in his life?"

He stared at her for a moment, then smiled. "No. I simply couldn't sleep."

"Well, I am glad you're here. I went to your room first, but you weren't in your bed."

"And for that I shall be forever sorry." He grinned, then his eyes narrowed. "What is it?"

"I want you to look at this." She set the paper down with a flourish. "What strikes you about this wording?"

He studied the page for a moment, then looked up at her. "Nothing out of the ordinary."

"Look at it again."

He did and again shook his head. "I still don't see . . ."

She came around the desk, leaned over and tapped on the paper. "Read this line, where it says I am to complete the collections."

"Very well." He read the line. "It says you're to complete the collections."

"And?"

"And?" He shook his head in a helpless manner. "And what?"

"It doesn't say I have to own the collections; nor does it say I have to be in possession of the collections. Only that I have to complete them."

He stared at her and, finally, realization broke in his eyes. "Good God."

"All we have to do is bring the three seals together, and the collection is complete." Triumph filled her. "The very moment we do that, the seal, and everything else, belongs to me, and I can promptly donate the seal to the society."

"Livy." He rose to his feet and grinned. "You've won."

"No, Sterling." She threw her arms around him. "We've won." A moment later her lips were pressed to his. Triumph mingled with passion, and desire exploded between them. His kiss deepened, and her arms tightened around him.

She slipped her hands under his dressing gown and pushed it off his shoulders so that it fell to the floor. She shrugged out of her robe, and it joined his. He gathered her nightgown in his hands, drew it over her head, and tossed it aside. Then he discarded his nightshirt, and their naked bodies pressed together in need and desire and victory.

She leaned back against his desk, and his mouth left hers to explore her throat and breasts. She ran her fingers through his hair and caressed his shoulders and his back, his muscles defined and powerful beneath her fingers. She let her head fall back and gloried in the feel of his mouth, and his hands and the warmth of his flesh. Her breath came faster, and she wanted him to join with her, to take her, to possess her. He suckled one breast, then the next, and she braced her hands on the desk behind her and arched toward him. His lips trailed lower to her stomach, and she moaned with the sheer sensation of his touch.

"I should lock the door," he murmured against her.

"Yes," she said breathlessly, but he didn't, and she didn't care.

He paused for no more than the beat of a heart and swept the items on his desk onto the floor save for the lamp on the far corner. In the back of her mind, a practical voice noted that the inkwell would leave a nasty stain on the carpet, but she didn't care. She sank back on the desk, her toes barely skimming the floor. Her legs fell open, and she ached to feel him inside her.

His hands caressed her breasts, and his mouth returned to tease her skin. His tongue traced a trail down her stomach and lower. She moaned and clutched his shoulders. He slid his hands lightly down her sides, then along the tops of her legs until he slipped his hands between her thighs. His fingers parted her, and his tongue flicked over her. Pleasure, pure and strong, shot through her, and she gasped with the intensity of it.

"Oh, God, Sterling . . ."

He toyed with her with teeth and tongue until she thought she could stand no more, and yet she wanted more. And wondered if he could feel her throb against his mouth. She hovered on the edge of bliss, and her fingers dug into his shoulders, urging more.

At last, he raised his head, straightened, and positioned himself at the entrance to her sex. He smiled down at her, stared into her eyes, and slowly slid into her. She thought she would swoon at the exquisite feel of him filling her, at the pleasure of being one with him again. She arched her back and wrapped her legs around him, pulling him deeper and deeper into her. Into her body, into her soul.

He pulled out of her with an agonizingly measured move, prolonging the pleasure, allowing her to feel every inch of him. He slid out until only the tip of him touched her. And she ached and throbbed and urged his return with the heels of her feet against his back. And when she thought she would scream in frustration, he drove hard into her, and she cried out with pleasure. His thrusts came harder and faster and deeper, and she rocked her hips against him, urging him ever harder and faster and deeper.

"Livy." Her name was little more than a groan from his lips.

Familiar, lovely tension coiled within her. She gripped his hips and met his thrusts with her own.

Without warning he withdrew, pulled her to her feet, swiftly turned her around, and bent her forward over the desk. For a moment she tensed, then aching need vanquished all reserve. He held her waist and slid into her.

She rested her forearms on the desk and lost herself in the feel of his joining with her. He drove into her again and again, her pleasure growing, spiraling upward with every stroke. She had never known, never imagined . . . And his pleasure was hers.

"Oh, God, Livy . . ." He thrust again and his body shuddered against her and the warmth of his seed flooded through her.

"No, Sterling, please . . ." She fairly sobbed with need and wanting. Wanting that place he'd taken her to before.

He curled around her, wrapped one arm around her waist, and slipped the other hand between her thighs, his fingers caressing her sex. He thrust into her again, and bliss exploded within her. Her body jerked and shuddered against his. Wave after wave of exquisite sensation washed over her, through her, and captured her soul.

He swept her into his arms, carried her to the sofa, and lay down beside her, wrapping his body around hers. Warm and comforting and . . . right.

She giggled. "So much for the stiff and stodgy Earl of Wyldewood."

He snorted back a laugh. "Well, stodgy anyway. As for stiff . . ."

She laughed and buried her head in his neck.

"Once more you have ruined me."

"Good," she murmured against him. She could stay in his arms like this for the rest of her days.

He idly stroked her hair and her back, and they lay together until her heart resumed its natural beat. At last she raised her head and smiled into his eyes. "I should be getting back to my rooms."

"Yes, you should." He paused. "We do need to talk you know."

She sighed. "Yes, I know, but not now. Not until this is all resolved."

"Very well. But then . . ." A warning sounded in his voice.

"Yes." She nodded. "Then."

She slipped off the sofa, quickly found her nightclothes, and threw them on. By the time she turned around, Sterling too had dressed.

He pulled her into his arms kissed her soundly once again then released her and gently pushed her toward the door. "Go, now, or I shall never let you go."

She laughed and moved to the door, grabbed the handle, and looked back at him. "Do you really think we've found the answer?"

"No, I think *you* have found the answer."

She met his gaze. "Thank you. For everything."

He grinned. "It's the least I can do."

She returned his smile, stepped out of the room, and closed the door behind her, her smile fading with the close of the door.

The least he could do. Because no matter what he said, she would always be an obligation to him, a debt unpaid.

And that was no way to start a future.

TWENTY-FOUR

"And that, Mr. Beckworth, is what I propose."

Livy sat in the director's office, serene, composed, and confident. She gave no sign of the enormity of the stakes involved and had presented her proposal with a calm authority. This was a woman any man would be proud to call his own. Not merely because she was beautiful but because she was intelligent and had a quiet strength about her. Sterling's heart swelled.

Merrill Beckworth, the director of the Antiquities Society studied her carefully. His wife, a lovely woman some twenty years younger than Beckworth, sat in a chair behind and slightly to the right of her portly husband. Sterling and several other board members had long suspected it was Caroline Beckworth who truly ran the society. Not that it mattered. The London Antiquities Society had an excellent reputation and was indeed one of the preeminent organizations of its kind in the world.

"I find your proposal most interesting, Lady Rathbourne," Beckworth said, his words measured. "Your late husband was a valued member of the society with a fine eye for antiquities. While few have seen his collections, their distinction is unquestioned." He paused. "I should tell you as well that we are aware of the odd stipulations of his will."

Livy smiled politely. "I daresay, by now, there are few in London who are not."

"No doubt." Beckworth nodded. "You are to be commended on your success thus far."

Livy's smile remained, but she held her tongue. And indeed it was her success. Sterling had provided the means and had been instrumental in acquiring the canopic jar, but it had been her idea to barter the Titian, and it was she who had recognized the loophole in the will. Even at this meeting, he had said little save initial greetings. No, this was her triumph alone.

"Your opinion, Lord Wyldewood." Beckworth addressed Sterling. "As a member of the board, that is."

"Obviously, as I accompanied Lady Rathbourne today, I am in complete support of her proposal," Sterling said coolly. "The seals in and of themselves are priceless but to have all three, well, it's an archeological accomplishment of unparalleled significance."

"To have the seals that might hold the key to the Virgin's Secret would greatly enhance the society's stature," Mrs. Beckworth said quietly. "And I daresay, increase our donations."

Beckworth sighed. "Funding is always a problem."

"I am well aware of that." Sterling's gaze slid from Beckworth to his wife and back. "Any number of donors I know would be quite impressed by the society's possession of such a prestigious collection."

"Quite right." Beckworth nodded. "I think Lady Rathbourne's proposal will benefit all concerned. And while I certainly have full authority in this matter, there is the question of having Lord Rathbourne's name on the collection to consider."

Livy narrowed her eyes. "I don't understand."

"Nor do I," Sterling added in a hard tone.

"If this collection were being donated as a whole, that is, if the set of all three seals already bore Lord Rathbourne's name, there would be no difficulty whatsoever. As it is, you are asking us to name a collection, two-thirds of which already belongs to the society." Beckworth shook his head. "It is most irregular."

"One would think, given the importance of this collection, the name on it would not matter," Livy said.

"One would think," Mrs. Beckworth echoed under her breath.

"Especially as my late husband was a member, and I believe patron, of this organization."

"Nonetheless," Beckworth said firmly. "I shall have to have the approval of the board."

"I cannot imagine any board member's objecting given what the society has to gain," Sterling said pointedly.

"Nor can I. However." Beckworth shrugged. "This is not a decision I can make without the board's approval."

"Then we shall simply have to get the board's approval," Livy said with a pleasant smile.

"I would suspect few of them are in town at this time of year." Sterling stared at the director. "Is it necessary to have the approval of all fifteen board members?"

"If we had them all in the same room a simple majority vote would suffice but . . ." Beckworth shifted in his chair, as if trying to find a comfortable position that obviously had nothing to do with how he was seated. "Lady Rathbourne, may I speak candidly?"

"Please do."

"Your late husband was not, I'm not sure how to phrase this, well liked. To have his name on a collection of this magnitude —"

"I understand completely. We shall simply have to hope the prestige of the society's possessing all three seals will overcome any distaste at naming the collection after my late husband." Livy nodded. "I assume a simple letter of agreement from each board member will suffice in this matter?"

"Yes, indeed, that will serve," Beckworth said with relief.

"We shall proceed with that at once then and contact you when we have the approval of the board members." Livy rose to her feet, and the other men followed. "Good day, Mr. Beckworth, Mrs. Beckworth."

Sterling studied the director. "I must say, I did not expect you to be such a stickler for rules, Mr. Beckworth."

"My lord." The director peered at him over the rims of his glasses. "*You* would have it no other way."

"No, I suppose not." Sterling nodded and bid the couple good day. A few minutes later, he and Livy were in a carriage returning to Harrington House.

Livy was remarkably quiet on the return drive as she had been all day. Initially, Sterling had assumed that the gravity of their mission had occupied her mind. Now, he wondered if there was more to it than that. He pushed the thought away. After last night, what could possibly be wrong?

They found Josiah waiting in the parlor for them.

"I have spoken to Mr. Hollis about your discovery, and he agrees that your plan will indeed meet the stipulations of the will." The young man paused. "He has also instructed me to continue to assist you in whatever way possible. I believe he has had an attack of conscience regarding his failure to disclose the time constraints although he claims it was an oversight on his part."

Sterling chuckled. "I suspect it was not an attack of conscience as much as financial considerations and his hope that Olivia will continue to employ his firm."

Josiah nodded. "That is my impression as well."

A thought struck him, and he studied the solicitor. "How did you know about this?"

Surprise colored the young man's face. "Why, Lady Rathbourne sent me a note this morning." He turned to Livy. "As per your request, I have arranged a meeting with your father's solicitors."

"Excellent." Livy nodded. "I should know what his estate entails before I decide what to do with it."

"We should be off then," Josiah said.

Livy turned toward the door.

Sterling stepped toward her. "Shall I accompany you?"

"No," she said sharply, then cast him a polite smile. "I should think your time would be better spent composing notes to the board members. As you are a member yourself, and you know them, whereas I do not, I think this request would carry more weight from you than from me. Don't you agree?"

"Well, yes —"

"Very well then." She nodded and accompanied Josiah from the room.

Sterling stared after her. He was right. There was something wrong. What on earth had happened? Last night in the library, well, last night was thoroughly improper and completely unexpected and probably quite mad as well as delightful and extraordinary and the stuff even the most sensible man's dreams were made of. He would never look at his desk in the same manner again. He had thought Livy had felt the same. No matter. At the moment, he had other things to do.

Several hours later, Edward, in his usual efficient manner, had determined the location of all the board members. A handful were in London but most were at homes in the country, in locations stretching from Cambridge to Winchester. Sterling had written fourteen letters, had included the need for an urgent response, and messengers had been hired to hand-deliver each one. Livy and Josiah had still not returned, which Sterling found bothersome but not of great concern. He turned his attention to perusal of Quinton's handling of family affairs in his absence.

It was late afternoon when Livy finally appeared in the library.

Behind his desk, Sterling rose to greet her. "Rather a long meeting, wasn't it?"

"Oh, the meeting was over hours ago," she said with a blithe wave of her hand. "Your mother was right, I can make no decisions about what to do with the inheritance from my father until the question of my late husband's estate has been resolved. Fortunately, my father's accounts and properties had already been put in my name. It's remarkable how easy matters can be when one doesn't have to do battle over them."

He frowned. "Then where have you been?"

"Apparently, several years ago, my father sold his house here in town and purchased a new one." She shrugged. "I have no idea why, nor do I care. But I have never resided there, therefore it carries no reminders of the past. It has seen better days, but once the painting is finished —"

"You're having it painted?"

"Well, I have no intention of living there as it is."

"I thought you were staying here until this was all settled."

"I can't possibly stay here for another twenty-one days."

He stared. "Why not?"

"Sterling," she began in a somewhat condescending manner, as if he were a small, rather dim, child, "didn't we agree that I can make no decisions regarding my future until all else is settled?"

"I don't recall agreeing exactly . . ."

"Besides, I have imposed on you long enough, and I don't wish for you to feel obligated —"

"I don't feel the least bit obligated."

"No?"

He shook his head. "No."

She studied him for a moment. "Nonetheless, I simply cannot make any kind of rational, well-considered decision about —"

"Us?" He raised a brow.

"Yes, if you will." She shook her head. "I cannot do that if every time I cross your path —" Her gaze shifted to his desk.

"What?"

She met his gaze firmly. "It was something Josiah said on our last voyage. I need to decide what I truly want and what I am willing to sacrifice to get it. At any rate, I have spent the afternoon hiring painters and looking at fabrics and employing all the people I need to get my house in order."

"You can't live there alone."

"I shan't be alone. I have instructed Giddings to close up that horrid house. He and the other servants have already begun moving into my new abode." She shook her head. "Oh, it will be terribly chaotic. But quite fun I think. I have never done anything like this."

"Livy." He came around the desk toward her. "I don't want you to go."

"I think it's best," she said with a patient smile.

"But what about the responses from the board members?"

"I have no doubt that you will keep me informed as to the progress. Sterling," she said firmly, "I cannot stay here, idly waiting for the responses. I shall go mad with nothing to keep myself occupied. This way, I shall be very busy, and the time will fairly fly by."

"But —"

"I do not wish to debate this. I have instructed Andrews to have my bags packed and delivered to my new house. And now I should be on my way." She cast him a bright smile. "Good day."

Before he could protest she swept from the room, leaving him to stare after her like an idiot. How had they gone from passion on the desktop to polite indifference? What had he said? What had he done? He had no idea, but he would figure it out.

He went over last night's conversation, what little conversation there had been. Nothing came to mind. Still, there must have been something. Some innocent comment on his part that she was twisting out of all proportion. Not that he could truly blame her.

Livy was a woman of extraordinary courage. But was she brave enough to abandon the dreams that had sustained her for a decade in exchange for the man who had once failed her? He had wondered, when this all began, what might happen when she no longer required his help, no longer needed him. Now, he understood that he needed her as well; he always had. And knew, in his heart, she needed him too. Not for his money or position but because they were meant to be together always. Because neither of them was complete without the other.

Ten years ago, the world, his world had shifted out of its orbit. Today, it was very nearly right again. His life — their lives — were almost on the path they should never have left. Almost but not quite.

Determination clenched his jaw. She could be as stubborn as she wished, but he would not give up until he made her see what he already knew. That regardless of triumph or failure, together they could face anything.

Especially the future.

Two weeks later, Olivia wandered through the rooms of her new house. Aside from the bedroom she was using at the moment, every room in the house was being prepared or was in the process of or had already been painted in light, bright colors. She had taken stock of all the furnishings, deciding what to discard and what to keep, and she had ordered quite a few new pieces. She was indeed extremely busy and at night fell into her bed exhausted. She'd been right, the house did take her mind off everything else. Everything but Sterling.

To date, none of the responding board members had objected. Waiting was both annoying and frustrating, but there was nothing to be done about it. Nothing she could do now but leave it all in Sterling's trustworthy hands. She wasn't sure precisely when or how it had happened but she'd realized she could indeed trust him not to fail her. And suspected she could trust him with her heart as well.

He had called on her every day for the first three days of her residence here and had sent daily notes apprising her of the responses for several days after that. Then his notes abruptly stopped. Even her requests for information were now being answered by his secretary. It was surprisingly distressing. And with every passing day, it was harder and harder to keep herself from marching to Harrington House and pounding on his door. Damnation, how could the man ignore her like this? Not that she hadn't set it in motion herself. Not that she didn't, perhaps, deserve it.

But putting half of London between them had been wiser than even she had at first realized. It had allowed her to put things in perspective, to indeed be calm and rational. To consider the questions she needed to ask and answer.

Was she being foolish, to let something as insignificant as a single offhand comment stand in the way of being with him? Regardless of his protests, did he indeed think of her as nothing more than an obligation? Yet another responsibility to be borne by the Earl of Wyldewood? Did the fact that he hadn't responded to her notes or paid another call mean that, once again, she had lost him?

No, not this time. This time her fate was in her hands. She had seven days until her quest was at an end. Win or lose, she would know she had done everything in her power to succeed. And even if she failed in beating her late husband, she had, in many ways, already been victorious. If for no other reason than she had refused to accept the fate he'd planned for her, refused to surrender.

As for Josiah's question, that still lingered in the back of her mind. What did she want? And what was she willing to sacrifice to get it? The answer to the first question was easy. Sterling. As for the second, she still didn't know. All she did know was that even though she'd lived without him for a decade, every day without him now seemed an eternity. And perhaps the answer to the second question was obvious as well.

Whatever was necessary.

Sterling stalked into the house and headed for the library.

"Andrews," he barked in passing, "have a footman meet me in the library. I need a note delivered to Lady Rathbourne at once."

"Welcome home, my lord, but . . ." The butler's voice trailed after him. "There is no need . . ."

"There is every need, Andrews," he called over his shoulder. "Never mind. I shall go myself."

There were still three days left, and he had succeeded. Now he would go to Livy, and they would end this nonsense. And begin their lives all over again. This time together.

He'd had a lot of time to think in the last fortnight. What he'd done wrong and what he needed to do now. And admittedly, it might involve groveling.

He strode into the library, set the valise he carried on the desk, and opened it.

"Did you steal that from Josiah?" Livy's voice sounded behind him.

He bit back a grin and turned toward her. "Admittedly, it might look like his, but it

472

happens to be mine."

"Where have you been?" The demanding note in her voice belied the look of concern in her eyes.

"My dear, Lady Rathbourne." He withdrew a handful of letters from the valise. "I have been to . . ." He pulled one letter free of the others and waved it at her and slapped it down on the desk. "Hertford." He pulled a second free. "Cambridge." He pulled free a third. "Oxford and . . ." He waved the final letter at her, then, with a flourish, set it on the others. "Aylesbury. That was this past week."

She stared at him.

"The week before last, I traveled to Warwick and Winchester." He cast her a satisfied grin. "We now have fourteen letters of approval from board members far and wide."

"You went in person to get them?"

"It became apparent to me rather quickly that the board members might be not be as prompt as was necessary in their responses, so I took it upon myself to call on them in person."

Her eyes widened, and she stepped toward him. "Then we are done? We have succeeded?"

"Indeed we have." He grinned. "And we

have much to discuss."

"Sterling, I —"

"No, Livy, allow me." His gaze was firm. "First of all, when I said in this very room that it was the least I could do, it was not a reference to the past but to the quite delightful interlude we had just shared."

"Oh that." She winced. "I might possibly have taken —"

"And while I can never truly make amends for the past, I do intend to spend every day for the rest of your life trying to do so."

She shook her head. "Sterling —"

He held up his hand to quiet her. "Secondly, it has struck me that I have never fully apologized for all that happened ten years ago. Nor have I ever begged your forgiveness. I do so now."

She swallowed hard. "Sterling —"

"A decade ago, I failed not only to come to your aid but to fight for you. I shall not make that mistake again." He propped his hip on his desk and studied her. "I have, as I said, fourteen letters of approval from fourteen board members." He shuffled through the papers on his desk. "Only this one remains to be signed."

Her brow furrowed. "Did we forget someone? Who is it?"

"Me."

"You?" She shook her head. "I don't understand."

"I will sign this letter only if you agree to
marry me."

She gasped. "Sterling, that's blackmail!
And no different from what Rathbourne did
to my father."

"It's entirely different. I love you."

She stared at him suspiciously. "You didn't
say that."

"My apologies. I love you, I have always
loved you, and I shall always love you. And
whether you are willing to admit it or not,
you love me. I would not do this were I not
completely convinced of that."

She scoffed. "Even so, this is most . . .
that is to say . . ." She paused and studied
him for a long moment. His heart caught,
and he held his breath. At last, she heaved a
resigned sigh. "Very well."

"Very well you will marry me or very well
you love me?"

She cast him a reluctant smile. "Both."

"You haven't said it," he said in a lofty
manner that belied his relief as well as the
most amazing feeling that might well have
been happiness.

She laughed. "Then I shall say it." Her
expression sobered. "I love you. I always
have. I always will."

"I knew it." At once he moved to her and took her in his arms. "You are mine, Livy, you have always been mine, and you shall always be mine."

She shook her head in a long-suffering manner. "I am not yours. I am not a possession. I do not belong to you."

"No, of course not, I didn't mean . . . No!" He pulled her tighter against him. "Bloody hell, you are mine. And I am yours. I belong to you just as much as you belong to me. That, Livy, is how it's supposed to be."

She glared up at him. "But —"

"Halves of the same whole. All these years I was only half-alive without you and never suspected. Now I know, and you know as well. You put me on your list even though you hated me."

"I never hated you," she murmured.

"No," he said in his best Earl-of-Wyldewood, pirate-hunter voice. "There is no debate about this, no argument. We belong to one another. For now and forever."

"I don't think I can be independent and married at the same time." She brightened. "Perhaps I could be your mistress?" A teasing note sounded in her voice. "The Contessa de Sarafini would certainly approve."

"I do not. And I don't want a mistress, I want a wife. No, I want *you* as my wife. Furthermore, I believe you can be independent and married at the same time." He stared down at her. "I believe you can do anything you set your mind to."

"I do not intend to be the image of a perfect wife ever again," she warned. "I value who I've become. I can —"

"Breathe?"

"Yes."

"It's of no consequence now, but I don't think you were at all perfect." He smiled at the woman who had long ago claimed his soul forever. Even if neither of them had realized it. "But you are now."

"I will not give up my list. However . . ." She paused. "I shall expect you to join me in crossing my items off."

He raised a brow. "Even the items with men chosen for their capacity for adventure?"

"I have crossed out their names already." A blush washed up her face. "And written in yours."

"Excellent. As for the others, well, I think we should take the children with us."

She smiled slowly. "Children?"

"Several I should think. A family of our own."

"Sign the letter, Sterling."

"Will you marry me?"

"There is nothing I would rather do. And thank you." She drew a deep breath. "For saving me."

"My dear Livy, you don't understand at all." He stared into her green eyes, the eyes that had haunted his dreams for a decade and would stay in his heart until it beat for the last time and beyond. "You saved me. I was lost, and you have found me. Dead and you have brought me back to life. No, it is you who has rescued me."

"We have both changed so much." Her breath caught, and her gaze meshed with his. "And yet nothing has changed at all."

"And nothing ever will." He brushed his lips across hers. "By the way, my love." He smiled. "I now have a list of my own."

Epilogue

Only a pool of light cast by a single lamp on the desk illuminated the room. He drummed his fingers on the desk. "It was foolish to have attempted to find the seal in Rathbourne's house. I regret that. It might have led back to us."

"Nonetheless, it did spur Wyldewood's involvement. Without him, Lady Rathbourne would never have come into possession of the third seal."

"Now the society has all three." He smiled with satisfaction. "Then this is the end."

"Not at all." His partner's smile matched his own. "This is only the beginning."

ABOUT THE AUTHOR

Victoria Alexander was an award-winning television reporter until she discovered fiction was much more fun than real life. She turned to writing full time and has never looked back.

Victoria grew up traveling the country as an Air Force brat and is now settled in Omaha, Nebraska, with her husband, two kids in college (buy her books!), and two bearded collies named Sam and Louie. She firmly believes housework is a four-letter word, there are no calories in anything eaten standing up, procrastination is an art form, and it's never too soon to panic.

And she loves getting mail that doesn't require a return payment. Write to her at P.O. Box 31544, Omaha, NE 68131.

www.ecletics.com/victoria

We hope you have enjoyed this Large Print book. Other Thorndike, Wheeler, Kennebec, and Chivers Press Large Print books are available at your library or directly from the publishers.

For information about current and upcoming titles, please call or write, without obligation, to:

Publisher
Thorndike Press
295 Kennedy Memorial Drive
Waterville, ME 04901
Tel. (800) 223-1244

or visit our Web site at:

http://gale.cengage.com/thorndike

OR

Chivers Large Print
published by BBC Audiobooks Ltd
St James House, The Square
Lower Bristol Road
Bath BA2 3SB
England
Tel. +44(0) 800 136919
email: bbcaudiobooks@bbc.co.uk
www.bbcaudiobooks.co.uk

All our Large Print titles are designed for easy reading, and all our books are made to last.